PRAISE FOR
A THEORY OF EXPANDED LOVE

"worthy debut"
—*Publisher's Weekly*

"Hicks adopts Annie's precocious voice skillfully and draws from it self-effacing humor, spiritual bargaining, and enough charm to fill the corridors of Vatican City twice over. This is an involving tale of religious evolution that reminds us that good faith is what sometimes grows out of defying convention and braving the unknown."
—*Foreword Reviews*

"Annie's disarming voice evokes nostalgia for a bygone era and hope for humanity in a weary, modern world."
—*Kirkus Reviews*

"an unforgettable heroine... a gem of a read"
—*BigPacific.com*

"a triumph"
—Deborah Hining, award-winning novelist,
A Sinner in Paradise

"Caitlin Hicks captures the inner workings of a twelve-year-old's mind with empathy and humor."
—Elizabeth Hein, novelist,
How to Climb the Eiffel Tower

A THEORY OF
EXPANDED
L O V E

a novel

Caitlin Hicks

To Darj. For everything. But mostly for love.

"The great advantage of living in a large family
is that early lesson of life's essential unfairness."
–Nancy Mitford

"It's all true, except what didn't really happen."
–Gord Halloran

"If the shoe fits, wear it."
–Marcelle Prudell Hicks

PROLOGUE
PASADENA, CALIFORNIA

April 14, 1963, Easter Sunday

Daddy said we were having lamb for Easter dinner.
    "You mean like 'Mary had a little lamb'?" I asked.
    "You mean like little lost lamb?"
    "You mean like–Lamb of God?"

PART 1
JUNE, 1963

CHAPTER 1
NOT ENOUGH

June 3 – Dear Diary, Before dinner, we said Eternal Rest for Pope John XXIII. A plane crashed off the coast near Alaska, and 101 passengers bit the dust. All those people got to see the Pope at heaven's gate. I hope some of them were Catholic, so they could get in.

It wasn't enough that there were thirteen of us born of the same two parents, living in a creaky old house with ratty grass and spilled tricycles in the front yard—across the street from the tennis courts of a ritzy Protestant girls' school in Pasadena. Or that our dog Sparky chased the cars and nipped at the heels of these privileged girls after school every single day, calling constant attention to our embarrassing rank in the neighborhood.

It wasn't enough that we were Holy Rollers in an obviously secular society: good, patriotic Catholics who found parking spaces by praying to St. Anthony, who could recite the old Latin Mass by heart, and dutifully learned the modern English version, word for word after the Second Vatican Council. Not enough that we went along with the flock and replaced the magnificent, time-honored, glorious Latin hymns with inferior folk songs led by guitar strumming, self-declared musicians who had no sense of rhythm. It wasn't enough that we were Navy Brats and every three or four years, in service of our country, we gave up our friends and favorite haunts and moved to a completely new military base, Whidbey Island being one of those places, where one of our brothers Buddy (Number ten), who weighed thirteen pounds at birth, arrived during a freak snowstorm.

Even being the second-to-the-largest family in the parish was not enough. (We were neck-and-neck with the Feeneys; they were ahead by one child, albeit a gimp). There were so many of us that the number of our birth was more important than our name. (I was Number Six). Certainly nobody but me cared that our mother had flaming red hair, white skin prone to freckles and sunburn, traits which I inherited, traits which made me stick out of the crowd I was born into, and every other crowd that ever gathered for anything for the rest of my entire life.

We did have the dubious distinction of being the only family in the whole school who fought communism every night by praying the rosary. The stained and weary lot of us knelt down in front of two statues and a chalice every night after dinner, counting fifty Hail Mary's, one Our Father and five Glory Be's with a string of beads when other kids were already finished with their homework and watching their new black and white TVs. It wasn't enough that the family's main galvanizing fear, the Cold War, was lurking mysteriously and darkly on the horizon somewhere in Russia, a war which made us bump our heads on the underside of our desks at school and crawl into a ball whenever the siren sounded. We had a bomb shelter, a hole in the ground with cement steps leading to a pit next to the garage, but this is where we would almost certainly be vaporized in the event of a nuclear holocaust because it wasn't deep enough. A dark, grave-like corner in which to huddle pathetically in mass panic; a hole that Mother and Daddy hastily expanded and stocked with canned vegetables (the soggiest, most barf-inducing food you could ever eat) after the Cuban Missile Crisis at the end of last year. And our *Bombs Over Tokyo!* Dad who wore a Navy uniform to work everyday (when not a soul we knew did military service) constantly reminded us that *Rank has its privileges* and that we were really nothing more than his own private "Mess Hall," mere props in his Last Supper tableau.

None of this was enough for us. Underneath it all, we had visions of grandeur and ambition as sprawling as we were. And suddenly, we had the chance to reel it all in.

It was 1963. You may remember it as the year President Kennedy was assassinated. With more than a dozen kids, our parents (following church doctrine by using abstinence as their preferred method of birth control) had already defined the word *good* as in: *Catholic*. In 1960, they also defined the word *staunch*, as in: Republican, by voting *against* the Catholic candidate for President. When Kennedy got shot dead, it was one of those things that my father silently praised God for, even though to the rest of the world it looked like a tragedy. Or, as our parents would say, lacking any other explanation, a tragedy that God intended "for His own mysterious reasons."

But Kennedy was shot at the end of November. The big thing that happened to us that year happened in

June.

The pope died.

That benevolent-looking, roly-poly guy in the white robes, Pope John the 23rd. And the whole thing nearly changed our fortunes. Because of his death, 1963 was the year we were the most famous Catholic family you ever heard of. 1963 was the year that the messy, lumbering lot of us finally earned some status in the world.

On December 7, 1941 our dad, Martin Shea, was 22 years old, an Assistant Supply Officer, a boot ensign aboard *The USS Pelias* stationed at a submarine base dock at Pearl Harbor. The night before, he and his shipmates hooted it up at a party on the beach, a luau at the Officer's Club. The evening was humid and warm, palm trees silhouetted against a moonlit sky, and the officers danced hula with the young ladies. Father Stefanucci, an Italian-born American priest, the ship's Chaplain, was "three sheets to the wind," apparently excelling at the hula.

But it wasn't until the next morning that their friendship really got going. Our dad was up just before 8 dressing to go to Sunday Mass, when General Quarters sounded. Beep. Beep. Beep. Father Stefanucci had a cabin across the hall from our dad, and hearing the alarm, peeked out the door, still in his pajamas, certainly not ready to say Mass. Beep, beep, beep, the alarm kept sounding. *All hands to your battle stations.* Our Dad, who wasn't yet our Dad, slapped on his trousers, quickly buttoning his shirt as he skipped up the steps to the main deck. Beeeep, beeeep, beeeep. There, he saw a plane roar by, level with the ship, covered with

Japanese markings. Bombs were already dropping in the visible distance, huge sheets of flame shooting skyward, the sound of droning airplane engines and the smell of burning oil filling the air. He ran back downstairs, two steps at a time. Father Stefanucci was still standing there, stunned and somewhat hung over.

"Why does everything have to happen where I am?" Stefanucci wailed, still glued to the spot. Apparently he was well traveled and things went wrong on his trips.

"Father, get a hold of yourself," our future Dad barked, as he steered Father Stefanucci back into his cabin and started yanking open dresser drawers, throwing clothes on the bed. "Get dressed! Where's your battle station?" That kind of talk usually snaps us out of it, makes us hup-to, and I guess it worked on Father Stefanucci.

Back up on deck and looking across the harbor, a massive explosion instantly gave way to walls of orange flames and billowing gray clouds as *The Arizona* was hit, three-quarters of a mile away. Bombs hailed over the scene, a huge explosion rocked *The California* and lit it on fire. The sky filled with black smoke, and the morning became dusky and thick, almost like evening.

So that was the big story about our Dad and Father Stefanucci. Together in battle on the most famous day of days—for anyone, not only in the US Navy, but also in the whole world. The thing that made it such a game-changer for us—the reason for all the excitement between June 3rd when Pope John XXIII died and June 21st when the Council of Cardinals gathered in the Sistine Chapel to vote for a new pontiff of the Holy Catholic Church around the world—was that Stefanucci was on the shortlist to become pope! His name was in all the papers as the first American Cardinal to be considered a candidate for His Holiness! Stefanucci's election would make 1963 a banner year for the Americans and the Catholics: Kennedy still reigned as the first Catholic President of the United States (it was only June, he wasn't assassinated yet). And if elected, Cardinal Stefanucci would be the first American Pope—ever.

For those two weeks, it was glorious for our Dad. And for us, his faithful extras. Suddenly we weren't on the losing team anymore. Our Dad and Cardinal Stefanucci had been best buddies. Since Pearl Harbor! And we, the whole unkempt gang of us, were suddenly his lifelong friends. After all, he came to visit us once on Whidbey Island, just before he became Archbishop. Buddy, who was barely out of diapers, was so desperate for attention that he hung onto Stefanucci's arm the entire night until he was extricated when the Archbishop tried to put on his cape at the door.

Daddy didn't waste any time telling the nuns and the Monsignor at St. Andrew's of his privileged position as the guy who might even have, *ahem*, saved Father Stefanucci's life. Because their story changed a bit after that. Now we saw them both on the upper deck, with our Dad yanking Father Stefanucci out of the way as the bullets rained over them. And the two of them panting heavily under the awning that protected them, their ears pulsing after the huge roar of an engine had splintered the air.

We stormed heaven that June, the month when the air is the sweetest in Southern California, when if you're a kid you just have to be outdoors, inhaling smog and eucalyptus scent kicked up from the leaves of the tall, elegant trees with multicolored bark. June, the month you create and star in magnificent adventures out back (re-enactments of Walt Disney's Davy Crockett), by the shed, or in the bamboo, or behind the bushes, or even downstairs in the bomb shelter until Mother calls you in for dinner. "Last one in is a hairy ape!"

That June, the June of 1963, all of us roused ourselves for 6:30 Mass with Daddy (to bribe God with our devotion). It was the month we all sat subdued and nodding in the Volkswagen bus on our way to church as the streetlights went dim and the sun rose like a blush around us. On Sundays, we went proudly to Mass *en masse*, better late than never as we trailed up the aisle, stretching the good Christian nature of other Catholics who knew how to get to the church on time. That June, at the doorway to the church, we saw for the first time ushers nodding approvingly as we filed up the center aisle. The faithful congregation, usually whispering disapproval, inched down the pew in their Sunday suits and high heels, smiling indulgently as we proudly, rather than sheepishly, created a conspicuous disturbance during the sermon.

One morning that spring, as my sixth grade class sat fresh and scrubbed with our hands folded on our desks, Sister Everista opened the day's proceedings directly to me with "Any word from the Cardinal?"

"Um, well," I said, gulping air and sensing a unique advantage. I took another breath. Unbelievably, I had the full attention of every single person in sight. There was only one thing to do.

I made stuff up.

He had called last night during the rosary, long distance from Rome. He recognized my voice. What a smart guy, no wonder they want him to be pope! So many voices to recognize and he got it right! From across the ocean! Dad got a special delivery letter in the mail with simply *The Vatican* as the return address: it was sealed with a red, wax seal and its embossed contents were a secret.

I never lied so much in my life, but how could it hurt? Our parish sucked it up just as much as we did; they were not above glory by association. In the end, when our prayers were answered and Stefanucci got to be Pope, I'd just go to confession. "Bless me, Father, for I have sinned, I told a few itty bitty lies."(Big deal!)

God would have to forgive me. You can't get any closer than the Pope.

CHAPTER 2
MOTHER'S SECRET

June 5 – Today at Religion time, Sister Everista asked about the news from the Cardinal. Everyone was looking at me like I was already a saint. I didn't want to say anything because I was still smarting from a spanking last night (so obviously I need more time in purgatory before I can be canonized), but I knew they were expecting something, so I told them, very casually, that our whole family was invited to The Vatican if he gets elected. The entire class sucked in air with "ooooooh!" Then Sister had us all pray for "God's will in matter of Cardinal Stefanucci and His Holiness, The Pope." At recess time, everyone crowded around me like I was Judy Garland! This Pope thing is really paying off.

Yesterday I accidentally discovered something even better than the mysteries of the rosary. A true secret, with getting-in-trouble danger involved. I was looking for Bitty, who was overloaded with babies in her stomach. I got a flashlight and went to the shed out back next to the bomb shelter. Bitty wasn't in any of the corners, but there was a cedar trunk with a lock on top. The trunk was open. My curiosity didn't even try to resist: if it was wrong to look, it had to be only a venial sin. I wasn't going to hell for this.

"You're never going to believe what I found!" I ran

back in the house and told Clara (#2), Madcap (#4), Jeannie (#7), and Rosie (#9), who were hovering over a jigsaw puzzle of Elvis Presley.

"What? What?" they clamored.

"Shhhh," I whispered, "It's a secret!" We traipsed past the laundry room where Mother was doing her seventh load of the day, and gathered in the dark shed with the flashlight, elbowing each other for a good view. It was hard to believe, but there were *photographs* of a skinny blonde man in an Army uniform with our very beautiful Mother. The name under her picture was not our Mother's name. It was Adamson. Mrs. Katherine McLellan Adamson. We looked at each other right in the eyeballs, letting it sink in. *Our mother was married before Daddy?* We were so shocked we didn't hear anything, not the sound of Daddy's car pulling softly into the garage, not the sound of his door slamming. Not even Sparky nosing the door open with his snout.

• • •

After the lights went out that night, we lay on our backs in the dark staring at the ceiling. I still had welts on my bottom, so at first, I was frozen still in my bed, listening for Daddy's voice at the door. Usually he made the rounds, his voice springing up out of nowhere, startling us out of a drifting sleep, his stern "Pipe down kids!" resonating down the hall. Jeannie (#7), Rosie (#9), and I shared one of the two big upstairs rooms. We could hear the sounds of Mother knocking about in the kitchen, finishing up the dishes below us. The uneven voices of John-the-Blimp (#3) and Bartholomew (#5) were muffled behind their closed door across the hall. Clara (#2) in her single room at the front of the house was already fast asleep, her throat making a soft rattling sound in the distance. Madcap's room, at the other end by the stairs, was not a proper bedroom, just a small rectangle under a skylight. She was probably reading a book with a flashlight. The light in the hallway flicked on. I imagined Paul (#1) sitting under its glow on the wooden storage box as he spoke softly into the telephone receiver. Usually we tried to stay awake long enough to hear the embarrassing "I love you" at the end. Every night we had to hear it to believe it. It was impossible to imagine Paul, with the exploding temper of a thousand mad Irishmen, sounding so gentle.

I was thinking about the expression on Daddy's face as he stood in the shed, looking at that picture of Mother in the embrace of the handsome soldier. We were hiding behind the boxes, peering up at him from the darkness. Rosie was breathing too loudly in my ear. And Daddy's face got this look on it—curiosity, maybe? A softness, staring at it for so long. And then he discovered us. He looked right into my eyes as Rosie squealed.

So tonight we girls had to talk about Mother's secret.

"That's why she gets migraines and has to take naps." Rosie offered. Rosie was just 7 years old, but she had her theories. "She's still sad."

"Yeah," said Jeannie, "maybe that's why she's moody all the time." Then Rosie's little voice came out of the dark in the corner again. "Do you think she really loves Daddy?"

"I think she does," I answered. "Hey! You know the picture of Mom and Dad in the corner of the den?

Their wedding picture?"

"Yeah," said Jeannie. "Mother wasn't wearing a white wedding dress! She was wearing a pink suit with flowers on the lapel."

"That's why! Her first wedding used up the chance for a proper veil!" *Right,* I thought, *I've got to see them*: the real white wedding pictures were probably still in the trunk.

"If the soldier didn't get killed, would you love him as our dad?" Rosie asked.

"We wouldn't even be born if he didn't get killed," I said. "We're half Dad and half Mom," I said. You have to slow down for little kids like Rosie when topics of this magnitude are discussed.

"I'm not half of anybody," she said defiantly, "I'm me!"

Then Jeannie said, "I think that's why Mom stays after Mass every Sunday."

"So she can be alone with her prayers for her first husband," I added.

"I bet she still misses him," Rosie said quietly.

How could you miss someone after they were dead for so long? I wondered. The soldier had been dead for longer than we were even alive. But it was true: when everyone else clears out of the church, Mom kneels in the pew reading her prayer book full of holy cards. (Gold edged, decorated on the front with Renaissance Blessed Mothers or scenarios of famous martyrs being shot up with arrows or burned at the stake).

"Maybe that's why she's so devoted to the Blessed Mother," Jeannie suggested. I hated to admit it, but I thought Jeannie was right.

The Blessed Mary *was* Mother's pet saint, even though she wasn't technically a saint. As we all knew, the Blessed Mother is well above the angels and saints. Chosen to be the mother of God, Mary managed to get pregnant without going through any of the usual channels. Even though we didn't understand what it meant, we *believed* in The Immaculate Conception, the Virgin Birth, the Holy Ghost--and were ready to be martyrs for it all.

I used to imagine the lot of us rounded up around a boiling pot of water in the jungle while pygmies gathered 'round trying to get us to chicken out of our Catholic beliefs. They'd be standing on their short legs, shifting their weight from foot to foot in anticipation, hands on their spears staked in the ground next to them, grinning like we do in front of our fried chicken dinner. I couldn't picture what would happen at the critical moment, when all the darkies, silent and salivating, waited for my response to, *You! Number 6! Articulate deception? Denounce it or we're going to eat you!* Would I stride confidently up to the steaming vat? Would I have the courage, knowing I'd be triumphant in correcting their pronunciation, but still ignorant of what Immaculate Conception or Special Dispensation, or any of it, really meant exactly? At the critical moment, would it boost my bravery knowing I'd be canonized a saint? That the drama of my scalding would ultimately be reduced to a routine martyr scene, printed on gold-edged holy cards and tucked inside my mother's prayer book?

No! *The Blessed Mother* would come to the rescue! Of course she would. (I would give up the golden image of my martyrdom on the holy card if she'd miraculously pull me out of the pygmy clutches at the last second.)

I was counting on it. She had a special mission in life: to intervene on our behalf, to whisper things into God's ear that would put us into His special favor or remind Him to show a little mercy. (God, being so perfect and capital "G," was somehow excused for doing dramatic and frightening things only He could be responsible for, like wars, disease, tidal waves, earthquakes and having shrimpy Africans boil little children alive just to prove their loyalty to Him).

It was easy to see how even God Almighty could get carried away with all that raw power. Clearly He needed someone to hold him back, so as a practical consideration, He created the gentler Blessed Mother. And we prayed to her, just in case we ever found ourselves surrounded by pygmies.

Out of thirteen children born to her, Mother named eight after Mary, the mother of God. Something must have happened; either some heavenly panic visited her or a secret holy pact was struck with The Blessed Mother because five of my *brothers* were given the middle name of Mary. Mostly the kids in the second half of the family got it. As if Mother was just too darn tired after the seventh birth or the ninth birth or the twelfth to dream up a second name.

The next day I caught Mother in the bathroom. I had been tracking her around the house so she would notice me. Last week I hid behind the coats then casually appeared wherever she was, pretending to be doing something. I found out that she took a nap every afternoon once the little kids were down. The rest of the time, if she wasn't sterilizing baby bottles or changing diapers, it was dishes or laundry. Or she helped the kids find things, saying "Dear St. Anthony, please come around, something is lost and can't be found." Sometimes she helped Clara (#2) or Madcap (#4) with their sewing when they got frustrated. She had these thick veins in her legs, and she wore beige stockings and thick shoes. I could tell when she was tired: she would sigh. And if she didn't take her nap every afternoon, she would get migraines.

But, there was only one place where I could always find Mother with no kids around: the bathroom. So I camped outside that bathroom door. Sometimes I asked her questions. Sometimes I just said "Hi, Mom" and read a book.

Today, I sat down on the floor and leaned against the door. I got my pencil and started doing my homework assignment.

Life is not fair, I started, reading over what I had already written. *Wanda only has one measly little brother. Sally has two. How long is it going to take for them to write a paper on their family? Am I being punished? I've got eight brothers and four sisters.*

Number 1. Paul is also known as Big Cheese, because his feet are big and he wears the same socks five days in a row, until they're stiff. And they stink! He's 18 years old.

Number 2. Clara is 17 years old and super bossy, but a very cool teenager (with boobs) and really nice when she's in a good mood.

Number 3. John-the-Blimp is 16 years old. When we're mad at him, we call him Fatso Freshy. He deserves it.

Number 4. Margaret is Madcap because she's

eccentric. She comes home late from school without a good explanation, cuts classes and hides things in her lunch bag. Even though she gets good grades and looks beautiful, she smokes cigarettes and dresses immodestly in short skirts and black stockings. She's 15 years old.

Number 5. Bartholomew is 14 years old. We call him Bart the fart 'cause whatever he eats makes him toot.

My hand was getting stiff from writing.

"Mom?" I called to her over the the transom window.

"Yes, Annie."

"Why did you name me Annie?"

"I named you Mary. Your father wanted to call you Annie. Saint Anne is the mother of Mary and the Grandmother of Jesus."

I started writing again.

I'm Number 6. Sometimes I'm known as Skinny Milink the Graveyard Dancer because I'm spindly like a bag of bones at the graveyard. Mother wanted to name me Mary, but Daddy won on that one and everyone calls me Annie. When Mother is mad at me she says, "Mary Ann!" I like Annie Shea, it has a ring to it. I'm glad they don't call me anything having to do with my red hair. I turned 12 on January 8th.

"Ok, Mom, why did you want to name me Mary?" I called through the bathroom door. There aren't many stories about me, but I wanted to hear one. And I *was* the first Mary, even though it's my middle name.

"It's Blessed Mother's name," she said, over the sound of the toilet flushing.

"I know Mom! So you named me after the Blessed Mother?" I had to yell so she could hear me. "Why?

Was there something special about me?" I was setting myself up for a compliment.

"If I gave you that name, I thought maybe Mary could always watch over you in a special way." Now I could hear the water running in the sink.

"What about the boys? Why'd you give Mary as a middle name to the boys?"

"It works the same way for the boys," she said. "The Blessed Mother can take care of them, too."

"Mary is not a boy's name."

"There are boys who have Mary as a middle name." Her hand was on the door handle.

"Oh, really?" I said as she opened the door.

"Really," she said, wiping her hands on her apron.

"Pray tell," I said, but she didn't answer. So then I looked back at my list.

Number 7. Holy Moley. Mother loves everything Jeannie does and she can do no wrong. (Jeannie is 11). If it wasn't a mortal sin to hate someone, I would hate her.

Number 8. Dominic Vo Biscum. When Mother told us his name was Dominic, John-the-Blimp said, "Vo Biscum" We said "Et cum spiri tu tu oh," and it stuck. Dominic is 9 years old.

Number 9. Rosie is short and sweet, and we can't help but love her. She's named after Saint Rose of Lima. Mother usually dresses her in the color rose. She's 7 years old.

Number 10. Luke is Buddy. He's six. He was named after the apostle St. Luke, the patron saint of artists, doctors, students, and butchers. (Butchers?)

Numbers 11 & 12. The twins, Matthew and Mark are 4 years old. They're named after the apostles. Darling.

Number 13. Jude is just 1½ years old. He's named

after St. Jude, the patron saint of desperate cases.

I finished the assignment. Daddy wasn't scheduled to be home for another two hours. I put my homework down and went out to the shed. I heard voices in the front yard; the boys were folding their newspapers for their paper routes. I listened for Daddy's car up the driveway. The coast was clear.

The shed, a drooping building made of dry, splintery wood that smelled like stale oil and grime, was attached to the back of the house. The door creaked. Inside, bursting sunshine lit the darkness as it poured through the doorway in a single line. I closed the door behind me, and waited for my eyes to adjust. Then I knelt down in front of the box. Now what? It would be just my luck that Daddy would come home unexpectedly and accidentally lock me in the shed.

The book with the photographs of Mother's wedding sat on top, where we had tossed it just as Daddy discovered us. I opened it and stood in the glow of sunshine coming through the slat. Our mother's face was so plump and smooth. She wore a white satin dress down to the floor with a veil to her waist and a big bouquet of flowers wrapped in a shiny satin ribbon. Her soldier wore the khaki uniform of the United States Army. He had a young face, too, was much taller than she was, and quite thin. He looked pleased with himself. His hand on her white dress gently touched our mother's waist. Her eyes sparkled. It was hard to imagine that the flowers she held had wilted and gone mushy and that the man whose face I saw was just a skeleton in some grave. I read the clippings.

Katherine Alice McLellan married Clifford Mary

Adamson *on my birthday*! In 1944, on January 8th in Milwaukee, Wisconsin at the chapel in the Old Soldiers Home. I was feeling really special about my birthday and my middle name when something white fell from the pile of photographs.

I held up the square white envelope in the beam of sunlight streaming through the darkness. Mother's familiar handwriting said *Feb 2, 1945* on the outside. Tucked inside was a makeshift wax paper envelope holding a thin clump of soft, blonde hair. Then I spied a hospital identification bracelet in the white envelope. Every one of us has one of these from our own birth, given to us by Mother for our First Holy Communion. I recognized it instantly. This one was made of blue glass beads with white beads etched in black letters, spelling "baby boy adamson." I touched it, feeling the love that put it there so reverently.

Suddenly, I had a thousand questions.

CHAPTER 3
BRIDE(S) OF CHRIST

June 6 – Dear Diary, Now I am the keeper of a very
big family secret. It's not enough that Mother was
married to someone we just found out about. I think
she had a baby, too! If there is a secret baby, I feel like
I have loved it for a long time. Even though it would
be older than me by now. I don't want to tell anyone.
It's my secret.

Yesterday I was home with a really bad cold. After
school, Wanda called and said the teacher read my
mystery story "The Bleeding Crucifix and the Next
Pope" out loud in class. She said it was really good and
everyone liked it. The only thing I got wrong, Sister
Everista said, was that Christ is not "magic." He's God.
Everyone was talking about our family friend, Cardinal
Stefanucci, being a candidate for The First American
Pope. I smiled a lot and got tons of attention. If this is
God's will, then let it be done!

It almost went without saying that once he got
elected Pope, Father Stefanucci would have to visit us. I
wanted to be on the altar with him, to hold the incense
and cross my hands over the heads of the faithful.
Because I was a girl, being a nun was the closest I could
get.

Mother gave me a wish book of all the orders of

Sisters. I flipped through the pages, looking keenly at the uniforms. The Franciscans, the Dominicans, the Sisters of the Sacred Heart of Jesus. I couldn't decide. The nuns at our school were the Sisters of The Holy Name. I didn't like their uniforms, and I didn't want to have anything to do with them. Their mystique had been depleted by daily contact.

At first I imagined myself in the various habits. The Daughters of St. Vincent de Paul wore long black wool dresses, white bibs and starched white hats folded into huge wings. I thought that would be cool, balancing that thing on my head and caring for the poor. Everyone in the family would be beam at the sight of me in one of those contraptions, and best of all, my red hair would be invisible! But I was shopping, no commitments yet, and the Carmelites started to look pretty good. Theirs was a chocolate brown habit with a street length sleeveless chasuble over their plain dress. The round, white capes were set off by the dark brown and framed their faces. A rope belt at the waist and a huge dangling cross completed the look. This outfit made them look more like monks. Bonus! I was sold. Secretly, I just wanted to be one of the guys.

In preparation for my vocation, I knew I was supposed to behave like a saint, which for a girl, meant to keep my head down, silently cross myself randomly and never get irritated at anyone. So I developed this nibbling mouth gesture, like I was praying under my breath, that I adopted in case someone was looking at me. I directed it at the numerous paintings and portraits of God and the saints hanging on all the walls of our home, making a point of stopping at each statue and doing a mini-genuflect. Sometimes I imagined we were all having a party: The Sacred Heart, St. Patrick, St. Anthony and St. Therese of the Little Flower, standing on the mantle around the chalice, interrupted by the clock chiming every fifteen minutes. I noticed for the first time that there wasn't a single room where some face of heaven wasn't looking out at us. Even in the bathroom. I felt the pressure of all of them, watching me and adding it all up. Sin? Devotion? Vanity?

But the vows. I felt a little constricted by the vows I'd have to take: Poverty, Chastity and Obedience. I was tired of being the poor family on the block. I didn't understand the need for Chastity. What is it really?) Obedience was another thing. According to Mother, I was always being "willfully *dis*obedient." Maybe I could sow my wild oats like St. Paul did. (Not sure what "sow my wild oats" really meant, but I knew I could probably do it!) I could go back to the nun's life after I had something to be sorry for.

On the other hand, I was kind of lured by the idea that I would be the bride of Christ. What little girl doesn't like to think of herself as a bride? Or a princess?

I began to conjure the wedding scene.

A white flowing gown, tight to my bodice and cinched at the waist (very grown up), a veil covering up my strawberry blonde hair and tiny white flowers around my head. Red roses across my arm. Gloves up to my elbows.

All thirteen of us, from Paul to Jude, plus Wanda, Sister Everista, Monsignor Boyle, and the nuns fill the pews. Families dressed in Sunday best stuff the church to overflowing. I catch a glance from Teresa Feeney.

She's steaming jealous, but I forgive her, because Why Not? Jesus is my fiancé; she'll never do better than that.

Daddy stands with me at the back of the church wearing his Navy Summer Dress Whites, which I love - the hat and gold bands on his shoulders and across his chest. He's a Commander and when you see him in the outfit, you just want to salute.

Maria Callas gently rolls out the soft notes of *Ave Maria*. I can tell by the back of her head that Mother has tears in her eyes at this very second!

Martin Caslow and Zeke Brody lead the boys' choir up the middle in white surplices over their cassocks, forming a semi-circle at the altar facing the congregation. All the boys who throw spit- balls in class and get smacked by the nuns look angelic up there. Two altar boys swing the incense --there's so much of it that grey clouds rise to the dome.

This is Stefanucci's first duty as the new Pope, and he's next in the procession. Decked out in gold vestments, huge glittery gloves and the tall Pope Crown tottering on his head. "Here comes the bride" begins to play on the organ. I'm getting goose bumps. A bunch of officers (friends of Daddy's) stiff and tall in white Navy uniforms walk up on either side of the pews and face each other. You can hear their shoes clicking on the marble floor. They pull out long swords and touch the tips to form an arbor. All eyes are on me as I go up the center aisle, walking under the swords on Daddy's arm.

I can't believe it. *Jesus* (in his best sandals, beige cassock and gold-edged chasuble) is waiting for *me*.

Jesus Christ!

The most famous man in the world. More famous

than Shakespeare! He's so tan (!) from all that time in the desert, his blue eyes twinkle at me affectionately, and his beard is freshly shaved around the edges. His teeth are so white he looks like a toothpaste commercial. He has that Christ glow around His head, so you know for sure it's Him.

I pass by His family in the pew, God the Father, God the Holy Ghost, the Blessed Mother, her cousin Elizabeth, her husband Joseph, the whole gang. And they're all hoping that Jesus has finally made the right choice : "*Two thousand years, and He picks this cute little red-head Annie Shea to be his bride. Yeah, she's feisty, we like her.*" His mother, The Blessed Mother, is so happy she's glowing, like you see around the head of Our Lady of Guadalupe. She glances over at my mother who has been staring at her. They exchange an inspired look of destiny and pride across the aisle. Daddy is now at the front; he gives me a kiss on the cheek and then, *Jesus Christ*, the bridegroom, reaches out for my hand. It's shaking.

Of course, Father Stefanucci, now the Pope, says Mass. When He asks for the ring, Jesus just snaps his fingers and it springs from the pillow and appears in his hands. It's kind of a surprise for the little kids, who are staring at the pillow when the ring disappears. Jesus is right there next to me, his arm around my waist, but he takes the white wafer on his tongue like it's perfectly normal to eat your own body and blood. Everyone is holding their breath for the moment when The Pope says, "I now pronounce you Husband and Wife. You may kiss the bride."

I've never been kissed before, but lately I've been

thinking about it. I've been sitting crossed legged in the closet kissing my two fingers like they were lips and I've practiced to where I'm pretty good now. When you kiss a guy you have to lift your face and look into his eyes. Then, just before he leans in and brushes his lips against yours, you close your eyes…

So that's what I do. I close my eyes and lean in…

But then… *"Brides of Christ."* Hey! That's plural.

Just then, I look around and see a line-up of brides behind me out the church and a mile long into the street, waiting their turn to seal it with a kiss. Agggh! I hadn't thought of that! They say "Bride of Christ" to any girl who wants to be a nun. That means that all the nuns of the middle ages, the Renaissance and beyond are already married to Him! Plus the modern ones. Think about it! The situation is pretty convenient for Him to have thousands and thousands of brides; He can read your thoughts and actions all the time, but you can't see anything He's doing. As a nun, you understand this going in. You turn a blind eye to all the other relationships that Jesus has with the other nuns. Right?

You act as if the idea is perfectly normal.

It's gross. Some of the nuns aren't even that good-looking. Even though their outfits cover up everything but their faces, I can tell. A big nose is big nose. Ugly is ugly.

Okay, maybe that's the point: that Christ loves even the ugly ones. But… married to them? The whole thing is creepy. Why would He set up something so sleazy as that? As a nun, I'm just another girl in a black wool dress and a white bib with wings on her head who has to bow and scrape to the priests, the monsignors, and the archbishops. I have to admit that things being what they are, I'll never be good enough to even be an altar boy, never mind getting to step behind the white gates up on the altar and dangle incense with the priest. I certainly wouldn't be the chosen one! I would just be one of his many nuns, all covered up in strange headgear. Besides, *I* want to be the center of the universe. *I* want to be Number 1, *I* want God to love *me* the most.

No, no, no, this nun thing is definitely not for me.

CHAPTER 4
HIM'S GOT

June 7 – Dear Diary, I wore my new dress today. Wanda and Carole asked me when I was going to Africa as a nun. I said there was a delay. Luckily I brought the nun book, and we looked at the habits. Wanda wants to wear the white wings on her head. Carole is a Doubting Thomas. BY THE WAY. Today I will sacrifice my diary in the service of Father Stefanucci becoming the Pope at the end of June. Instead of saying "Dear Diary," I will say "Dear Jesus" and write letters and prayers to God. This is, from now on, a prayer book instead of a diary.

The day was as gorgeous as it could be. No smog, the sun squinty bright like it is at the Rose Parade, only hot, and I should have been excited at the sight of the waves. We were on a sandy beach that stretched for miles. But there was dread and danger everywhere. Scary music played in the background, the kind that makes you know something bad is going to happen. Mother and I were barefoot; I could feel the sand between my toes. I wanted to run, but nothing in my body worked like it usually does.; I couldn't even move a finger. The iron pot was as round as a witch's and as big as the backyard swimming pool at Clarkie Franklin's house next door. The water wasn't hot enough yet, but the fire burned under it. I was first in line! In my mind, I read the headline: *Youngest nun ever to be sacrificed.* Then I felt something tugging at my foot. Through sleep mud, I heard Daddy's voice.

"Annie, do you want to get up with me this morning? It's time to get dressed." The fear at the pit of my stomach evaporated as I understood that I was in my own bed, that Jeannie and Rosie were dark lumps in theirs.

Yes! Yes I'd love to go with you to Mass this morning! I thought right away. *And you can bet I'll be saying a special thank you prayer to the Blessed Mother.* I was out of my pajamas in one second. I felt the warmth sitting in the pile of them, and the cold in the room.

"This is a special day, Annie," Daddy said as we backed out of the driveway. "You'll pray for me, won't you?"

It always feels special so early in the morning when there's a little bit of chill and no one on the road. You can hear the tires rolling over the asphalt. Cars parked in front of the houses sweat with condensation as the first light of day creeps up. When we pass our neighbors, I imagine them stirring in their beds, still sleepy and exhaling bad breath clouds. In winter, the street lamps fade one after another as the sun rises all around us. The smell of fresh manure wafts up from the manicured lawns on Orange Grove Boulevard and tiny blades of recently sown grass poke up through the soil in early spring. A calm euphoria, the feeling of promise and a comfortable goodness, fills the air. I love these mornings. Especially when I'm the only one who gets up for 6:30 Mass. Because on those mornings, it's just me and Daddy.

Today is Friday. Mass on the first Friday of each month for nine consecutive months guarantees the "grace of a happy death." If you do the novena, the deal is, God will make sure you won't die in your sleep or get killed in a car crash without first saying you're sorry. At the very least you have the chance to clean the slate since your last confession. You won't go to hell. That's the guarantee. It's like buying an insurance policy without having to pay anything. The only thing you sacrifice is your sleep. I had five more Fridays to go.

Today, he said, was his last day at work for the United States Navy. It was the last day he was going to have to work for idiots who bossed him around just because they were above him and had a higher rank.

"But Commander, that's a high rank, isn't it Daddy? Don't you have people you can boss around?"

"I've been in the Navy 21 years, Annie," he confided.

That's what I liked about Daddy – he told you things that were on his mind, like he forgot that you were only 12 going on 13. And when he told you, it's like he was giving you this responsibility to take his side. And you didn't want to let him down.

"In the beginning, I rose quite quickly, during the war," he said. "At Pearl Harbor I was a boot Ensign, but by the time I met your mother I was already a Lieutenant." We were at the corner of the majestic Arroyo Seco Bridge and the road to downtown. The sun was glowing on the horizon. The air was warming up; there were more cars on the road. Pasadena was waking up to her day.

"In the Navy, there's a whole social aspect to getting ahead," Daddy confided. "But with so many kids, it became impossible for your mother. People have their expectations, but it's a different reality when there are 5 children at home under the age of 7. You can't just drop everything and get gussied up for a dinner party. Don't ever tell her this," he paused. He looked over to me as if deciding whether or not his secret would be safe with me. He smiled, a bit sadly. "She wasn't cut out for it. It's a disappointment. But what could I do? I love your Mother."

So Mother wasn't inclined to playing Navy wife to Hoity Toitys? I had to agree with him there. I couldn't imagine her dressed up. There's no way she would wear high heels. For one, her bunions were as big as her toes from standing on her feet all day.

That's the problem with Dad, you can get going on a topic, but sooner or later it always comes back to the same thing: how the kids slowed him down, or used up all his money, or took away his golf time. It made me feel guilty and sad. Now he was resigning from the Navy because he didn't get promoted. And he didn't get promoted because Mom and us kids were hanging off his neck, relying on him to get bargains on massive amounts of food and keeping him from important cocktail parties. I couldn't help thinking about the photograph of Mother in the hospital with that mystery baby on her lap. Daddy acted like it never existed. If I had a baby that disappeared, I might not think impressing other Navy wives was an important thing to do either.

"But Dad," I said, "didn't God want you to have so

many kids? If it's the kids' fault, or if it's Mother's fault for having so many kids, it's really God's fault, isn't it?"

"God is never at fault, honey. And it's not your Mother's fault, either. It's just a disappointment, that's all."

We got to the church doors just in time. The priest was already up on the altar. Mr. Sanchez, who attended Mass every morning since his wife died two years ago gave Daddy a stiff salute.

"Good morning, Commander. Any news of the Conclave in Rome?" he asked,

holding the huge wooden door open for us.

"Nothing yet, Sanchez." We stepped into the cool church and hushed our voices. "God's will be done, whatever it is."

When we got home the house pulsed with the sounds of morning: coffee percolating on the sideboard, the screen door slamming as Bartholomew (#5) put stuff in the VW bus, steam hissing from the iron as Madcap pressed her dress. I melted butter on my steaming bowl of cream of wheat, excited at the prospect of an adventure: we were all going to play hooky from school and drive to China Lake with Daddy for his last day in the United States Navy.

We filled the whole front row of the main conference room at the Naval Ordnance Test Station while a bunch of guys in uniforms gave speeches about our dad. Luckily we had training about how to sit still, from having to go to Mass every Sunday. Mother had to take Jude to the doorway and put him down so he could toddle around. I love how babies are disobedient, how you can't always get them to do what you want.

They just need what they need. Jude didn't want to be cooped up in a room with a bunch of boring old Navy officers, and because he was still a baby, all he had to do was wiggle to get a little bit of freedom. But once they learn how to talk, you can control them by telling them stories. They'll believe anything.

Anyway, the Admirals and officers gave Daddy a plaque and he got up to the microphone.

"It's not so bad that I'm retiring," he quipped, motioning to the lot of us, "I've got my own private mess hall here, in case I get homesick for you guys. Heh, heh, heh." Everyone laughed with Dad. "Once a year on April 15th, I thank the Lord for these kids. I never pay taxes 'cause I've got so many deductions." Laughter again. Maybe Daddy was retiring to become a stand-up comedian. He was saying things like, "Damn the torpedoes, full speed ahead!" as the punch line, or "Praise the Lord and pass the ammunition!" As Jude ran through the aisles with Mother chasing after him, everyone was laughing, like they do on TV when Phyllis Diller tells a joke. Then Rosie (#8) called out from the front row: "Don't give up the ship, Dad!" The crowd roared.

There were a couple of cakes with 7-minute frosting (my favorite) and they had to cut really small slices so all the kids could get a piece. All the Commanders and Captains were standing around the cake table, having coffee, patting Daddy on the back, and bending over and shaking the hands of the little kids. There was one guy who'd survived the war, standing on one good leg. The other leg was just a folded pant leg. He had a cane and was dressed in a long khaki coat, so you didn't really notice it, unless you were short. But I could see that Matthew (#11) was trying to figure it out.

"Him's got only one leg!" he blurted. The room went silent as all faces turned towards little Matthew, age 4, and his big voice. A smile escaped from Daddy, and then he suppressed it. Hopefully no one else saw. We all felt sorry for the guy with only one leg.

After that, we stretched out in a line in front of the enormous metal anchor out front of the building, in birth order. Paul, aka *Big Cheese* (#1) at one end, and Mother holding Jude (#13) at the other next to Daddy in his Navy dress whites. We squinted into the sun as the photographer snapped a picture.

As soon as the car doors were shut, the windows were rolled up and we rolled out of the parking lot, Daddy led the charge. "Him's only got one leg!" he said laughing heartily, egging us on. "Him's only got one leg!" The carload of us were killing ourselves with laughter, barreling down the highway towards Pasadena.

Dear Jesus, The big surprise was, John-the-Blimp announced that he had decided to join the seminary! No offense to you, but John-the-Blimp is not priest material! He just wants some of that residual glory going around about Father Stefanucci possibly becoming the pope. Surely you know this, and you're just letting him work it out on his own. Right? Right?!

CHAPTER 5
JEANNIE OVER THE LINE

June 8 – Dear Jesus, Things are out of control all over again, and it's making me feel twitchy. First of all they've got some weapons called Titan nuclear missiles near Tucson, Arizona. Daddy is up in arms about them; he's going ballistic even though he thinks they're a good idea. Do we really need these? This nuclear bomb talk is scarring me for life, not to mention all the children in my class who are bruising themselves as they fly under their desks in a panic whenever that siren starts to blow. And now Mother is prejudiced against me. She sticks on Jeannie's side whenever we disagree. I don't mean to quarrel, but I try to keep myself from living in a pig sty! Jeannie immediately tattles: "Mother! Annie took my Peds off the fan and did something with them!" So Mother calls me in. I haven't the slightest about her Peds!!! And then, she tries to chop me low by telling EVERYONE in a loud voice WHAT I AM DOING AND WHERE I AM DOING IT. SO YOU SEE HARDLY ANYTHING IS PRIVATE. EVEN MY WRITING IN THIS DIARY. I AM YELLING!

Now that Daddy didn't have to work at the U.S. Navy anymore, we were all recruited into helping him get customers. First of all, he decided to quit smoking his pipes because the American Heart Association said smoking is bad. But the important thing is, while he was quitting smoking and deciding to retire, he bought an American Motors dealership. Therefore, we had to help him send out "Under New Management" announcements. He didn't own the dealership yet—they were waiting for the paperwork to go through—but Daddy said it would be a good time to introduce himself. So Daddy and Mom and the older kids sat around the dining room table on a Saturday afternoon, putting cards in envelopes—hundreds of envelopes —boxes of envelopes—for Daddy's new job.

There was all this sickening talk about John-the-Blimp's unexpected "vocation" and how glad God in heaven must be. I sat there, forced listen to it while my hands quickly moved over the post cards. You could tell Mother and Daddy were just bursting with pride, and John-the-Blimp wallowed in it like a sparrow in a birdbath on a hot day. He had just turned 16, and with this announcement he'd get to be up on the altar for all the special Masses and holidays, with everyone whispering and smiling approvingly. He was even allowed to take his cassock home.

It wasn't like his personality would change now that he was going to be a priest. For instance, he was still fat, and he still held the record as the quickest one to snitch anything edible. This morning the idea that he was now going to be a priest didn't stop him from hiding my geography book as I tore through the house looking everywhere for it, while the whole family waited in the idling car, late for school. It didn't stop him from saying, "Annie, are you having a geography test today? Would you be missing your book by any chance? It's right here!" in front of everybody. Then, producing the book, it didn't stop him from gloating ("If it was a bear, it woulda bit you!") then smacking me on the back of the head as I climbed into the bus.

So now he makes this dramatic entrance wearing his cassock as we sit around the dining room table stacking envelopes.

You think you're God's best buddy now? You're still John-the-Blimp! *There's no way I'm going to confession to you: you need to ask God's forgiveness for all the harassment you do to us All. The. Time.*

"John, would you do all of us the honor of opening this gathering with a prayer to Almighty God?" Daddy asked him. *Like we need his blessing to stuff envelopes!* John opened his arms like he was up on the altar. I felt like I was going to suffocate.

"I have to go to the bathroom," I said quickly, before he could get started, and ran down the hall and up the stairs to my room, slamming the door. *Jesus, Mary and Joseph.* I just wanted to get out of there and catch my breath. And have some privacy for once. If I had to say anything it would be this: Leave me alone. Let me be. Clara and Madcap were so lucky to have their own rooms. I went down the hall to Clara's room, hoping she'd let me sit there. Sometimes she was in a philosophical mood and she'd say things about her exciting life as a teenager or let me try on her clothes or use her nail polish while we listened to her clock radio.

I knocked on her door at the end of the hall. Her bed was neatly made and there were three yearbooks next to her bed. I opened one from 1960 when she was a freshman, looking for her picture. The girls in the black and white photos were so grown up. High school was so daring. There was a club for everything I wanted to do but knew I would never be able to do in real life because it was probably bad for your soul. Like Drama. Which ultimately would lead to Hollywood, a "den of iniquity," according to Mother and Daddy. At St. Andrew's High there was a Drama Club with twenty five girls! A singing club. Even a dance club. Those were things I really wanted to do, but they were absolutely useless in terms of getting ahead in the world and making points in heaven. I closed the book, more irritated than ever. I went to my bedroom to find my diary, because writing down how I was feeling would at least make me feel better.

In the bedroom, the first thing I noticed was Jeannie's bed creeping over the line again by about a foot! She does this on purpose, so *she* can have more space. Her little kingdom around her bed is so perfect. I could hear her in the closet, the hangers making little tinny sounds against each other. *Why isn't she downstairs stuffing envelopes like the rest of us?* Mother probably gave her a dispensation for helping in the kitchen. Mother *always* favors her. So now Jeannie stepped out of the closet with my new dress on that I just made! The dark blue shift with the bib around the neck. I worked so hard on that one. The one I wanted to wear to Candy Kohler's pool party.

"Take off my shift!" I accused her.

"You said I could try it on." I pushed her bed back to her side of the room, right on the line we drew on the floor. Something crashed to the ground. I didn't care.

"And keep your bed on your side of the room!" I yelled. Finally, some satisfaction. Jeannie went over to the crashed shards.

"Now you've done it," she accused me. "It's my statue of the Sacred Heart that Mother gave me! Look what you've done! It's all broken!"

"Well, don't put it on your bedstead that's a foot over the line next time!" Yeah, that felt good. She walked over to a small shelf above my bed, with my collection of porcelain penguins. She took the Daddy penguin and threw it to the ground and stomped on it. It splintered under her sneaker.

"There!" she screamed triumphantly.

That's it! The one thing Mother gives me, and Jeannie deliberately breaks it. I rushed over to her, yanking on her hair. She still had my dress on, so I started unzipping it off her back. She swung around and pushed me away.

"Don't touch me!"

"Take my dress off!"

"Make me!" My arm went back to smack her face, but she was already in action, lunging at me. We both toppled to the ground, socking and pinching and straining. If I'm wiry, Jeannie is strong, but I couldn't seem to get a grip on her as we rolled over each other. My legs flailed under her; I felt a sharp pain on my arm near my elbow, like glass stabbing me.

"Owww, Jeannie!" She leaned across me, her arm just within reach of my mouth. I opened and chomped down. She screamed and walloped me across the face. The floor around my arm was wet. We both sobbed, and I twisted my whole body with a great effort to topple Jeannie. When I rolled over, it was Daddy, pulling her up.

"She broke my statue, and then she bit me!" Jeannie blurted in short breaths, her chest heaving.

"She deliberately smashed my penguin!" I blubbered. Blood dripped off my arm. "And she's wearing my new dress without permission."

"You said I could try it."

"I did not!"

"Did!"

"Did not!"

"It's my new dress! I'd *never* let you wear it, you big ape!"

"Pipe down kids!" Daddy's bellowing voice shut us right up.

"What are you doing up here, *fighting*?" he asked. "While the rest of us are downstairs, working hard to put the food on the table, you're up here bickering over a dress?"

"Look at my Sacred Heart!" Jeannie knelt down to assemble the pieces, which by now were swimming in my blood. "She broke it!"

"Annie, that's a statue of the Sacred Heart. How could you go to Mass with me on First Fridays and then break the very statue of the Sacred Heart?"

"Her bed was over the line!"

"This is not Christian behavior."

"It was accidental!"

"It was not!"

"I was pushing your bed back over the line! Where it belongs!"

"Annie, you should be ashamed of yourself."

Like it was all my fault!!!!! Like Jeannie is Miss Perfect.

Holy Moley. Holy Moley, Holy Moley I said over and over in my head. Then Daddy launched into a poem, directed mostly at me. As if *eloquence* was of any use at this particular moment.

Here lies the body of William J
Who died maintaining his right of way
He was right, dead right as he sped along
But he's just as dead as if he were wrong.

Daddy stood there like the ref at a boxing match. We held our corners, sweating and breathing our way to our next move.

"You're both going to get the glue out and put that statue back together, one piece at a time." I held my elbow, dripping with blood, but even that wasn't enough to make him notice *my suffering*.

"You're not coming out of this room until you've apologized to each other." As he walked out the door, his shoes crunched on my broken penguin. But of course, what's a penguin statue compared to the Sacred Heart?

Their theory was, "Don't let the sun go down upon your anger." The sun wasn't even close to going down, but saying you're sorry when you're not is like eating cold vegetables—it makes you want to throw up. "I'm sorry" I quipped sarcastically and slammed the door. I didn't even wait for her feeble squeak. As I was going out the door I turned back into the room for the phony "will you please forgive me," and I saw her, pushing her bed back over the line.

I am not sorry! And this is not the end of this.

CHAPTER 6
MONSIGNOR BOYLE

June 10 – Dear Diary, Today I read an article in a magazine. It said, "Test your talent." I drew some pictures. One was a bulldog. I thought they were just like the ones in the magazine. I sent the bulldog away for the test to "Test your talent." Last night, this young singer named Barbara Streisand sang on The Ed Sullivan Show. *Mother says she's got what it takes. Also today JFK signed a new law, equal pay for women and men. Mother says that after a woman gets married, she should never take on a job—her job is in the home— and if you take a job outside the home, you will get used to the money and you won't be able to give it up when the babies come. Just a reminder, only 11 days left until the Pope gets elected!*

A week of fantasizing about becoming a nun produced what I thought was a well-developed story of me, at 12 years old, becoming the youngest nun ever. I knew the class could not resist; they would burst into applause at my announcement. However, after my depressing realization that nuns are donkeys compared to the stallion glory of the priesthood, I had to come up with something to replace the nun story. I had their attention as long as I had a connection with Stefanucci and the Pope, but all this lying was making me dizzy, and there wasn't time to make up anything before class!

45

I now dreaded Sister Everista's question, *Have you heard from the Cardinal?* Unbelievably, she went straight into Math after the opening prayer.

What a relief! My guardian angel really *was* looking out for me.

But just a few minutes later, our pastor Monsignor Boyle came to visit. We all stood, freshly attentive; there's nothing like a visitor to break up the boredom of school.

"Good morning, Monsignor Boyle," we said in singsong unison. Sister Everista stood beside him, fawning. She always acted like she was the luckiest woman on earth whenever the Monsignor visited her class, and today I think she was blushing. I used to wonder if Monsignor could tell (was she flirting with him?) but I'm pretty sure it didn't even occur to him; he always had this air of being the most important person in the world. He *expected* preferential treatment. And he acted like we all loved him. Let me set the record straight: we didn't *all love him*; he used to grab my nose and pretend to pull it off after Sunday Mass if I accidentally stood too close to Mother. I could hardly wait until Cardinal Stefanucci got elected Pope; I would get some grown-up respect then.

"Good morning, class," Monsignor Boyle said, "I understand that we have with us a close family friend of Cardinal Stefanucci." *Oh, no here it comes*, I thought. *What do I say now that I don't want to be a nun?* "And, that Cardinal Stefanucci," he continued, "may be called to ultimate service by Jesus Christ our Lord to lead the Catholic Church as His Holiness, the Pope."

When he put it like that, it seemed like centuries

of the Catholic Church, all the nuns, priests, bishops and cardinals with all their vestments, incense and gold chalices from the ages came into the room with him and stood there, staring at me. And they could see that I had been lying. Not only was I rejecting the nuns, I had been making up stories to satisfy my own vanity. (*Vanity, vanity, vanity!* Mother always warns.) Right now I was caught, and Monsignor Boyle was going to expose me in front of my entire class! My face started feeling hot. The whole parish would know! I was turning the color of my hair. I glanced over at Wanda, my best friend; she looked terrified. I stood up next to my desk, staring at the floor. Monsignor walked closer.

"And I hear you report anecdotes directly from Rome?" *Busted!* What could I possibly say now to justify my lies?

"Well," I began, trying to think on my feet. Wanda rolled her eyes.

"You're actually talking to the Cardinal?" Monsignor interrupted me, gently and curiously. I searched his face, confused, still unable to speak. "The Cardinal is phoning the family?" Now he sounded like he really wanted to know. (!!!) Wanda looked hopeful. Monsignor was waiting on a word from me.

So I went with it.

"Yes, Monsignor! Last night when he called the house, the gossip was that my father's best friend, Cardinal Stefanucci, reported that he almost had the critical percentage of cardinals on his side." The Monsignor seemed pleased; I was so relieved I was gushing.

"He's an intelligent man," he said, strolling the

aisles, "And he's quite personable."

"Yes, he *is* very intelligent!" I exclaimed a little too eagerly, as if I was the keeper of intelligence standards.

"I met him myself, once, in Rome," he went on.

"He came over to our house *twice*," I bragged, my voice getting louder.

"Oh? What's he like, then?" Ooops! (I was probably 6 years old when he visited. I don't remember him well enough to recognize him on the street).

"He's... taller than me," I blurted, trying to think fast. "And he wears a purple gown with a beanie on head."

"Cardinals wear red, my dear, a red cassock, a red mozzetta over the rochet and a red biretta on their heads."

"He wasn't... Cardinal... yet when he last visited us, so... I think he was wearing civilian clothes." *Oh, God help me! Civilian—that's what Daddy says for non-military people.* But Monsignor didn't seem to notice my gaffe.

"It's not the clothes that make the man. It's his soul," he said, walking up to me and grabbing my nose. (!) He held up his clenched hand, showing his fat thumb between fingers on his fist.

"Got it, he said, "Ha, ha, ha!" (Like I was 5 years old and I would believe that he had pulled my nose off!) My face was practically vibrating with humiliation.

"If the eyes are the windows of the soul, what is the nose?" he grilled me. *What??? There's something religious about the nose?* Wanda was shaking her head.

"It smells sins?" I guessed. Now she looked down at her desk, holding her head in her hands. *The nose is the pantry of the soul?* That didn't sound right. I had to change the subject.

"There's something else," Monsignor, I said, emboldened by panic.

"Yes, my child?" by this time he was roughing up the stiff crew cut on Todd Zimmerman's head.

"He gave me his blessing."

"His blessing?"

"To become a Carmelite nun." The class gasped. Monsignor turned towards me.

"Did he?"

"I'm going to be the youngest nun there ever was." A collective "Oh!" Monsignor smiled.

"Do the Carmelites know this, my child?" He could have been chuckling.

"When the Cardinal gives his blessing, I think the nuns know."

"What about your parents?"

"They said, 'You have my blessing, my child.'"

"And the convent? For the youngest nun ever— where would that be?" Now he was smiling indulgently, humoring me. I had to top that.

"Africa!"

CHAPTER 7
FATHER PIERRE FOR SUPPER

June 11 – Dear Diary, President Kennedy got on television and gave a speech about civil rights. He said segregation "is morally wrong," and he's Catholic, so he should know what's morally wrong. Today the soldiers with guns made sure that two black students could go to a white school in Alabama. I don't think I would like to be the black students. No one wants them at their school. Who would their friends be? Speaking of school, I made an idiot of myself today in class. I ask you: If the eyes are the windows to the soul, what is the nose? That's a new one. Now I have to go to Africa as a nun. Why did I say Africa?

Why *did* I say Africa? It was a seriously dangerous place. On Sunday nights, while Mother prepared dinner, we watched Mutual of Omaha's Wild Kingdom, where we learned about the lions and tigers of Africa—especially how they stalked and killed their prey, voraciously ripping them apart as they lay dead on their backs, their legs splayed, their necks broken, their innards exposed, twitching and hemorrhaging on the savannah. We watched boa constrictors swallow mice whole and squeeze them down their throats. We watched hyenas tear off the skin of zebras while they were still running. It was bloody and disgusting, but we couldn't look away. Daddy subscribed to National Geographic and missionary magazines (all of which lay strewn around the house), and from these we saw the little black barefoot orphan babies with no underpants on and skin so dark it was hard to see their expressions. We pored over photos of wooden lips and ear lobes of walnut brown women carrying water on their heads and holding their babies in a sling; we saw the headdresses, the spears and tribal dances of the men. Under Africa's clear skies I would without a doubt, get third-degree sunburn on my nose to within inches of my life. And sooner or later we were bound to have the ultimate showdown with the pygmies.

Maybe I was thinking "Africa" because a couple of weeks before, a missionary priest from The Belgian Congo had come to visit our parish, and Daddy invited him over for dinner.

Our family often hosted men of the cloth for evening meals. It was a chance for the priest to entertain himself as we did the "exotic" things, routine to an enormous family (like wolfing back an ungodly amount of spaghetti or pork chops in 3 minutes flat). And for Mother and Daddy, a rare opportunity to be acknowledged for all the "thankless work" they did for "you kids." The guest seemed to know his role: there was the expected amount of congratulations at what seemed like Daddy's achievement in fathering and providing for all these children, the understanding that we were an exceptional Catholic family in action. Mother was always in a good mood, Daddy sat at the head of the table in his Captain's chair, regaling our visiting Padre with jokes, mostly about priests and rabbis trying to get into heaven. There was no such thing as punishment when we had a guest; no kids would be strapped with the belt or sent to bed without supper, and we would have something really good to eat, like barbequed steak and French fries. I could finally be a member of The Clean Plate League, as I could spit my canned vegetables into my milk while everyone else was trying to get the priest's attention. We were trotted out on our best behavior as we set the table or loaded the dishwasher or did our homework without complaining. We were the actors, and we loved the stage of a priestly visit.

Leaning out the upstairs window I could see Father Pierre striding up the walk in skinny black trousers and I felt a lurch in my stomach. He didn't look anything like the balding, full-bellied Monsignors we usually hosted. His blonde hair parted in a cut that reminded me of Steve McQueen. He wasn't my idea of an African missionary priest. He looked like a movie star.

"Jeannie! He's coming up the driveway!" Jeannie was changing from her pedal pushers to a summer shift dotted with large sunflowers. We were all trying to wear something that said Africa. I had painted all the faces of the Little Kids with native-looking orange and yellow stripes. Dominic had taken his shirt off and we went crazy painting his chest. I wore my dark green pedal pushers; I didn't want to be one of the natives.

Kids from all corners stomped down the stairs, pounding on the hardwood. Even baby Jude, still trying to get out of the playpen, bounced up and down with "Ennnh ennnh ennh!" Bart threw open the front door and the little kids poured forth. Out of nowhere

Dominic streaked by with native markings on his white chest, calling *Aaaaaaahhhhh! Aaaaaahhh!* as if he were Tarzan, swinging from the vines. Then he disappeared. I looked down at him, flat on his chest where he'd accidentally belly flopped at Father Pierre's feet. I waited for the knee-jerk whimper. But I saw in his expression that Dominic suddenly understood he had an audience; he screwed up his face in determination to stop his tears. The little kids came screeching to a halt, pressing themselves as close as they could to Father Pierre, who smiled as if genuinely pleased. Dominic pulled himself up, grabbed Father's hand and dragged him towards the kitchen. I could tell this priest was a mark. It was going to be a good night.

Just then Clara came sashaying down the steps like she was balancing a book on her head. You could tell she was trying to impress the Padre. As the eldest girl in our family, she knew how to dress up like a lady. Usually she sat on a stool in the kitchen chattering while Mother made supper, in her blue plaid school uniform skirt and bobby socks, dusty from the day's activities in the school yard, but that afternoon she put on nylons and a straight skirt with a soft green top that looked so tight it might have been a second skin. It had the effect of highlighting her curvy, bosomy shape so that even I had to stare. She wore a string of Mother's pearls. She smelled of perfume and her nails were painted a coral color. She stepped gingerly down the steps in heels like she was a debutante in her big "ta da!" moment. I just stood back and sighed. With her long eyelashes and big green eyes, her short bubble hairdo and her soft skin, she looked so glamorous. Very Jackie Kennedy. A feeling of pride welled up in me: this was *my sister*. I had never seen the two things, glamour and bedlam, in the same room at the same time, but there they were as Clara entered the room, like a vision of heaven or *Seventeen Magazine*.

Just then, Mother pushed open the pantry door into the dining room, wiping her hands on her apron.

Father Pierre reluctantly shifted his gaze from Clara then pulled a hand-carved black statue from his pocket and offered it to Mother.

"*Voila* the Madonna," he said in a French accent as he held it up for her.

"The Blessed Mother of The Congo?" Mother asked, hopefully.

"Hand made by the natives."

I was shocked. The Mother in the statue had huge boobs pointing straight out. She was pregnant, but she already had baby Jesus on her lap and her lips were enormous. Not sure how they were going to explain that in Catholic terms. Our mother put the little statue on the mantle next to the Sacred Heart.

"Do they serve Martinis in The Congo?" She eyed Dominic, hanging from Father's arm, the orange and yellow paint on his chest smudging Father's sleeve.

"*Mais, non, Madame* Shea," he said.

"Would you like one, Father?"

"*Mais, oui, Madame* Shea," he replied, delight almost leaping out of his mouth. "May I help?"

"Why don't you make yourself at home?" Mother turned back into the kitchen. Dominic swung from Father's arm. Luke fired rubber bands from the couch; poison arrows from the African jungle. They whizzed by; Luke is a terrible shot.

Just then all the lights went out in the house. The dishwasher, splashing in the pantry, stopped. There was silence where the egg beater had been making a drilling noise. The record player, wound down on the chorus of an Andy Williams song: *Can't get used to loowsing yoouw.* We all shut up, standing where we were, looking at each other, waiting for a diagnosis.

"Fuse!" yelled Paul (#1) from upstairs. He sounded annoyed "Turn off the fan! You've overloaded it again!"

• • •

"All hands on deck!!" Mother announced. She yanked on the bell rope, *Clang! Clang! Clang!* As Daddy carried in a tray of steaming steaks, the smoky smell of burning meat and sizzling fat wafted into the room.

In the living room, Jude clung to the playpen, his stinking diaper still full and smelly. I looked around: Clara sat poised on the edge of the couch giggling shyly with Father Pierre. Madcap was nowhere to be seen, and Bartholomew never helped with the little kids anyway. I was next in line. Jeannie, who was fully capable, was probably in the kitchen, kissing up to Mother. I picked up Jude and carried him at arm's length into the bedroom, deposited him in his bed while I warmed up the water and wet a washcloth.

"Hey, Jude! Jude-y Jude-y Jude-y! We're gonna clean up your *diaper!*" You have to talk to babies like that, getting excited about things like pooping and getting into jammies. Tone of voice is everything.

As soon as I laid him on his back, his plump little legs kicked vigorously. With one hand, I unfastened the diaper pins and opened the diaper hamper. The unmistakable smell of steaming pee was unavoidable. I dropped the whole diaper into the diaper hamper and put the lid back on. Jude was not easy to help. I held him under the faucet, rinsing his little bottom and trying to soap it up. When the water hit his skin, he yowled. Everyone calls me Skinny Milink because I'm wiry, and wiry can be strong. But Jude was fat and heavy, almost propelling himself out of my arms. Finally I got him back on the bassinet, but it took all my strength to hold him there with one hand, as I pinned a dry diaper on him.

"Hey, settle down," I said, like I was his best buddy. "We don't want to miss out on the missionary from Africa!" A giddy delight lit up his face. He squealed and giggled, reaching up to me like I was his savior. I pulled him up and swung him onto my hip, one leg on either side.

We all stared at the heaping plates of steaks, a huge bowl of hot French fries and a plate of pale green beans in water. This was the best and worst part of supper. Best because of the anticipation, the mouth-watering food all stacked up. Worst because of the forced waiting while Daddy served everybody, in order of birth. First the priest, then Paul, Clara, John Madcap, Bart. Six people had to be served before me. I was starving.

Okay, not like the little black babies in Africa starving. America starving.

It was almost unbearable. Each plate passed from hand to hand around the table. *Hey! He just served Jeannie!* Surely Daddy was just testing me. When he sat down to his own full plate and asked Father Pierre to begin with the prayer, I caught Mother's eye as tears spilled down my cheeks.

"You forgot Annie!" Mother announced, and all eyes focused on me, wallowing in self-pity at the end of the table. The more I tried to hold back my tears, the more they poured forth. Father Pierre glanced at me and a reluctant smile crept up on his face. Gaaaaa! Couldn't I just once hide my feelings?

"It's all gone!" Bart teased, "There's none left for Annie!" he gloated. He leaned over, practically yelling in my ear. "You're going to have to go to bed *hungry*."

I picked up his elbow and smashed it on the table.

"No elbows on the table!" I announced. Instantly, he smacked me with the back of his hand across the face. I shrieked and burst into tears.

"Bartholomew!" Mother said sharply.

Father Pierre began the prayer over our meal. At the "Amen," it was as if we had all been on the starting line and someone had just yelled, "Mark, set, go!" The clinking sound of knives and forks, of swallowing and gulping air between bites was pretty much all you could hear as we harked it back. A rare moment of relative silence, and then we came up for seconds.

"You forgot to say Eternal Rest!" Rosie blurted. As far as I knew we were the only family who recited a prayer for the dead as part of grace over meals. Normally this was another mortifying, unavoidable detail of living in a Catholic family of 15, but tonight we had an audience and he was a priest, so we felt proud. *"May their souls and all the souls of the faithful departed, through the mercy of God, rest in peace, Amen."* Once again, our voices died down to silence.

John-the-Blimp punctuated the quiet with a deep,

grumbly burp. Instead of being embarrassed, he sat there, satiated, like he was proud of his accomplishment. "It's better to burp and be in shame, than not to burp and be in pain."

"John!" Daddy said.

After the table was cleared, we had to say the rosary, so the Communists could be eradicated. Father Pierre knelt down in the middle of the living room. Mother came rushing in, having just put Jude in his crib in the back bedroom.

Then Daddy gave us the lecture about Communism. Again. Just last year there was some kind of showdown with Russia a few miles from the coast of Florida, and for a few nights we went to bed worried if we were going to get bombed to smithereens. Tonight Daddy was an expert on Our Lady of Fatima (who was really The Blessed Mother dressed up as Our Lady of Fatima). This version of The Blessed Mother appeared to three little kids while they were tending sheep. Their message: "Unless a certain number of people say the Rosary, Russia will spread her errors around the world."

As Daddy said this every night, I often asked myself, *Who would these "certain number of people" be?* We were the only family in the whole of North America doing this as far as I could tell. Not a single soul at our school did it. The nuns never admitted to doing it. The priests and Monsignor—if they were saying the rosary, we'd be getting "rosary this" and "rosary that" lectures. So then, the fifteen of us were holding off World War III? On the other hand, maybe it was working. I haven't ever seen any communists around Pasadena.

We started the rosary with Jude down the hall, still

fussing. *Our Father, who art in heaven, hallowed be thy name.* It was bad enough that Jude spent the whole afternoon with a poopy diaper, trying to get out of the playpen. Now Mother was putting him to bed early when we had a special guest. How fair is that? Suddenly Jude shrieked and burst into pitiful wailing. All faces turned towards Mother, but she had her head down as if she didn't hear, fingering her rosary.

Daddy raised his voice trying to drown out Jude's cries. We took our cue and went along. Our voices rose fervently, all of us reciting the Catholic Church's loudest group Hail Mary, but Jude just got more desperate.

I glanced up at Father Pierre. *Did he understand what was going on?* We all knew the drill, our parents had done this with each of us, but tonight we were on display, the exceptional Catholic family. This wasn't supposed to happen.

"Hail Mary, full of grace the Lord is with thee…" I couldn't help but think: what would the Blessed Mother do if it were Jesus in there instead of Jude? "Blessed are thou among women."

By the third decade of the rosary, Jude sounded scared. Maybe he thought no one could hear him, or worse, no one was there. How could Mother stand it? I was itchy to go back and calm him, but I knew I'd lose my place next to Father Pierre.

If someone didn't go now, Jude would go to the next stage.

When babies go beyond rage and panic, the next level of crying is inconsolable. They go on for hours, in a trance. It finally stops when they wear themselves down. They start sucking in the air and whimpering and trailing off. They lie down, thumb in their mouth and fall asleep, exhausted. I couldn't bear to listen to it anymore. Or however long it took until "he learned." Besides, I knew there was another reason for his crying: his diaper was probably soaked with pee and his raw bottom was stinging him. I got up and started towards the back.

"No, Annie, let him go." Daddy ordered me in his Commander voice.

I could barely hear myself squeak. "I'll read him a story until he falls asleep."

"No, Annie. He's stubborn, but he'll learn." I looked around, hoping for some solidarity. Every kid in this room had been through this first hand, whether or not they remembered it. I looked at Dominic, who was nine. When he was Jude's age, he kicked so hard in his high chair that Mother tied his foot to the chair with a sock, then left him in the room by himself for hours, closing the double doors behind him. No one in the house escaped his rage that day.

"He'll cry himself to sleep in a few minutes," my father continued. "Just wait."

I stood there, not daring to disobey him. Jude's voice thickened; he wailed, a long, inconsolable sound. It was excruciating. Everyone was too cowed to do anything about it. Even Madcap, usually somewhat of a rebel, had her head down. And I could hardly believe this was the first time it occurred to me, but suddenly, it seemed all wrong.

I looked at Father Pierre straight in the eye. He wasn't doing anything either. It just made me mad. Here we were, showing off how good we were, what perfect Catholics and we couldn't even pick up a crying baby and comfort him.

"Do you let your little orphans cry themselves to sleep like that in Africa?" I blurted. He was certainly surprised, and I could hardly believe I had just said that. Everyone looked as stunned as I was, so I took advantage and ran out of the room. *You just come and spank me!* I didn't dare say it, but I slammed the door and ran down to Jude's room. The sight of me just made him scream louder. I picked him up and laid him on the bassinet anyway. His diaper was soaked and his bottom was raw.

CHAPTER 8
SHEA FAMILY MOTORS

June 15 – Dear Jesus, I looked through the Bible today, calling to mind thy sufferings and death. I always enjoy looking over this part of scripture. They really tortured you. Maybe that's why the littlest always gets left in the crib to cry himself to sleep—Mother and Daddy are preparing us for when we're going to be tortured. Last night, after dinner and the rosary, all the kids watched Walt Disney. The show was The Son of Flubber. *I was not feeling well. I kept praying to you not to let me have the flu. But I guess it was your will that I suffer. I ran to the bathroom with that horrible feeling and spit up. You gave me this penance and I am offering it up for your glory. I already offered up some of it all over the bathroom. Usually it's disgusting to even get near the toilet, but when you have the flu, it doesn't seem so bad to have your mouth wide open right next to the bowl. Mother cleaned it up. I hate the flu. But it's probably not as bad as getting crucified.*

When the Cardinals met at the Sistine Chapel in 1963 to elect a Pope, there were eighty three of them, including Cardinal Stefanucci. It was the largest conclave ever, a fact I thought might be God's clue to us that our favorite Cardinal would win. The Feeneys were still ahead of us in standing in the parish, they already had 14 children and there was no sign of

Mother having another baby, but if Cardinal Stefanucci became the Pope, Teresa Feeney would have to hold her tongue.

Almost two weeks after Pope John died, the day after school let out for summer, but before the white smoke went up to announce the decision of those eighty three cardinals, a Soviet astronaut was launched into space and Daddy opened up his new business. We all went down to celebrate the Grand Opening of Shea Family Motors, a car dealership with one set of gas pumps.

The day before, we spent the whole time after school blowing up balloons and baking cookies. In the kitchen Jeannie and Clara were in charge of making the dough and putting cookie sheets in the oven. The baking smell of warm sugar permeated the house. Even the little kids stayed up past their bedtime, decorating cookies with red, white and blue sprinkles, to go with the color of the AMC logo. Mother let us listen to the radio and we heard the count down to the top ten best songs for that week on the radio. We sang along with: "Do You Want to Know a Secret" and "Can't get used to losing you" ("gonna live my whole life through, dunh dunh, lovin' you"). On the dunh dunh everyone nodded their heads in unison like piano keys being plunked at the same time.

Madcap was in charge of painting the signs: "Grand Opening!" "Welcome!" "Under New Management" "Let's Make a Deal!" I liked art, too, and I added small daisies to each sign to give them an artistic look.. Daddy wrote out a list of what he wanted the signs to say and we used a real brush and red paint on white butcher er. "Big Sale!" "Price Reduced!" "One owner!" There was always an exclamation point, because you had to generate excitement. Buying something big like a car can be a thrilling event in a life and people in a frenzied state are usually good impulse buyers, Daddy said. Bartholomew and John-the-Blimp took care of the balloons, piling them into a corner and stringing them together. Sometimes John popped a balloon and everyone jumped in surprise.

Mother gave the twins a job which highlighted their strengths. Namely that they were the cutest two little guys you could ever lay your eyes on, and when they were both dressed in shorts, knee socks and small ties, everyone had to say "Awwww!" even if they didn't say it out loud. So Mother asked me to put them at the entrance to the lot next to a table of doughnuts. They were going to soften up the customers. That night, at bedtime, their little suits ready at the bottom of their beds, they fell asleep, repeating to themselves, "Welcome to Shea Motors. Would you like a doughnut?"

Dad got Paul, John, and Bartholomew company uniforms—short-sleeve shirts with buttons up the front and pointed collars with the logo of Texaco on the pocket. When the first batch of balloons was ready, Daddy took the three of them down to show the boys how to pump gas, clean off windshields and check the oil.

He put a crucifix in the office right above the till, and a statue of the Blessed Mother next to the coffee urn in the show room where people would make deals to buy their cars. There was a large family photograph, the one taken on the day Daddy retired from the U.S.

Navy, with all 13 of us lined up outside the big anchor at the China Lake office. This photograph was framed and placed in the center of the table in the showroom.

Everyone knows how to rub a car until it sparkles and cleaning windows is a reward unto itself, but I really wanted to learn how to pump gas and check the oil.

But the next morning we were told to put on our Easter dresses and shoes. Mother said we had to introduce ourselves to whoever came onto the lot. If we saw someone seriously looking, we had to politely excuse ourselves and get Daddy. The big girls—Clara, Madcap and me—were supposed to read the brochures on the new Ramblers and memorize facts about the cars. If we helped sell a car, maybe we could get some kind of commission.

Daddy said American Motors had the mid-size high performance luxury compact market to itself, and he was going to sell a lot of cars. The prices on the windows of the cars told you right away which ones were used and which ones were new. There were only five used cars, with prices from $175 to $850. The feature car, sitting in the middle of the lot cost $2,665. We were going to be rich enough to be able to afford wall-to-wall carpets once we sold all those cars.

Daddy had to give up 6:30 Mass because he had to open the garage at 7:00 to sell gas. He wanted to be there on the first day, to make sure it all went smoothly. First impressions are lasting, he kept saying. Besides, God wanted him to succeed, and sometimes you have to skip Mass to do it.

I called Wanda the night before, inviting her and

her family to come on down.

We all got out of the Volkswagen bus at 9:00, Saturday morning, spilling onto the lot. The effort of it felt like we were bundling up for Sunday Mass. But there was no one there, and the place looked worn and dingy in contrast to the three, new, shiny automobiles and five used cars. (A Ford Falcon, an old Austin Healey, a Volkswagen bug and two others I didn't know the names of). "Start small and think big" was Daddy's motto, which he repeated when he saw me looking forlornly at the lot, surrounded by multi-colored, triangular flags that blew in the breeze. Me and Madcap hung around together, looking like Easter morning in our chiffon dresses, poised to receive the hordes. The smell of coffee in the urn made me hungry. Paul, John, and Bartholomew stood at attention behind the glass in the indoor showroom, their feet apart, their arms folded across their chests, waiting for their first customer. A lone red Volkswagen bug tooled up to the pumps and Paul, John, and Bartholomew descended upon it. Paul lifted up the hood and checked the oil, John-the-Blimp went to the window to ask if they wanted Regular or High Test, and Bartholomew brought the tan cloth and the Windex for the windshield.

The twins lolled about in close proximity to a huge box of glazed doughnuts and already there was sugar down Luke's vest and crumbs on Markie's face. They looked green and uncomfortable, and their small hands were full of bitten doughnuts.

Finally around 11:00, there was a rush. A bunch of families from the parish arrived, and I fully expected Daddy to gather in their midst and say some kind of prayer. Instead, he took them to the Ambassador and gave a speech about its luxurious interior, its vinyl bucket seats, head rests, and color coordinated shag carpets. He invited them to sit inside while he told them about the dual chamber master brake cylinder, separating the front and rear brakes, so that in case one failed, the other brake would come to the rescue. Daddy said AMC had made the car of the future. It was also lighter than the 1962 Classic and had a V-8 engine. Every other car manufacturer, Daddy said, was playing copycat with their new compacts. AMC was a truly visionary company. I felt pride by association, even though nobody seemed to want to buy anything.

What I noticed particularly was that the men got in the car, moved the gearshift and pressed all the buttons, while the women strolled around doing small talk with Mother. I could tell her feet hurt; she wore canvas sneakers with white shoelaces and kept wanting to sit down. Clara and Jeannie strolled the lot with Jude on a hip, until a group of boys from the high school arrived, and the next thing you know they were all gathered around Clara in a circle. In the farther reaches of the blacktop, where the used cars sat glinting in the sun Me and Madcap hung out, making smart comments about anybody who walked onto the lot. I held the brochure in my hand, ready to tell people about The Ambassador, but I really wanted to take one of those cloths and rub the shiny cars until they were good enough for Jesus to parade into town on a Palm Sunday. There was enough room for him and three of the apostles in the new Ambassador, and I wanted that automobile to glisten like a jewel.

Suddenly a new group of people parked their cars on the street and stepped out. Wanda and her dad. Right behind them was the Feeney station wagon full of a bunch of kids of all ages. My heart sank. Wanda had obviously invited them. The little kids from both families didn't know any better and soon they were chasing each other around the lot, playing hide-and-seek behind the gas pumps. Paul and John had discovered the switch that made the car lift up and down in the bay, and its growling sound started up as the huge metal frame went slowly up from the floor on a pole towards the ceiling. Daddy was in the lot giving his speech to Mr. Feeney. Mother and Mrs. Feeney chatted amicably in the showroom around the coffee urn. One of the Zimmerman boys drove up and stepped out with Teresa Feeney and opened the door for her, like she was stepping out on a red carpet. Her hair was exceptionally smooth, new bangs across her forehead and a shoulder length flip. Suddenly I was glad I had worn my Easter dress. I waved to Wanda, trying to seem friendly, although I was disgusted that she had invited the Feeneys.

Wanda's father walked with his hands in his pockets, past the cars, looking at my signs with the daisies. This was my chance to use my newfound knowledge of the Ambassador. He had stopped at the Ford Falcon, which looked to me a lot like the Ambassador.

"Hi, Mr. Anderson," I said.

"Hi, Annie," Mr. Nowakowski greeted me. "Quite an operation here!"

"That's right, Mr. Nowakowski. AMC is the car manufacturer of the future." Madcap sidled away from me.

"Did you see the new Ambassador, Mr. Nowakowski? It has curved glass and push button door handles. It's Rambler's newest car, the car of the future," I added, trying to remember the bit about the brakes.

"I'm attracted to it," Mr. Nowakowski said, smiling.

"It has vinyl bucket seats, Mr. Nowakowski."

"Thank you for pointing that out, Annie. That's quite a feature."

I liked Mr. Nowakowski. It was usually the weekend whenever I came over to Wanda's house and Mr. Nowakowski would be home from work, wearing slacks and a casual sweater. He'd see me and say, "Oh, hello, Annie!" as if he was surprised, but delighted. "Ready for some catch?" Then he'd disappear into the bedroom and emerge with a leather mitt on his left hand and a softball nestled in its grip. The other mitt, my mitt, was under his arm. I always thought, *He wants to play catch with* me? But it made me feel in demand. Then he'd say something silly to Wanda about playing with her Barbie dolls for a few minutes while he ducked outside with me. He didn't have the best arm in the world; but I got to be a pretty good catcher because of Mr. Nowakowski. He used to say he liked my "spunk." Wanda told me he always wanted to have a son, but since her mother could only have one child, he had to make do with Wanda. Whom he loved dearly. Because of my hair, I never tried to dress up in girlie clothes unless I had to (for Sunday Mass), so I think he liked the tomboy aspect of my character.

"Actually, if you can keep a secret," Mr. Nowakowski said on the lot, "I'm hoping to get a car for Wanda's mother for her birthday."

"That's some gift, Mr. Nowakowski," I said, trying to sound positive. But the fact that someone could even think of buying a car that cost $2,600 as a *birthday present*, made me feel envious and depressed. Of course, Wanda's Dad was a lawyer and had only one daughter to spend all his money on. Their house was normal to fancy, with carpets and a lanai and a bar for cocktail parties. They always had fresh flowers artistically placed on a shiny black piano that no one ever played. Their kitchen had shiny marble counters and a dishwasher that always worked.

"Do you know about the brakes?" I asked, putting aside my martyr feelings.

"What about the brakes?" Mr. Nowakowski said.

"Well, they're split up, so if one gives out, the other can act as a back up," I said, proud of myself for remembering.

"Hmmmm," he said.

"You don't want a gas guzzler," I told him.

"No, I don't, Annie."

"Then the Ambassador is your car, Mr. Nowakowski. Elegance and efficiency," I said, getting the hang of being a car salesman, "Remember the Double E." I'd just learned "efficiency" when I was reading the brochure. "Fuel efficiency." I already knew elegant.

"Let's go have a look," he said.

So I brought Mr. Nowakowski over to The Ambassador. I invited him to sit inside and touch all the gadgets.

"I'll go get Daddy," I offered, "He can tell you all

the technical stuff." But Daddy was over at the Ford
Falcon, extolling its virtues to Mr. Feeney, right in the
middle of a whole lot of words. Who else would know
about the cars? I ran to get Paul, since he was the eldest
and he was going to work at Shea Family Motors.

"Hey Paul, do you know much about the
Ambassador? Mr. Nowakowski wants to look at it. I
only know the stuff in the brochure." Paul shrugged,
but he went out to Mr. Nowakowski. I could see him
leaning over and talking to Mr. Nowakowski in the
front seat. I thought, how do boys know so much about
cars?

Later, I found out that they talked about how easy
the car was to wax and shine. Paul hadn't even looked
at the brochure. I knew more about it than he did! Mr.
Nowakowski decided to put down cash for the car while
Daddy was shaking hands with Mr. Feeney. Daddy was
so excited, he rewarded him with a commission of 1
per cent of the sale price. $26. It would have been rude
to question Daddy's reward to Paul in front of Mr.
Nowakowski, so I waited until the end of the day when
everyone had left.

"Daddy," I said.

"Yes, Annie."

"I think you're missing the boat," I said, using his
own phrase.

"Oh?" He asked, smiling, quite pleased with
himself and the day's success, the bulk of which was the
outright sale of the Ambassador to Mr. Nowakowski.
Daddy didn't even have to bargain over the sticker
price, since Mr. Nowakowski took the cash out of his
pocket, while saying, "remember the two E's."

"Yes," I teased Daddy with my voice so he would listen. "Since it's Shea Family Motors, I've thought of a slogan to go with the family photo."

"What is it, Annie?"

"Shea Family Motors," I said, like I was an announcer on the radio. "The family that drives together stays together." Daddy looked up from the adding machine and cash box, where he was counting the day's take. He grabbed a piece of paper and a pencil and started scribbling.

"Shea Family Motors," he said, "Our family means business."

"Or how about this," I suggested: "Shea Family Motors: Cars of tomorrow for the family of today."

Then Daddy said, "Today's family, tomorrow's car. But it's more than selling cars," Daddy said. "It's everything about cars. Gas, clean windshields, oil changes, tires rotated. It's a business. With a family feeling."

"How about this one?" I ventured. "Shea Family Motors. A family business with a family feeling."

"I think I've got it," he said. "Shea Family Motors. We mean business about family. That's it!" he said, triumphant, scribbling the slogan. "Annie, you've got quite a head on your shoulders."

"Daddy?" I said, now that he was for sure in a great mood. "When Mr. Nowakowski came on the lot, I was the first person to talk to him. He's Wanda's Dad, you know. Wanda's my best friend."

"Aren't you proud of Paul?" He asked me. I could see this forming up to be another one of our one-sided conversations.

"I told Mr. Nowakowski about the dual action brakes," I insisted, determined to keep his attention, "and the bucket seats and the fuel efficiency."

"A cash sale!" Daddy exclaimed. "I taught Paul the routine yesterday with the Sales Manager, when the buyer wants to bargain on the sticker price, but we didn't even have to use it on Mr. Nowakowski."

"Dad."

"That's the kind of time you need a lawyer," he chuckled. "When he wants to part with his money. Heh heh heh."

"Dad? Will you please listen? I read the brochure while we were waiting around for someone to visit the lot. That's how I knew what to say. Mr. Nowakowski told me first that he wanted to buy a car for Wanda's mother. I told him about the bucket seats and the dual action brakes. Then I went to get you, but you were talking to Mr. Feeney."

"Out with it, Annie. What's the point?"

"I sold that car to Mr. Nowakowski. Paul only talked about how to make it shiny. I deserve the $26."

"Hmm, Annie. I'm proud of you for telling Mr. Nowakowski about the car. But in this business it's all about closing the sale. Paul closed the sale. Mr. Nowakowski pulled out his cash and put it on the table for Paul."

"But I was the one who went to get Paul! Mr. Nowakowski would have given *me* the cash if I hadn't volunteered to get Paul.

"I see your point, Annie. What you don't understand is that Paul is going to grow up and be the breadwinner for his family. You won't have that pressure as a female;

you can get an education and a job as a secretary. That's why Paul is working at Shea Family Motors and you're not. He's getting important training for his role as a man in society. I set up the commission to give him an incentive to be a good salesman. He's going to work for me. That's why he deserves the commission."

"Dad! I deserve the commission!" I said, stamping my feet.

CHAPTER 9
FERTILITY

June 16 – Dear Jesus, I really need a room to myself, so I don't have to constantly be on watch for someone wandering onto my territory and claiming it for themself! If it's not Jeannie, it's Rosie, with her piles and piles of dirty clothes all around her bed. I am so sick of all the junk everywhere! Can't we for once have a really pretty place—not all trashed up with diapers and newspapers and laundry everywhere, and pots all over the place when it rains? Maybe wall-to-wall carpeting in the living room? I realize these are all selfish wishes, because "if wishes were horses, beggars would ride." Please note: my novena for a single room ends Thursday at 2:00 pm.

Life itself flowed relentlessly on Madeline Drive in Pasadena while we waited for our family friend to be elected pope. Fertility blossomed continuously, sloppy and voracious, inhabiting every living thing right under our noses and without our permission. It became an atmosphere surrounding us, a ripe smell, the confluence of hot sun, of throbbing, unknowable forces that populated the known world and permeated our subconscious. Grass creeping around the bricks on the walk up to the front door. Roses sprawling in the formal, weedy beds at the side of the house, an overgrown patch prickly with red, yellow and pink flowers about to bud, in full bloom or falling like confetti onto the ground. The bamboo on the border to Clarkie Franklin's yard sprouted green rods furiously, and no one tried to cut it back. Vines over the ancient wooden arbor swelled with leaves and then hung with purple flowers, and it didn't occur to anyone to trim them until the arbor itself groaned in the middle and slunk under all the weight. My dog Sparky went sniffing around the neighborhood as far as the vacant lot to the north and South Pasadena Avenue to the east and Orange Grove Boulevard to the west. These excursions produced litters of pups, who were born more deeply mutt than he was. We only knew they were his offspring because in each litter, there was one in his spitting image: short and squat, black and white, a bib around the neck and a striped tail that curled up over the rump. Because we were Catholics, we would never spay or neuter our pets. Sparky would return from these excursions trotting proudly, his tongue hanging out, panting in quick puffs, later exhausted and spent as he lay down at the side of the house in the sun and napped the rest of the day.

School was out for summer. Candy Kohler had sent out invitations to a co-ed pool party and girls-only slumber party, the first ever co-ed social get-together for our class. Now I wished I hadn't said anything about being a nun. I really wanted to go to Candy's party and fit it in with everyone else, like a regular person.

Wanda had already "blossomed into a young lady" as Daddy said when she came over for lunch last weekend.

"How's Wanda?" he asked with sudden interest

when she walked into the dining room. It was after breakfast on Saturday, the coffee going cold in the cup in front of him. He stood up from his Captain's chair and opened his arms to give her a hug. She'd been my best friend for four years, all of a sudden Daddy notices her? (and gives her a hug!). When was I going to "blossom"? I was still flat, flat, flat. My nipples looked like mosquito bites pasted to my white, bony chest. It hadn't occurred to them that it was time to begin training for their ultimate role in life (nursing babies). But I could see it coming. I had just turned 12, and soon we'd all be teenagers. I had to seize my life and live it before I was exiled into the convent. I got to thinking about what I should wear in the pool.

Every month *Seventeen Magazine* came in the mail, addressed directly to me, courtesy of my oldest cousin, Jake McLellan in Northern California (a son of Mother's sister). He wrote me letters on blue paper with small handwriting, bragging that he was going to take me out of the nunnery and marry me. I pored over its colorful pages, pretending to belong to this ultra hip world where nun was spelled n-o-n-e, and meant nothing left. Nuns of all shapes and sizes wearing bizarre black clothes and living together in delusion of their special status in fantasy relationships with Jesus Christ was like aliens in outer space to the glamorous people in *Seventeen Magazine*. In last month's issue, there was a promising but ultimately useless article called "How to win arguments with your family." More amazing, it featured a voluptuous model with Wanda breasts and a tanned midriff, casually wearing a two-piece bathing suit with squarish bottoms. When I got

Candy's invitation, I knew *everyone* was going to be wearing a two-piece.

It wasn't often you really needed something, especially clothes, in our family, and no one had that particular thing. This was the case with the bathing suit. There was nothing to hand-me-down. I had gotten too tall in the waist for last year's one piece and Madcap was still wearing hers. Mother had to take me on a shopping trip before the party. It would be just her and me, a spectacularly rare indulgence, and my one chance to get a two-piece bathing suit.

"In case you have any ideas," Mother warned me, "There's no way you're getting a two-piece bathing suit, Annie. They're immodest." She slammed the door to the VW bus and climbed behind the wheel. It was a given that other kids had more liberal parents than mine; lately I'd been noticing Daddy scrutinizing the length of our school uniform skirts and getting into fights, especially with Madcap, about how short is modest.

"As a young woman, it is your duty not to lead the men astray with your immodesty," Daddy lectured Madcap, who routinely rolled up the waistband of her skirt so it was well above her knees. "Lead us not into temptation, but deliver us from evil." One of the advantages of being a Christian who reads the Bible is the convenience of little memorized phrases to whip out during arguments. But Madcap lived outside the lines at our college prep school and was determined not to let Catholic fear of everything handicap her style.

After they yelled at each other, after Madcap said "Expand your mind, Dad," after Dad said "You're so broadminded, you're flat-headed," and finally after Daddy put his foot down, Madcap unrolled her waistband so her skirt hem hung just above her knees. Long enough to get out the door. Then she rolled it right back up.

"Mary Hucklebee and Wanda wear two-piece bathing suits," I said to Mom.

"I don't care what the other kids are wearing," Mother shot back.

"But their belly buttons don't show!"

"I won't buy one for you, and I forbid you to wear one."

Well, the model *next to* the two-piece model in Seventeen Magazine was wearing a blouson suit. I suppose I could be that model at Candy's party, unless by some fluke both my parents had a conversion to paganism. I found a blue and white striped blouson with a navy blue two-piece underneath. The bra was completely flat. My plan was, at the party, I'd take off the blouson top, exposing the two-piece suit underneath. I could stuff the cups with Kleenex and give myself Wanda breasts.

At the store, I held it up on the hanger.

"I kinda like this one," I said, gambling that Mother wouldn't get what I was doing.

"That's what you want?" she asked, skeptically. I shrugged. Mother bought the suit and confiscated the bag. When she plopped it on my bed the morning of the party, the bra had been sewn into the lining of the blouson with tiny stitches. She was worried about *sexy*, which went hand in hand with sin. But sexy was not anywhere near me and my skinny, flat, child's body with frizzy red hair and freckles. There was no danger whatsoever of anything sexy about me, even if my midriff was bared.

Mother also tried to forbid me to shave my legs, but it wasn't against any Catholic dogma, so her arguments didn't have the sticking power of the guilt of generations. The hairs on my legs were soft and blonde, hardly visible; I didn't understand why everyone was shaving, but they all were, and if there was one thing I wanted, it was to fit in. I would have grown a mustache if they were all doing it. To deter me, Mother said if I shaved, those fine hairs would grow back bristly and dark, maybe even red. This, I seriously considered.

I hated my red hair. Lumpy and frizzy and no amount of curling it could get it to be normal. It grew too far down the back of my neck, so if I got it cut short, there was always this peninsula of red fuzz below the hairline. Luckily I didn't usually get a good view of it. And it was orangey and red at the same time; it didn't match anything, but there was no avoiding it; people noticed it and would try to be witty. "Better red than dead." "Your hair is blushing." "How'd you get sunburn on your head?"

Nevertheless, I locked the bathroom door and found one of Daddy's shavers behind the mirror in the cabinet. Since I was lathering up my legs, I took off my underpants so as not to get them wet.

As I began to shave my legs, wouldn't you know it, a new horror presented itself, of all things, dark red hairs growing in *down there*. What? Hairs? What use are hairs down there? No one ever said anything about hairs down there! In a fit of disgust and panic,

I tried to shave the rogue reds away, but in my haste I shaved a chunk of skin, producing copious amounts of blood, which leaked over everything. Also the toilet paper stuck onto the wound, but it didn't seem to do much good, as the deep red liquid replenished itself generously, each time I dabbed it with a new gob of T.P.

"Mother!" I called at the top of my lungs from the bathroom. "*Mother*! I'm bleeding to death!"

"What in the world is the matter?" She came from the kitchen, looking puzzled, closing the door behind her. "Oh, don't worry about this, honey," she said when she saw the blood. Then she reached up behind the mirror and pulled out a thick bandage from a box called "sanitary napkins." She handed it to me.

"This is a really thick bandage, Mom, how do I keep it on the wound?"

"It's not a wound, honey."

"I cut myself trying to shave my legs! For the party." Too mortified to say anything about the hairs.

"But your legs are lower on your body. This is not your legs."

"I know, Mom!" She tried to get me to take my hand off the toilet paper. I recoiled.

"It stings!" I held the bandage over the wound while she attached it with white tape. Neither of us could bring ourselves to speak about the hairs. Some were still left. She had to have seen them.

"How do you say, 'I told you so' without saying, 'I told you so'?" she asked me as she helped me wipe up the blood.

The next day after school, Mother took me to her bedroom and closed the door. She had something important to tell me. About growing into a young lady. *Ok*, I thought, *she's going to elaborate about getting breasts.* It was humiliating beyond words that we both saw my new hairs, but maybe she could tell me about them. It's possible I might have to go to the doctor.

Instead, she read to me from a booklet. "Remember that the body is the temple of the Holy Ghost. You must have higher standards as a woman; you've got to hold it up for everyone. *Noli me tangere* and *Kyrie eleison*. Don't touch me and Lord have mercy. Call upon the Blessed Mother if you need help. One day you'll give birth. Something's going to happen to you to prepare you for being a woman. The road to hell is paved with good intentions."

"But what are you talking about?" I kept asking. I couldn't picture what on earth she meant.

"Don't be afraid of it," she tried to reassure me. How could I be afraid of it? I had no idea what "it" was.

"Madcap," I asked her in her cubbyhole room by the stairs. She sat against her bedstead under the skylight. "Mother said something is going to happen to me to prepare me for being a woman. But she wouldn't tell me what it was."

"It's your period," Madcap said.

"What's a period?"

"It's something that happens when you're old enough."

"How old is old enough?"

"All the girls get it."

"What is it?"

Maybe it was the hairs. God's disgusting punishment for being born a woman. The nightmare was expanding. Did the Blessed Mother have hairs down there? I'll never look at her statue the same way again. And why do they call it "your period"?

It was the Sunday, June 16th, the afternoon of the coed pool party. I arrived early at Candy's house, so I could grow my fake breasts in the privacy of her bathroom. She answered her front door in a short shift just like mine, only hers was red and white with a flower pattern.

"You wearing your two-piece underneath?"

"Yeah," she said, "I got it yesterday! Wait 'til you see!" She already had the music up, "heartache on heartache, blue on blue." We passed through her movie star living room. I say that because it looked like servants had just dusted everything. It was glamorous and the air was cool in there. I looked around, amazed. How could there be nothing broken or scuffed? Where were the laundry baskets? She had a baby brother, but I didn't see any playpens or broken toys. Where did they keep their religious magazines? Their *National Geographics*? And what about the statues? Should I be worrying about Candy's soul? The white couch was spotless and puffy; the glass and mahogany coffee table didn't have one fingerprint. A shiny vase of orange and green Bird of Paradise posed next to the armchair. On the carpet you could see the tracks of the vacuum cleaner where it had laid the rug flat. There was a lot of space in Candy's living room, and it was so quiet. They couldn't actually live here. They must have another house.

In Candy's bathroom I wrapped toilet paper around my hand until it was a thick wad, then I pulled it off my hand and stuffed it in against my skin. The paper seemed springy but I kept balling it up and squeezing it down so it would fit. By the time I was finished with both sides, the whole roll was pretty much used up. Outside, I heard voices and the thumping and splashing of the boys cannon-balling into the water.

I had a look at myself in the mirror. Okay, this was kind of fun. I had breasts, from the looks of it. They were lumpy, but the effect was grown up. It felt kind of good to stick out on the top. I turned sideways. Oh my god, the board bandage kind of stuck out down there! Maybe I could stuff more toilet paper in my swimsuit bottoms to make it all the same. I opened the cupboard under the sink, looking for another roll. Inside, just another box of sanitary napkins and a plunger. Suddenly these sanitary napkins were everywhere. Why are they called napkins? They're bandages.

"Candy!" I called. No answer, just the sound of Teresa Feeney's voice outside the window on the patio. Teresa Feeney, of The Famous Feeney Family. Unfairly gorgeous, six months older than me with silky long hair down her back, right now wearing a Hawaiian style two-piece bathing suit, out of which her Wanda breasts emerged seductively. Teresa Feeney who sizzled with envy as I soaked up the Cardinal Stefanucci attention. She and her brother Christopher stood around the table pouring Kool Aid into their plastic glasses and crunching on potato chips. Teresa nibbled daintily, like the chips were dirty or something. Why did Candy even invite her? I hated Teresa Feeney (scratch that; I'd go to hell if I really hated her. Instead, I *disliked* her as much as you possibly could without committing a sin).

"Candy!" I yelled louder this time.

"What?" from the kitchen.

"I need more TP!" I looked through the slats out at the pool and lanai. Teresa glanced towards my window. I closed the slats, hoping she didn't hear that last part. Candy finally came to the door.

"Wow, I thought I put one in there," she said. "Here's another." She plopped two rolls onto the counter. I ripped and stuffed and smoothed. "It's my party and I'll cry if I want to" played through the walls.

Candy's pool was modern, with blue tiles that gave the water a turquoise sky look. It wasn't off in the distance behind a chain link fence, past the blacktop, like ours had been at our old house in La Canada. Hers was part of the side patio. This added to the movie star aspect.

"Hi, Wanda," I said. She sat on the steps in the shallow end, sitting coyly like Marilyn Monroe.

"Hi, Annie!" She smiled. *Can't say much here with the boys watching.* She looked me up and down; I shrugged. Her yellow hair seemed blonder than usual, her lips red and full, and her two-piece was tight around her breasts; you could almost feel the weight of them. Her skin looked so soft, I felt like touching her. Karen, usually tom-boyish had these really tan legs that you just had to look at; they went all the way up to her small, round butt and her yellow two-piece was even tinier than Wanda's. She had just recently sprouted some low-lying hills on her chest. With their shirts off, the guys looked a bit skinny and bony, except for Villelli who couldn't decide who he wanted to stand around, Wanda or Teresa. He was older, (held back in fifth grade, so his muscles had a chance to grow). "My boyfriend's back / he's gonna save my reputation / hey la, hey la / my boyfriend's back."

I dove into the pool. When I came up for air, the Kleenex had popped out on one side. I went underwater to stuff it back in, but the soft paper had been saturated and was already coming apart. I surfaced again and went down again to grab the little pieces floating here and there. Up again for a breath, my fist curled around the wet mass. Teresa Feeney called across the pool.

"Hey Annie, what's going on there?"

"Underwater tea party," I said, gulping air. Thankfully I thought of that.

I took a deep breath, submerged myself and pushed off the wall to the far end. If only I could stay down here until everyone went home. I swam to the deep end and approached the ladder, hoping to escape. Teresa Feeney stared down at me through the clear water from above. She had gathered her brother, Christopher Feeney, Paul Villelli and Tom McColloch who crowded around her. I know they all saw it. One Kleenex breast still intact, the other, my usual flat self. I pulled up out of the water. *Don't you dare say anything* I mentally bored into her.

"How's that nun bathing suit holding up?" she asked. Then I had to walk past them towards the bathroom, hoping there was nothing clinging to me.

At 10:00 that night, Mother pulled the VW bus into Candy's driveway. John-the-Blimp stepped out wearing his official priest camouflage, the cassock. His triumphant expression as he approached the door reminded me of Sparky, trotting home from his excursions. *Go away John-the-Blimp, I already have a guardian angel. You're not saving my soul from sin. You're embarrassing me, wearing that cassock everywhere.*

Thank God the boys had gone home by now. The rest of the girls sat around casual and relaxed in their nightgowns, wondering why I couldn't stay overnight at a slumber party.

"Why are you leaving?" they pressed. How could I tell them it was just my Mom, worried about modesty and chastity, two-piece bathing suits, mortal sin, and temptation. I myself wasn't sure what any of that had to do with a slumber party, but I had to come up with some better explanation for my mother's refusal to let me stay over.

"I've got to get back early to receive a call from Cardinal Stefanucci," I said, as the doorbell rang.

"Ooooh," everyone crooned, except for Teresa Feeney. Now I had to finish the conversation before Mother and John got in the room.

"Yeah, he's scheduled to call at 10:30 our time; gotta go! Bye!"

When Mother and John arrived, I had already gathered my wet bathing suit and towel. I grabbed Mother by the hand and started to drag her out the door.

"Thank you so much, everyone!" I chirped cheerfully. But Teresa Feeney stopped all of us in our tracks.

"You forgot your party favor, Annie!" Right. She held out the pink bag. I grabbed for it; she let it drop. So now I was scrambling on the floor at her feet.

"Thank you," I said, just to be polite. "Bye, Candy,

great party!" I was at the door.

"And you're rushing off to get a call from The Vatican?" Teresa asked loudly. "*Really*? Cardinal Stefanucci is going to make a *personal* call to you, Annie?" She said that last bit like it was as unbelievable as it seemed. All voices hushed; all eyes switched towards me.

I was busted. Mother would deny it, and of course John-the-Blimp had no idea whatsoever. Now everyone would know what a fraud I was. The whole glorious few weeks were over and I would never live down the humiliation of having lied to everyone. All the friends I made loaning out the nun book would just laugh at my fraudulent ambition. Even Wanda—I don't see how she could still be my loyal friend. The blush started at my chest and spread quickly up my cheeks. My eyes felt hot.

I glanced at Mother, who, by the expression on her face, was figuring it all out. She looked at me in the eye sternly, and then to Teresa, and then to everyone. She opened her mouth and she said, "Yes. We're waiting for a call from Cardinal Stefanucci. It's getting so close to the vote, and he wants to check in with the family." Approving chatter erupted all around.

You could have pushed me over with a feather, as Daddy would say. I was struck absolutely, completely, and utterly dumb. I stood there with my mouth open. John-the-Blimp flicked his finger on my earlobe and said, "Oh, really? Sister Skinny Milink," he said on the way to the car.

"Flummoxed," Mother said when we closed the doors. "You were flummoxed." Mother was a graduate of Marquette University, and she had a great vocabulary. The words she used were accurate to within point 01 percent of expressing exactly what was happening. She liked to say things like "hee-bee-jee-bees" and "discombobulate" and "flabbergast." She liked the sound of "persnickety," "kit and kaboodle," "lollpalooza"and "gee gaw" and she thought college was worthwhile; it prepared you for marriage. "If you're perspicacious, as you are, Annie, then higher education can give you the knowledge to converse with your husband at his level." Another of her caveats regarding marriage was "never take a job once you're married— you'll get used to the standard of living two incomes provide and you'll be tempted to work outside the home when really your God given mission is to have babies."

This time, I didn't mind Mother's sharp sermon about telling the truth. About how one lie leads to another until you're a fly, paralyzed in a spider's trap. It was clear that I was a fly, squirming in a spider's web, but I was a giddy-with-relief fly. Mother had saved me so totally from complete ruin. And Teresa Feeney humiliation! Ha, ha, I got away! I didn't want to ask Mom how she could lie for me and still have a clear conscience; I didn't care. *Bless me father, for I have sinned! Amen.*

God was still on my side.

CHAPTER 10
LOST BOYS

June 18 – Yesterday the Supreme Court said that public schools are forbidden to say prayers in the classroom or read the Bible. Too bad for their souls, but we are exempt because we are a Catholic school. I saw an ad in the paper that said if you want to be an actor, sign up here. I would LOVE to be an actor! But Daddy and Mother say, "Hollywood is full of sinners, so forget about it, Annie."

I am in so much trouble. We left Dominic behind at Disneyland. It was hours before we even noticed *he was missing*. It was all my fault, but I won't get spanked tonight because it's too serious; everyone is rung right out from crying; we can't help thinking about Dominic all the time, and Mother is just shaking from it. But I know exactly when he got lost. Right after I told him how great he looked up on that wall pretending he was a statue of the pope. I was so sick of having to be responsible for all the little kids! I already had the twins to watch out for. So I tried to ditch Dominic. *Jesus, Mary and Joseph, save my soul.* He's so gullible. Once he had his arms outstretched, pretending he had on one of those triangular pope hats, I told him to close his eyes, and then I ran around the corner and put his leash in Bart's hands. I said, "Not it! Dominic's your charge.

Not it!" I tore out of there, dragging the twins, Markie and Buddy behind me. I don't know how long Dominic stayed on that wall, playing Pope Statue. Where was his guardian angel, anyway? It's times like this when you count on those guys. But since they're conveniently invisible, they can go AWOL any time they like and no one can tell if they're on duty or not.

Can you imagine how many kids get left behind at Disneyland every year? There have to be a few of them. Among all those hundreds of cars in the parking lot, there's probably enough to form a club. Maybe the club could be called "The Left Behinds" or "Disney Orphans." How many of the stories could possibly have a happy ending? I'm repeating myself, I know, but the weird part is, when we lost Dominic, it was *hours* before we even realized he was gone.

We had our guard down because the little kids were in harnesses, to protect against this very thing. Ever since Mother had more than three "under her feet," she and Daddy had straps that fit around our shoulders and clipped together at the back. Whenever we were in public together, they walked us like dogs. People stared, but nobody got lost.

But not today! Everyone blames me for losing him. I was distracted by Clara in one of the stalls. She was sobbing. Gulping sobs while *her* charge, Luke stood patiently outside the toilet, attached by the leash under the door.

• • •

We had met at the restrooms after lunch, before going on any more rides, like we agreed in the beginning.

"Think of Christmas," Dominic kept repeating to the twins, trying to convince Markie and Mattie that they could fly like Peter Pan. You can tell the twins anything; they're just 4 years old, not very tall, and even more gullible than Casper the Friendly Ghost.

"You can fly, Markie!" Dominic enthused.

When I came out of the ladies' room, Dominic was sprinkling invisible fairy dust over Markie's head. Mattie stared wide-eyed up at his twin, balancing on the wall. He was next in line to try. The toes of Markie's little shoes perched at the edge of the wall and he looked waaay down at the ground, his small body quivering with the courage he was gathering to leap off.

"All you need is trust and a little bit of pixie dust," Dominic goaded. "You can fly! Markie, you can fly!"

"Stop!" I said, running to the wall. "Markie, don't jump!" I yelled, holding my arms out to him. His little body lifted up and fell into my embrace. I grabbed on tight. Whew. That would have been broken legs.

"I can fly!" Markie exulted.

"Dominic!" I frowned, struggling to keep my balance against Markie's squirming torso. "Someone's going to end up crying!" I was still thinking about Clara, in the toilet stall, her pants at her ankles, weeping.

Dominic loves capes; he had a towel remnant around his shoulders, so after I put Markie and Mattie on the ground safely, I told Dominic that he looked like Cardinal Stefanucci. He was still standing on the wall when I said, "Pretend you've just been elected." That's when I put his leash in Bart's hands and ditched him.

Bart was hanging around the door to the women's

restroom, waiting for a skinny blonde who just went in. His pants were sticking out in the front; he musta had a carrot in his pocket. I put Dominic's leash in his hand and said, "Not it!"

That's the last I remembered of Dominic.

• • •

As I lay in bed, picturing Dominic's big ears against his recently shaved buzz cut and panicked about him going missing, I got the feeling that someone was at the door to our bedroom.

Jeannie and Rosie, over there, exhaling in tandem from their beds, were sound asleep. I was just drifting off, too drowsy to wonder who could possibly want what after everything today. I waited for a voice. Whoever it was stood there, as if listening. Footsteps quietly walked over the floorboards. Towards my bed. Suddenly I was wide-awake, even though my eyes were slammed shut. I froze. Then I knew this person was standing right next to my bed. I could have opened my eyes up to see who it was, but I didn't. I wanted to see what was going on, and my curiosity got the better of me.

Hands pulled back my covers and began touching my chest and doing little squeezes where my breasts were. I shifted under the covers, like I was going to turn over. The hands stopped, but stayed. Slurping sounds with my mouth, and more shifting around, to suggest I was in danger of waking up; I turned over. That worked; the footsteps retreated.

I waited in the dark, *what the heck was that?* My heart was beating in my throat. I felt a strange glee that I had been witness to something forbidden. At the same time my chest burned red with embarrassment. I held my arms around my torso, to hide. My thoughts raced: the person who did this had no idea he was being observed—even though my eyes were shut. I was sure it was a sin what he had done. What was he thinking? I was barely allowed to touch my own breasts, and they're on my body! Had this person done this before? Maybe he thought he could get away with it, but this would be the last time! I wasn't a Tattle Tale per se, but I remembered something Our Lady of Fatima said. "More souls go to hell because of sins of the flesh than for any other reason." I had to do something right away.

I rolled off my bed and stepped quietly downstairs, trying to avoid the creaking step. The house had quieted down and I could only hear water rushing in the shower. There was a light coming from Mother and Daddy's bedroom. I padded down the hallway and peeked in. Daddy stood over the basin in their adjoining half bath and reached for Old Spice from the shelf over the sink and poured some into his hands, then patted his cheeks. So it was Mother in the shower. I walked back down the hall and waited until she turned the handle on the door.

"Mother," I said, as she stepped out, steam wafting into the hallway. Her head was wrapped in a turban towel, like a tower.

"What are you doing up?" Little wet wisps of hair curled up around her neck. Her face was flushed from the hot water.

"I've got to talk to you," I whispered.

"You're in enough trouble already. Just go to bed

94

now," she said, shaking her head.

She walked ahead of me; I stopped. It would be so easy to go back to bed. I felt queasy in my stomach. I knew I had to tell her this.

I followed her flopping slippers and her quilted red bathrobe that covered her large bottom. In comparison to mine. I'm only saying in comparison to mine. I'm a skinny runt and she's grown 13 babies in her body. She has a right to have a big butt. Daddy pulled his bathrobe around him as he stepped out of his room. When he saw Mother he opened his arms and gave her big, long hug. She rested her head on his shoulder, quietly sobbing, I think. I waited until they separated.

Daddy looked down, passing me as he went down the long hall away from their bedroom, to the bathroom. I was surprised he didn't take this opportunity to give me a lecture about Dominic. I imagined him using the word shirking.

"Goodnight Daddy," I called after him, as if to say things would seem better in the morning. In the bedroom I sat down with Mother on the side of her bed. She kicked off her slippers, and I could see the varicose veins on the side of her feet by her ankles, just below her pink nightgown. Somehow the familiarity of that reassured me. She'd know who it was, or she'd know how to find out. She'd have a talk with him. He'd go to confession. God would forgive him. No one would go to go to hell over this.

"I was almost asleep," I told her once she got in her room, "but I was really awake. Someone came into my bedroom and put his hands under the covers."

"Alright, Annie," she said, taking her hair down off

her head. "It's been a big day." Like I'd been making it up.

"Mother, he put his hands on my body."

She stopped and looked right into my face.

"You said *his* hands."

"I didn't open my eyes, so I don't know who it was."

"How do you know it's a he?"

"I think it was a he. Why would a she do that? A she already knows what breasts feel like."

"Alright, Annie," she said again, drying her hair with the towel. "You go to bed now. Say your prayers."

Like I hadn't been saying my prayers? It was too creepy and I didn't feel like going back to my bed.

I couldn't sleep. Who was it? It could have been Paul, John-the-Blimp, or Bartholomew. I had to be a really bad sin, because almost everything about the body is a sin. Especially the breast parts. Maybe someone else, like your husband, can touch them after you're married in the church, like Daddy grabs Mother, and every act is a sacrament so it's okay. But until that day, it's strictly off limits.

• • •

Earlier in the day, we had been screaming down the Matterhorn and then we were driving home from the land of Mickey Mouse and Donald Duck; I had a window seat in the back and I was counting the dashes on the freeway, 63, 64, 65, 66, trying to be the first to get to a hundred, but being slowed down by Madcap who was at 79, 80, 81 and thinking about Clara and what was wrong with her to cry like that in the restroom stall in the middle of the Magic Kingdom? I glanced at the back of Clara's head sitting in the seat right in front of me. Her hair told me nothing.

Then Daddy pulled off at a Texaco gas station just before Madcap got to a hundred. The heavy metal door of the restroom swung shut behind me. It was disgusting as usual, the small room smelling sour, the dirty tile floor piled up with paper towels, the cracked toilet seat. The water was cold and the soap, small white crusty granules that melted in your hands.

In the bus, Mother counted heads. Then she did the list, and I heard that panic overlay in her voice, naming every single child as she looked at all our faces. "Paul, Clara, John, Margaret, Bartholomew, Annie, Jeannie, Dominic."

"Dominic, where's Dominic?" No one said a word, but we looked at each other. No Dominic anywhere.

Mother and Daddy always said that when they had another child they didn't have to divide their love into an even smaller parcel because of the new baby or have less time to pay attention to the rest of us. No, a new baby meant there was *more* love to go around. I think it was their response to a nosy lady in the parish who thought Mother had too many kids, after Rosie was born. It was one of those bits of logic that at first seemed great. But if you thought about it, it was like, "Yeah! That makes sense! Maybe. Kind of." I called it *A Theory of Expanded Love.* In my mind, it was a just theory, because a new baby, except when it was sleeping or sucking on the bottle, had to get attention right away or it would start to cry. So everybody else got shunted to the background, too bad, tough luck. "I'm over here sterilizing bottles or feeding the new baby, or changing its diaper, shut up, do the dishes, get out of here, I need a nap." You yourself might have once been a darling newborn, but right now you were a toad or a cockroach, just something useless and in the way and maybe even ugly. Daddy loved to brag about how many children he had because it added to his accomplishments. Now he was the father of 13 kids, and all the old "You've got how many kids?" "What, your own mess hall?" jokes came out again. The new baby made everyone else invisible while Mother became more irritable, had less time, got less sleep, needed more help. Adorable at first but ultimately a big shift in the order of things. A new baby meant you were on your own; you had to figure it out because Mother and Daddy for sure weren't going to be there for you—they were too busy with the new baby! The other idea they had was "Always count heads before you leave to go anywhere" and "Don't ever leave the kids in the car. Even for a minute." That day, they proved themselves wrong on all counts.

"Dominic is missing," Mother announced, a fact that had already occurred to us. But her saying it made it dreadful. Daddy had a crazy look; his eyes lit onto each one of us.

"Is he in the restroom? Clara! Could he be in the restroom?"

"No," said Clara, "I looked in both." She shook her head.

"Who had Dominic?" We cowered, no one daring to speak. "Who had Dominic?" he bellowed.

"Bart did," I squeaked. "I gave him to Bart at the restrooms near the Matterhorn."

"You did not," Bartholomew said.

"I did too! I put his leash in your hand!"

"Liar!"

"You're the liar, Bart!"

"I never had his leash!"

"You were staring at that girl with the slimsy legs!"

Bartholomew burst out of the bus, walking around in a frenzy. "Dominic's nine, he doesn't need a leash!" He was 14, lanky and pimply, too big for his clothes. His voice sometimes high and sometimes big and low, Bart was full of a buzzing energy, like he had a bee in his bonnet.

I personally know he was looking at a girl, I saw him stare at her with his mouth open. I put that leash in his hand, saying, "You're it! Dominic's your charge!" Now, pressed on all sides by warm legs and within bad breath distance of Madcap and Jeannie, I pushed my way out the open door of the bus. Bart was pacing, looking at his feet.

"Don't forget about the big boobs!" I yelled at him, jumping onto the asphalt. He looked up at me and rushed at me, pushing me to the ground.

"What were you doing?" Daddy yelled. Bartholomew shrugged. "Where did you last see him? Bartholomew. Answer me!"

"In the restroom! He was with Annie. Annie was dragging around with the twins. I thought maybe Dominic was helping her with the twins," Bartholomew said.

"He didn't say anything to me!" I yelled at Daddy. "You lost him!" I screamed at Bart.

"It's your fault!" he screamed back at me.

"Get back in the car," Daddy barked in his Commander-in-Chief voice. We shut up and took our places. He turned on the ignition, shifted gears and gunned the gas. My hands were vibrating and tears streamed down my cheeks. No one said a word. We could practically hear each other's thoughts. Or at least the breathing. Baby Jude had no idea; he was the picture of fidgety, but then he noticed there was something not right. He looked from face to face, searching for *what* was wrong. It was more silent than I have ever experienced in the company of my brothers and sisters altogether. Ever.

The red light before we went on the freeway went on for hours. Then Mother pulled out her rosary from her purse. *In the name of the Father, and of the Son, and of the Holy Spirit,* she began. All our voices soberly chorused those words we know so well. After just one Hail Mary, it was such a comfort; it felt like we could actually save him.

And while we were reciting, I pictured Dominic on the Jungle Ride with his high forehead and green eyes. He was moving his ears like the elephants do, and we were laughing. He's skinny on the top but squarish on the bottom with short legs—his body is a giraffe; his ears are an elephant.

I remembered him at home, naked in his white skin, his swinging pee-pee between his pathetically skinny legs, wanting to go down the back of the bathtub twice in a row for the Jiffy Bath. He's a bit too old for the Jiffy Bath, but I let him slide down since he was already soaped up. A slide down the back bathtub wall is only a few seconds. I was so glad right now, that I let him. It could have been his last fun moment. Did someone steal him? He was a desperate character, always trying to please everyone. Someone could have easily lured him away, just by paying attention to him. *Oh, Dominic.*

I imagined Dominic back at Disneyland, lanky and lost among all those hundreds of hairy-legged daddies in shorts. I thought he'd be missing us. I thought he'd be crying and lost.

But he was not.

We finally arrived at the Disneyland parking lot. Mother and Daddy locked us up in the car, took five steps and came back to get us. It would have literally been Purgatory, and I'd never have to atone for another sin, if we had to stay in there, waiting. But they realized their mistake. Mother opened the doors, barked orders as we spilled out; we were to look after our charges, and everyone was to stay on the leash. "The family that prays together, stays together," Daddy said. Then we said a prayer to Dear St. Anthony, who is, after all, the perfect saint for this kind of situation, as he is the patron saint of lost causes. We invoked The Blessed Mother and St. Jude. Then we hurried, all of us running with little steps together; our immediate goal being the ticket booth, which glowed against the darkening sky, like a beacon up there.

Daddy talked to the ticket booth lady, who had a blonde beehive hairdo, and she got on the phone while we pressed our faces against the glass. We had a while in the cool dusk, hemming and hawing outside the ticket booth, watching her mouth as she spoke words we couldn't hear into the phone.

I tried to see Dominic in everything we did that day, but it was hard. I don't even know where he sat in the car as we sang "I love to go a wandering" and "The

Ash Grove" altogether as we tooled down the Pasadena Freeway. We were a whole family with no one missing while we sweated under the overcast smog, waiting for The Teacups, but I couldn't remember seeing him, exactly. We weren't thinking *treasure these last moments with Dominic* when we went down Main Street, inhaling the smell of cotton candy. We piled into the Skip Jack, and I don't even know where he was sitting. Where was Dominic on the Jungle Boat ride, with fake hippos and alligators rising up out of the swamp at a totally unrealistic speed while water dripped off their teeth?

And I don't remember him when giant Mickey Mouse and Donald Duck came lumbering by. I remember Markie barfing after eating too much cotton candy on an empty stomach. And this girl about my age sitting on the bench in broad daylight, popping zits on her boyfriend's cheeks. Even though we weren't paying attention to Dominic all morning, he was with us then. Maybe that's what Mom and Dad meant by "more love going around." You kind of love them in the background to everything, even if you don't have time to have a good look at them, or even notice if they're on the same ride with you.

Beehive hairdo talked to Daddy through the glass, making gestures with her hands, and shortly a couple of guys in overalls came up to the booth with walkie-talkies. Daddy had to describe what Dominic wore. He had to ask Mother, who asked me.

"Red shorts," I said, "a green short sleeve shirt with a collar. Tucked in. Green like Peter Pan. Buzz cut. Sneakers."

Mother told how tall.

I said, "Big ears like Dumbo."

Mother said, "Annie!"

Bartholomew said, "The car doors are open on both sides."

"His head is the car," said John-the-Blimp.

We followed them back into Disneyland. Markie yanked on his tether, practically pulling me down. We actually split up the twins—Jeannie took Matthew, so I only had one twin as my charge.

I thought about Tinkerbell the whole way over there. Too bad she wasn't a saint, she might have some pull with God here. She was in the same realm as my Guardian Angel, only our parents didn't believe in Tinkerbell. Meaning, they thought she was made-up, while they wholeheartedly and sincerely believed that we each had this invisible angel hovering around us 24 hours a day, trying to help us get into heaven. An entire heaven of characters, several different kinds of the Blessed Mother, three persons in one God—why couldn't there be elves and fairies, too? Maybe there are, and we just can't see them. We never get to hear or see the Guardian Angel, and all the miracles happen in Europe where we'll never go. But sometimes I think it would be so great if you could sit long enough in the garden, just looking. You might find the little hideouts belonging to the fairies and elves. Or even the elves themselves. With Tinkerbell, at least you can see the light of her and hear the tinkling sound.

We went first to the restrooms by the lunch booth near The Matterhorn. This is where we agreed we would meet if anyone got lost. There was no Dominic

CAITLIN HICKS

here. The girls went into the Ladies room and the boys went into the Men's room, looking under all the doors. No Dominic. I felt sick to my stomach.

I made up a prayer to his guardian angel and his namesake saint, St. Dominic (the patron saint of astronomers)—and to Tinkerbell—to bring him home. Since Tinkerbell was such a favorite of his. It couldn't hurt. It wasn't like I was praying to false gods. Walt Disney is practically a god. And Disneyland is, after all, practically heaven.

But it gave me an idea. Dominic admired Peter Pan for refusing to grow up. Dominic enjoyed creating the happiness of the thing that made the children fly. He loved saying "Think of Christmas!"

We were on Main Street, peeling our eyes into all the stores and whistling. Three notes: two high, one low. It was how we find each other in public. Whee-whee, whir, whee-whee, whir. People wondered, but we knew that if Dominic heard this whistle, we'd find each other.

"Hey!" I said, "Do you know where Peter Pan is?"

"Really, Skinny, that's enough. We're not looking for Peter Pan."

"But that's where he is! Dominic is with Peter Pan.! He's *a lost boy!*"

"Annie!" Mother said. "It's not the time for puns."

"Like in the story! Dominic is totally crazy for Peter Pan. He has tights and a hat. He jumps off things all the time, thinking he can fly. He volunteered to read Peter Pan to the little kids before bed for the past month. We're at Disneyland where Peter Pan hangs out. If we find Peter Pan, we'll find Dominic. I'm pretty sure!"

So Daddy stopped people right in their tracks, asking, "Have you seen Peter Pan?"

"Or Tinkerbell," I said. "They go together."

It was getting darker and darker, and all the lights started to glow like a party around us. A big spotlight cut a swath of white against the dark sky behind the castle up ahead. Seeing it, I felt more and more sure. We all trudged up the steps inside the castle. We heard an announcement about Tinkerbell.

Inside the rooms of the castle, it was this flowing sea of shorts and purses and summer dresses. I started to doubt if I would even recognize my own brother; there were so many legs and feet and sunburned faces and the red toenails of mommies in cotton skirts. At the top, there was a window out to the square below. And at the window there was a slouching kid in a green shirt and marine haircut. It was Dominic.

"Dominic! Dominic!" I squealed. "There he is!" But he couldn't hear me. His arms were hanging out the window, holding him up, and his knees were bent. We were a crowd ourselves, but we pushed through the people traipsing around. "Dominic! Dommy!" Me and Jeannie mobbed him, along with the twins, Matthew and Mark, everyone hugging him and saying "Vo Biscum!" John-the-Blimp whacked him on the back of the head—we all had to touch him to believe he was real and alive.

His face lit right up. "I'm hungry, he said. "Do you guys have hot dogs?"

"Where were you?" Daddy asked him gruffly. You would have thought Daddy would be grateful to God for saving his lost son, but instead he was instantly irritated to see him. "How did you get separated from Annie?" He demanded. Everyone was talking at once.

"We said a whole rosary for you!"

"Mother counted heads, and you were missing."

"Petow Pan," said Luke bouncing in Clara's arms.

Daddy was angry, practically screaming at him, which ultimately silenced the rest of us. The people who normally stare because of the leashes were staring because of Dad's military voice and the fact that there were so many of us huddling around this one child with white chalk knees.

"Why didn't you wait there? Like we told you!" Daddy barked. Bartholomew, at the periphery, inched a little closer.

"I did." Dominic said quietly, looking at his feet, "I waited a long time." Then he started sucking in sobs. We were all afraid to hug him because Daddy was so mad. But Mother opened her arms and wrapped her purse around him and patted his head until he calmed down. Daddy stood back, clearing his throat and pacing.

"We'd never leave you," she said, right after having done just that. She was crying ,too. That seemed to energize him. He looked around, realizing he had an audience.

"Now I'm really *A Lost Boy*!" He unraveled, like a metal handle on the back of a toy going in circles. "Captain Hook? He's a high school guy in a costume. I'm really hungry. I've been waiting for Tinkerbell," he said, pointing out the window. "Look at that!" Just then the fairy light flew across the square. "Does anybody have any popcorn?"

Luke had been saving a hard candy in his pocket that he had already sucked on. It had fuzz on it, but when Luke held it in his fat little palm, offering it up to his big brother, Dominic popped it into his mouth and smiled. Then he ruffled up Luke's hair.

Downstairs in the square, in the cool, under the lights, Daddy bought Dominic two hot dogs with all the mustard, relish, onions, pickles and ketchup. He wolfed it back, and we watched him eat it all. Then we got him French fries, and then a cotton candy cone. No one was jealous of him, even when John-the-Blimp snatched some of the pink cotton candy. We said another rosary on the way home in the car, and the twins fell asleep on my lap, one on either side, drooling on my shorts. I held Dominic's hand, as he nodded off to sleep on his own shoulder, waking up every time his head drooped. He let me.

When we got home, Jeannie and I helped the little kids get their jammies on and everyone went straight to bed. Except for the hands.

The following night, when we all knelt down for the rosary, I thought maybe Mother might say something to the boys about what happened under my covers, but she didn't. She could have, because she had everyone's attention. But she just thanked the Good Lord for Dominic being returned to us. It would have been embarrassing for me, to tell in public that someone was trying to feel up my breasts in the dark, even if it was a chance to make an example for the rest of the kids. As I was falling asleep, Jeannie said,

"What's wrong with Clara?"

"I don't know. Maybe it's her boyfriend."

"I think they broke up."

"That Todd guy?"

"I don't know who he is."

"She's really mad and upset."

Then there was a long pause as we thought about Clara. Rosie was making puppy-licking sounds in her small bed in the corner, so I could tell she was drifting off. I heard Daddy's footsteps outside the door. He had no reason to say "Pipe Down Kids." The wood creaked under his feet.

"Good night, girls. God bless you."

"Good night, Daddy." I could hear him on the stairs.

"Jeannie," I said.

"Yeah?"

"Someone came in last night."

"In where?"

"In here. You were asleep. He didn't know I was awake."

We both lay there in silence. I wasn't sure I could tell her what he did. Even though it wasn't my fault, it made me feel ashamed. After a while Jeannie said, "Annie, I know who it was."

"The hands?" I asked.

"Yeah, the hands."

"How do you know?"

"I just do."

"Who?" I asked her again. I was pretty drowsy, waiting for her answer, and then it was morning and Daddy was tugging on my feet for 6:30 Mass.

Dear Jesus, Mother had us move our bedroom downstairs, away from the boys. John-the-Blimp and Bartholomew helped move our table, chairs and a chest of drawers. Jeannie and I took our clothes on the hangers and carried them down the steps. We didn't move the beds, we just switched places. Mother changed the sheets. It was all done by the afternoon. We had quite a time because Jeannie wanted her bed here and I wanted it there. As usual, she was backed up by Clara, Madcap, Mother, and John-the Blimp. As usual, only Rosie was on my side. And she's only 7.

When I run away, they are going to miss me. They are going to be so sorry.

CHAPTER 11
CAMP HOLY HILL

June 20 – Dear Jesus. I don't know if this is good or bad. They are going to have a new red hotline between Washington and Moscow in case someone gets trigger-happy with the nuclear bomb. It's just to stop everyone from being blasted to smithereens if Khrushchev loses his temper, or if the translator isn't too good. But more importantly! In a few more days they're going to scour the Sistine Chapel for vagrants and then lock all the Cardinals in. The Cardinals are going to be trapped in there until they elect the Supreme Pontiff and Vicar of Jesus Christ on earth. Are you going?

No one in my class suspected, but at our house, there was no news whatsoever out of the Vatican. If truth be told, we were just as ignorant as every other family in the parish—only *we* knew we didn't know anything. Other than one phone call our father made to the archdiocese of Baltimore to Cardinal Stefanucci when the pope died, it was all made up. Even so, throughout the month of June, we added an extra prayer at every meal to get the cardinal elected pope; it was supposed to be a typhoon of begging that would overwhelm God into doing our bidding. I was a Doubting Thomas as to whether or not it would work, but maybe if I threw in my "vocation" as a nun, the group effort would get him elected. I could drop out once he became Pope.

Clara didn't seem to notice anything about the impending celebrity sweepstakes we were hoping to win, what with her slamming doors, crying and running off in a huff whenever she and Mother had a fight. She ditched the last two days of school and she and Mother went to the doctor. When they got back, it was even worse. What the heck was the matter with her? After a flurry of cleaning up, I happened upon her sitting on the floor amidst a stack of magazines, staring at the Life article with pictures of deformed Tha-lid-o-mide babies. I had to stare at them, too. Somebody had made a huge mistake. All those mothers trusted the government and their doctors that the drug was perfectly safe.

"What are they going to do with those little babies?" I asked Clara.

"What do you mean?"

"They won't be able to sit up. Or do anything normal. Luckily they're so cute." She just stared at me.

Cuteness is definitely a survival technique for babies, but I wasn't even sure their mothers would want them, with hands growing out of their shoulders and feet attached to their hips, and some of them, no legs at all. I wondered if something like that had happened to Mother's "Baby Adamson" and that's why he's disappeared.

The summer stretched in front of us with six little kids needing supervision. The only way to deal with it was to start a military camp. Jeannie liked the idea too.

Every Navy Brat knows that the foundation of good conduct is reward and punishment. I felt the call of this instinctive understanding when the first thought I had was lickable gold stars. Mother's found some in her secret cupboard and gave them to me. Campers got stars for going to Mass and saying random prayers for Cardinal Stefanucci, and we named ourselves Camp Holy Hill. I was the Founder and Chief Counselor. It was a role I was born for: I felt a surge of happiness when things were in order and everyone was busily doing my bidding. "All hands on deck!" I loved making them scramble to line up in front of me with that one. Campers got demerits for anything I deemed demeritable, but mostly for neglecting obligatory chores and leaving anything messy.

In the beginning, it was bliss. I'd tape the signs up to greet the campers as they entered the dining room first thing after 6:30 Mass in the morning.

Good Morning, Campers. Today we are serving French Toast. I know, this made it sound like utopia camping, but it wasn't really because of a certain level of obligatory chaos: one of the twins always ran in stark naked and the other chased him, a superman cape tied around his neck. Or somebody whined, "Big Bully," "Fatso Freshie," "Stinkin' Diaper!"

"Please. Sit. Down. And say grrrace." Rosie stood in front of the signs and pointed out each word as she was reading them. Plump and short, she reminded me of our next-door-neighbor, Mr. Franklin, when he watered his lawn in bare feet. The widest part of Mr. Franklin's body is his waist, and you wonder how he got the shorts up around himself. He looks like an egg with legs. Rosie is like that, only shorter. She doesn't have glasses, but it's like she's always wearing thick ones, and there's this glassy reality between her and what she sees.

At first, everyone loved the routine.

"Stomach in, chest out, shoulders back!" I barked as we all stood in formation on the front lawn. They looked straight ahead while I inspected them. These are two of the best parts of the Navy—drills and blind obedience.

"Jeannie! Bathroom detail! Shape up or ship out!" I picked up a thin stick off the ground and hit them on their bare arms and legs, like my ballet teacher does to me.

"Dominic! Mow the front lawn!"

"Rosie! Vacuum the hallway and living room! Now! Let's hear that sucking sound!" I loved how clean the house was—in the ten minutes between morning chores and lunchtime. The demerit system worked for the first few days, but soon there was a lot of abandonment of deck swabbing and other forced cleanup jobs. Our home resumed its natural state of chaos and we went outside.

In the front yard, we played Statues, where we froze whenever a car went by then discussed whether or not the people in the car were fooled.

"The driver of the car didn't even look!"

"Yes he did."

"No he didn't."

"He did so!"

"How could he? He was looking at the cigarette he threw out the window."

"The motorcycle guy waved! He thought we were real."

"His girlfriend on the back looked confused."

"How could you tell? They went by so fast."

"*I* do! *I* do!"

I had them do wheelbarrow and relay races around the house until they couldn't walk. It wore them down so they would sleep at night. And at bedtime, the big attraction was The Jiffy Bath.

Each Jiffy Bath only lasted about 39 seconds. The little kids had to stand around naked, hovering in the corner until it was their turn. Rosie, first in line, stripped herself down to nothing and sat on the back edge of the bathtub, which was half-full of warm water. I splashed her and she soaped up. Then I said, "Okay, mark, set, go!" and she slid down the back of the tub into the water, rinsing off the soap and splashing around. She stepped out into an open towel, which I wrapped around her, as Buddy scrambled over the tub and perched himself at the back. I had put a pile of clean jammies outside the door. Once they were all snapped up in their buntings, they brushed their teeth and I combed their wet hair and inspected their beds.

Then we all sat around on the bed for stories. That was my favorite time of the day; they looked so fresh and sweet. The dust and dirt had been washed away, they smelled of shampoo, their wet hair was plastered to their scalps, their skin was soft ,and their eyes shone.

It was the perfect time to indoctrinate them about Cardinal Stefanucci. I reminded them how Daddy met Stefanucci at Pearl Harbor, with the ships blowing up and bullets from the Japs whizzing by.

"Bombs over Tokyo!" Dominic yelled triumphantly.

The next morning, we all dressed up as Cardinals. I attached towels to their shoulders with diaper pins.

Then I explained that the congregation outside in St. Peter's square waited for our decision, and they were all praying for the Will of God.

"What's the Will of God?" Markie asked.

"It's what God wants."

"Doesn't God want everything?"

"*I* do! *I* do!" Jude.

"Okay," I said, "Now is the moment of truth. You are the Cardinals who are deciding the fate of the Holy Catholic Church." I handed out tiny slips of paper to them and gave them each a crayon.

We bowed our heads and I said, "Okay. The person to vote for is Cardinal Stefanucci. Do you want him to be pope?"

"Yeaay!" they all yelled.

Alrighty, then. Mark an "S" on your ballot." I drew a big S on the paper. "Like a snake." All heads bent down, hands furiously scribbling.

"Nucci!" baby Jude blurted. "*I* do! *I* do!"

So it was done. "*Habemus Papam*! I said after counting the folded paper ballots. "*Habemus Papam*!"

"What's that mean," asked Dominic?

"It means, 'We have a pope!'"

"Popem! Popem!" Jude exclaimed, bending his knees and bouncing up and down.

So of course we had to make the smoke come out of the chimney so the people in St. Peter's square would know. We didn't have a chimney, but we had a magnifying glass under the silverware drawer in the kitchen, where every little rubber band, miscellaneous cork, pencil and breadcrumb was stored.

Outside on the brick walk I magnified the sun's

rays onto the voting papers. Pretty soon it got so hot, the paper burned, smoking black smoke. That got me worrying—maybe we've jinxed it with the black smoke. And it's not a good example to play with matches in front of the little kids, either. But I couldn't stop myself from burning all the papers with that magical band of sunlight, pushing away all the little hands who wanted to try it too.

We all piled over to the vacant lot, saying "*Habemus Papam*!" I carried Jude, sucking his thumb. The vacant lot was our favorite hang out, with a small cave covered in rose bushes and bumpy land, bricks here and there, stunted bushes sticking out of the dusty earth and dirt-filled cement rectangles. This wasteland stretched for an entire block. It was where we spent hours on sweaty weekends, adventuring as Swamp Fox.

Now we threw branches into a pile and picked up a stick in each of our hands and ran around this pile. At first we called out "*Habemus Papem*! *Habemus Papem*!" Then, because I couldn't resist, I screamed. So then we were all screaming at the top of our lungs. Big screams. Let it all out screams.

I led them around the pile, "Pretend you're in a horror film! Scream like they're just about to get you!" There we were, screaming and screaming! It felt so good to vent. We sounded like Bloody Murder.

But Dominic wasn't screaming. He huddled over the magnifying glass, trying to start a fire. It was hot and smoggy, and pretty soon a strand of smoke curled up in a wisp above the leaves. It flickered and then immediately expanded into a bigger cloud of grey smoke. I ran over to the fire to stomp it out, but he had grown it on a pile of dry oak leaves and it was already multiplying. I looked around for help, feeling like I was in the dream of a biblical wave on the horizon and how impossible it was, because of my leaden arms and legs, to run away. It was the middle of the day. At the Conway's house, where I babysat all the time, the lights were out, no car in the driveway.

"Dominic! Help me! Stomp!" We stomped amidst all the screaming, but the dust was being kicked up and the fire was growing.

Then there were sirens everywhere. Mother came running down the block in her apron, making the sign of the cross. Her hands were coated with flour. She could hear us screaming. She could see the smoke. She could hear the fire trucks.

CHAPTER 12
HABEMUS PAPAM

June 21 – Dear Jesus. I just have a little something to say. I never learn anything when I am spanked into it. And I'm getting too big to be spanked, even if there was a fire. Everybody had their panties in a bunch over the screaming, but that's what saved us. Someone called the fire department when we first started screaming. When am I going to improve in others' eyes? Mother says I'm bossy; Clara says I'm selfish; Daddy says I act too much. Please help me to be perfect and pleasing to you, as well as to others. We were just trying to announce that it's almost Pope time!

We had a Papam, alright, but it wasn't the Papam we wanted. It was a disaster, a complete, unmitigated disaster, for me and for the Shea family, formerly the church darlings. It went like this: it was a Friday morning, June 21st, and the church was full to brimming. Everyone was there, to pray for the election of our pet Cardinal, Francesco Stefanucci. The conclave had been voting for two days, and they already had six ballots.

Monsignor Boyle said Mass. His sermon was predictable: if it's God's will, then Cardinal Stefanucci will become pope. Otherwise, we have to look in our hearts and continue with the work of the Lord. Now that it was down to the wire, I could see both scenarios. The winning: we'd have continued super star status in the parish, the Pope would be the first pope to visit Pasadena, and we'd be in all the Catholic newspapers and magazines. We could milk it for years.

But if he lost? Shame to the bones. Humiliating beyond the beyonds. We'd be shunted off to the corners again. The Feeneys would still reign as Best Catholic Family, and Martin Feeney would win the Christmas stamps contest, like he had the past four years. We would still live in the same tumbledown house, which was unbearably messy all the time. Sure, our dad had retired and he didn't wear Navy uniforms around anymore, but we'd still be forbidden to do all sorts of normal things and I'd have to keep cleaning both bathrooms every Saturday, whether I liked it or not. On top of it all, there would always be the enduring memory of our family's failed attempt at stardom lurking in the back of everybody's minds. Whenever they saw any one of us on the playground, or at Mass, the thought would be there. *Who did we think we were to dare such glory?*

When I thought that Monsignor couldn't possibly drag out his sermon any more, Father Pierre genuflected onto the altar and climbed up the steps into the sermon booth. Monsignor Boyle turned around to face him. A buzzing rose up from the congregation. I started to blush, even though nothing had happened. Monsignor Boyle held his hand over the microphone until it squeaked and we had to hold our ears. When he turned back to us, he was nodding. As Father Pierre descended the pulpit, Monsignor Boyle spoke, his voice booming through the microphone.

The magnificent expanse of the Roman marble columns stretching the length of the church on either side framed the hopeful faces of the congregation. The dome above our heads seemed to stretch to the heavens, contributing to the picture of our insignificance.

"*Habemus Papam!*" he said, but no one exhaled. All faces hung onto the silence. I heard Daddy clearing his throat. My eyes fastened on the marble star on the floor in between the pews.

"God's will be done," said the familiar Irish brogue of Monsignor Boyle. I looked up as he paused again, his eyes lighting here and there as he made eye contact with the parishioners. He locked his gaze onto Daddy. I could almost make out a staring path in the air between them.

"Giovanni Battista Montini," he said slowly and clearly, as if we needed to hear it spelled out, "the Archbishop of Milan, is the new pope of the Roman Catholic Church. He is to be known as Pope Paul the VI." There was a loud, collective, "Aaaaahhh!" from the congregation and an immediate buzz of voices all whispering together. I felt dizzy. My chest heaved up and down as I gasped for air. My ears were ringing. And then someone right behind me started clapping. What? Clapping? Everyone in the church followed, all the parishioners and nuns and altar boys, who took the time to come to church that day. A huge ovation. I couldn't help myself; I started to cry. Real tears came down my cheeks as fast as I wiped them from my face.

"Too bad," someone whispered a little too loudly, "it wasn't meant to be." The voice had a twinge of self-righteousness in it and was coming from just behind me in the pew. I looked over my shoulder. Teresa Feeney! She must have been hoping and praying against Father Stefanucci just as hard as we had been praying for him. Teresa Feeney's prayers worked!

I had to sit through the rest of the Mass in the front row with Teresa's gaze boring into my skull—the most humiliating 20 minutes of my life. I thought about the black smoke from the burning ballots, maybe God noticed that. Then there were the lies I told to the class, to Monsignor Boyle, and the to rest of my girlfriends. I wish I could take it all back and clear off my soul once and for all, but to confess it would double my shame. God knew I didn't really want to become a nun. Maybe He wanted to teach me a lesson.

How could I have believed with all my heart that my fervent wishes would reach the heavens? And be granted? How could we have thought that our unruly and socially inept family deserved any kind of special treatment in this world? Even if Father Stefanucci had been elected pope, we would never learn to get to church on time, our shoes would always be scuffed, our lunch bags would still be stocked with one peanut butter and jelly sandwich wrapped in wax paper everyday and maybe an apple—very rarely, two Oreo cookies. We sucked back our food in 30 seconds after we all said grace at supper like a barnyard of turkeys, because if we weren't fast enough, someone else would get there first. John-the-Blimp would always be the undisputed King of Burps, cassock or no cassock. The twins would move through our lives as The Darlings, the decoys, the two who always attracted the focus, no matter what else was going on. There was no reining us in or teaching us manners or getting us to clean up after ourselves. Maybe it was just too much of a reach, even for God. Maybe we really were unworthy. We were descendants of Adam and Eve, born with original sin. Why should I be surprised? We were stained, damaged goods from the get-go. What was the point of it all?

How could Teresa Feeney look so cool, be so neat, know what to say? How could she be from a family as big as ours and so smart in school but without the mandatory nerd personality to go with it? Our Paul, supposedly brilliant in math and science, wore white shirts that were almost transparent (you could see his right nipple), short sleeves that showed off his bony elbows, white plastic pen holders in his breast pocket with blue ball point ink stains everywhere. He smeared his giant boogers on the hallway wall like he was proud of them. Worse than that was, they stayed there for a whole week—nobody noticed them, or if they noticed them, weren't significantly disgusted to do anything about them. I finally had to clean them off. How could our whole family be so oblivious to common decency?

The very moment Monsignor Boyle said, *Habemus Papam*, our destiny shifted. We had to finally face it, own up to our origins. Accept ourselves as individuals in the family to which we were born, and make the best of it. As parishioners, the seas no longer parted for us as we trailed into Sunday Mass, tardy again. We went back to being an annoying aberration of a Catholic family, distastefully big, living the letter of the law, tolerated but not loved—perhaps an entertaining spectacle (like a circus act) but not an envied one. Monsignor Boyle stretched out our humiliation by giving sermons on every aspect of the new pope for the next month at Sunday Mass, but even the importance of this began to fade.

We had been dazzled by the promise of being chosen and elevated to the heavens, but with Cardinal Stefanucci's defeat, our wings melted and our eyes opened to the sprawling and unbearable fullness of our own lives.

That moment was an end of something about all of us, even though we didn't really understand what exactly had happened. Sitting there in the church we couldn't have understood how Clara's disastrous story would unfold, a story there was no turning back from, a story that would affect each and every one of us. We couldn't have foretold that we were indeed mortal; that even famous people of the highest glory in the land could be taken down in a few seconds under the sun that shone on us all, riding in the back of an open car in Dallas.

Our whole world was about to change.

PART 2
JULY–DECEMBER, 1963

CHAPTER 13
BITTY

July 1 – *Holy Mary Mother of God, I can see nipples on our cat and her stomach sticks out on both sides, really big. She's waddling now and I'm pretty sure she's going to have kittens soon. I want to ask you a very childish thing. When is it going to happen? Will you let me be the first one to know?? Please don't tell Jeannie first.*

Clearly my strategy had failed, appealing directly to God. Well, as long as I was breathing in and out, I wasn't going to continue this losing streak. I had learned my painful lesson. Number 1, no more lies. And Number 2, I had to switch my attention to the Blessed Mother. It was a crossroads moment; I could feel the pivotal change stirring around me. I had to pledge my allegiance to the holy Mother of God and implore her for favors, except when emergency matters required executive decisions from the very top. Jesus probably wouldn't even notice me on my knees over there in front of her statue; I'd be just one less person tugging at his robes. He's got enough to do. But the Blessed Mother? To begin with, there are probably way less people clamoring after her. I could feel the instant improvement of my chances with this simple brainstorm. I felt the surge of hope, a residual rush of future glory.

Then one morning, after 6:30 mass, Daddy took me to Glendale to drop off the ownership papers for a used car he had sold.

The man who answered the door had paint drips all over his pants, overflowing onto his sandals. On the walls of this big room where he worked hung enormous paintings of the insides of flowers, as if he was close enough to be a bee. The paintings were huge, filling up an entire wall, and the colors were magnificent! I could easily imagine myself to be the bee, buzzing over these luscious reds, oranges, yellows and greens! And also the artist made big decorations out of found things, like ropes and rusted cans that were flattened. He called them "sculptures." Against an entire wall, car doors that had been smashed up in accidents leaned side by side. He had begun a painting of one of the doors, and it was dusty with a deep purple color; strangely the smashed parts were the most interesting to look at.

I wanted to touch everything I saw. The place was splattered with all the colors of his paintings, with brushes in stained jars, piles of magazines and scraps of metal and torn images from these magazines stuck on the wall here and there. It was a mess but I didn't get the instant feeling that I wanted to put everything away. Instead, I had to keep staring at it all. Inside me, electrical impulses were bouncing around, and yet I felt so comfortable here, almost like I could live here. I felt thirsty for what I was feeling, but the thirst had snuck up on me and there I was, standing in the middle of the ocean, parched for more.

All the way back in the car, I chattered about the

beautiful paintings. I wanted to do that all day—paint pictures with bright colors and make things.

"Well, Annie," Daddy interrupted me, "people are attracted to art because it can be beautiful, and the soul craves beauty, but it's important to remember what's really important in life. It's not the physical beauty of a piece of art, which is temporal, it's the beauty of your soul, which is eternal."

"I know Daddy, I know! But art can be your work when you're alive, can't it?!" I expected him to tell me about the temptations that painting and creating interesting shapes would offer and why it would be bad for my salvation. I couldn't think of any famous artists, but the artists of the Renaissance made religious paintings that were turned into holy cards by the Catholic Church. Maybe the church needs more of those. If I learned how to make portraits of saints, there would be no temptation danger. Not like in Hollywood, where unsavory sinners and tempters lurked around every turn. I was willing to give up any ideas I had about being an actor on the spot, if I could just do that.

"It's difficult to make a living as an artist, Annie," Daddy said. "People don't need art. They need food and transportation and schooling. But art is not essential for survival." I hadn't thought of this. It was so disappointing what he was saying. "When the economy is on a downturn, you can't sell your work." People only buy what they really need."

I felt like screaming. How could something so instantly dazzling be unimportant? This feeling was jumping around everywhere in my body; I was practically trembling with it. It felt more real and essential than the saints themselves. Even the idea of my guardian angel, who followed me around like my shadow pal all my life, receded in my imagination. I was meant to feel like this, wasn't I? If God hadn't meant for me to want this, He wouldn't have made me feel this way.

"I wouldn't recommend it for you," Daddy summarized. "Why not think about becoming a secretary? Secretaries can make a good living."

I thought about the Russian female astronaut who last month became the first woman in space. Aside from wondering why they're sending people up in spaceships and making such a fuss about it, I was proud of that woman. Because she wanted to go tearing into space in a rocket. That was her idea of a great life, and she stuck with it. At least she got a chance.

We don't call ourselves House of Bacon for nothing. That Saturday, as I inhaled the smell of bacon fat sizzling on the flat griddle, I heard this high-pitched screechy "meow, meow, meow," a small, short sound coming from the back porch. It sounded like someone was choking Bitty. I ran out. She was clinging to the screen door, hanging on for dear life by her paws, with a little mouse in her mouth, and out of the mouth of the mouse came this urgent tiny sound that somehow pierced the morning, *"Meow, meow, meow!"* I pushed open the door, and Bitty put the thing down at my feet. I reached down to pick it up off the cement. Of course I was a Muscle Head for thinking it was a rodent— it was a kitten. The creature was wet and its eyes were sewn shut. Bitty had staggered around the corner so I followed her with this tiny warm lump in my hand.

Bitty was my cat. A while back, Paul (#1) had rescued her from an experiment at JPL (Jet Propulsion Lab), and I had laid claim to her. I was a mark for small creatures with limited IQ and a cuteness factor and I immediately pitied her, imagining the lab experiments she was probably subjected to. Attaching electric charges to her to see if her hair spiked. Or maybe they just let her float around in zero gravity and bang into things. They could have done anything to her. I didn't have to get in a fight over ownership rights, like the Russians were doing over Cuba, or like Jeannie and I do over everything, because there was a certain inevitable neglect which followed anything new to the house after a few days went by. The new thing, if it was alive, could give you attention and make you feel chosen and important, but sooner or later, it also demanded that you look at it and give it a stream of your energy and focus. The cat was so small and insignificant looking that we called her Bitty. I liked her immediately because she had orange and white fur. She was a marmalade cat and our hair practically matched.

Once the novelty of her small face and thin meow wore off, I was the one who fed Bitty and patted her. We had our own language; I'd call her in a high-pitched squeaky voice, "Here Bitty Bitty!" She was never far away. I'd pick her up and flip her over on her back and hold her like a baby suckling at my non-existent breast, gazing into those yellow marble eyes as if she were my very own. I got her to purr within ten seconds of the flip. Once she accidentally ran past the feet of Mother or Daddy while they were closing up the house for the night and somehow, out of fifteen beds, she found mine and slept next to my face until Daddy shook my feet for 6:30 Mass.

So like this, we became the two sustaining members of the Mutual Admiration Society. She wasn't very big. Maybe her growth was stunted by the experiments at JPL, and by the time she got pregnant, she still looked like an adolescent kitten. When her belly swelled up and her titties started to show, she could hardly walk around without falling over. She tilted to one side then caught her balance, lurching to the other side. Once she got to the other side she listed back. She walked in a sort of stumble and lollop. Mother said she would hide herself when "her time came," and Mother would know. In spite of this very credible source, I was just beginning to think independently. I created a number of havens from cardboard boxes lined with newspaper and put them in corners, under the beds, in closets, and around bushes, just in case Mother was wrong.

Now Bitty jumped up onto the wooden chair with the old cushion and lay on her side, furiously licking her butt, her back leg jutting way above her head. Lick, lick, lick, lick. I realized she had rejected the box I had strategically placed in the corner of the porch, but I grabbed the towel in it and rubbed off the baby kitty in my palm until it wasn't so wet and put it down by her belly of ten breasts, hoping the kitty would know which one to suck on. Bitty had ruined the cushion; it was now covered with blood and shiny goo. A dark little ball slowly inched out. A head. Lick, lick, lick, lick. Then the body slid out. Bitty stopped licking. She seemed exhausted. The kitten just lay there. Clara pushed open the screen door.

"Aren't you getting ready? The photographer is going to be here." A new mumu she had just sewn billowed around her.

"Yeah, but look at this! Bitty is having her kittens! Stand back, but you can look." Clara crouched down. I picked up the second one and rubbed it off and put it next to the first one.

"Okay, that one is Number One and that's Number Two," I said, pointing to the two lumps. Just then the head of another kitten emerged.

"Where's the Daddy cat?" Clara asked. I shrugged.

"Mother says that animals don't have souls, so it doesn't matter if the dad never shows up." I proudly shared my knowledge of my very own cat with Clara.

"They're born out of wedlock," she added. "

"Clara, there's no such thing as out of wedlock in the animal world. They don't get married!"

"How convenient for them," she said.

"We can baptize them anyway, just in case." I added. "Besides, they'll learn everything they'll need to survive from their mother, so you don't need to worry."

"I'm not worried about them," Clara stated. "How many do you think she has in there?" Then she picked up the ends of her mumu and sat down on the floorboards next to me.

"They usually come in litters," I replied, stating the obvious but feeling like an expert. "The Catholic Church is probably going to be proud of Bitty, once she gets them all out. Maybe she'll have five."

"Maybe," said Clara sarcastically. "Maybe the Catholic Church will make her a saint."

So the two of us, Clara in her huge mumu, and me starving for my bacon breakfast, sat and watched Bitty push out a total of seven kittens and lick off the shiny bag around each kitten. Once I knew there were seven, I re-named them all after the seven sacraments: Baptism, Confirmation, Holy Eucharist, Penance, Extreme Unction, Holy Orders and Matrimony.

I went into the house and put on my dress for the family portrait between the births of Extreme Unction and Holy Orders, and after Matrimony was born, our human family stood out on the front lawn and had our picture taken, with Mother and Daddy in the middle and Jude on Mother's lap. I stood next to Clara, her eyes wet, in the back row. I held her hand and squeezed it when they snapped the picture. I thought about Bitty.

She was another creature altogether, and she never said one word in human language, but she trusted me, a non-cat, well enough to give me her firstborn. She jumped up on the screen door with her baby in her mouth and dropped it off at my feet! She knew I would pick it up and take care of it. She wasn't afraid of me at all! She wanted me to watch her during the birth of six more kittens. And you know what I think? I think she was proud of herself.

CHAPTER 14
CINEMATHEQUE WITH MADCAP

Dear Blessed Mother, Thank you for the sign! It was truly exciting to watch Bitty give birth to all those kittens. You could tell it hurt, but she did it anyway. I am now confessing to you, in the hopes that I can finally come clean. I am sorry to disappoint you, but, in spite of my success with Camp Holy Hill, I don't want to be a nun. There, I said it. I just couldn't keep on pretending, especially after being with Bitty giving birth. I realize I want a man who will love me and hold me tight. I want a baby. I want to be a mother like you. I want a good husband like Joseph and a sweet baby like Jesus. Did you want a baby when you were 12 years old?

We were all kneeling around the statues in the living room. The air was cooling; my lungs hurt from gulping smog at the Pasadena Athletic Club swimming pool this afternoon. The Blessed Mother's frozen expression on her tiny plaster head was sweet and wistful, but the song "Puff the Magic Dragon" was distracting me from the mysteries of the rosary. I looked down at the Hawaiian hibiscus flower pattern on my mumu. Clara's was just like mine from the same pattern, but in different shades; come to think of it all the girls had mumus on. The fan rotated in front of us, spraying cool air over there then whooshing back over to here. The little kids wore their lightweight cotton pjs and had post-Jiffy Bath wet hair. Jude squirmed on Mother's lap. Everyone slouched back on their heels. Even Clara sat in the armchair behind us, her flowered dress piled up in front of her. Daddy didn't seem to mind the lazy piety we demonstrated. Madcap knelt antsy next to me; we had planned to see a movie at Cal Tech Cinematheque together after the rosary.

"Let's say some extra prayers for peace," Daddy announced as we neared the end of rosary. "And for Clara. She's going to be going away for a retreat," Daddy said, "with the Sisters of Saint Isabella. She'll be staying with them for a few months in a place called Ventura. Hopefully, she'll be back in time for Christmas."

So Clara's going to become a nun! I slunk back on my heels. Everyone turned their heads to Clara, who was looking down at her lap. It wasn't quite right. I couldn't tell if she was happy about it, or what.

"We'll miss you, Clara!" Buddy said, getting up from his excellent position at the corner of the couch and putting both his arms around her legs.

"Yeah, why are you going away?" Rosie said, as she immediately moved right into his excellent position on the couch.

"She's going to be a nun, I bet," John-the-Blimp offered. I turned towards Clara.

"That's a great order, Clara, the Sisters of Saint Isabella," I said. "Their habit, the rope around the waist." Right after those words were in the air, I felt something was strange here. I couldn't figure it out. A retreat?

"Clara is going on a retreat to ask for God's blessing

and forgiveness," Daddy said.

She's going on a retreat to ask for forgiveness? I had to ask myself. All she has to do is go to confession. Why does she have to go to Ventura to ask for forgiveness?

"What's a retreat?" Buddy.

"Yeah, a treat?" Markie.

"Tree! Tree!" Jude.

"Hey, can we get a treat, too?" Buddy.

"A retreat is a time away, a chance to say prayers and ask for God's help in your life." What was he hinting at? Forgiveness for what? Everything he said sounded like we were at a sermon. Clara's silence made it all seem rehearsed. I watched her for a clue. Her mousey brown hair puffed up around her round cheeks. Although exceptionally coiffed for such a casual gathering, she seemed resigned and sad, and kept puffing up her dress on her lap in front of her, looking at the beautiful colors of her mumu.

"When is she going?" I asked.

"She's leaving Sunday. I'm going to drive her up the coast."

And that was that.

After we were dismissed from the rosary, Madcap and I slipped out to go to Cal Tech for their movie program. As usual Madcap looked beautiful; she had shampooed her hair before the rosary and stood over the heating vents combing it dry with the cool air coming up from the basement. Straight black hair to her waist. Mine was still bunching at my shoulders, wiry and uncontrollable. It would never look like hers. I wasn't really that interested in the movies themselves; I was there to sit next to her while Madcap flirted with the boys. No one seemed to notice me. The boys had their eyes on Madcap and that was fine with me. I felt invisible, but right next to the action. I wanted to soak it all up so that when I was old enough to go out on a date, and tame my red mane, I'd know what to do.

The films were in black and white. That night we were watching *Birth of a Nation*, a long one with lots of silent anguish on people's faces, many extras, horses running across the screen, and gunfire. The Ku Klux Klan, grown men running around in white sheets and pointed hats, burned huge crosses. I was hungry for a snack; I wanted to go to Bob's Big Boy and have the salad with bleu cheese dressing; I had just enough money for that and it was calling out to me with cartoon speech bubbles hovering around my pocket, reminding me how hungry I was. Madcap laughed or sucked in her breath with an "oh!" at all the right times, and we were all swept up by the marching orchestra music. In the dark at first it seemed cool between my legs, and then my panties seemed wet, so I went out to the restroom.

Just as I locked the door behind me I noticed a dispenser on the wall above the sink. Sanitary Napkins, it said, 5 cents. I didn't want to think about the hairs "down there" again, but there it was. A nickel! For a napkin? That's outrageous. It costs as much as a loaf of bread. And what do we need napkins for in a restroom? Then I remembered: maybe other girls shaved their hairs and cut themselves, too. That's embarrassing, but kind of comforting. But 5 cents! What a gyp.

When I pulled down my capris there was blood all over my underpants! The blood wasn't from the shaving; that was weeks ago. It was coming out from between my legs. From inside my body. *Oh, my God I am heartily sorry for having offended thee.* This called for immediate prayers, directly to the source. I wiped myself with toilet paper, which promptly soaked up more blood. *Oh, my God! Please don't make me die. I'll go to confession about the lies, I promise, I promise, I promise!* Luckily I was wearing the mumu. I stripped down so I could rinse out my underpants at the basin sink. I wrung them out almost dry, put them back on, and stuffed gobs of Kleenex in my underpants. I remembered to say a prayer. *Dear Mother of God, you guys have my attention. I'll do anything. Have mercy; I'm only 12 years old!*

Madcap was still in the dark, watching the movie.

"Psssst, Madcap. C'mere."

She glanced over at me, frowning. "What?"

"You gotta come."

"What? Gimmie a hint!"

"Shhhhh." Someone said behind her.

"It's urgent!" I pleaded, whispering across a couple of other people sitting in the aisle seats. *I'm dying in the most embarrassing way.* Maybe I could beam that thought over to her. I waved my hands again and again like c'mere! c'mere! and she finally got up, squished past the knees of the two others and went with me. I locked the ladies room door behind us. It was just the two of us in there.

"What? What is it?"

"I think I'm dying of something."

"Sick to your stomach?"

"I'm gushing blood. Down there."

"You finally got it!"

"What?"

"That's your Period."

"Oh… my period?"

"The thing Mother hinted about."

"But it's just coming out of my body, down there. I stuffed my underpants with tp."

"That's your vagina."

"What's your vagina?"

"You know how you go wee-wee and bo-bo?"

"Duh."

"There's another hole down there. It's a vagina. It's in the middle. Girls have three holes and boys only have two."

What? This was just unbelievable. I had another hole down there? And blood was coming out of it right now? I felt a bit dizzy, trying to understand.

"Don't worry, you won't bleed to death," Madcap said. It's the beginning of growing up."

Well, not exactly the beginning, I thought, remembering the hairs. "But what's it for?"

"It's for when the baby gets made in your stomach."

"But what's the blood for?"

"It's for the baby when its growing inside you; it comes out when you don't have the baby."

"I don't get it. I've never had a baby, but the blood is coming out anyway."

"Every month, it prepares for a baby."

"How long does it come out for?"

"I don't know, three days, or five. Sometimes I get cramps."

"Cramps?"

"Yeah, cramps like when you have hard bo-bo

and it won't come out. Sometimes you get cramps. It prepares you to give birth."

"The blood prepares you for giving birth?"

"The cramps do."

I stood there looking at myself in the mirror, disliking this growing up thing altogether. I had an inspiration. No wonder Peter Pan didn't want to grow up! On second thought, Peter Pan was a boy. He didn't have any of this weird stuff to deal with. At least I don't think they have to deal with this stuff. Do they? Maybe they probably grow hairs down there too, and have other weird bodily secrets.

"You have to get some sanitary napkins and a belt," Madcap, said, all business now. "Oh look, they have some here. Do you have 5 cents? Or a dime? You can stuff one of these in your underpants even if you don't have a belt." I reached in my pocket and felt the shape of a quarter in my hand.

"Aren't we going to Bob's?" I had just enough money for their little salad with the bleu cheese dressing.

"We could go to Bob's." Madcap said. "Dwight usually likes to go after the movie."

Hmmm, I thought. *Salad? Or sanitary napkin? Bleu cheese dressing? Or blood all over my pants?* I pointed to the dispenser.

"How long do these napkins last?"

"If you just stick it in your underpants, it'll probably last at least until we get home."

"I've already got a wad of Kleenex in there," I said, "maybe the Kleenex will last until we get to Bob's." Madcap shrugged.

I held onto my quarter.

CHAPTER 15
TIED WITH THE FEENEYS

Dear Jesus, Is that what you really want? I'm speechless. The blood thing is totally impractical. Also, do the nuns have to have periods, since they don't have babies? If you said no, it still wouldn't tempt me to be a nun. I thought I wanted to have a baby, but it's all pretty disgusting. Did Bitty's kitties come out of her third hole?

On my way to ballet class in South Pasadena, right across from Vons supermarket, I pedaled my bike with a white basket on the front. When I turned the corner onto South Pasadena Avenue I slowed down to look at this thing happening that I couldn't quite figure out.

I had my cloth bag with me, the pink one with my leotard and white tights and black ballet slippers. I had spent my babysitting money on the lessons—a necessary sacrifice for my new saint and glory campaign. Ballet is graceful and feminine; I could already sense approval from the Blessed Mother, Queen of the Heavens. To begin with, a ballerina looks like a princess. Also, I liked the idea of the stiff, bouncy skirts I'd get to wear at a performance. And once I learned how to do the movements, people were going to applaud me thunderously. I wanted it so much my stomach ached.

Mother hardly even knew I was taking this class;

she was probably having a nap right this minute. Which she deserved. Still. Most great ballerinas started when they were two or three, but I had to be old enough to babysit before I could even study. I was the eldest and tallest person in the ballet class; everyone else came up to the middle of my arm. Parents sat on the sidelines watching their darling toddler or five-year-old do pliés and bunny hops. Other girls my age in ballet were in the intermediate or advanced classes—luckily not at the same time as me; I would have died of shame, passing them in the hall. The teacher was strict; she poked me and struck my thighs and hips with a pointed stick as if I should know better being twelve-going-on-thirteen.

But right in front of me on the sidewalk a German Shepherd on his hind legs, was prancing behind a white terrier mutt who was attached to his bottom, in other words, two dogs were stuck together at the butt and going in the same direction. They looked like they were in the wheelbarrow race at the Girl Scouts' picnic. I had a book of dog stamps at home so I was at least able to identify the breeds. The terrier was yelping; its front paws running in a trot, like it was on a hampster wheel. The little dog kept glancing around at his butt, terrified and embarrassed, even as he tried to escape from it, like he might be thinking: how did I get this other dog stuck to my butt? *How did he?* I asked myself. *How did that happen, exactly?*

Then I saw someone run out of one of the houses— it was Mr. Devon, the doctor, chasing them both with a cup of water in his hand, which spilled over the edges. As I passed Peggy Cullen's house, I could see her between the curtains of the huge glass window gawking at the dogs as they yelped by. I straddled my bike and waved. Peggy was about our age. She and me and Jeannie sometimes played together in the summer, even though Peggy played in the tennis tournaments at Westridge School across the street and lived in a neat house with rugs and non-stained couches. She stepped down the red brick walk between her short and exceptionally green lawn.

"Can you figure that one out?" I asked. "How'd they get stuck?"

"Yeah," she confided, coming right up to me and whispering. "That's how grown-ups do it."

"Do what?"

"You don't know?"

Mr. Devon stepped in front of the dogs, and with one hand grabbed the small terrier by one paw, stopping them both from going any further. Then he poured water over the bridge of the dogs' butts. That poor little dog whined and slunk away, its tail between its legs.

"That's how adults make babies," Peggy said like she knew.

"What?" I tried to imagine how that would work. "That's disgusting. They get naked?"

"They strip their clothes off and put their private parts together."

"Gross!" I looked at her to see if she was pulling my leg. She shrugged. So it was true! This was just getting worse and worse. What humiliation will they think of next?

When I got to the door of the rehearsal hall, the little girls in their pink tights were already at the bar, in first position, completely unaware of what lay in store for them once they got big enough to start growing hairs down there. Mrs. Smider was waiting for me, her pointed stick in hand. I was hoping she wouldn't notice the bulge in my tights from the sanitary napkin, or if she did, that she wouldn't call attention to it. And I thought: Mrs. Smider knows all about this. She has hairs down there. She has a period, too. She's old enough to have a husband. Not only has she been kissed and knows what that feels like, she knows all about "doing it." She's probably "done it" herself a few times.

Everything looked completely different to me now.

When I got home, Mother was in the bathroom. I thought I heard her barfing.

My first thought was: I hope she doesn't give the flu to me. One thing about the flu in our family: when one person gets it, it's just a matter of time before everybody is spitting up all over the place. Then I felt sorry for her. I hate the flu. And now that we're talking about it, when does Mother ever get to have any fun?

She was kind of quietly barfing. Then I heard her turn on the faucet, probably washing her hands. And I think she just sat there on the toilet with the lid closed. She was kind of talking to herself softly. It made me wonder about the guy she was married to before. Although why would she be talking to him in the bathroom?

"Hey, Mom, are you okay in there?" I called to her. But she didn't answer this time. "Mom?" She used to tell me how she admired the Blessed Mother because the Blessed Mother "pondered things in her heart."

So maybe Mother had been pondering and ended up talking to herself.

"Mom? Is there someone in there with you? The next thing I knew, the door was opening and she came walking out. I looked up at her with my books on my lap as she closed the door behind her. She just smiled down at me.

Maybe she *was* talking to her first husband in there.

"Were you... talking to someone?"

"I *was* talking with someone," she admitted.

"Really? Who?" But Mother didn't answer. Strangely, she was standing still there, just having a conversation with me. "Is she—or he—still in the bathroom?" I asked, trying to see in through the crack in the door. Her hands were in her apron pockets, one on each side of her stomach.

"No, he or she is right here." She patted her belly.

It took a moment for it to sink in. I stood up, and my books fell to the ground. I put my arms around her.

"Oh, Mom! A new baby! When is it due?"

"March, next year."

"Number 14! A boy or a girl?"

"Only God knows."

"Oh, I hope it is a girl!"

A new baby. Mom was going to have a new baby. This would change things.

Now we would be tied with the Feeneys.

CHAPTER 16
A SURPRISE FOR ROSIE

July 13 – Dear Blessed Mother, Somebody important from Washington went to Russia to talk about a treaty on nuclear bombs. He brought three tons of American equipment to set up the red telephone hotline between Washington and Moscow. I hope it works, because I have been losing sleep over the possibility of being turned "ashes to ashes and dust to dust" ("if the Lord won't take you, the devil must") under a mushroom cloud while I'm dreaming. Good thing we're still saying our rosaries for the Russians, because you can't trust those commies. Clara's been gone for about a week, and we all miss her. But something fun and exciting is about to happen, and it's an absolute secret. Rosie is having a birthday party on the weekend, (July 13) and she doesn't know anything about it.

Rosie is the smallest in her class of seven-year-olds, and somehow, looking at her short self amidst her lanky classmates, I realized that when Rosie was born, Daddy and Mother named her perfectly. Rosie, to me, seems like the name of someone you treasure and love.

The best part about Rosie is her brown eyes. They're soft looking, like a deer. When she looks up at you, quietly and patiently, you just wonder what she could be thinking. Being that she's so small, has such big eyes, and goes around a little shell-shocked about everything, you can't help but feel sorry and affectionate towards her at the same time. She lives in the same mess and chaos we all do, but she gets lost in it. That could be it. Maybe there are just too many of us, too much noise, too many saints who are perfect in the midst of too much dirty everything everywhere you go, and the whole scenario is overwhelming for Rosie.

At home she drifted, like a lazy shadow on a hot afternoon. As if she was waiting for something to happen. Which it usually did. Rubber band fights broke out regularly after school, with somebody crying at the end, or being put down for a nap. Once, she went missing for a few hours and I found her in the tool shed, standing next to the boxes in the dark, sucking her thumb. She had been playing Hide 'n Seek and was still hoping someone would find her.

Everyday after dinner, you had to light a fire under her butt, and you had to say to her, "Rosie, it's time to do your homework now." Maybe she was on the couch, recovering from the rosary and all the images of Christ being walloped by a whip on his bare back or having huge nails pounded into his hands. That kind of violence could be tough for a seven year old, especially if you have a good imagination. I'm not sure how I got through it myself; I was always cringing at all the blood and torn flesh. But Rosie would sit there, staring at nothing, holding her patch of blanket. All that was left of her babyhood was about 4 inches of unraveling, faded green/yellow plaid cloth. She held onto it wherever she went and didn't even try to hide it. Everyday as we counted heads after packing into the Volkswagen on the way to school in the morning, on the list to check was "Rosie's blankie." One of us would gently take it out of her hand and say something like "We're just going to take your blankie and keep it safe so it will be here for you when you get home from school." The expression in her eyes, as she looked back at all our faces surrounding her in the car every morning, was terror.

So I'm not sure, but maybe Mother noticed this about Rosie and thought a surprise party would bring her out of herself.

I jumped at the chance to try making something for her birthday. Ever since we visited the artist in Glendale, I began seeing things, like the shape of the branches on the oak tree and how they looked like bony arms scratching at the sky. Or the shades of gray and brown on the bark of the Eucalyptus tree. I couldn't wait to put something together, out of some rocks and twigs and white paint from a watercolor set that I bought with my babysitting money. Everyday after school, I went down to the bomb shelter; I got this feeling inside of me, a certain excitement. No one knew where I was. As I walked down the steps to the lower level, I could feel the coolness of the cement against the earth surrounding me. I always hid the ingredients in the bottom shelf of the cupboard, behind broken pots and old newspapers. I pretended I knew what I was doing, like the artist.

Then, Mother said it was my job to find Rosie's friends in second grade, so we could invite them. The problem was, at school it was only Graciela and Rosie. She and her little friend trailed around together in the schoolyard, on the periphery of the action, (good use of "on the edges," Annie!), quietly watching tetherball or marbles from the side. So I reported that to Mom. Mom said, "In order to have a party, Annie, we have to invite *someone.*"

So Rosie and I sat together on the couch with her class group photo and I pointed, "Is she your friend?" And Rosie shrugged. "How about this boy? Do you play with him?" We did get to one boy named Roger and when I said, "Do you like this person?" She emphatically said, "No!" and started kicking her legs out, and crossed her arms, and turned her head away from me. But if she got a sort of pleasant look on her face, I would ask her that person's name and write it down. That's how we got the list of the nine kids for Rosie's party. We also included Clarkie Franklin, the littlest of our next door neighbor's three kids, who carefully picked his nose in public, like he was trying to figure out what, exactly, he was going to fish out of the darkness in there. And then he got this satisfied look on his face when he got the gob on his finger. You had to look away with Clarkie.

As Rosie's birthday got closer, I worked away at her present. Back at the bomb shelter, I found some curly sticks from the oak tree and green acorns (the kind with the hat), and I glued them to the top of a flat rock. By about Thursday I had the idea to paint some white onto the rock and a few spots on the branches.

When Rosie woke up that day, she stumbled out to the dining room table in her rumpled bunting, looking for her presents, because that's how it's done at the Shea Family Home. A stack of presents first thing in the morning, and you know you were really born in this family and someone noticed. Cake at dinner with candles and the song. But there was only one present at Rosie's place that morning; pea green pedal pushers and a yellow top with a daisy for show. She didn't even get filler presents like socks or underpants.

Rosie didn't say anything about the lack of presents that birthday morning. Maybe she had faith that the one pedal pusher outfit was due to the bunny. She had to appreciate the fact that getting a bunny of your very own in a family of thirteen children was truly a unique and special event and didn't require presents of a more ordinary nature. I thought Rosie getting a bunny was so rare as to be practically unbelievable, but as it turned out, the bunny was part of the master plan. It was a decoy trip to get Rosie out of the house. While Daddy and Rosie were gone getting the bunny, all her friends came over in their party dresses with presents. We set the table, blew up the balloons, and got the cake out of hiding. I had invited Wanda to sleep over and help me with the party. This was the kind of thing we both loved to do.

Mother, Madcap and Jeannie made the cake and cleaned off the picnic table under the oak tree out back. Jeannie answered the doorbell and wrote out the nametags. Wanda and I handed out party favors, yellow crepe cups with jellybeans, nuts, and Chex cereal. We made Jello the night before. The pigs in a blanket were puffing up in the oven

Back at the bomb shelter, I kept looking at my creation before I finally had to cover it up with wrapping paper. I really appreciated the natural quality, how it looked like an oak tree with snow on it, clawing the sky. Rosie could put it on the ledge by her bed and see it whenever she wanted. Finally, I wrapped it in newspaper that I had painted myself to look like the pants of the artist, splattered with every color of the rainbow. I counted the minutes until Rosie could open the present I had made for her. Even Wanda didn't know what I had done.

Everything went off without a hitch, as the cowboys in the Westerns would say, until Jeannie ran back and said, "She's here! They're parking the car!" It was a moment of breath-holding. We all ran to our seats at the table. Wanda and I sat shoulder to shoulder, and when we saw Rosie coming around the corner, holding this trembling white creature in a black cage, all the voices cried out "Surprise!"

Rosie's mouth dropped open, and then she burst into tears. I felt so sorry and happy for her at the same time and I ran over and knelt down and hugged her, and then I looked back at what Rosie saw. A whole bunch of kids in pastel dresses and huge stack of colorful presents on the picnic table. Balloons on strings bobbing over the presents. A big cake with seven minute frosting and seven candles in the middle of the table. Our bouncy dog, yipping and barking while all of Rosie's classmates chattered like a flock of birds. It was like a painting. Everything that your eyes looked at was sparkling and new.

Graciela, in a blue pastel Easter dress, white socks and white First Communion shoes, ran over to greet Rosie. Her skin was nut brown and her eyes were almost black, so the contrast was sharp and pleasing. I kept staring at her. She looked like a present, too. No wonder Rosie liked her.

"Look what I got, Graciela!" Rosie said. Then they huddled.

There is nothing quite like a brand new toy, still smelling fresh and plasticky, with no smudges, dressed up with its wrapping paper still around it. Every time Rosie opened up another one, a checkers set, a Barbie doll, a toy bracelet, I cringed when they bunched the paper up to throw it away. I wanted to smooth it out so I could use that beautiful colored paper in my next art project. But mostly I couldn't wait until she ripped off the paint-spattered newspaper and discovered my own, first artwork.

Finally, Madcap handed her my present. It was an unusual shape and Rosie stared at it. Just as the wrapping paper fell from her hands, a little smile began at the edges of her mouth.

"What's that?" Jeannie asked.

"It's a… sculpture!" I said, "I made it myself." Jeannie grabbed it from Rosie by the stick. In her hand, the stick dislodged from the rock and fell on the table, breaking into pieces. Rosie looked at me like she had been stung by a bee, but was so stunned by the surprise of it that it didn't occur to her to cry. I stopped breathing.

"It's not a sculpture," Jeannie announced. "It's just a rock and sticks!"

I could feel my neck getting hot. I tried to swallow, but I had to finally gulp in some air. I looked around to find Mother. She was walking over towards the garbage can by the side of the house, her arms full of wrapping paper. She had missed the whole thing. I sat down so

I wouldn't fall over. Then, I saw her stuff all the torn, beautiful wrapping paper into the garbage can.

And then I realized something: even if she had seen my present to Rosie, Mother might also have thought it was "just a rock and sticks."

"You broke it!" I cried, my eyes stinging. It sounded so infantile and obvious, but couldn't think of anything else to say. Rosie inched over to me from where she was standing. Her little palm slipped into my hand. I looked down at her. She looked up at me. I whispered into her ear.

"We'll fix it, Rosie, don't worry."

• • •

That night I woke in the dark because I was cold. Somehow my pajama top was gathered around my neck and my covers were down at my waist. I pulled them up around myself, shivering. I was drowsy and not sure if I had imagined a shadow in the doorway. Was there someone creaking on the stairs, or not? The house was so still except for the usual sounds of sleep breath, the snoring and gurgling of Jeannie and Rosie. The moonlight shone through the slats onto the floor like it was daylight. It felt like the whole house was frozen in that eerie moment.

I curled up into a ball and tried to go back to sleep. Even saying Hail Marys didn't help. There was a panic alongside me, as if something bad had happened to my guardian angel, and then I started to think about how Daddy used to drive to China Lake alone in his car for The Navy and I would be afraid he would never come back. I heard the clock chime two times in the living room, the lonely sound of the bell being struck and echoing against the silence. I imagined it sitting there on the mantle protected by all the statues. And I had this idea then and there that the statues were empty, that all the saints had fled somewhere and we were all alone under the stars and the moon.

The universe was way bigger than it had ever been.

CHAPTER 17
MEETING AARON SOLOMON

July 28 – Dear God, Yesterday you went on a killing spree. Two airplane crashes in one day. In one of them, twenty-six Boy Scouts from the Philippines died on their way to the World Scout Jamboree in Greece. Then, at about 5:30, you killed Bitty. Obviously the Blessed Mother would never let this brutal murder of a beloved being happen, so it must have been You who did this. HOW CAN YOU LIVE WITH YOURSELF? You killed my beloved friend and cat through a man and his motorcycle. As you probably know, if you were paying attention, this is what happened. I got home from ballet at 3:45 and went downstairs (the basement) and I petted Bitty (for the last time). I fed her out of the baby doll bottle that I was feeding the baby cats with. I said "Bye" and left. I didn't know it, but I would never see her alive again. Then I went to ballet. As I was riding my bicycle up the street on the way home, Jeannie called out to me that Bitty was dead. I thought she said, "Daddy is dead" so at first I was relieved it was only Bitty.

Jeannie told me that Bitty ran across from the other side of the street and a motorcycle hit her, but she kept running through a slat in the Hamilton's fence. Then she fell over and died. I went to see her, lying on her side, and it began to sink in. Her mouth was open. I could see that she was stiff. I looked at her for the last time. "Bye, Bitty!" I said, petting her fur, which was still warm. I left her out there all night but maybe I should have covered her up. Bartholomew saw her in the morning and put a cloth over her. We both stood there, staring at the cloth. Bart put his arm around my shoulder.

> *This is the next day. I am crying very hard. I loved Bitty, but I know I will never see her again, even in the after life where I will meet you. I AM SO SORRY IF YOU DID THIS BECAUSE OF THAT PRANK I PLAYED ON JEANNIE. I AM TRULY SORRY, SO SORRY FOR EVERYTHING. PLEASE LET BITTY COME UP TO HEAVEN WITH ME! PROMISE ME!*

After Clara left and Bitty died, I learned the word "morose" and realized it was me to a T. So I became more determined than ever about ballet, to get my mind off my dead cat. I got to class on time and just put myself at the mercy of the stick, trying to twist myself in whatever way I was hit. I did math homework first, since it was my weakness, and looked after Bitty's Seven Sacraments, feeding them with the baby bottle and changing the newspaper in their box. They were getting bigger, but their mother wasn't around to show them how to lick themselves clean. Their fur was a mess, all matted and stuck with bits of poop and pee and the soft food that I now put out for them. I couldn't imagine anyone wanting to take them home. But right after Bitty died, I did have the common sense to put a marmalade kitty—Matrimony—into a litter of another cat who was nursing kittens and she accepted it as her own. I made a plan to pick her up in four weeks, when she would be old enough. (I figured she'd learn to clean herself because her adopted mother would show her how). She looked like a miniature Bitty.

Then one day I got a letter in the mail from Clara. I couldn't believe she was writing to *me*.

Dear Annie, Why don't you come up and visit me? I really miss everyone, especially the twins and Jude. I heard about Bitty and I am sorry for you. Please ask Mother and Daddy if you can come up the next time Daddy comes to visit. I left a little gold pin next to the lamp by my bed, could you bring it? Mother must be getting big with her new baby. Love, Clara.

I found out from Wanda, who lately had been hanging out with Teresa Feeney, that Mrs. Feeney was pregnant again. Apparently Teresa Feeney said "The Shea Family has not caught up with The Feeneys yet because we have a little sister named Philomena who is in heaven." When Wanda said that, my heart was broken into hundreds of pieces. First of all, Wanda was my best friend, and now she was hanging out with *Teresa Feeney*! Secondly, once Mrs. Feeney gave birth to their next child, the Feeneys would reign forever as the largest family in the parish. They'd have sixteen kids, including the one in heaven. At some point you have to acknowledge that you're beat. You have to retire. I mean, Mother would have to have two more babies just to catch up! And then she'd have to get pregnant for nine months and have another one, just so we could rank. Her varicose veins would pop.

Mother was maybe three months pregnant then

(this one would be #14) and her stomach was beginning to stick out. When she climbed up the step to get into the VW bus to take us to school in the morning, she grabbed the steering wheel and hoisted herself up to the driver's seat. I handed her Clara's letter through the window.

"Do you ever worry about Clara, Mom?"

"She'll be fine in Ventura. The Sisters of Saint Isabella are lovely. What's that pin?" I had attached Clara's pin to the collar of my white uniform shirt, just for safekeeping.

"Clara asked me to bring it to her if I go up on the weekend. May I go with Daddy? Please!?"

"We'll see, Annie. You go to class now." She put the letter from Clara onto the seat next to her bulky brown purse and shifted the gears, pulling out of the parking space.

The next morning when Daddy shook my feet to go to Mass with him, I turned over to go back to sleep. Whenever I do that, I feel guilty for about five seconds before I fall into heavy dreaming again.

"How's my little nun?" He asked me, and the guilt beamed through my groggy dream. When we slipped out of the house in the dawn light and closed the back door behind us, I could hear Mother's slippers shuffling down the hall. Daddy backed the Rambler out of the driveway and I stared at his familiar neck, recently shaved and smelling of Old Spice.

"Dad, can I go with you to visit Clara this weekend?"

"Are you still thinking you've been called to serve the Lord in the contemplative life?" He asked me.

When Daddy has something on his mind he doesn't usually hear anyone else. (And he uses words like "contemplative" to make it sound official and enticing, but I know it just means the life of a regular nun in a convent, and being disciplinarian to a bunch of farty kids at an inner city Catholic school.) I was tempted to say what I know he really wanted to hear, but I was really trying to be truthful and obedient, now that Bitty died. It was clear to me how much power God really did have, and how much he could hurt me if I didn't mend my ways.

"Hmmm," I said. Daddy continued the conversation with himself.

"I've always thought that it would be nice to have at least one vocation in the family. Out of so many, surely the Lord has called one into service."

"What about John-the-Blimp?"

"How many times have I told you to call him by his Christian name?"

Ha! Now we were actually having a conversation.

"Okay, John, then. What about John? He's going into service for The Lord."

"John the Baptist was a contemporary of Jesus. He was a very devout man."

Yeah, I thought, *and he got it right where it counts, in the neck.* "I know, Dad," I said. "His head was given to this lady named Salome, who danced for Herod. It came on a plate. I got an A in catechism from first grade up. Now I'm in sixth grade."

There was a silence as the light changed to green.

Daddy cleared his throat. "John's vocation may come later, Annie. He may be too young right now to commit his life to the Lord." The devil must have been in the car with us because I felt like being sassy.

"John's vacation was showing off with that cassock. He wore it everywhere—right up until Father Stefanucci got defeated."

"It's vocation, Annie. John's vocation is something he has to work out with God himself."

Ha, ha, I thought. I got him on "vacation." He was listening. But I could feel the disappointment in his voice. I knew how I, too, was letting him down. I tried to imagine his proud gaze upon me in the short veil and knee-length black skirt of a postulant habit, standing in a line of future Brides of Christ before God and all eternity. But when I blinked and saw the image of his hands clapping vigorously, there I was, center stage on graduation day, Officer Candidate School—standing at attention on a football field in a white uniform with brass buttons, saluting in the sunshine, a band playing upbeat marching music. Tuba and trumpets glistening. Or! How about this: standing in formation on an aircraft carrier with ocean and sky behind us on the horizon under a steeple of raised swords. Drums, bugles, wind blowing dramatically as I receive a medal of honor from the President! Maybe someone else in the family will step forward and fulfill Daddy's Catholic destiny.

"You'd like the Sisters of Saint Isabella in Ventura," Daddy said, just as the president's hands were on my lapel.

"May I go?" I let him think I was excited about the sisters. "I could ride up with you!"

"Clara is praying for her own soul," Daddy said

solemnly. "She doesn't need visitors right now." What was going on here? Should I press him for details? But the thought of asking about the contents of Clara's soul was too embarrassing.

•   •   •

That Saturday morning Madcap rolled back my covers.

"Get up, Annie."

I could smell the bacon. I opened my eyes and looked around at the two other rumpled beds. Everybody else was already at breakfast.

"We're going to visit Clara," Madcap whispered, even though there was no one within hearing range.

"Great! Daddy gave permission?"

"Shhhhh!" She dug into my drawers, holding up pedal pushers and shirts. "Get dressed. We're going to Cal Tech together. At least that's what we're going to say. We're really taking the bus up to see Clara. You have something to eat; I'll pack a lunch. Do you have any money left from babysitting?" I went into my top drawer and grabbed up the bills and coins: 5 dollars and 65 cents.

I'd never hitch-hiked before, but Madcap stood with one hip tilted up and stuck her thumb out as the cars whizzed past us on Orange Grove Boulevard. If anyone stopped, we were to say "Greyhound Bus Station on Walnut Boulevard." It was windy and crystal clear blue, but warm. An invigorating morning, on top of the fact that what we were doing was absolutely forbidden. The only downside was that we could get caught. I stood behind a telephone pole, hoping it wouldn't be a murderer who decided to stop. We both wore pedal pushers and sleeveless shirts. I brought an extra long sleeved shirt in case it cooled off. With the warm wind, I was hot. Madcap's waist length hair blew around like a flag, rippling in the wind. It didn't take long. A blue Ford pick up with a surfboard sticking out of the back pulled over and Madcap hopped up into the cab like it was the most ordinary thing she could ever do. I emerged from behind the pole. We squeezed in next to an older guy at the steering wheel who was, I dunno, say 20 or so.

"Where you going?" The guy was dark haired and had a fuzzy, unshaven face.

"Greyhound bus station," Madcap said. "Walnut Boulevard."

"I know it," the guy said, "I drive past it every day." Madcap's arms were touching his arms, we were so close. I huddled next to the door and stared at him while he drove, memorizing his details in case he tried anything and we would later have to testify. His shirt and pants were caked with mud and white dust. His hands had paint stains on them, and he had two fingers on his right hand that were shorter than the others. When he looked over at Madcap, I could see that his eyes were blue. Wanda would say that he was kinda cute.

You could always count on Madcap to chatter. She yammered about the surfboard bouncing around in the back of the pick up and the paint stains. He worked in construction, he was an only child, he used to go to South Pasadena High School, and his name was Aaron Solomon. She tried to impress him by telling him we were from a family of thirteen children. I'd been noticing lately that whenever we were out in public, the conversation inevitably turned to how many children there are in our family. The statistical nature of our existence has that circus act factor, fascinating—like a man covered in tattoos is fascinating. Or the fat lady.

"Thirteen kids? Wow," Aaron Solomon said, "your mother must be busy!" Everyone thinks they're so clever when they find out how many kids in our family, but they're only clever to the extent of saying, "Your mother must be busy!" Sometimes the men say, if my Dad is there, "You must have been quite busy." And then they all laugh like they're congratulating themselves on their superior wit in telling some joke that only they understand, wink wink. Anyway, the next thing I knew, Madcap had her hand across my lap, reaching for the door handle.

"So where are you going on that bus?" Aaron Solomon asked. He smiled at Madcap, with a little twinkle of energy. I felt like I was watching a movie. They never even knew I was there.

"Ventura," Madcap said.

"What are the chances? Ventura! I'm going there! Why are you going?"

"I'll tell you if you tell me." Her sweetest smile.

"I'm meeting some guys at C Street Beach, and we're going surfing," he said, tapping his stubby fingers on the shiny steering wheel. Madcap paused.

"We're visiting our sister who lives there now." I was glad she was in charge, as I hadn't a clue about what to do. My real feeling underneath it was that I wanted to go with this guy. I wanted him not to be a low life on the wrong side of the law looking for victims. Here was my reasoning: Number 1, if we went with him, and he wasn't a murderer, it would save us bus fare. Number 2, there actually was a surfboard in the back, so his story about surfing might be the truth. But it was so hard to know. It could be a decoy.

"I could take you both," he suggested.

He could take us both and drive off a cliff with us! All the bad kidnap thoughts rose up at that suggestion: Don't talk to strangers, don't ever go anywhere with anyone in a car. Never be alone with a man until you're of a certain age (were we at that age yet?). Don't hitchhike. If you make the mistake of getting in the car with someone you don't know and they try something, just jump out of the car, even if it's going full speed ahead. Madcap looked at him directly. She cocked her head and made a face at him.

"I get it if you don't want to go with me," he said. Then he shrugged, all the while smiling with those white teeth. Now I was noticing his tan. It seemed like a long minute we were waiting for Madcap to make up her mind. I kept looking down at my lap, hoping she would not ask me for advice.

"So you're just going up there by yourself, then?" She asked.

Yes, Madcap! That's what he said!

"Once we get there," he kept smiling, "I'm going to meet up with the guys at the beach. And like I said, we're going surfing. Why don't you and your little sister come along?" Little sister. I cringed, even though obviously I was Madcap's little sister.

"I don't have a bathing suit," Madcap offered. "And besides, we're going to Ventura to meet with our sister."

"Bring your other sister!" I watched him mouth the words and felt myself caving in. Actually his mouth looked pretty cute, too, and what he was saying sounded exciting. I imagined the sunset and surfers with muscular chests, the sand stretching for miles, but I was still knee-jerk thinking, *body parts in the back.*

"Have you ever gone surfing?"

"Once," Madcap said. "I swallowed a lot of water, but it was fun anyway, getting smacked by the waves. It was my first time." What? Madcap went surfing? When was this?

"Your first time? Aww, I missed your first time?" he said, with mock disappointment in his voice, smiling at her like she knew the secret he was talking about. Madcap knew, alright; she looked at me and rolled her eyes.

"Afterwards," he said, "we sit around the fire and drink beer." If he drinks beer, he's even older than I thought, he's at least 21. That's old.

"Is Clara old enough to drink beer?" I blurted. Madcap looked at me sideways. It was the first and only thing I said up until then. It hurts being stupid.

"We usually make a bonfire on the beach," he added, just to put me over the top.

Oh my god, he's talking about being on the beach when it's dark!

"Okay," said Madcap. "We'll drive up with you. Could you drop us off at the mission before you go surfing?"

"Sure!" He said a bit too enthusiastically. "I know right where it is." Just as I imagined our violent end in the sand dunes at dusk, Madcap agreed to go with him!

Then he said,

"Isn't there a home there? For unwed mothers?" Madcap ignored him and at that moment he quickly turned the wheel away from the bus station. We were in it now and there was no turning back.

• • •

Aaron Solomon, it turned out, got cuter as the miles whipped past. I think that happens if you stare at somebody for too long. Madcap generously shared our peanut butter and jelly sandwiches with him, and he stopped once to buy proper picnic things for us like cheese, salami, bread and Big Hunk, jujubes and Oreos, and then we ate them like we'd been friends for years. There was no need for me, really, as they seemed to be hitting it off just fine. (Whatever that really means— hitting what? Off to where?) Madcap handed him bits to eat and the both of them sang along with the radio. "You've really got a hold on me." "Up on the roof." I was tempted when "Ring of Fire" came on, but I pretty much kept silent, wondering how he lost the tips of his fingers. Where did those finger bits go? Did they fly off his hands, or just kind of hang there by a thread, as it were? Did he put them in the freezer? Why didn't he sew them back on? Not that I really wanted to know. Up until we got on the Ventura Freeway I was worried he was taking us to Angeles Crest Highway where only the trees could hear our screams. I looked in the glove compartment for a gun, and everything fell out on the floor, pens and rubber bands and official car documents, a Swiss army knife, and little flat packets with round shaped rubbery circles. Candy?

"Can I have one of these?" I asked. Madcap looked

over at me with her eyes wide and her eyebrows arched.

"Ooops, sorry!" I said, blushing, not sure what she meant by that. Aaron Solomon reached over with one hand still on the steering wheel, trying to stuff the things back in. All his fingers on that hand were the same length. Madcap put his hand back on the wheel.

"I'll put everything back, you drive!" She beamed at him.

It was a glorious California day, sunshine all around and the radio on full blast. "Fun, fun, fun now that daddy took the T-bird away." The windows were down and Madcap's hair rippled dramatically in the breeze. Aaron Solomon and Madcap had to yell at each other over the sound of the motor and the cars going past.

Once we got out of the city, nearer to Ventura and driving next to the water, the air smelled like salt and dead fish. We drove past little houses at the base of the mountains, small towns, really, nothing like the bustling, smoggy city of Pasadena. The blue water sparkled on the left, white caps on top of the waves rolling in and in and in. "Little Surfer, little one, make my heart come all undone, do you love me, do you surfer girl?"

As we passed California Street, Aaron Solomon said, "I'll drive you up to the Mission, but I want you to see how easy it is to get back here to California Street. We call it C Street beach. You just take Main Street to California Street. Turn down towards the beach."

He dropped us off at The Mission. We pulled up next to the heavy wood front door, a white stucco building with a tower and a cross on top. I stepped onto the pavement and stretched my legs while Madcap gathered her purse on her lap.

"See you later?" He asked Madcap from the driver's seat.

"Maybe," she said, hopping down. "If Clara wants to."

"Clara!" He called to me. "Don't cha want to see me surf?" Now he had that flirty look on his face, and he was directing it at me.

"I'm not Clara, I'm Annie. Clara is the one we're visiting."

"Thanks for the ride!" Madcap said, waving.

"My pleasure." He was leaning down from the steering wheel looking at Madcap with those big blue eyes. "If you don't make it to California Street today, how can I reach you?"

"You live in South Pasadena?" Madcap asked.

"That's the story," he said, smiling that big smile again.

"My Dad's name is Martin and we're in the book. Martin Shea. We live on Madeline Drive, across the street from Westridge School."

"Westridge! I know Westridge," he said, elated.

"You can call me."

"I'll call," he said, and blew her a kiss.

CHAPTER 18
SISTERS OF SAINT ISABELLA

Dear Blessed Mother, You gave me all the signs, and I was too stupid to notice a single one. You've really got to help us here.

"There's Clara!" I practically shouted. I was so excited to see her. I could tell it was her by the little flip of her duck tail down the back of her short hair do. She stood up from a chair and turned around to greet us as we entered the living room at the convent. I took one look.

"Clara!" I said. "Are you pregnant?"

"I am," she said, holding her hands on her belly. My jaw dropped. Clara opened her arms up for a hug. Madcap ran up to her and embraced her. I stood off to the side and grabbed her hand, then squeezed. Her breasts were huge, like melons.

What the heck? I thought. *Clara is pregnant?*

No wonder our parents sent her up here; they didn't want anyone in the parish to know! That would definitely affect our rank at St. Andrew's. It was as unbelievable as it was scandalous. No wonder Daddy was talking about confession! Clara had been naked with some guy already!

She put her private parts together with him, I thought. *Oh, my God! Oh, my God!*

But I didn't have the heart to tell Clara what she

already knew, namely that she was a mortal sinner, casting a black mark on a perfectly upstanding Catholic family. And if she hasn't already gone to confession, she's in real danger right now. She could cross the street and get hit by a motorcycle, wham! And end up in the fiery inferno with the devil. I felt so sorry for her. She was overly glad to see us; her eyes were red and swollen from crying. Happy tears, she said. "Thank you, thank you guys so much for coming up here. I've been so lonely. I've just been unbelievably lonely."

"We met this guy," Madcap said unable to hide her excitement.

"I miss everybody," Clara wailed. "Jude must be getting big."

"Yeah, but I see him everyday, so I can't tell how much he's grown.

Then Madcap said, "How long before your baby is born?"

"They say I'm due at the end of November. Did you get my letters?" She looked at both of us eagerly.

"I did, Clara," I said. "But you didn't tell me."

"That's why we're here, Clara," said Madcap.

"How could I tell you, Skinny Milink? You wouldn't have come."

"We hitchhiked!" Madcap could barely contain herself. "After that letter, I knew I had to do something drastic."

I was standing next to Clara, and she seemed warm. Warm and moist, almost as if we were in a sauna and little steam clouds were rising all around her.

"We hitchhiked with this really cute guy." Madcap gushed.

"He wasn't a murderer," I added. *We're in so much trouble*, I thought. *How are we going to get home?*

"Watch out for the guys," Clara said. "You'll end up here, trapped with no communication to the outside world. You won't be able to use the phone. Daddy will come up once a week to lecture you."

"He lectures us anyway," Madcap said.

Clara led us down the hall to her room. It was simple and neat, two beds with barely an aisle between them. Hardly any stuff, just a white bedspread, a pillow and a crucifix on the bare stucco wall, and a one-bulb lamp next to the bed.

"This used to be a nun's room," Clara said. I took a breath, trying to comprehend the implications for Clara. A musty smell and the cool stillness of the bare room made my heart race, the same kind of panic I felt thinking Clara was gone forever from our lives. I noticed a small window framed by a simple piece of wood high up on the wall, but you couldn't see the sky outside. Just some wood beams, probably on the archway in the courtyard. The sun was blasting outside, but it was all shadows in Clara's room. I looked at Madcap whose eyes darted around like a trapped animal. She shifted her weight from one leg to the other and back again. She pushed against me like she does when she wants to go to the restroom and we're at the Cal Tech movies together.

"Let's get out of here," she whispered to me.

"My roommate, Bee Bee, left the day before yesterday, to have her baby at the hospital." Clara said. "I don't even know what happened."

"What do you mean?" I asked. "What happens

when a person has a baby?"

"I mean I don't know what she did with her baby. If it was a boy or girl." This was completely new territory for me. *What she did with her baby?* Why is that a question? Mothers cuddle their babies and change their diapers. But I hadn't thought about it in terms of Clara. I assumed we would bring the baby home and Clara would have it all to herself. But then, everyone would know. She was here because they were trying to hide the fact that she was pregnant.

"Hey, can we see the inside of the chapel?" I asked. I was wondering if she had thought about going to confession. Seeing the confessional might remind her and save her from the jaws of hell. Just in case. You never know what second you're going to go.

The cool ambience of the interior was so familiar. This one had a Spanish feeling. Blue and red votive lights under a large wooden statue of Our Lady of Guadalupe. Statues standing on shelves at eye level, looking down on the faithful. Instead of marble, it was stucco walls and terra cotta tiles on the floor. The church itself was a long hall, with wooden pews stretching on either side of the central aisle. The altar at the front had a small, golden fort-like building in the middle of it, where they put the Eucharist. Silver candlesticks framed the gold box. The whole thing just took you over, with its musty wood smell, its statues and chandeliers and Stations of the Cross up and down the walls, framed in gold wood frames with a small crucifix atop each one. Dark, thick wood beams stretched across the ceiling. Two of the statues had real clothes on them. There was an American flag at the front. The confessionals stood at the back, dark wooden cubicles. It looked like the doors probably creaked. We sat down in one of the pews.

"They make us do the chores," Clara whispered. A nun sat in a pew near the front, muttering to herself. I tried to get a look at the habit, but all I could see was the veil, reaching half way down her back.

"Laundry, dishes, sinks, and toilets," Clara complained, all wound up. "At least I get to do my homework. The nuns—all they do all day is pray. Apparently the namesake of this order of nuns, St. Isabella, was going to be married off to a prince of Germany and she refused. She wanted to be a virgin for Christ." Clara recounted this story sarcastically, sounding scandalized that anyone would want to waste her life as a virgin. I was shocked, too, but only because we didn't exactly use the word virgin in casual conversation, except in reference to the Blessed Mother.

Just then, Clara grabbed my hand and held it under her rib. A fish swam around under her skin. You could see it poking through.

"She's kicking!"

"How do you know it's a girl?"

"I just know. I had a dream."

"Who's the dad?" Madcap turned around and faced us. "Can I ask?"

"I haven't told Daddy or Mother. They just pass judgment. And I'd never be able to see him again."

You want to see this guy again? I thought.

"Todd Zimmerman?" Madcap knew all the names in Clara's world.

"You'll never guess."

"Steve MacDonald?"

"We went to the prom together. No, not him. He's a good Catholic boy. He's shy."

"Someone you like?"

"You gotta like someone to let him take your clothes off."

"Oh. Who, then?"

"You can't ever tell." Clara looked at me. I just shrugged. This was way over my head. I mean, when were they ever alone together long enough to get their clothes off?

Madcap turned to me. She gave me the look.

"I promise!" I said.

"You gotta cross your heart, and hope to die."

"Cross my heart," I said.

"Hope to die," Madcap said.

"Cross my heart and hope to die!"

Clara opened her mouth to speak, then closed it again.

"You can tell us," Madcap said.

"You want to!" I blurted. There was a silence. Madcap got serious.

"Who was it, Clara?" She put her arm around Clara's shoulder. Clara started crying again.

"Christopher Feeney."

"*Christopher Feeney!*" We both said in unison. A bit too loudly. The nun turned around.

"Shhhhhh!" Clara said. But I kept thinking, *Christopher Feeney? Christopher Feeney?*

"He gave me his choir pin. He said he wanted me to be his girl."

"Christopher Feeney is pretty cute, but I would

never think he could get you pregnant," I said.

"It doesn't take much," Clara replied instantly. I wilted with shame, thinking about even taking off my training bra in front of a boy. Clara had breasts. How much more excruciating could it be with real breasts?

"I have your pin," I said, unfastening it from my collar. Clara helped me take it off. Her belly bumped me as she looked at the pin longingly, as her hands reached across under my chin. I was glad to get rid of it, now that I knew.

"I'm pretty sure he's a cad," she said. "He doesn't know about the baby. If I told him, he would for sure drop me like a hot potato."

"Are you sure Christopher Feeney doesn't want to marry you?" I asked

"Don't even say his name. You promised."

"Sorry." *How old is he anyway? How old do you have to be to be a daddy to a baby?*

"Of course he doesn't want to marry me. Christopher Feeney is too cool. Having a baby is not cool."

Clara's words fell out of her mouth, like the last leaves on a barebones tree just before winter. I could feel the leaves settling on the cold ground, but I didn't know why I was so sad all of a sudden. It felt like a desertion, like we were the last two people on earth. Or maybe the last one. I kept thinking how we are all so entranced whenever Mother brings a new baby into the house. Clara, especially, gets really sweet when the new baby is so little and its tiny hands can only curl up, and it's little mouth moves like it's tasting air. It's a time that feels like we're in a fairy tale with whimsical drawings;

the baby still smells so good you can put your nose right up to its scalp, and there's a softness that makes you want to keep coming back and sniffing. You kiss the baby a lot and it lets you. But Clara's words ruined that moment like a rainstorm can wreck a new dress. As if everyone was home having supper and we were walking in the downpour, listening to the silverware and glasses clink and the happy chatter inside walls where we were not welcome.

Why not just bring the baby home? We could all raise her. What's one more mouth to feed? In the beginning, it's a tiny mouth, and Clara could nurse it on the cheap. But I didn't say anything. Obviously, everyone would know if Clara brought home another baby. I kept bumping up against that fact. And there was another thing here that no one talked about but it was bigger than Clara's baby belly. It was shame. I think I was trying to protect Clara from all the shame that we found here when we opened the door and walked in. When we realized why everyone was here: To hide. Why should a woman feel embarrassed for something like this? She can't help it that she's the one the new baby sticks to, and not the dad.

"It's selfish of me to even imagine I can keep her. That's what they tell me."

"What do you mean?" Madcap said. "It's your baby."

"What are my options?" Clara asked, hopeful. Madcap shrugged.

• • •

We walked outside into the sunshine, into a courtyard, the buildings covered with red Spanish-style roofing. The convent was surrounded by a brick wall on all sides, mossy in some places, flowers in others. Little statues of the Blessed Mother and Saint Isabella perched in tiny arched shelves in the wall. Short palm trees and tall cactus plants sat in the dry earth gardens. I wondered where the nuns were. Madcap walked slightly ahead of us, touching her fingers on the walls as we passed.

It was the weekend, so visitors mingled with the other pregnant girls who waddled around with their big, small, and medium-sized bellies out in front of them. A few strolled with someone else. Obviously, their parents. Pent-up was a word that came to mind, with all the bellies. I imagined the little babies crouched up and sucking their thumbs inside their young mamas and wondered if they were feeling steamy and sad, like I was.

I sat on the edge of a flat bench under the shadow of an oak tree, holding a folded page in my hand in Clara's handwriting. It was notebook paper, lined in blue.

"I am growing this baby for the family that could not have children," said her handwriting. This was the side of the page that said all the things she could give to her baby who was in her stomach, if she gave her baby up to a complete stranger for adoption.

"I am giving her love and my best wishes for a great life with parents who can afford to bring her up."

"I am heartbroken to give her away, but there is not much I can do. How can I raise her?"

The paper was wrinkled from dried tears.

"Let's go to the beach," Madcap pressed.

"I can't leave here. But I really want to."

"You can, Clara! What's stopping you? Look over there. It's not locked." Madcap pointed to the gate. Parents came in and out of the very gate since we arrived.

"I'll get demerits."

"There's only so much laundry. And once it's done, it's done."

"Easy for you to say."

"At some point," I said, "don't you get time off for being pregnant?"

"We're all sinners, here. We have to do our penance, is the idea."

"Let's go, Clara! What are they going to do?" Madcap said, pulling her by the hand towards the gate. "They won't even know you're missing!"

"How can I go like this? I'm an embarrassment!"

"You're pregnant. No one knows you're out of wedlock."

"Could we pretend I'm married?"

"We could!"

CHAPTER 19
SURFIN' USA

Dear Blessed Mother, I'm counting on you. I just made one bad decision: to go with Madcap. The rest of what is going to happen can't be my fault

We escaped from the courtyard one at a time, playing Nonchalant. It was a game that Jeannie and I had practiced to perfection when we were posing as twins in the front yard to passing cars during Camp Holy Hill. Cats do it all the time, especially when they're protecting their territory. Maybe they have a growly fight, their paws flying and scratching and then one cat just walks away, very stealthily, if you can move and be still at the same time. "Oh, I'll just sit here and lick my right shoulder," he says with his body language, just before the bigger cat pounces. "There's something really engaging about my paw, now that you mention it." The big cat crouches, but Nonchalant cat pretends he's not the least bit afraid. That's the secret of Nonchalant. It takes bravado, but has to look natural.

All three of us stood preening by the gate, somewhat hidden by a big cactus. Madcap said I should go first, while she stood on the lookout for nuns. I opened the wooden gate and waited outside. Cars whooshed past me on the neat, one-way street. Neat, meaning it looked like it had been swept the night before by the shoe elves. No oil stains or cigarette butts. The rusty latch lifted behind me and a couple of parents walked out. I stared down at my feet, like the cat suddenly interested in his paws. When the couple was ahead of me, I looked up. The mother held a purse around her with both arms, like she was hugging it. She couldn't really keep up with her husband, whose strides were very long, while hers were very short. Actually she made me think of a Chihuahua, her steps were so short, chasing after a Greyhound.

Whenever I see grown ups in a couple, I always marvel at how the man is an acceptable number of inches taller than the woman. How does it happen that of all the men in the world a woman meets this one man who is an acceptable number of inches taller? They fall in love and then they get married. You look at every couple and the story is exactly the same. He's 6' and she's 5'6". Or he's 5'6" and she's 5'2". It's seems extraordinarily coincidental to me. This couple broke that rule, in favor of him being exceptionally taller, like he was on stilts. She was tiny, diminutive, as Mother would say, small bones and short steps in high heels, trying to keep up with him. The top of her head came up to his chest. She looked like a reporter rushing after a basketball player for an interview.

"It's what she deserves," he said.

"Maybe God will forgive her," said the Mother, sounding like she hoped it would really happen. "She's so young; I hope she survives holding the baby in her arms."

"Don't go soft on me now, Georgina. She's got to understand the consequences of her behavior. This will be a good lesson for her. Think of what a good life the baby's going to have. Two grateful parents in a stable home, who are otherwise deprived of offspring." He sounded like Daddy does just as we're about to get spanked: repeated logic, familiar language, righting a wrong. After hearing the tall man's tone, I wished I had noticed their daughter when we were in the courtyard. I felt like I should go in there and tell her we were going to the beach, that she could come with us and have a great afternoon and let it all slip away for a few hours.

The voices and footsteps of her parents faded as the two of them grew smaller and smaller down the block. Clara and Madcap slammed the gate. Madcap grabbed Clara's hand, dragging her across the street, big belly and baby and all. There were no cars on the street. So the danger of Clara getting smacked into hell by a car was sidestepped, if only for this crossing.

"We've got to get away from here as fast as we can," Madcap said, taking long steps. We all walked quickly in silence, only the sound of our footsteps on the pavement. Clara brought up the rear with her waddling. At the end of the block, the triumvirate of us came to a halt. (Sister Everista would give me points for use of that word—triumvirate!)

"Which street did we take to get here? Can you remember, Annie?" I shrugged, disappointed that I hadn't been paying attention, like that policeman had told me to do, when I went for the Ride-along in his patrol car. If you're a policeman, you know what block you're on every minute. Instead of remembering street names, I had been staring at Aaron Solomon.

"We just have to get to C Street," Madcap said

urgently.

"Oh, jeez, it feels good to be out of there!" Clara said. A breeze blew at us, throwing our hair back across our faces. I had never been this far from home, and it hit me what we were in the middle of doing. We had just kidnapped our sister from the convent where she was exiled to repent for her sins of the flesh. We had hitchhiked with a complete stranger and were now hundreds of miles from home. No one knew where we were. We had no way back.

Instead of being afraid, I felt exceptionally lucky to be alive. Really wide-awake. My skin tingled. My heart beat easily in my chest. I wanted to run and sing like an opera star, at the top of the scales. I grabbed Clara's hand and started skipping but immediately tripped on a bit of heaved cement. I caught myself without actually falling, my arms wildly flailing as I righted myself. For a second. Then I tripped and stumbled again. This time Clara held me up. We both lost balance and grabbed the air, then each other, struggling to stay upright. I almost tackled Clara to the ground as I tried to grip her for balance, my arms whipping around like a rag doll in all directions. This hit me as hilarious beyond hilarity, and we couldn't stop laughing.

Then we turned a corner, ending up on a street with shops and a café. We could see the ocean in the distance past the pier. The blue horizon, the waves, the fresh air altogether overwhelmed me with their glistening beauty. The sky in all its soft blueness seemed closer to the heavens, like it had opened its arms for us. A few wisps of clouds tickled at the edges.

"I made a wrong turn," Madcap said, still laughing.

"We'll never get to the beach. So what!"

"Let's get a shake," Clara suggested, "I've got to sit down." Her whole manner had relaxed and perked up at the same time. Black metal chairs huddled on the sidewalk.

"They're laughing, the chairs are laughing," I said, and that bust us up again.

"I have an idea!" Madcap said. "Let's do get a shake!"

"Surfin' USA" was playing in the café, loud enough to be heard in the kitchen, adding to a sense of drama and purpose in the world. And we were the California Girls they were all singing about. The tall and short couple sat across the café, eyeing Clara. I tried not to listen to them, hoping they hadn't noticed she was one of the "unwed mothers" at the convent. I just kept sucking on my straw, creating that slurping sound at the bottom of the glass.

"Mary was an unwed mother," Clara said.

"Shut up! Clara," I whispered, "They'll hear you."

"What do you mean," Madcap asked. "The Mother of God was an unwed mother? Wait a second. Joseph was the husband, wasn't he?"

"Joseph was the stepfather, but they weren't married. So technically, Mary gave birth to the Baby Jesus out of wedlock."

"You mean Joseph doesn't count?" I challenged her.

"You have to consummate the marriage, or it's not a marriage. According to the rules," Clara continued. "Right, Madcap?" Madcap frowned and rolled her eyes. It had never occurred to me to wonder about The Blessed Mother. She was the highest of the high, no one was more blessed than The Mother of God.

"I'll tell you something," Clara said, sounding like she was gearing up to win a round on the debating team, "trying to understand the Immaculate Conception is like trying to get truth out of Donald Duck. They're always talking about a virgin birth. But even if Mary was impregnated by God the Father, she still never married Him. And there's no mention of Joseph actually marrying Mary. So therefore, Jesus was born out of wedlock."

What? I thought? *That would make Jesus a bastard, wouldn't it? And isn't this blasphemous?* I crossed myself. *Bless me, Father, don't let her go to hell.*

Just then Madcap got up from the table. Her long hair swung side to side across her back then touched down just below her waist as she stood next to the table of the Tall and Short couple. I cringed and put my fingers in my ears. What could she possibly be saying to them?

The next thing you know, we were all piling into the back of their Lincoln Continental convertible on the way to California Street Beach. We sat squished together, Clara chattering confidently about her pregnancy to the basketball couple, the wind swirling our hair into our faces.

"My fingers are too swollen to wear my wedding ring anymore," she shouted to the backs of their heads in the front seat.

"Really?" said the tiny lady, glancing at the profile of her husband, whose head just grazed the top of the car roof.

"What a lovely wedding we had at the Ventura

Mission just ten months ago! The flowers were all red hibiscus, how unusual, but can you imagine how glorious against the white dress?"

"What's your husband's name?" Basketball man asked, glancing back at us.

"Thomas Melvin," Clara said right away. (She was such a liar!).

"They already have the baby names picked out," Madcap chimed in. "Elvina, Alexa, and Rosalyn." I sat somewhat dumbfounded. I'm not sure why Madcap pretended that Clara's baby was going to be named one of those non-Christian names. When you're born, you need a saint looking out after you. Mother and Daddy gave each of us our own saint at baptism. Mine was Saint Anne, which started out in Hebrew as Hannah. I wish they had named me Hannah, but there is no such thing as a Catholic Saint Hannah.

"Where does this Thomas Melvin work?" Mrs. Basketball asked. He was sounding a bit skeptical by now.

"For the Navy!" I blurted. Both Clara and Madcap looked at me. That shut them up.

"Oh, the Navy!" said Mr. Basketball. "I know a few officers at the China Lake Bureau."

Ooops, I thought. *That's where Daddy used to work.* I glanced askance at Madcap then back to Clara shaking my head.

"Right," I said. "He doesn't really work for the Navy, per se, he works, well, he supplies... you know... stuff... to them."

"What kind of stuff?" Mr. B looked at Mrs. B. A little smirk crossed his lips.

"Ping pong balls!" It just came bouncing out. Clara and Madcap collectively sucked in their breath at the same time.

"Ping pong balls?"

"Yeah. And golf balls!"

There was a bit of silence after that. So all three of us fabricated a cozy story for Clara and her unborn beach ball. The couple didn't mention anything about their daughter, languishing back there at the Convent of the Sisters of Saint Isabella, but Mrs. B seemed overly pleased with Clara. She kept saying how young Clara looked.

"I'm almost twenty," Clara reassured her. If only they knew! Clara was really racking up the sins.

Once we unloaded from the car and crawled over the rocks at the edge, the first thing we did was kick off our shoes and burrow our toes into the warm sand. Madcap and I ran towards the shore, screaming. No one heard us but each other; the wind whipped ferociously and surfers straddled their boards, bobbing over waves that swelled under them. A few white caps broke closer towards the shore, but the surfers weren't catching them. Everyone was facing the horizon, waiting for the perfect wave. There were ten or fifteen of them dressed in dark wetsuits up to their necks and leaning forward as if they were propelling themselves by sheer willpower towards Hawaii.

The waves were swirling, powerful and effortless, churning over and over producing furious, white bubbles. The spray that came off the top of them as they unfurled was like a mist. Then one surfer tilted the nose of his board around towards the shore and paddled with both arms, trying to catch up with the wave. He tucked his board into the rushing cylinder of water and stood up, his legs bent to keep him steady, his arms stretched out sideways. I had to watch his breezy, exhilarating ride, until closer to the shore when he turned the tip back towards the horizon and bobbled over the ridge of water. The spent wave crashed in white suds and crawled up the beach, rushing towards me. As the tide pulled back to the sea, I ran down to the wet sand, stepping on little holes and bubbles under the receding foam. Even though the sun made me squint, the water was a cold shock to my feet. The sea was chasing at my ankles like a yipping dog and I was in a game with it, squealing as I tried to outrun the rushing tide.

"Clara!" We hollered to her in the distance, our voices on top of each other. It felt like the moment when you first see the birthday presents on the table and you realize they're truly for you. When you wake up and you know that today is the day you were born, the one day you are truly special, and all day and you are going to get the attention you deserve. My body was tingling full of it. I felt such joy. "Let freedom ring," I said, hugging Madcap and humming the notes. I waved my arms to beckon Clara down towards us, but my voice was beat back by the air roaring around us. So I screamed louder.

"Clara! C'mon down!" What a feeling, as if in the splashing of the waves and the whirling wind, I was heard by no one and yet contributing to the sound of all things in the universe. I was part of its beating heart. I felt myself standing smack dab in the middle of the solar system, gloriously zapped by an electrical connection with everything alive. The rocks and the water, the wind, and the sun.

A large pier stretched out on our left, hundreds of dark legs underneath it like a centipede with a flat back, its feet in the water. Three seagulls floated on a breeze over a breaking wave. I was thinking that Jesus would probably be a pretty good surfer, but He would have to get some shorts. Madcap stood next to me on tiptoe, one hand holding her hair back and the other making an awning over her forehead to keep the sun out of her eyes. She scanned the horizon.

"Can you see him?" I shouted.

• • •

The waves thundered magnificently, rolling over in that blue tunnel shape with white crashing foam chasing the heels of the surfers. We couldn't do much but sit on the sand for a good view, the three of us huddled against the wind like three rocks doing the important work of the centuries, just being. We were mesmerized by the warm sun and glistening water and whipping wind, and I could have sat there all day, watching the guys paddle on their stomachs to catch the swell, pushing themselves up onto their feet and then balancing, dipping and steering their boards as they cruised down the wave. I loved seeing them head over heels when the water flipped them over and bounced their boards in the crashing foam like plastic toys.

I wanted to do it myself. It seemed so wild. Being on the beach, you were captured in the whole world of it, an experience that stretched as far out as you could see. The open sky seemed to extend to China, or Russia or heaven. Each puny wetsuited surfer was so small out there, bobbing around in the enormous sea. I could feel my muscles jumping, getting ready to leap and run and swim and surf the waves as my mind chased around in my head, bumping up against the limits of my land-locked life in Pasadena. Santa Monica Beach was a freeway excursion that took the whole day, once a year, resulting in blistering sunburn. Could I ever get to the beach to learn? Where would I get the board?

I was shrieking with delight and excitement on my own interior planet as Clara and Madcap talked into the wind. It was such a glorious blue day, but Madcap couldn't console Clara, and Clara couldn't stop crying. Her face looked so sad. Madcap's arm so skinny. I wanted to hug her, but a hug from me seemed irrelevant. I wasn't part of her suffering and I had no experience to relate to hers. Standing there on that wide beach, under that big sky, how could it be that Clara seemed so trapped?

Aaron Solomon came striding up the sand, holding his board under one arm, water beaded up on his black wetsuit, his hair dripping, his eyes blue like an open sky, and he smiled an extremely white, happy smile. He walked confidently up to Madcap, who stood to greet him. It looked like he was going to put his arm around her and kiss her, but they both stopped short of each other, smiling into each other's faces. Madcap held her shoulders back, and I was proud of her, thin and strong, her long black hair streaking down her back. I moved closer to Clara and put my arm around her anyway.

"You made it!" Aaron Solomon beamed at Madcap.

"How could we miss this!" She gestured to the waves, yelling above the wind.

Give Clara a minute to dry her eyes, I thought, but Madcap turned and said,

"Here's my sister, Clara. She's gonna have a baby! Her husband's in the Navy, and he's out at sea right now. She misses him."

Lately I had been noticing how easy it seemed to be to just make things up. Madcap was almost as good at it as I was.

"How do you do, Clara," said Aaron Solomon. He reached out his free hand to her and she stood and shook it. So I guess Madcap was convincing.

"I'll be alright!" Clara yelled, the effort of which seemed to lift her spirits. Aaron Solomon motioned to the truck, parked at the edge of the beach, behind the rocks.

"I'm gonna put my board down in the truck!"

So the three of us girls huddled in the cab, waxed paper on our laps, munching on leftover candy bars and Oreos. We watched Aaron Solomon peel off his wetsuit and dry himself with a huge beach towel. I was beginning to like the look of his hairy legs.

CHAPTER 20
LILY

Dear Blessed Mother, Aaron Solomon is really cute. Did you send him to us? That was a good move!. His eyes are blue with long eyelashes, just like Jesus'. And to think he was a suspected murderer for most of the trip.

We peeked around the corner of room 216, like the Three Stooges, one head on top of the other. The first thing I noticed was the crucifix above the bed. *What kind of situation do they have Jesus in now?* I wondered. Even though anything is possible with God, for some reason there is no Standards Department when it comes to making crosses and statues, and sometimes, Christ can look pretty twisted on the cross. This crucifix, regular wood and painted gold around the edges, looked sort of Renaissance. Christ didn't look too uncomfortable, except for the nails. His eyes were closed and He looked like He had already expired, so I relaxed a little. At least He wasn't suffering anymore.

Clara's roommate, Bee Bee, had given birth here at St. Francis hospital yesterday. I was excited to see the baby. And talk to Bee Bee to find out what it was like. Did it hurt a lot, like they say?

Against the far wall, an unusually tall bed on wheels held up a girl about Clara's age lying on her back. Short brown hair. Her head hung limply onto her chest, like she was dead. Or had fallen asleep sitting up.

Clara walked up to within inches of her friend and blew softly into her face.

"Bee Bee? It's me, Clara."

Bee Bee sat right up.

"Oh, Clara," she said and promptly burst into tears. "It was horrible."

Clara hugged her over the metal railing on the side of the bed. "I thought I'd never see you again."

Clara and Bee Bee, I thought. It had a funny ring to it. Bee Bee had a small face with a cute, turned up nose and crystal blue eyes. Her name was so perfect for her.

I waved as Clara introduced us. "These are my sisters, Annie and Margaret," she said.

Madcap rushed over and shook Bee Bee's hand.

"They brought me here with a surfer," Clara enthused.

Bee Bee's big eyes were puffy and red. She was doing this thing: rubbing her fingernails with her thumb nervously. "I want to see my baby," she wailed, "but they won't let me. They took her away right after she was born."

We just stood there, dumbfounded at such a preposterous idea.

"It's kind of raw down there. Everything's swollen."

Wow, swollen was an excellent description. Her breasts were bigger than Clara's, practically bursting out of her gown. They looked weighted down. Her body was so thin in contrast, she looked unnatural and freakish. She should ask the doctors about that. It couldn't be normal.

"It stings to pee," she added.

Now I was staring at Bee Bee. She was just maybe five years older than me, like Clara, yet she already knew everything there was to know about being a woman. And she wasn't happy about it at all. She crossed her arms like she was giving herself a hug, and scratched at her ear. She looked worn down and edgy, circles under her eyes and bloated cheeks from crying. She talked to Clara like Madcap and I weren't even there.

"We could get a wheelchair!" Madcap offered to nobody and everybody.

We all stood there in silence.

"I feel like half of something, Clara. You can't imagine how empty." Bee Bee looked down at her hands. Clara hugged her. What else could she do? I tried to think of something, but it was hard to listen without welling up. Madcap turned towards the hallway.

"I'll go get that wheelchair," she said.

"Did you sign the papers?" Clara asked after Madcap was out the door.

"I was sleepy from the drugs!" Like Clara was accusing her.

"But you did sign the papers." Clara stared at Bee Bee. All you could hear was the buzz of the hospital machines. After a pause she said, "It's too late, isn't it?"

"They kept me in a room all day!" Bee Bee cried, rocking herself back and forth. "By myself with the priest. I kept telling the man that I did not want to sign the papers."

Clara watched her friend, long enough for me to notice the squeaky sound of nurse shoes coming down the hallway. Finally she said, "But you did sign them, didn't you?" She said it carefully, like she was playing pick up sticks and she didn't want a single thing to move.

"He just kept at me, saying, 'It's for the baby's sake.'"

How can they do that? Just take your baby from you? Isn't that kidnapping? I thought. Just then a man with shiny legs shuffled past the door, pushing a metal pole. A bag was attached to the pole with water in it. When he passed, it was shocking and science fiction at the same time. We saw his bare bottom, in broad daylight. The back of his gown was wide open, but he didn't seem to notice.

"I just want to hold my own baby," Bee Bee said. She didn't see the shuffler, or maybe she was just used to him strolling past in that flimsy tent he was wearing.

"Let's go to the nursery," Clara said, determined.

"Maybe your baby is still there," I interjected. They both turned towards me, considering this.

"Even so, they won't let me see her."

"I don't see what's stopping us," Clara said. "It's on this floor."

Madcap came back into the room with a wheelchair. Then everyone's attention was on the floor, where nothing was happening. It felt like the principal's office and we had just got caught ditching Mass. Suddenly Madcap clapped her hands together and turned to face me. "No one's going to suspect you, Annie," she said. "You be the scout!"

"What? Me?"

"That's what we're saying," Clara chimed in.

I didn't want to go—way too suspenseful. But they had a point. I was a runty 12. What would I be doing in the nursery?

So I walked as casually as possible towards the sign that said "Nursery." I tried to relax my mouth, but my heart was pounding and I could feel every beat. The man in slippers and flyaway gown was right behind me; I could hear his mutterings, like he was breathing down my neck. I turned to look at him. His eyes were wet and rimmed in red and he looked right through me, like I wasn't there. Surely he had escaped from somewhere! A nurse walked down the hall towards me, looking stern and purposeful. What was I going to tell her when she asked me why I was on my way to the nursery? I couldn't think of anything. We locked eyes.

Just then, the man behind me fell over in a clatter, pole and all. He lay on his back, his legs willy nilly in the air looking like someone had slapped him out of his dream. I almost laughed because it looked so comical and it was so unexpected, but then it hit me that he was a grown up, who probably knew a lot more than I did, and he was lying on the floor with his private parts visible to practically anyone because he had lost his balance. It looked like he couldn't even remember what he knew. He really needed help, and I had no idea how to help him. The nurse ran towards him. Suddenly everything was abuzz; the intercom started barking orders. Code this. Doctor that. I realized this was my chance. So I continued walking, as nonchalantly as possible, towards the room with all the babies.

Around the corner at last the Nursery came into view. All these little creatures were brand new, and they didn't know anything. They were lying on their backs, too, needing help just to stay alive. What a strange place this was.

I felt like I had arrived at the Promised Land. It was a huge room filled with small metal beds side by side. It looked like the hospital was preparing for a population explosion, or maybe this was a factory in baby heaven, before they send them down to earth from the assembly line. Each little bed had a glass box held inside the metal frame with a soft looking blanket, and there was a baby inside that cradle. You could only see their heads. I stared through the large glass window into the room, feeling close to something that was both magical and strange in its uniformity and orderliness. I relaxed a little knowing they were all dealing with Mutter Man and his pole out there in the hallway and I wasn't going to get into trouble any time soon.

Between rows of bassinets, a nurse was helping a lady take a baby out of one of the beds. The woman wore heels, a tight green skirt the color of a turtle's back and a matching jacket. I could tell she had never put her arms around a baby before. She held the baby away from her, like it might be a china vase and she was afraid of breaking it. A baby just naturally snuggles up to your body, and you can hold him in the crick of your arm. I know all about that, from holding all my little brothers and sisters, from changing their diapers and feeding them. When the lady pressed the baby against herself she giggled. What was so embarrassing about holding a newborn baby?

Then I noticed that someone was standing next to me. I jumped, but it was only a man in a suit, looking like he matched the lady with the baby. He had a short haircut, slick with Brylcream, probably.

"That's our baby girl," he said, beaming. "She was born yesterday."

Wow, that was quick, I thought. *The mother is already out of bed. She's wearing heels. Why is Bee Bee all bruised up and swollen with milk and this lady is in a fashion show?*

"Yesterday?" I asked. "Your wife isn't in bed resting or anything. You're taking her home already? That's amazing."

"Yes," he said, "the Good Lord has brought this baby into our lives. A young teen mother who got herself in trouble is probably right now thanking God that she doesn't have to deal with a screaming baby twenty-four hours a day. She can finish school and have a future."

Oh, I thought, *babies don't scream twenty-four hours straight; does this guy know anything? For instance, right now his baby isn't screaming.*

"What's her name?" I said instead.

"Her mother gave her the name Lily, but we want a Christian name. We're going to name her Christine."

"Christine! What a beautiful name to go through life with!" I said. Lily was a good name, too. I felt so curious about this couple. I guess I had never seen an adoptive mother before. I wondered if she would have the same feelings of love for this baby as our mother has for us. I stood there watching as the woman brought her Lily/Christine out to her husband.

"No honey, you hold her," he said as she approached.

"I know how to hold a baby," I piped up. "I have a lot of practice with my younger brothers and sisters. I'm from a big family—13 children." The mother was looking at me, so I said, "I change diapers and stuff all the time." I shrugged like it was nothing. The Dad was listening, too. "You have to hold the neck and the head, especially when they're this young," I said as if I knew everything. "Their neck muscles aren't developed yet." I must have been convincing because the mother smiled and held her baby out to me.

So I tucked the baby under where my breasts would be. She naturally fit. I inhaled, trying to smell that cozy smell they have. I knew she couldn't see yet, but she looked out at me like she was wondering what the heck had just happened.

"Lily Christine," I said.

"It's just Christine," said the Dad.

Christine looked squished, with a wrinkled forehead and patchy scalp. I could see the indentation on the top of her head where her soft spot was. I had to wonder why babies don't remember anything. This baby could go through her whole life and never know how odd she looked when her mother first met her. She'll probably never know anything about her real mother, either. It seemed like such a shame all around.

As I held her, she made this licking gesture with her mouth and we all stared at her as if she was doing a magic trick. After a few moments, I gave her back to the mother. Pretty soon the baby was nibbling at her breast through her jacket. The mother offered a finger, and the baby started to suck it.

"Ohhh!" We were all surprised into speechlessness.

"Thank you," Fashion Lady told me.

"My pleasure," I said. I crossed myself and kissed my thumb for extra blessings as I watched them walk down the hall towards the stairs, the mother taking short steps because her skirt was so tight, her high heels clicking on the floor. Both of them still arched over the bundle in their arms.

Then I felt a sharp knock on the back of my head. Madcap whispered at me through her teeth.

"What have you been doing?"

"I just saw a couple take their baby home."

• • •

The four of us stood in front of the window of the nursery, with all the babies lined up. Three of them were crying. One started it up and then the other two chimed in. Bee Bee stretched her neck up. From her wheelchair she had to lift her chin to see in. By now tears were just naturally flowing down her cheeks. Clara had her hand on Bee Bee's shoulder.

Then the nurse saw us at the window. She put the baby back in its bassinet, but it was still kicking and screaming and getting redder against that white blanket. More babies started crying, but the nurse ignored them. She pushed the door open and addressed herself to Bee Bee, like they knew each other.

"You're not supposed to be here," she said, looking down at Bee Bee in the wheelchair.

"Just tell me which one she is."

The nurse looked at down Bee Bee, then at me, then at Clara, then at Madcap. She took a breath in. Her face relaxed into a frown. She looked official: a white nurse cap, her hair tied back at the nape of her neck. She had spit up on her shoulder and I could smell it. But she seemed kind.

She shook her head.

"I know I signed the papers," Bee Bee offered, "I know it's too late. Just let me see her."

The nurse looked resigned, like she didn't have any good news for us at all. We waited. Then her face brightened.

"What did you name your child?" she asked.

"Lily," Bee Bee said like a reflex. "I named her Lily."

The nurse turned around and we were all staring at her white nurse-bottom, walking away from us.

I felt dizzy. Even though my eyes were open, everything was suddenly blurry. I leaned against the wall. I was going to die of the sadness I felt.

"Are you crying, Annie?" Madcap asked me incredulously.

"No." I looked down at my shoes, then at my fingernails, like they knew something.

But Clara and Bee Bee and even Madcap waited hopefully. I could see their mood had changed. The air seemed lighter where they stood.

"I can't believe it, she's going to find her!" Bee Bee said. Clara squeezed her hand.

But how could one moment of seeing your baby be enough? The moment is over so soon, and then the baby is gone for the rest of your life.

We could see the nurse going up and down the rows, looking closely at the names written on a small card on all the baby bassinettes. More babies were hollering by then and I was glad I couldn't hear them. Clara put her hand on Bee Bee's back and smoothed it up and down, something Mother does when we're gaping over the toilet with the flu.

But I was wondering how could the nurse be doing

this? *She knows that Lily has just left the building with her new parents.* Then I had a thought. *Maybe she's stalling so they can get away undiscovered!* I turned on my heels and ran outside, hoping the parents hadn't gotten into the car with their new baby yet.

The parking lot was almost as full as the Nursery. Cars everywhere, sunlight glinting off their windows and bumpers. I could see the warmth of the afternoon in an almost invisible wave above the asphalt. The dry heat was everywhere. My socks against my ankles felt overly warm and thick. I waited and watched. There was no movement anywhere, only the sounds of muffled traffic on the other side of the building.

Lily was gone.

When I got back, most of the babies looked red and angry. The nurse was pointing to a quiet baby who was probably the farthest away possible in the room.

"They found her!" Bee Bee said, thrilled. "Look what a good baby she is!"

"I wonder if the nurse is going to get in trouble," Madcap said. "It can't be good that they're all screaming."

The nurse took the baby out of the bassinette and brought it to the window and held it up, for Bee Bee to see. I couldn't imagine the noise in there.

"Lily, Lily, Lily," Bee Bee cooed. Now Bee Bee's face was pink and flushed, and her eyes shone with pride. She grinned joyously, like it was Christmas morning.

Right where her nipples were, her mother's milk began seeping through her gown.

CHAPTER 21
VOICES

Dear Blessed Mother, please don't let me bounce out of this truck. They put me back here 'cause there was no room for me in the cab once Clara decided to go back with us. She's really big! It was a good thing Aaron Solomon tied down the surfboard; that gave me something to hold onto. Listen, will you please take Jesus aside, and especially God the Father, and tell them what really good girls we usually are? I'll offer up the suffering of how freezing I am back here to weigh in our favor. Also, it would help if it's not dark yet by the time we get home. I can't be responsible for what kind of trouble Clara's got into, but I can see her point about her baby. Daddy is really going to be mad. FYI: I'm too big to be spanked; I don't know what he's going to do.

The light had faded from the sky when Aaron Solomon's truck rolled up the driveway. Luckily, he lived close by, as only one of his headlights worked. Shadows gathered as Sparky came barking down the brick path, so there was no way we could sneak in unnoticed. I stepped over the back gate of the truck with my foot on the fender and jumped down onto the asphalt. Looking behind me, I saw Madcap reach up and kiss Aaron Solomon. On the lips! Then he drove off and the three of us were on our own, Sparky looking up at us with his tongue out. Across the street the tennis court was quiet and dark. It was Saturday night—the Westridge girls were probably having some kind of summer debutante ball for all I cared.

We walked up the driveway to the back of the house, Sparky trotting up after us. My skin tingled from the sun and hours of cold wind, and I felt seasick from all that bumping around in the back of the truck.

The little kids came storming down the hall when they heard the screen door squeak open. No one was expecting Clara and when they realized it was her, they mobbed her, with Jude toddling towards her, then attaching himself to the back of the twins who were hugging Clara's legs.

"Clara, Clara!"

"Oh, Clara look at you!"

"Clara's back!"

They were supposed to be in bed by this time, a bad sign, meaning I hadn't been there to give them their Jiffy Bath. But their hair was wet and they had their jammies on so maybe Jeannie got extra points for doing my job. Bully for her. I went hitchhiking to the beach in Ventura and watched surfers!

"Where's Daddy?" I whispered to Dominic.

"I dunno, he took Bartholomew with him in the car in the afternoon."

"Where's Mom?"

"I'm right here." She spoke up sharply as she stepped out of the kitchen, pulling off her yellow rubber gloves, still sudsy from doing dishes. "Where have you been?"

For the tenth time today, I was dumbfounded into silence. I waited to see if this was a rhetorical question, or if there was any room for a story. We were supposed to have been at Cinematheque, but of course, with Clara here, we could only have been in Ventura at the Mission. Now, the question was, should we tell we hitchhiked? Maybe I wouldn't have to say anything. I hoped Madcap and Clara had their story straight. They might have had a chance to rehearse something in the cab on the way home. I was still shivering.

"Jeannie can you put the kids to bed? Say a short rosary with them and some extra prayers for Clara, Madcap, and Annie here." Then she said, like I was the first business of the night, "Annie you go up to your room right now. Too bad you've missed supper. You're grounded. Madcap, I'll deal with you when your father gets home."

Great, I thought. I can already feel Jeannie gloating.

"We got a ride in a pick up truck from a friend who surfs in Ventura," Madcap inserted. "When we heard he was going to Ventura, we decided to go see Clara. We didn't have a chance to call you."

"Clara," she said, ignoring Madcap's explanation, "come in and sit down. You must be tired after that ride. In a truck?"

"Oh, Mother!" Clara threw her arms around Mother, their stomachs touching each other, (Clara's bulging, Mom's not so much). "I've missed you so much!" Mother hugged her somewhat stiffly, but she and Clara padded off together towards the living room, and it was the weirdest sight—neither of them screaming at the other.

I got upstairs into my room and grabbed a long sleeved shirt to put over my arms and then quietly (so as not to creak the boards) tip toed to Madcap's small room at the top of the stairs. There were no lights on and I could see by her shadow that she was standing on the wooden bedstead, stretching up to the skylight, smoking a cigarette. The white smoke wafted up and out towards the night sky, which seemed blue, although it was dark outside. I loved the dry smell of it, because I always smelled it with Madcap in her room like this, and it was kind of exciting. You could see little twinkling stars through the space between the window frame of the skylight and the roof. I climbed up next to her on the headboard, so we wouldn't be heard.

"Is that good or bad, Madcap? Mother and Clara aren't even yelling at each other."

"I don't know, Annie. Daddy must have driven up today. When he arrived, Clara was nowhere to be found. She should have said something to the nuns."

"I think escape was her only option," I said.

"Mother didn't seem the least bit surprised to see her. Daddy must have called from the Mission. He's on his way back now."

"What's going to happen to her?" I asked, really hoping she would know.

She exhaled white smoke with a fish mouth, shaking her head.

I lay down on Madcap's bed and squished myself to the side by the wall so there'd be enough room for both of us. I closed my eyes. Images of the day swirled around in my mind. The waves and the brilliant sun, the contents of the glove compartment, the small alcoves in the wall surrounding the Mission, the crucifix with gold around the edges. The tips of Aaron Solomon's fingers. Even the bum crack of Mutter Man and Lily's tiny lips, the shiny floors of the hospital, and the smell. I awoke to the sound of voices downstairs. My skin was tight and sore, my arms wrinkled with dryness, my face hurt. Sunburned again. At first, I only heard the words that rose in volume.

Daddy's voice… "bringing *shame* on the family."

"What about the boy?" Clara asked. "He should be ashamed, too."

"Who is the boy?" Mother asked.

"What difference does it make to you? Is he gonna marry me? At 17 years old? Besides, no one would believe me."

It was pitch dark. I stretched my eyes open to let any light in, and only when I sat up and turned my head behind me did I see the face of the electric clock, whose hands glowed white at 11:20. I looked for Madcap's form in the dark. I could feel that she wasn't there. The room seemed empty. It was pretty late, but it was a Saturday night, and I didn't know if the big boys had come in yet. I would have heard a motorcycle if Paul was home. John was too fat to have a girlfriend; I imagined he had gone to bed already, but there was no way to know. The house was quiet except for the voices downstairs. Where had Madcap gone?

"Don't you understand that once you show yourself at the school your reputation is ruined? And so is the reputation of this family!" Now Daddy was yelling. I imagined him getting red. He was probably pacing.

"I don't care about my reputation."

"That child is going to live a good life with its adoptive parents. You'd rather shame your father and mother and throw away your education and good upbringing than go to confession and do your penance?" Daddy's angry voice didn't leave much space for anyone else to respond.

"And what are you doing for that child? How are you going to raise that child?"

I heard a murmur of Clara's voice, as she tried to say something, but he interrupted:

"Maybe you should have thought about that before you lost your willpower in the presence of this young man. I for one am not going to raise that child; I didn't bring it into existence. Your mother and I have enough on our hands with all of you."

I was shocked by Daddy's statement. It was like turning a beggar away at Thanksgiving just because you don't want to pay for their meal. You want familiar faces around the table. Would Jesus do that? I don't think He would. Would the Blessed Mother? I listened for what Clara might say. Maybe she was as shocked as I was and couldn't form a sentence. Then I heard Mother's voice.

"The sisters of Saint Isabella are kind women, Clara," she said more gently. "Don't you want to finish your education? If you keep this baby, how can you finish high school?"

I hardly heard another word. Something inside me was evaporating like neon leftovers of fireworks against a black sky. How could Mother be against Clara, too? It would be so easy to take this baby into our family! Maybe Clara could finish high school from home. She's a senior already. I could volunteer to get her assignments from school. Okay, so we'd have to show our faces to the student body and admit our sister has fallen in God's eyes. But hey! St. Paul the apostle strayed before he repented, and now he's a saint. That's what confession is for. Otherwise, what? Leave Clara doing all the hard chores while the lazy nuns pray themselves into ecstasy? Waiting until she has the baby and they take it away from her at the hospital? Like they did to Bee Bee? And let's think about the baby for a change. Are adopted babies really as happy as real babies? With fake parents? It has to have an effect.

Daddy must be trying to "teach" Clara something. Maybe he thinks if she gets away with it then Madcap would get pregnant out of wedlock, and next thing you know, bingo! I'd be expecting a baby without a ring on my finger. Oops, then Jeannie! (She'd probably have twins.) Watch out, soon as Rosie started to grow breasts she'd be pregnant. All his daughters, pregnant like the plague and no one married in the church. He'd have twenty grand children before he could say "Bless me, Father for I have sinned." We'd be the famous Christian family that started a runaway ex-Catholic population explosion. We'd be the rabbits of St. Andrew's High School.

Of course, I wouldn't do it. The part about having no clothes on is pretty much a guarantee for me. Madcap can see what a jam this is and she wouldn't do it either. There's too much humiliation. I would be so embarrassed to be pregnant in front of all my friends. They'd all be able to picture what I was doing! Which I would never do in the first place! How can Clara can say she doesn't care about her reputation?

Teresa Feeney, watch out, I'm going to look you in the eye while you're getting all the medals for A's in math, and

Science. And my stare is going to say, "Look what your brother did to our sister Clara."

No one even knows Christopher Feeney is doing it! And he's getting away with it. Clara should tell, for justice sake. He doesn't have to go through any of this. It's not fair!

Everyone's a phony.

I walked back to my bedroom and lay on top of my covers.

A sound woke me up. Something was grazing the window. It was still dark, no moon. There it was again. I got up and walked over, lifted the wood frame by the handles. I stuck my head out.

"Hey, Skinny!" I could barely make out someone thin looking up at me. It was Madcap. She whisper-spoke.

"The doors are all locked, can you let me in?"

"I thought you were grounded!"

"Shhhhh! C'mon!" She motioned to the back of the house.

I tiptoed down the stairs as quietly as I could. A few creaks. Luckily we were at this end of the house while Mother and Daddy slept at the front. I had no idea what time it was. I opened the door to the hall and then stepped through the laundry room to unlatch the lock on the back porch. Shadows of piles of clothes lay still on the floor around the washing machine. Just as we closed the screen door, I could see headlights beaming up the driveway. The Rambler pulled into the garage, it's red tail lights glowing.

"Get in!" I pulled Madcap's sleeve. "It's Daddy's car! What time is it?"

"About three thirty in the morning."

"Three thirty in the morning!"

"Why is Daddy out at this time of night?"

We hurried up the stairs. There was no time to figure it out. I was in my bed when I heard the doors close, and Daddy's footsteps walking the floors. I listened for Clara's snoring down the hall, but I couldn't hear a sound.

The next morning, I slept through 6:30 Mass.

CHAPTER 22
MAN THE RAILS

August 4 – Dear Blessed Mother, Didn't you hear my prayers in the back of the truck? I went through the whole day thinking I had gotten away with it!

When Daddy got home after Mass that Sunday, he said, as he was taking off his tie, "It's a good thing you're not in the Navy. You'd be keelhauled." He kept asking where Madcap was. I had the feeling she was in trouble. Did Daddy find out we hitchhiked?

Usually no one really cares where Madcap is. She gets away with it because there are so many of us, and because she's daring. Most of the time, she's part of the wallpaper. She comes in, and she goes out. But today, there was something in the air.

At supper, just in case, I kept my head down and set the table, making sure I remembered all the stuff Daddy likes around his throne at the head of the table: his coffee cup, cream and sugar, his special knife, Tabasco sauce. His martini, which was in his hand. My mouth was already watering; we were having spaghetti, my favorite meal. I could see the steaming pasta in the colander in the sink. The smell of bubbling tomato sauce permeated the kitchen. Garlic bread sizzled in the oven.

"All hands on deck!" Daddy called. He had that

urgent, commanding sound in his voice, which usually resulted in a general hup-to; no one wanted to be the one, the straggler he might single out at times like this.

"Man the rails," he said and we all knew that meant we had to go to our place at the table and stand behind our chair at attention. Like we really were on a ship in the Navy. Sometimes this was fun; we'd puff out our chests and look sideways without moving our heads and pretend we'd just gotten back from the barber and all of us had buzz cuts and sailor hats. The last time he had us do this, it was when everybody was afraid of the atom bomb from Cuba.

Tonight, I thought Daddy was going to tell all of us what Clara was really doing up there in Ventura with the Sisters of Saint Isabella. After all, Clara was like the Blessed Mother: far from home in her time of need, pregnant and without a proper husband. But no.

"Annie and Margaret, come up here," he ordered us in a clipped voice. Everyone quieted down, as Margaret and I shuffled closer to Daddy. It's amazing how just a little hint of menace can get the room so quiet you could drop a pin and it would sound like an orchestra. You have to stop breathing when Daddy means business like this. You have to watch his face and pay serious attention. Otherwise, it could be you on the wrong end of a paddleboard.

I tried to shrink in size. Most of the time it's as if no one really sees me—or cares whether or not I'm in the room. I'm a number and I have a place. You try all the time to get noticed but when Daddy's voice sounds like this, there is nowhere to hide.

"Yesterday," he began, and my stomach sank to

the depths. His voice for sure had that sound to it. "Margaret and Annie left home with a stranger and took a ride in his truck all the way up the coast to Ventura."

"He wasn't a stranger!" Margaret cried out.

"Without permission," Daddy said, cutting her off.

I stood to the left side of Daddy, and Madcap stood to the right. She was doing something with her eyes, squinting them, and her face wasn't scared. She had a look on it like she was angry. I put my head down, looking at my bare feet, which were sunburned.

"Do you know what happens to girls who hitch hike?" Daddy barked at Madcap.

We were going to get it.

It was a familiar moment. You know you're going to get a beating, but it hasn't started yet. You have to wait for it, but you really wish it was over. Or, you just hope it doesn't go on too long. Maybe he'll hit you just once for show. So everyone will know. An example. I usually pray for that, while I'm sweating it out. It's never worked. This is where the Blessed Mother and Jesus could improve their act; it's definitely a weak spot. Maybe they have a policy: "Do not respond to panic prayers."

"Margaret, who is the older sister of the two here," Daddy said, gesturing "didn't tell Mother where they were going. Instead, she and Annie hitchhiked in a truck with a stranger."

"He wasn't a stranger!"

"For hundreds of miles." When he added it all up like that, it sounded bad. But he was making it all Madcap's fault. I felt sorry for her. My bosom buddy, close pal, and life long friend. On the other hand, maybe I was off the hook.

But Madcap was going to get it. It was so quiet. When Daddy took a breath, I could hear the arm of the Baby Ben on the mantle moving from one second to the next.

"Then, after disrupting Clara's holy retreat," Daddy continued, "the three of them ran away—again— without telling the nuns where they were going. These things are very, very serious. Even dangerous," he said, shifting his weight on his feet.

"Do you hear me?" he asked rhetorically.

"We hear you," John-the-Blimp offered. Everybody immediately mimicked him.

"We hear you."

"We hear you."

"It is forbidden to leave this home without telling anyone where you are!" Daddy was working himself up even more. "Do you understand that?" Nodding all around. Sheep. We were all sheep, especially when Daddy got like this. "For your own safety, never get into a vehicle with a stranger. Do you understand? Never." Buddy and Dominic mouthed the word, "never." Daddy's manner softened ever so slightly. He waited.

"Never…"

"Never." Jeannie and Bartholomew piped up, and then everyone decided it was a good idea to say "Never."

When the group died down, Daddy took his cue, lowering his voice for effect, "But the worst part of it was—Margaret put her soul in danger and led her younger sister Annie down the path with her."

I myself wasn't worried about my soul. All I did was

pray to the Blessed Mother on the way back. But it was the worst thing Daddy could accuse Madcap of doing. Putting her soul in danger.

Jude started kicking his feet in his high chair where he was still waiting for his dinner.

"Eat, eat!" he said, laughing and kicking and looking around the table, trying to catch the glance of any one of us. The twins nervously giggled. No one else moved.

"Pipe down!" Daddy bellowed. Mother leaned over to Jude, touching his small hands.

"Shhh, shh," she said gently.

I waited. The story wasn't over. There was this big part about Clara being pregnant. I was wondering how he was going to handle that one. And besides, the heat was really hot on Madcap, and I felt sorry for her. Even though Clara was the obvious sinner.

"Put your hand out, Annie," he ordered me. *Me?* I thought? *I was just going along!* Then he unbuckled his belt in front of everyone and pulled it out of the loops.

My cheeks burned a bright red. I started shaking right away. My chest was going up and down and I couldn't hide how hard I was breathing.

At least he wasn't going to make me pull my pants down in front of everyone.

"Never leave the house without permission. Never get into a vehicle with a stranger," he repeated. The sound of the silverware against the plastic plates and his china coffee cup pierced the silence, as he started to push all the dishes and silverware away from his place. So he wouldn't hit them with the belt. "Even if your older sister tells you it's okay, it is forbidden."

"Now, hold your hand out in front of me." There was a collective sucking in of breath around the table where everyone was standing at attention, as Daddy wrapped the belt around his hand. I stretched my hand out, palm up, like he told me to do. Maybe if I were obedient, he would go easy on me. He lifted his arm up over his head and slapped the belt down on my hand like I was a horsehide.

"Owwwwwwwww!" I said pulling my hand away. "Owwwwwwwww!" My eyes started to water from the sting. I started jumping around on my toes.

"Even if it wasn't your idea, it was wrong to hitchhike. It was wrong to leave the house and not tell your mother where you were going. I'm going to give you something to think about. Bring your hand back there." I kept thinking: *I just have to bear it until he stops.* But I couldn't put my hand out; I backed away from him.

"Get over here and put your hand down on the table!" He grabbed my hand and laid it down, palm up on the table. Then he lifted his arm and let another one down. *Whack!*

"Two!" he said.

"Ahhhhhhhhhhhhhh! Owwwwwh!" I had to cry out. I caught a glimpse of Rosie at the end of the table next to Mother. Her saucer eyes were frozen in terror, and her mouth was wide open. Mother got up and went into the kitchen. My neck started to get hot.

"Put your hand back there," he commanded me.

"No!" I said, backing away. "It hurts!" He grabbed my hand again and laid it down on the table.

"Of course it hurts! I'm doing this for your own

good. So you won't forget!"

"Three!" he yelled and everyone winced as the belt came down. "Don't you ever leave the premises without first getting permission, do you understand me?" I burst into tears at the sharp pain radiating on my fingers and palm.

"Yes!" I said. *Just don't hit me again, please.* "Yes, I understand!" I couldn't hide the panic in my voice.

"Put your hand back there," he said. "And leave it there!"

Everyone standing around the table began to shift in their places. The twins were crying and rocking. Jude stared, perfectly still. Rosie slipped her thumb into her mouth and started sucking. Buddy put his head down on the table and covered his ears.

"I'm sorry! I'm sorry!" I said, "I won't do it again, I promise!" I held my hand limply in front of me. He motioned me to put it back on the table.

"Put it there!" he yelled at me. My hand felt like it was about to fall off, and I couldn't stop crying. Madcap was just a blur across from me.

"I said I was sorry! Daddy, please!" I pulled my hand away and the belt hit the table. I fell to my knees, sobbing.

"Mother!" I cried. "Mother! Help me!" The door to the pantry pushed open and Mother appeared in the dining room. Behind her, the door swung on its axis. She stood at the other end of the table with her arms crossed.

"That's enough, Martin," she said. "I think she's learned her lesson."

But it wasn't enough for Daddy. He had to teach

Madcap a lesson, too. He turned to her.

"Can I be excused?" John-the-Blimp dared to ask. Meekly. Daddy snapped his head back towards the table.

"You will stand at attention until you are excused. Do you understand?"

"Yes, sir!"

"Put your hand here on the table in front of me," he said to Madcap, his face getting redder. I looked up from my crouch on the floor in front of Daddy. Madcap was shaking her head. She pushed Daddy aside and stepped around me.

And she turned and walked out the door, slamming it behind her.

CHAPTER 23
COMPLETELY DARK

August 9 – Dear Diary, Jackie Kennedy had a baby named Patrick Bouvier Kennedy and everyone was excited because she's like the queen of the United States of America. Then they were all worried because he was born five weeks early. He was only two days old when he died today. I'm pretty sure he was baptized.

When Madcap slammed the door, she went running out into the night.

"You come back here!" Daddy yelled after her. I heard his footsteps down the steps on the side porch. But Madcap was fast and Daddy returned a few moments later, puffing and sweating.

Dinner was ruined. Mother put the spaghetti out on the table and started serving. John-the-Blimp grabbed a plate, starting the bucket brigade. Bartholomew and Jeannie filled in, handing each plate around the table when it was heaping with spaghetti and tomato sauce and a little bit of salad. It was the first time I noticed the boys ever helping mother at dinner. I wasn't hungry anymore and I went to my room and lay on the bed, tenderly holding my throbbing hand under my arm, listening to the sounds of forks and knives on the plates. It was a weird silence; no one was talking out there. I guess I wasn't too old to cry myself to sleep.

For a moment I wondered how cold it was outside and if Madcap was hiding in the bushes. But she had a girlfriend named Tessa who lived nearby, with modern parents who would probably let her spend the night. Worse comes to worst, she could just wait until everyone was asleep and throw a pebble at my window. I'd always let her in.

Maybe I deserved to be punished for running away. It's true we could have been kidnapped. It's true that hitchhiking is stupid and dangerous. But Daddy was really mean. On the other hand, I was so proud of Madcap that she defied him! I felt exactly like doing that, but she had the guts to actually do it. At the same time, I was scared for her. What is she doing out there in the night by herself? Eventually, she has to come back. What's Daddy going to do when she comes back?

I must have fallen asleep, because when I woke it was completely dark. My hand still hurt, and I was cool; my top was unbuttoned and my covers down. I'm not sure why I woke up, but then I had the feeling that someone had been there by my bed again. The thought of it gave me goose bumps. There was a dog barking down the street. The house was quiet and I kept really still and listened as hard as I could. I thought I heard footsteps upstairs in the boy's bedroom, but then there was a soft knock on the windowpane. It was Madcap outside. I tip toed into the hallway and let her in the back through the laundry room. She didn't say anything, and we both froze when we heard the clock in the dining room, chiming on the forty-five minute mark.

"What time is it?" I whispered.

"Almost one." As the sound of the chimes lingered, we hugged each other for a long time. Right away I started crying. I thought about asking her to stay with me for protection.

"Shhh," she held her finger over my mouth. Then she crept upstairs, but it's impossible to get all the way up without making that third step groan.

The next morning at breakfast "Hello Mudda, Hello Fadda" was playing on the transistor in the kitchen when Daddy announced that Madcap was grounded for a month.

CHAPTER 24
LETTER FROM CLARA

August 28 – Dear Blessed Mother, It's hard to get any sleep around here; everyone is a priest in a pulpit. Martin Luther King gave a speech at a march on Washington, D.C., his deep voice going up and down in a barrel, like he was telling a scary story at Halloween. Daddy says he's rabble rousing the Negroes. He turned off the television, saying "Propaganda." Crowds as far as the eye could see, wall-to-wall Negroes and a few Whites holding placards with writing on them. The sun was bleach-hot; legs and feet marched by the camera and people sang "We shall overcome." If you had to go to the toilet, you'd be in trouble. I wasn't sure what the Negroes wanted, since the Civil War supposedly freed them from slavery. Daddy said that they spend all their money on shiny cars like Cadillac, Lincoln and Chryslers. His experience selling cars at Shea Motors makes him an expert. But he says their houses are small and they live on a street where the windows are broken and the front yards are full of garbage. "Buy a cheap car, save your money for the house." Although he wouldn't mind taking their money if they wanted to buy a car from him. He has a gray Rambler. Plus we have a Volkswagen bus for transporting the hordes. Our house is big, but it isn't exactly sitting in the middle of a fine trimmed lawn. I think Daddy is against the Negroes because he's afraid of them because of where he was raised. We have 2 negro girls in our class, Martha and Martha (we call them 'the two Marthas') and Tall Martha is the funniest person I have ever known. I wonder what she thinks about all the people marching.

Also, Nikita Khrushchev gave another speech about burying us with a shovel again. We should stop calling them Commies and talking about bombing them, because, as Daddy says, "Mother monkeys love their baby monkeys." If you imagine mother Russians loving their baby Russians, they seem just like us and the monkeys.

I got a letter from Clara. It had one of those new zip codes on the front.

August 4th, Monday after your visit

Dear Annie,

Thank you so much for riding in the back of the truck so that I could sit in the cab. Please tell Madcap and Aaron Solomon THANK YOU for those few hours of sun, sand, and freedom. Before Daddy and Mother lowered the boom. I hate them; I'm sure you heard all about it. Daddy for being so inflexible and Mother for not standing up to him—although I could see she was torn. It's no wonder they never fight—Mother always gives in.

I can't believe this is happening to me. It was so fast and seemed like hardly anything, in a way. I really liked Christopher, and then we were alone. But I'm keeping myself busy; after the chores I do my schoolwork so I can take the SAT test and get into a good university. The nuns let me out of the mission to go to the library and I look forward to it—every afternoon.

Is it still a secret that I am having a baby? Because here's another: I'm going to keep it. I haven't told anyone yet, except for Bee Bee. She's excited, even though she's no help whatsoever. She writes me letters from Orange County, and she's very depressed about losing her baby. But she makes me strong, because I don't want to have the heavy sorrow of it in my life. I don't know how I'm going to do it alone, but I am going to try. Just let them try to take my baby from me.

The baby is due on December 4th. Now that I'm closer to delivering, I've been researching labor and the actual birth. I wish Mother would tell me what to expect. Bee Bee was no help; they just gave her drugs to knock her out. Glad I had the chance to see Bitty give birth to all those kittens and just get up and walk away after having a bit of a nap.

In a way it's very exciting. I've had a lot of experience taking care of the little ones, so I won't be at a complete loss when the baby I'm holding is my own. I'm trying to find out by sleuth if there are other girls who want to keep their babies; I think the YWCA will take me in. I do need a bit of money, though. I've got to go. Write me with the news about everybody.

– Clara

P.S. I wish you could come up and be with me.

CHAPTER 25
SOMEONE YOU LOVE

September 16 – Monday. Dear Blessed Mother, The 16th Street Baptist Church in Birmingham, Alabama was bombed on Sunday, and four little girls were killed in the bombing, just because they were black. I think a bunch of white guys in tent hats and sheets called the Ku Klux Klan did it. Could you imagine being somewhere and not being able to hide because your black skin gave you away? I bet Father Pierre feels that way about his white skin, because he's in Africa.

I'm so confused about everything.

When school started in September, we got Mrs. Parry for the 7th grade. I sat behind Chris Zimmerman in the second row, third seat from the front, with a view of the sky through the windows. My seat was directly in front of his best friend, Michael Kort, and they were constantly shooting spitballs at each other and getting them caught in my frizzy hair, which acted as a magnet and was right in the middle of them.

If you picture Mrs. Parry, this is what you'll see: thin, tight skirt, short, dull brown hair. A longish nose. Always carrying the pointer with the missile-shaped rubber end. Disciplined and stern, she showed no favoritism and demanded perfection. Unlike the nuns, who could be easily impressed by my superior knowledge of catechism. Mrs. Parry always caught me telling Zimmerman and Kort to "Stop it!" and it looked like I was the problem. But she gave us a good first assignment after summer. "Describe someone you love."

I thought of Daddy right away. Even after what he did when we hitchhiked, and even now that I'm almost 13, I look forward to him coming home from work. Jeannie usually hogs the kitchen around dinner, and therefore Mother dotes on her and acts like I'm bad, when I'm only avoiding the kitchen because it's useless. Jeannie knows where everything is, and it makes me look stupid. But Daddy can usually tell when something is wrong with me. When I was younger he would sit me on his knees and try to cheer me up saying things like "You can catch more flies with honey than you can with vinegar" and "Smile and the world smiles with you, weep and you weep alone." Or he'd try to surprise me by opening his knees and letting me fall through them, and then catching me at the last minute, and then we'd both laugh and pretty soon it was time for dinner. I had to think about how to describe him, so I wrote everything down that came to my mind right away:

My Dad was a Commander in the U.S. Navy for 20 years. That's where he gets this phrase he uses a lot, "Rank Has Its Privileges." Now he's the owner of a garage and car dealership. He has 13 children and one on the way. He always looks at the bill. "The family that prays together, stays together," is his motto.

When they invite him to speak at Holy Name

Society brunches, he tells the faithful about Our Lady of Fatima and how daily rosaries can stop Communism. I like going to the brunches because they serve bacon and eggs with tater tots, which we never have at home, and I get to eat them while he talks.

My Dad likes a bargain. If he gets one and brings it home, for example, a flat of strawberries at a "steal," or the last tree on the lot on Christmas Eve for $3, it's all the news for the next few days.

He taught Clara and Rosie how to swim by throwing them right in the pool and letting them figure it out.

He farts often, but he almost never says, "Excuse me."

He likes his martini at the end of the day. Also Bob's Big Boy restaurant. He especially he loves Bob's Bleu Cheese dressing, also my favorite.

"Judge not lest ye be judged" and "Practice what you preach" are things he says a lot. At the same time, he thinks Angela Davis is dangerous and that Martin Luther King, Jr. ought to be kept in jail in Birmingham, Alabama.

How to Make Friends and Influence People by Dale Carnegie is one of his most treasured books. He also likes *Conscience of a Conservative* by Barry Goldwater.

My dad thinks he is right about everything. He likes talking about religion and politics from the head of the table, sharpening his rusty skills as an ex-member of the college debate team on anyone within hearing range.

I have never heard him apologize to a mortal. However, he repeats this prayer every day of his life: "Oh my god I am heartily sorry for having offended thee… and I detest all of my sins…"

To my Dad, "Thou shalt not kill" means that if you murder someone you will be doomed to eternal damnation and hellfire (unless you say you're sorry before the last second of your life); however, war is okay if you're on the right side (not the Communist side).

Whenever he sees a young couple holding hands, or kissing, he says, "That's young love in bloom." When he sees black smoke coming out of one of those pipes on the big trucks, he says, "That's not really pollution, it just looks like it."

When he puts his foot down, it stays down.

There were things I couldn't really say in the 7th grade out loud. I left out how when I was little I used to wet my bed. When Mother changed the sheets in the middle of the night, Daddy held me against his shoulder, even though my PJ's were soaked. Because what would people think when they found out I wet my bed? Even though I was younger then. Also, I probably shouldn't tell them that Daddy farts. Teresa Feeney's Dad probably doesn't fart. So I took that one out. Also sometimes at breakfast and supper, if for some reason, everything isn't on the table by the time he sits down, he scolds Mother and looks disappointed. So I didn't mention that. Other than that, he never fights with Mother over anything. So I wrote that down. But is that weird? They don't ever argue.

There was one more thing about him that was really

bugging me. That phrase, "When he puts his foot down, it stays down." I didn't explain it in my composition. Daddy put his foot down when he drove Clara back to the mission that night, so that no one would know she was pregnant. That's the only explanation; it matters so much to him that our family wins the championship of holiness in our parish. He'd rather have her clean toilets for the Sisters of Saint Isabella than be home with us now, when she is creating a baby in her body. It's embarrassing, alright, that they did those disgusting naked things in the dark somewhere, but now that it's done, Clara and her baby are much more important than keeping the parishioners at St. Andrew's from knowing that Christopher Feeney got our sister pregnant.

Sending her to the mission, Daddy is forcing her to give up this baby like, no problem, she'll have plenty of babies later to make up for it. Like this baby *doesn't* count just because it was conceived 'out of wedlock'. And if no one finds out, it will be like the baby never even happened.

Speaking of 'out of wedlock'... If Clara is right, the Blessed Mother should have given up baby Jesus for adoption, because he was conceived out of wedlock! If she had done that, Jesus would have grown up with imposter parents and he probably wouldn't have become The Messiah. Where would all us Catholics be now?

Also, Mother? It seems like Mother might know some things, after having thirteen children. They should be best friends right now, Clara wearing Mom's pregnancy hand-me-downs, Mom telling her what she should expect and giving her a pep talk about the labor pain.

And suppose I were the person who was pregnant, for instance? Not that I would ever be. I wouldn't, but suppose.

Daddy would send me back, too.

This thought stopped me right in my tracks. I always felt I was his favorite, if I can be vain enough to assume that in such a large family. I never thought he'd do something like that to me; I'd just have to talk to him, like we did in the mornings before Mass, and he would understand. But now, I realize that if I were in Clara's position, Daddy would send me back, too. He would send me away and say I wasn't his daughter anymore if I didn't do what he wanted.

When Daddy came home that afternoon, he opened the front door. Usually he comes in the back, but I think Mother was out front getting her loaf of Hollywood bread from the Bread Man. Every night Daddy usually goes straight to her after work and hugs her and grabs her bottom, and she shrieks and says "Marty!"

I was sitting in the corner of the living room on the red chair with my knees in my chest. He had to pass me to get to his bedroom where he always hung his jacket. The twins had just gotten up from their naps and stumbled sleepily into the room, one after the other. Thumbs in their mouth, their blankies dragging.

"How's my favorite daughter named Annie?" He asked me, but I didn't fall for it this time. I'm his only daughter named Annie. He took off his jacket and flung it onto the couch. Markie climbed up, Matt reached his arms up across the cushions. His little legs pushed off the floor, and he hoisted himself up.

"Do you know what your father did today?" I hadn't gone to Mass with him since the belting at dinner, and I had been keeping my distance.

"I'll give you a hint," he said, "it has four wheels and begins with a 'C.'" Then he did a pretend tap dance in front of me, as he loosened his tie and hung it on the doorknob. My lips couldn't help but go up at the corners, even though I was determined.

"That's right, Miss Smile and the World Smiles with You. You get the prize—a brand new bicycle. Going, going...." He stood there, holding out one arm in a gesture that presented me as the star. I looked the other way.

"Gone! Sold! To the highest bidder. Annie you must recognize opportunity when it comes knocking on your door. Opportunity has passed you by this afternoon. However, I will not let you go away without knowing what all the excitement is all about. Your father sold two automobiles today! Yes siree Bob! Not one, but two! Two! Two! Two cars in one!" He punctuated his monologue by patting the heads of his two sons, sucking their thumbs on the couch.

I was all seriousness.

"Annie," he said, looking at me in the eye, "we made some money today." He walked around the room, took up the space, like me and the twins were the big audience. His voice was louder than usual.

"The first one was a Ford Falcon. The buyer: A young chap with two children and one on the way. A used car. And you know what sold him? Besides the price." He paused, giving me a chance to answer. I looked away. "Room for six passengers. I told him I was the father of thirteen children. That's what sold him. For a man with a family of four, I told him, a car that has room for six passengers is the car of the future."

The twins were waking up; their eyes lit up with Daddy's excitement, and I wasn't budging. I kept my eyes down. But Daddy was on a roll.

"The next buyer?" Daddy looked at me, still down in the mouth. "An older gentleman, who could afford the sticker price of $1,250 on the new Rambler American. I detected his means by noticing his attire, and he detected my confidence. I led him to the automobile of his final choice, like a lamb to the slaughter. Annie, confidence is contagious. That's what sold the second buyer."

I got up and walked into the dining room and sat down in a huff. Clara is one of those 13 children he's bragging about. But he just put her out of his mind. We weren't on the same wavelength. He sat down next to me and told me this poem, hoping it would inspire me.

The tree that never had to fight,
For sun and sky and air and light,
But stood out on the open plain,
And always got it's share of rain,
Never became a forest king,
But lived and died a shabby thing.

It was a good poem, if I took it at face value, or if anyone but Daddy was reciting it. But things looked different to me.

I wasn't going to instantly believe everything he said, like I used to.

CHAPTER 26
ANNOUNCEMENT FROM
THE PRINCIPAL'S OFFICE

November 26 – Dear Blessed Mother, How did you let this happen? Please pass along the message to Jesus. Have mercy on all of us!

You couldn't have suspected it, especially if you based your suspicions on the kind of day it was. A sunny day after the rain, everything crisp and shiny. Even in Pasadena, there were a few trees whose leaves changed to yellow and orange, reminding you that it was fall. Later on, as the sun beat down, the smog stretched its fuzzy dirt across the horizon and made the sky whitish, but right then, it was perfect.

I couldn't wait for recess. All our 7th grade heads were bent over our shiny beige desktops, penciling in a Geography assignment. Mrs. Parry walked up and down the aisles checking on us like inmates. Static scratched the wall to the right next to the clock. I heard fumbling. Someone cleared her throat.

"This is an announcement from the Principal's office. We have been informed that President Kennedy has been shot. It is not known if he will live. Please pray for his recovery."

Mrs. Parry marched to the front and put the pointer on the ledge next to the chalk. "Continue with the assignment, boys and girls." Then she opened the door and let the steel grasshopper leg on the top corner of the door pull it shut. A murmur rose up from all of us. Who would that be? I wondered, the person who continued with the geography assignment after the announcement that the President has been shot?

At recess, Sister Everista stood on the cracked asphalt near the lunch tables, in her black robes and thick rosary jangling from her leather belt. Her eyes were red from crying. I walked past her, thinking that her face would somehow answer some of my questions. What did she know about the President that made her cry? I'm pretty sure she never met him. I was sorry he died because he was a Catholic, but I wasn't sorry because he was a Democrat. Sister Everista obviously couldn't see through Kennedy's Catholicism to the truth of his political mistakes. I wondered if God considers being a Democrat a sin. Maybe it's a big sin, and maybe the President was being punished.

After recess we processed into the cool church, single file, all the grades, from first grade to eighth grade for a mandatory student body noon Mass. We were going to storm heaven with our prayers. All four grades of St. Andrew's High School joined us. It wasn't long before Monsignor came to the pulpit and we heard that "shot" had been changed to "assassinated." President Kennedy was really dead, and we were all let out to go home. It was hard to understand. Since he was a Catholic, he would be up in heaven right now, enjoying the big pay-off. If he managed to go to confession before he was shot down. But the shock of his death was much more real. Everyone was talking about it. On the radio, in the newspapers, on television, everywhere. Nobody said anything about heaven in the world outside our parish.

I was perplexed and a little bit frightened that in the clutch, not only did our prayers fail, but the doctors couldn't save him either. Modern medicine was so smart. They had drugs, and they could operate. Their machines could keep you going when you were just lying there with your heart stone still. Why couldn't they put him back together again, with stitches and somebody else's blood flowing through his veins? He was the most famous man in the land. Our country was the luckiest in the world. What happened?

I felt guilty; could it have been my fault?

Madcap was going out at night and sneaking back in at all hours, and sometimes, I had to cover for her. Which meant that I was committing venial sins every time anybody asked where she was. I always said she was in her room, doing her homework. I didn't even know where she went. Sometimes she ditched school; she'd duck out of line when the student body filed into the church on special days. Aaron Solomon would pick her up. And sometimes, she didn't get back until after everyone else had gone to bed. I don't know how she got away with it, except I was part of it. Sometimes when she came in, waking me up by throwing seed pods at my window, she seemed silly and talkative and sleepy at the same time and her breath smelled like Daddy's breath just before dinner, after Mother and Daddy had their martinis. I sat in Madcap's room at times like this, trying to stay awake, while getting information from her about what she had been doing. Just in case. I was afraid for her. If anything happened, how would we ever know where to look?

And Wanda told fibs to her parents, too. Like the time we both went to the store to get Abba Zabbas instead of making her bed and arranging her dolls that had real glass eyes and fancy costumes.

Her mom pounded on the door, "Is your room cleaned up?"

"Spic and Span!" Wanda had said, as we chomped down on the chewy taffy, giggling. "And no, you can't come in!"

Wanda thought confession was embarrassing, so she never went and I felt scared for her soul, just like I did for Madcap. What if Wanda died without getting the chance to wipe the slate clean? But she had a point— the priests could recognize our voices, we were both sure, or maybe they could see us through the screen. We both hated the idea that they had all the nasty details to our personal lives. When you have to tell private sins to a man, and you're a girl, well, that's why they put the confessional in the dark. I myself have to close my eyes and say it. I usually rehearse my sins so I don't chicken out. I say them in a list, trying to sound very matter-of-fact about it. *I hit my sister, I told a small lie, I borrowed a red scarf from my other sister without permission.* Your soul is like the blackboard and confession is the eraser.

Lying seemed like a necessary thing, an unavoidable consequence of being in the world where there are so many rules. It's bad enough that God can spy on your every thought. There's no privacy at all, once you figure in the church and confession and your parents knowing where you are at every minute. Other people had to be doing it, too, and if everyone else is telling stories, it wasn't just me—how could President Kennedy's death be punishment for *my* sins?

But there was some good news on the horizon—Cardinal Stefanucci was coming to visit on Thanksgiving. We were all given extra chores to tidy up the house before he got there. I had to wipe off the smudges and boogers on all the doors and walls. It took a few hours, but when the stuff came off, the doors around the handles seemed to glow, and I looked at them every time I passed, feeling like I had accomplished something.

On Monday, November 25th, schools all over the country were closed to observe the funeral. Televisions beamed out of all the houses on our street. Branches of the redwood tree reflected through the picture window, and it was hard to see the TV screen because there was so much light.

Jacqueline Kennedy walked bravely between her brothers-in-law, Robert and Edward, down the street towards St. Matthew's Cathedral for the funeral mass. She wore a black hat and I could see the breath in front of her in white clouds under her black veil. I was afraid someone was going to shoot her out in the open like that.

The coffin was draped with the American flag, and I imagined the President's body inside, stiff yet jiggling in the dark under the lid, rolling along behind magnificent white horses, with men in dark uniforms sort of bouncing atop their backs. The hush of the huge crowd staring in silence could almost be heard through the television. On the steps outside the cathedral, Jackie leaned over and whispered something to John-John.

And then the little boy saluted. He was only three, a year younger than the twins.

Mother sat on the couch in her apron, wearing the usual thick-soled shoes and tensor stockings, sighing. Maybe I was too young to notice the last time, but I can't remember her ever being this tired. Drums and bagpipes floated their squeaky, sorrowful music all the way out to California from Washington, DC. The guns went off, soldiers stood at attention in white gloves, the eternal flame was lit, and we heard the final lonely notes of a bugle playing "Taps." I held my hand over the hard surface of Mother's tummy to feel the baby kicking, and I thought how Jackie is like the Blessed Mother. She is the woman who loves the most important man in our country, but who has to suffer while everybody else watches her.

• • •

On Thanksgiving day Daddy pulled up the car into the garage and Cardinal Stefanucci stumbled out of the grey Classic Rambler, looking like a regular, ordinary priest in one of those black and white collars and a lumpy black sweater. He was a tall, wide man, and his grey hair was just barely covering his scalp in strands across the middle of his head. I didn't really recognize him; the last time we saw him all I noticed were his new Archbishop gowns. Now it was his rosy, puffy cheeks, a round belly, and Frankenstein eyebrows. He was an important man, and he took up a lot of space. But he looked so strangely frail. I had this image in my mind of God's right hand man, the potential Pope, glorious at the altar with all the gold garments, the chalice over his head and incense around him, but here was this old guy with greasy strands that he combed over the shiny bald spot. The strength in him had already faded, but we were still going on with the myth.

He came in through the laundry room and kitchen with the usual welcome: one kid on either side, hanging from his arms. I shook his toasty warm hand. Even though he wasn't married, he had a shiny gold band on his left ring finger. I wondered if we had missed something—are Cardinals married to the Blessed Mother, just like nuns are married to Jesus? He was older than Daddy, and the skin on his neck sagged in the middle around his Adam's apple. And those bushy eyebrows (I almost forgot about them) they hung over his eyes like an awning. And they were still black! There are a lot of places to look when you first meet our family, but Archbishop Stefanucci looked me in the face and said, "Pleased to see you again, Annie." I'm pretty sure Mother told him my name just before we shook hands. For some unknown reason, I curtsied, blushing as usual.

By that time, the house was filled with the cooking and baking smells of Thanksgiving. In the kitchen, the cutting board was covered with flour, and so were Mother's hands. Her powdery, white fingers pinched the crust against glass pie pans. Usually it was Clara helping her at supper, but this time, Mother had specifically invited Madcap and Jeannie to be the ones to make the thanksgiving dinner together. They opened and closed the refrigerator door, cleaned up the dishes in the sink, washed the bird, salted, stuffed, and baked it like this had always been their job. If you had mentioned the name Clara they would have said, "Clara Who?."

"Would you like to sit here, Father?" I asked Cardinal Stefanucci, pointing to the couch, full of newspapers and unfolded diapers. I scrambled to push them aside—after all the cleaning, it was still a disgusting mess!

"Anywhere you want me," he said affably. That cheered me up. Maybe he didn't really notice. So I sat him on the end of our extra long brown striped couch. (Good at camouflaging stains). The weight of him tipped the couch a bit, so I smoothed out a pillow in the center to encourage him to sidle over to the middle. Then I went back into the kitchen to get his martini. I wanted to make small talk with him, to make sure he remembered me for when he would come into our classroom and be introduced as my personal friend. I had to prepare him for his role as the Pope candidate who phoned me all the way from the Vatican and recognized my voice out of all 13. If he came unprepared to our class, it would only take one question from Sister Everista to expose me as a liar. I would never get to ride on the parish float. My latest essay would be disqualified from the "Christian Leadership" contest.

When I delivered the Cardinal his martini, Jude and the twins were creating a catastrophe waiting to happen.

Jude was a sturdy little guy, close to the ground, and now that he could walk he was somewhat dangerous. He was trailing around after the twins, trying to knock them over. The twins weren't like normal kids, who fought with each other—they hung around together, I'd say within six inches of each other, like they could

241

sense when the other had gotten just maybe six *and a half* inches away, enough separation to make them uncomfortable, and then they would both look around and find the other and head towards each other. They didn't say much, either, but usually knew exactly what the other meant.

Right then, they invited the Cardinal to help them create an epic battlefield for their plastic war soldiers on the floor in front of the couch. Markie held a mass of gray and green soldiers in his arms as Matt cleared away a space on the worn rug.

"Annie!" Mother called me from the kitchen. "Set the table!" The way she pronounced that one word *Annie* told me that sitting with the Cardinal on our lumpy couch was akin to lounging by a pool when everyone else struggled to lift rocks in a prison work camp, bleeding from chains and dying of heatstroke under the sweltering sun.

"Maybe we can talk later," I said to the Cardinal, standing up. "We were all praying for you to win, you know."

"God's will be done," he said quite happily. "If I had become Pope, I wouldn't be here now. And I'm enjoying myself."

I cleared off the magazines, schoolbooks, pencils, dirty cups, and boxes of rubber bands from the dining room table.

"Salt and pepper, bread and butter, cream and sugar, knife, fork, spoon, napkins," I reminded myself. After the places were set, I counted again to make sure I had the right number of table settings. Thirteen kids, minus Clara, plus the Cardinal and Daddy and

Mother. Fifteen altogether. Daddy sliced the steaming white breast at the head of the table; John-the-Blimp ran up next to Daddy, bowing to anyone who would listen and watch.

"Dad! Look at that bird!" he said urgently, pointing out the window. We turned instantly and stared into the sky past John's finger. As we looked away, he grabbed a morsel of meat.

"The disappearing bird!" He taunted, slamming the door behind him. "Now you see it, now you don't!" he called down the hall.

"Supper's ready!" Mother put the pies in the oven, wiped her hands on her apron and sighed. Madcap and Jeannie brought bowls of steaming beans and mashed potatoes from the kitchen and set them in the middle of the long table. Now I was really feeling sorry for Clara; she was missing all this. Paul emerged from upstairs; John reappeared and snitched another bite before sitting right next to Daddy. Daddy smacked his hand.

"Enough, John!"

Rosie quietly climbed up onto her chair and sat like an honor student with her hands folded on her plate. As usual, she wore cotton candy pink and glowed like a pastel carnation on the mantle. Dominic, Bartholomew, the twins, Buddy, pulled their chairs out from under the table, scraping them on the wooden floor, as we took our places around the steaming food. Conveniently, Cardinal Stefanucci sat in Clara's empty spot. We all quieted down and folded our hands to say grace. This moment, the few seconds before grace, is one of the few actual incidents of silence in this family, and for this I am grateful to God. The Cardinal looked around.

"Where's my favorite niece?" He asked, and the silence bounced around the room. "I've been waiting patiently for her to come in the door at any time. But I'm not sure I would have recognized her." He looked at Madcap, but his expression remained quizzical. "She must be quite a young lady by now."

I was hoping I was his favorite niece. I sat up straighter and made noise with my knife and fork. Jeannie nudged me and I thought, *Please God, don't let it be her.*

"Who is your favorite niece?" John-the-Blimp asked.

"Clara," he replied. "We always played checkers whenever I visited."

I looked up from my plate at Daddy. He was staring across the table at Mother. I could see from their expression that neither of them knew what to do. Madcap was smirking.

"She's at the Mission in Ventura!" Markie blurted out.

The jig was up. There was only one reason that teenage girls went on retreats with the Sisters of Saint Isabella. Now I knew that.

And I knew what Mother and Daddy were probably saying in their minds. They were probably thinking *Out of the mouths of babes.* Now, they had to tell the Cardinal, the man who was almost the pope, that their daughter was pregnant.

But that's not what happened. Daddy cleared his throat and said,

"Clara sends her regrets, Father." (We all still called him Father, even though he was now Cardinal). "She's on a retreat with the Sisters of Saint Isabella. In Ventura."

The Cardinal glanced back and forth from Mother's face to Daddy's face. Finally he said, "A retreat! Wonderful! I'm just sorry I missed her. God bless her." He looked to Mother. "And keep her safe and healthy." Mother nodded. A weak smile appeared on her face. Then Daddy spoke.

"In the name of the Father, and of the Son and of the Holy Ghost, he began." We all chimed in.

"Bless us oh Lord and these, thy gifts which we are about to receive from thy bounty, through Christ our Lord, Amen." Then we prayed for the souls of the faithful departed, including President John F. Kennedy.

"Please bring Clara home safely," Daddy added at the end.

Then, like the starting line at the races, we opened our mouths and filled them with turkey, breadcrumb and sausage stuffing, gravy, cranberry sauce, and mashed potatoes at a shoveling pace.

This was the beginning of the Thanksgiving weekend. With the clanging of the silverware and the breathing sound of fifteen people wolfing down food, with the warmth and the light, with the idea that other families were also gathered around a steaming table giving thanks to the Lord, we could only feel happy being so large and familiar and altogether. Everyone was safe, everyone was here (except for Clara), and we had a very special, top-notch guest. We had our rituals, and we had the weekend. We had a visit to Long Beach to go Christmas shopping for our Kris Kringle on Friday. We had four nights with no homework. Four nights to gather around the Advent wreath and watch the candles melt the darkness around them. Four nights with all our voices reciting the rosary as we pictured the magic of the shepherds on a crisp night full of stars, and the wonder of the special baby being born.

Amidst the cacophony of voices and silverware against hard plastic plates, Daddy tried to make a big story out of our Kris Kringle ritual. Probably to distract the Cardinal. I kept feeling the silence of that cover-up moment about Clara. Then Daddy said, "At some point, with all the kids underfoot, Katherine and I decided that Kris Kringle would simplify things at Christmas. We write each child's name on small pieces of paper and put them into a hat. We pass the hat. Everyone picks a name out of the hat. And that person is their Kris Kringle." Daddy smiled at the Cardinal.

"Do you want to participate?"

"Wait, first tell him what he has to do," John blurted out.

"You have to be nice to your Kris," I said immediately. "You have to keep their name a secret."

Jeannie added, "Your Kris is your special person. All through Advent, you're responsible for them."

"Yeah!" Dominic yelled from the far end of the table. "You have to do things for them!"

"Clandestine and mysterious things, sometimes," Bartholomew added.

"Like you make the bed for your Kris and leave a scribbled note with only the letters PX written on it." Rosie said, swaying back and forth on her chair.

"Or we send anonymous cards in the mail, or leave a piece of candy under their pillow," I said.

"Sometimes we arrange for someone at school to hand them a note with hints," Jeannie said.

"Hints?" Cardinal Stefanucci looked at Jeannie.

"Hints as to who you are." I answered before she had the chance.

"Ah," he said. "Hints."

"On Christmas morning, everything is revealed." Daddy concluded.

"If small prayers qualify as 'things,' then I'll participate," Father Stefanucci said.

"You have to get them one present for Christmas," Rosie said. "At Long Beach."

"Just one present," Daddy said. "That's the point of it. But you could get it anywhere you want."

So the Cardinal said, scratching his awning eyebrows, "Count me in."

The hat was Daddy's Navy Commander hat, the white one with gold braid. All the torn, folded pieces of paper were bunched up together in the well of the upturned hat. Daddy started with Father Stefanucci, who tucked the paper into his pocket once he read it. Then Paul.

"By the way," said Paul. "If you pick your own name, you have to put it back."

Clara was next and Mother picked for her. Daddy held his hat above each person's head as they reached up. The twins and Jude couldn't read, so Mother helped them, taking the paper out of their fist and then whispering in their ear. When it got to me, I felt all the papers before choosing one.

"C'mon, Annie," Daddy said. "Pick one."

I dropped that one back in and fumbled for another. I opened it up.

"Clara," the paper said. My heart sank. How was I going to be a good Kris for Clara? Mom would never let me go to Ventura to visit again.

Jeannie was next, Number 7. Her eyes widened and she said a quiet, "Oh!" So she probably got Father Stefanucci. I could tell because right away she started serving him the first piece of apple pie. Then she really gave it away when she said,

"If someone had you as PX, where would she send letters to?"

Then things got ridiculous. It was as if Jeannie's question gave all the little kids permission to ask the Cardinal anything. Buddy, who had been unusually quiet piped up:

"Father Nuchie, can you be the Pope if you don't have the hat?" A hearty laugh from Father Stefanucci.

"Of course you can, my son. That hat is a Papal tiara and it celebrates the tradition of the papacy. But it doesn't affect God's intention in choosing someone to represent His church."

Just then Dominic came in with a couple of towels draping down his back and a rosary around his neck. His hands were folded. Because he didn't have the cassock, and his legs were spindly, I thought he was trying to be a Catholic Superman.

"Ah yes, the cape," the Cardinal said. "I should have worn my vestments."

"If you're Pope, are you still infallible if you're not wearing the pointy hat?" I asked.

"Annie!" Daddy remonstrated. "The hat has nothing to do with being infallible."

"The pope is God's representative on this earth," our friend Cardinal Stef began. At that moment, Rosie became unusually bold, blurting out this excellent question, "If you stand in the freshold of the Jewish Church, would God bring the lightning?"

I used to have these lightning thoughts myself. At my First Holy Communion, I wondered if God would zap me if I touched the Holy Eucharist even a smidgen with my finger. I was so curious on the day of my First Communion that I snuck my finger into my mouth after I received the wafer on my tongue. I put my head down like I was praying, hoping that God and everybody else would be distracted by all us little girls in our white dresses and bridal veils and white socks and white shoes. Nothing happened whatsoever. It's just a matter of time for Rosie before she understands that God doesn't go around electrocuting Catholics whose curiosity gets the better of them.

Rosie mispronounced the word, but what she meant was, would God strike you dead if you put your toe onto the threshold of a synagogue? I wanted to know the answer to that myself. I looked over at Madcap. Suddenly she was paying attention. I think I know why. Aaron Solomon is Jewish, and I'm pretty sure Madcap wants to be carried over the threshold by Aaron Solomon. Although she's kind of young to get married. But a threshold is a threshold, and a girl's ears perk up whenever that word is mentioned.

"I don't think you'll get any lightning if you stand in the doorway of another place of worship," our friend

Cardinal Stef laughed. "Unless there's a thunder storm in the neighborhood."

"So what about the people who stepped through the doorway when it was a mortal sin to step over?" I asked. "What if they died without going to confession? They're in hell now for all eternity. Then the Pope just changes his mind and makes it not a sin. Is that right? So now people can step over willy-nilly and it's not even a sin?"

"We do have to acknowledge that people of other faiths can be good people who worship God in their own way," he answered, scratching the shelf of his eyebrow. "That's the message of the Pope's ruling."

But my head was spinning. I couldn't keep up with it all. Then Rosie turned the whole thing on its head with a real gasser.

"You should get the Pope to try out for the Rose Parade. Cause it looks like he's got a pretty good wave from the balcony!"

That one really cut us up. Leave it to Rosie to ask a question about The Rose Parade. We all started imagining the Pope in all his gold lamé outfits cruising along Orange Grove Boulevard at the front of the St. Andrew's float, waving at all of us on New Year's Day. I closed my eyes, imagining myself in a sparkly gown, God's princess, dramatically throwing roses out to the adoring crowds.

Then we had to help clear the table. Paul didn't have to help because he works at Shea Motors and as long as he has a job, he doesn't have to do chores. Madcap and Jeannie got off because they helped in the kitchen before dinner. It was me, John-the-Blimp, and

Bart who got stuck with the disgusting leftovers As I stacked the dishes in soapy hot water, I noticed again a white plastic plaque hanging by a string on a nail over the sink, splattered by numerous meals. "Thank God for dirty dishes, they have a tale to tell. While others may go hungry, we're eating very well. With home and health and happiness, I shouldn't want to fuss, for by this stack of evidence, God's been good to us."

Cardinal Stef sat in the living room, reading *Green Eggs and Ham* to the twins before their bedtime. We all knew this book by heart. Our lips moved as his pulpit voice boomed the rhyming words; the twins kicked out their legs up and down against the couch, like they couldn't wait to read the next line. I was looking forward to the rosary; it would give me time to figure out a strategy for when someone in my class asked about the phone calls from The Vatican and the embossed letters to Daddy. In school, after the Thanksgiving break, they were going to ask those questions, and I had to be prepared. But The Cardinal excused himself, saying he was just now feeling a bit under the weather, and could Daddy drive him home? Okay, I said to myself. It's Thanksgiving weekend. Tomorrow's Friday.

I have until Monday to hatch a plan.

CHAPTER 27
THE BASE

November 30 – Dear Blessed Mother, Can you see what's going on here? The Hands are still after me! Shouldn't you be putting this on God's radar? It's embarrassing enough to say anything and have Mother act annoyed, like I was making it up. In the meantime, I've been trying to stay awake so I can see who it is coming into my room, but I got really tired. So I brought my pillow down onto the floor on the other side of my bed, to hide. A sound woke me up and I could see some feet from where I was under the bed, but I couldn't tell who it was. I think he got scared when I wasn't in my bed, because he just hurried out of the room. I heard him trying to sneak up the stairs, but that third step creaked like it usually does. So it IS one of the big boys! There aren't many things you can really call your own in this family, but before this, I would have said my bed was really mine. My very own bed. Mine! Obviously even that is up for grabs. Maybe Madcap would know what to do. If I could say something to her.

"Whooooaoaaaaa!" Mother took a curve around South Pasadena Freeway. I scrunched into the turn, squishing Rosie and Jeannie against the window. We passed a VW bug chugging along in the slow lane.

"I'm squished!" Jeannie called for mercy. But when

mother swerved the bus the other way, Jeannie leaned into us. On my right was Dominic and on his right, Buddy. Flat pancakes, all.

"Whoooooohhhha!" We all said, laughing. Everyone was in a good mood, except for Mother, at the wheel. She was all eyes and ears on the road. The day was crisp and sunny, leaves floating on the occasional breeze.

It was Friday after Thanksgiving, one of the most exciting days of the year. Christmas was coming, we had a little bit of money in our pockets, and school was out. I had saved my babysitting earnings for the Commissary at The Navy Base in Long Beach. During the year, Daddy shopped there for groceries, because it was cheaper there, a perk for being a retired Commander in the U.S. Navy.

But today we were going Christmas shopping. It was an annual family outing. I could feel all the energy bouncing around inside our vehicle.

Normally, all 13 kids could fit into the *V-duby yew*, with room for Mom and Dad. This year, Daddy drove the Rambler with Paul to store the groceries and to hide all the presents we bought for each other, so the proper secrecy around Christmas could be maintained. The rest of us took the bus with Mother. Since Clara wasn't there either, it seemed like there was lots of room.

Jeannie and I clapped our hands and smacked them together in a game I learned in the first grade:
"Myyyy boyfriend's name is Able
He used to set the table
Now he works in the stable
Down on the Bingo farm."

"Okay, that's enough, kids," Mother said.

What's the deal with Mom? I thought. Other than when she has her migraines, usually she's a pretty good sport, and I can tell when she's enjoying herself. Today, though, she didn't get us singing "I love to go a wandering" by just starting it up with her beautiful voice. She didn't ask us things like, "Who lived in the Emerald City? Buffalo Bill?" To which we'd all say in unison,

"Noooo!"

"Saint Peter?" To which we'd all shout a resounding,

"Noooooo!"

"The Wizard of Oz?" To which we'd all say,

"Yeaaassss!" Then we'd start singing, "We're off to see the Wizard, the wonderful wizard of Oz. He really is a whiz of a whiz because of the things he does…" It was a favorite way we had of starting up a trip in the car.

Maybe Mom was worried about Clara. When was the baby going to come? Did Clara sign the papers? I didn't want to think about it, even though it was all I could think about.

Finally we were there. Mother downshifted, and we slowed to the grinding sound of the engine as we approached the gate. I loved the feeling of being admitted past the lifting arm, like we really belonged to this place. I even had a picture ID that said I was a "dependent" of the U.S. Navy, in case anybody asked. Daddy was ahead of us and I could see him as he slowed down at the booth. The guard looked at the sticker on the windshield, and then he put his white, gloved hand up to his forehead in a crisp salute to our Dad. I could see through the windshield that Daddy handed the guard a small card, probably his "Shea Family Motors, We mean business about family" card. Nowadays, he was handing these out to everyone he met, even in the grocery stores. But the base was Daddy's territory; I didn't have to feel embarrassed here when he did that. The guard looked at the card and smiled. The long arm with red and white stripes lifted and his Rambler inched forward. The bus was next, this time the guard saluted to Mom. Once the bumper of the bus got in front of the arm and it went down again behind us, we all broke into applause and yelled, Yeaaaaaaaay! Whoo! Whoo!

"Pipe down kids!" Mother tried to shout, but it wasn't nearly as threatening as when Daddy said it.

As we drove through the base towards the commissary, sailors fresh with new haircuts walked in twos and threes in their Navy blue uniforms. Giant striped candy canes painted in red, white and green covered up the windows on the huge stores that faced the parking lot. Outside, evergreen and flocked white Christmas trees huddled in two groups, instant forests on the asphalt under the fall California sun.

Out on the dock a huge ship stretched from end to end with the number 135 on the bow. Two huge stacks, three turrets with about ten or eleven guns sticking out on each side pointed into the sky. The shimmering water stretched beyond it.

"That's what's called a heavy cruiser," Daddy said. "The USS *Los Angeles*. It was just decommissioned on November 15th. "

"What is decommissioned?" Rosie.

"It's done its duty ,and they're going to mothball it to San Diego."

The ship was massive. It was hard to imagine the force of the blast that would come out of the enormous guns. The sound alone, the sudden ear-piercing blast along with the earthquake feeling of the ground shaking beneath you. When we were on Whidbey Island we heard jets flying low all the time, roaring up, droning overhead and fading into a faraway sky. Sometimes I woke from dreams of them, the hot, sudden sound piercing the world, shattering my eardrums, shaking my body to alertness in instant fear.

"The sound of freedom," Daddy would always say. He and Paul walked towards the ship. Everybody knew that Paul wanted to enlist. Daddy discouraged it. "Go to college first," he'd say, "then you can join as an officer." Looking at them stroll towards the floating hulk that seemed to stretch a few city blocks, as they were dwarfed into the size of plastic toy soldiers, I felt proud. Proud and protected. Daddy was right, no one was going to destroy our way of life as long as the Navy was around. Not even the Communists in Cuba.

We split up, once again. Daddy went shopping for groceries and everyone else paired off to go to the store with all the toys. We were to meet back at the cafeteria at noon. I was in charge of Rosie, meaning I had to help her find a gift for her PX with the allowance that Mother gave her this morning. And I had to find a present for Clara. Inside the grocery store, "Deck the Halls" and "I'm Dreaming of a White Christmas," added to our excitement. Even though we were in California, we wished for snow every year. We ached for it, and the song made it especially poignant. Even though there would never be a white Christmas in Pasadena; even though none of us had ever even seen a snowflake. When the song came on, we sang along, like we were missing the good old days.

Rosie had Jude as her PX, so getting a present would be easy.

"Here's $2 for Rosie," Mother had said, digging in her big bag for the bills. "I'm sure you can find something for that."

She grabbed my hand and put the bills into my palm and closed my hand around the bills. I hugged up to her, because it seemed like she could use a hug, but she pushed me away. At times like this, it's like I, Annie, am not even there. I'm just the person doing the errand. She had so much else to think about. Oh, well. It's great to have a phrase you can just pull out for times like this. *She must be under the weather*, I thought.

We walked along the rows of toys. I steered Rosie away from the dolls, 'cause I knew she wanted a Chatty Cathy and it would really wreck it up if Rosie saw her PX carrying that doll to the cash register. She would know it was for her, since she's really the only one left who's of an age to get a doll. Actually I wanted a baby doll myself. I should have been growing out of wanting a doll, but there it was.

We got a die cast metal toy car for Jude. In the end Rosie chose a Lincoln Continental because she liked the creamy green color.

It was already lunchtime, so I walked Rosie by the hand to the Mess Hall, where the smell of hamburgers, chocolate shakes and French fries was almost

CAITLIN HICKS

unbearable. Steam wafted up from the stainless steel containers full of food, as customers inched along with their trays. The lines were long. Mother grabbed a high chair for Jude and commandeered a group of tables. We sat waiting while Daddy and Paul went up to the counter and ordered for all of us.

I was so hungry, my mouth was watering and I had to keep swallowing my spit. We sat at the empty table looking at each other. John-the-Blimp couldn't just sit there, he had to swat Bartholomew on the back of the head and flick Dominic's ears. All three of them ended up having an arm wrestle (which of course John-the-Blimp won). The twins both kicked out their legs repeatedly under the table to the point that they were kind of moving in unison from the shoulder up. It was all you could see of them, since they were so short. Luke got a pen from Mother's purse and was drawing on a napkin. Mother quietly asked Madcap to deal with the baby while she went to the restroom.

Me and Jeannie played this game where you take all the stuff on the table, the salt and pepper shaker, the sugar packets, ketchup, silverware and arrange them in the middle, then you sort of push back, all the while looking at what you've done, like you've just made a painting and you say, "Your move." Then she moves those things around and says something like, "Gotcha." And you say, "Oh I didn't see that! Good move." And then you change something small and give her the next move. Like that. All the while studying the pieces intently. Pretty soon everyone else is looking at what you're doing, trying to figure out what the game is all about. But there are no rules, so the joke is on them.

At last Daddy and Paul carried four trays full of burgers, fries and shakes to the table. We tore off the wrappers and fell silent as we wolfed down our burgers and inhaled our fries. I was breathless afterwards, still hungry even after my shake.

"The cook said, '*How* many burgers?'" Daddy recounted to us proudly, "'What have you got, a team?' So I said, 'My own private mess hall.' Heh heh heh," He concluded. Then he looked around. "Where's your Mother?"

"She's in the restroom," I said. It had been a while since she had excused herself from the table. We were all finished and her burger was still sitting there. I wanted the fries. Madcap was trying to wipe Jude's face; he had ketchup and mustard all over, and he hated his face being wiped, so he was shaking his head side to side as she tried to dab with a wet napkin. Daddy said, "Annie, can you go check up on your Mother?"

"Sure, Dad." I was glad he didn't ask Jeannie. I am older. He pointed to the sign that said, "Restrooms."

When I pushed open the door, I thought Mom would at least be washing her hands by now, but she wasn't. I bent over and looked under the doors. Her shoes were there under the last stall.

"Mom? It's Annie. We're wondering why you're taking so long. Daddy sent me in."

"Annie, can you do me a favor, honey?"

"Sure, Mom." I heard some fumbling in the stall.

"I'll get you a quarter. Do you see a box on the wall there?"

"Yeah, Mom. I know what it's for."

"Can you get me a sanitary napkin?"

"Sure, Mom."

"Here's the quarter." I saw her hands come out under the stall, holding a quarter. I took it and went to the machine, inserted the quarter and turned the knob. The machine clinked, dropping two dimes in the square change cubby. At the same time, a plastic package with a thick napkin fell into the rectangular area at the bottom of the machine. I grabbed it.

"Here's the napkin, Mom." I handed it to her under the door. Was Mom having her period while she's pregnant?

"Thanks. I think I'll need another." Her hands appeared under the stall once again with another quarter.

Another one? I thought. *Wow, she must have heavy periods.*

"Are you having your period, Mom?" As soon as I said it I felt ashamed to have dared ask her such a personal question. She didn't answer. I felt so embarrassed. What an idiot I am! *Geeze. Shut up, Annie. Of course she's having her period.*

When Mother finally emerged from the stall, the color had drained out of her face. As she washed her hands, I had to stare at her. Something about the way she looked made me feel strange. She seemed sad and vulnerable, and I don't remember ever noticing that about her. Looking at her, I felt afraid.

"I'll be okay, sweetheart," she said, as if reading my mind. But she wasn't looking at me. She was looking at herself in the mirror. She held onto the side of the sink with both hands, bent her knees and sat down on the floor. Her feet were in front of her and her knees bent so I kind of saw under her dress before she had the chance to drop her knees in front of her.

"Can you get your father, Annie? Just go get him, please." I pushed the door open and ran out to him as fast as I could.

"Daddy, Daddy!" I yelled from across the large cafeteria. I waved my arm in a "C'mere" gesture. "Hurry!" Daddy dropped his burger and we ran together dodging the tables and chairs back to the hallway. I stood at the door to the Ladies' Room and pushed it open for him. He went right in.

He took his keys out of his pocket and handed them to me. Then he lifted Mother off the floor and held her in his arms.

"Go up to the cashier at the cafeteria and ask for a nurse," he commanded me. "Tell her it's an emergency. Give the keys to Paul. He knows where the car is parked."

Later, we didn't go back to the store like we had originally planned. Things had changed. We waited around in the commissary while Mother and Daddy were at the infirmary.

Then Daddy drove the Volkswagen with Mother in the front seat, and Paul took the Rambler home instead of Daddy. There was no explanation as to the change of plans. It was quiet in the car. Creepy quiet, like we were all jammed in a dark closet where the only light was through a crack at the bottom of the door. Spiders were silently weaving their webs around us. Hungry rats waited in the corners for all of us to fall asleep so they could start eating our toes. We tried to keep as still as possible so nothing worse would happen.

No one else knew what I saw. What I kept seeing. The dread I was feeling. As if a black widow had just climbed up on my knee and was ready to sting me with her poison. I kept remembering the blood on the floor. I have never seen Mother cry before, but I know she was crying because her cheeks were wet. Sometimes Daddy reached his arm across to her and touched her face. She didn't say one single thing the whole ride back.

Then, instead of driving home, Daddy stopped at Huntington Memorial Hospital. He got out of the car and went into the hospital with Mother still in the front seat. Some guys in white outfits came out with a wheelchair and Mother got down off the front seat and sat in the wheelchair. She tried to hide the blood, but the back of her dress was stained with it.

Daddy went in and we sat in the bus outside the hospital.

"What's wrong with Mom?" John asked when Daddy got into the driver's seat of the Volkswagen.

"She's not feeling well."

"Will she be alright?" Madcap spoke for all of us.

"The doctors are going to have a look and see. I'm sure she'll be fine now."

"When is she coming home?" Jude was sucking his thumb, sitting on Jeannie's lap.

"Let's say a prayer, for your Mother," he said.

"Hail Mary, full of grace," we all began in unison.

I might have known this for a while, but when Daddy said "I'm sure she'll be fine now," it was the first time I consciously realized that truth could be told in fractions. That's why they make you promise to tell the truth "the whole truth and nothing but the truth" when you swear on the Bible. People are probably going around telling part truths all the time.

It made me think of the time when everyone was afraid that the bombs from Cuba were going to blow America to smithereens. Everyone was worried about it. We weren't so afraid for ourselves because Cuba was close to Florida and we were in California, way on the other side of the country. Still it would be sad to lose all the people in Florida and all their pets. Even though I had never been in Florida. One night, during the week that it was the topic of everyone's conversation, as I was drifting off to sleep, I said, "Daddy, are they going to drop the bomb?"

"There's nothing to worry about, Annie. They'll never drop the bomb. It will be a long time before anyone destroys our way of life," he said confidently, like he had some inside knowledge. He had survived Pearl Harbor, so maybe he knew about these things that happen on ships out at sea. For example, when they're all out there, deciding whether or not to send the bombs—maybe there's a button on all the ships that's purposefully stuck, so the button doesn't work when you press it. Maybe the sailors think they're following orders, but they when push the button and it doesn't work, the bomb doesn't go off. Maybe Daddy knows better.

Maybe things are going to be okay.

CHAPTER 28
LIMBO

December 4 – Dear Blessed Mother. Thank you for keeping our Mother alive. She has so much love in her heart for everything. She brought all of us into the world. If you look at a Cardinal and think about what he did with his life, and then you look at our Mother? No comparison, even if he is a Cardinal. By the way, did her baby go to Limbo?

It's easy to love a baby, so I don't know why it surprised me that Mother was so sad when she lost her fourteenth. She still had all of us. It wasn't even born yet, and the baby didn't have a name. None of us knew what sex it was, until Mother came home after the weekend. Then we found out it was a girl, although Mother never said anything. We just found out. I don't know if I overheard Madcap telling Jeannie, or if it just seemed so perfect that it was a girl and then everyone agreed that it had been a girl. Daddy said it was a miscarriage. The fetus was about the size of a newborn kitten and it weighed as much as a bowl of Cocoa Puffs in milk. Newborn kittens are pretty cute, but they sure are small. A lot of women have miscarriages. A lot of babies never get born. Daddy says, "it's a baby who wasn't meant to live." So why was Mother so sad about this one?

Something had tilted in the universe, because

when we got home from the hospital, we learned how fantastically awry things had become. Daddy got an urgent call from the rectory. Cardinal Stefanucci had a heart attack on Thursday night after Thanksgiving dinner at our house. And while we were shopping at the base, he died. Just like that. It felt like the whole world was splitting at the seams; children were being sucked into manhole covers; pigeons were exploding; people inside photographs began to move.

The only thing we knew how to do in response to all this was say Hail Marys. The sound of our voices chanting the same thing over and over became a relief with its familiar, hill-and-vale sound. If we prayed, we could feel boredom in the face of frightening circumstances. It was a way of being normal. And of course we poured our thoughts and fears into the prayers. For Cardinal Stefanucci's soul to enter the gates of heaven (I think he was pretty much a shoe-in). We prayed for the soul of Mother's lost baby, although it had done absolutely nothing wrong. We prayed for Mother. I prayed for Clara—her baby was still alive, as far as I knew.

I had two urgent questions for God. Number 1, Why did He let Father Stefanucci die? If someone had been in the room when he had that second heart attack, the Cardinal would be alive today. Instead the nurse was probably on the telephone, or doing her nails and didn't notice that he had stopped breathing. Just a little detail like that. God is so good at those details. He wasn't paying attention!

And Number 2, after all the kids Mother brought into the world, why did God let that baby die even before it was born? Every time I thought about it, I started to feel mad. At God. It was probably a dangerous way to think, but I couldn't help it.

Then I wondered what happened to it. Did it just get flushed down the toilet with all that bleeding? Or what? Where was that teeny baby whose kick I felt while watching President Kennedy's funeral? I felt so sorry for Mother. Why didn't they baptize the baby and give it a name and have a proper funeral? That way it wouldn't be in Limbo while the rest of us were across the way, waving from Heaven.

The least that God could do now would be to let Father Stefanucci intervene and get that baby out of Limbo. It's so unfair! You're hardly even a person, and you'll never be able to really be in heaven. And it's not your fault. It's God's fault.

Once Mother came home from the hospital on Monday, there was an expectation that things would go back to normal, but she stayed in her room with the shades drawn. Daddy asked Mrs. Hopkins, a kind, thick-hipped woman with squishy-sounding nurse shoes to help us with dinner and laundry. Everyday he went from Shea Family Motors, back home, then to the rectory so he could hear the latest details on the rosary and the funeral. By that time Daddy had regular employees, including Paul, on regular shifts to make sure the drivers could get their gas.

When the day of his rosary arrived, the entire parish came to pay their respects. The Mayor of Pasadena, the Mayor of Los Angeles and a few cardinals were going to be there. When Daddy drove Stefanucci to our house for Thanksgiving in his Rambler, I didn't know this, but Cardinals have big black Cadillacs with chauffeurs. And today, a few Cadillacs pulled up in front of St. Andrew's tower. All the boys wore their suits with the ties. It was the first time Jude had a tie on, and he kept pulling it off.

The Cardinal's body was laid out in a heavy looking coffin in the center aisle at the front. The dark and shiny wood glistened with gold fixtures along the side. From a distance, you could see Father Stefanucci lying on his back on a huge white pillow with his hands folded across his belly. He had a white pointy hat and a white cassock with red and black colors for accent.

Mother walked up the center aisle on Daddy's arm, her head down, a black see-through veil over her face. I was right behind her. When she genuflected, she bumped the pew and spilled her missal, stuffed with holy cards of the martyrs, all over the marble floor right next to the casket. I turned beet red as I gathered up all the holy cards. I handed them back to her when she had a chance to sit down. But when I went to genuflect myself, I noticed another card. It was a faded snapshot of Mother sitting in a wheelchair in front of a window, looking down at a bundle like a huge bandage, in her arms. The walls were white and shiny and reflected off a flash in the window. I couldn't make out her expression. It looked like she was wearing a white hospital gown. The picture said "Feb1945" on the white jagged edge at the bottom. I looked closer. I could see a very small hand just up out of the blanket, held in the cup of her palm. It was a baby's hand, but it wasn't grabbing Mother's finger, like newborn babies usually do. It loosely rested there, in the palm of her hand. Now I thought of the blue bead bracelet and the lock of baby hair I had discovered with Mother's wedding pictures, months ago. Here was a picture of the missing baby! And I knew that every time Mother went to Mass, she looked at this photograph, and prayed for this baby, which must have been hers. But right now we were all in the middle of a Rosary for a very important man who had died unexpectedly. I couldn't stop thinking about that hand. I was just dying to know what happened to that baby.

To my left was the casket holding our friend, Cardinal Stefanucci. When I got closer, what I noticed were his hands, which I had held when we were introduced at the entrance to the kitchen on Thanksgiving. They were draped with a rosary. He still had the ring on, and I could see the veins; they made his hands look like the bark of a tree.

I had never seen a dead person before. He was completely drained of anything, although you might be able to imagine that he was asleep, except he didn't breathe. It was hard to look at him. He was so still. He would never open his eyes again, or talk, or read *Green Eggs and Ham*. Already, I couldn't remember the sound of his voice. Only on Christmas day would we find out who he had picked for Kris Kringle, because that person wouldn't get a present from him on Christmas morning.

It was standing room only in the church. There was a lot of murmuring as everyone filed up to have a look at him. And it's not like they caught a glimpse and then walked on. Some of them stood around and stared; a few reached out to touch his hand. Were they curious as to what a dead hand felt like? The nuns filed up together in a black swish, looking somber and official, each one crossing herself when she passed him. Jeannie put a small wrapped gift into his coffin; he must have been her PX. It was really sad. He wasn't even there.

All the guys processed up the aisle in cassocks flowing to their shoes, like they were being canonized. John-the-Blimp and Christopher Feeney held the cross and swung the incense. Daddy was next in line, followed by Monsignor Boyle and a few Cardinals, all dressed to the max in flowing robes.

Mother's eyes were red and puffy, and I stared at her, wondering what she was really thinking. She reminded me of Jackie Kennedy dressed in black walking behind the coffin. Then I wondered if Mother was thinking about the funeral of her first love. She must have had a service for her soldier husband, and it would have been fancy, incense and honor guards in uniform with shiny shoes, saluting and folding up the American flag and giving it to the widow, just like at President Kennedy's funeral. But Jackie Kennedy was holding it in for the whole country. Mother was not holding it in. She stared at the floor, tears streaming down her cheeks. I was glad there was a real funeral going on around us, otherwise I would be terrified, because of what was on her face. Her mouth was slack, her eyes dream-world staring. It was as if she wasn't even there; she was somewhere else, far away. Daddy looked so important and official lighting the candle. Normally I'd be enjoying this privilege of my father up on the altar, but today everything felt creepy and weird.

We sat in the front two rows right next to the

open coffin, as if we were truly the Cardinal's family. Once everyone had settled into the pew, I realized I was trapped in the seat next to the aisle, with a dead body, maybe 12 or 15 inches away. Even if it was Cardinal Stefanucci. He lay there like a heavy weight. Even though he was probably as light as a feather, floating around heaven right now. (Unless he had a few outstanding sins and was burning in Purgatory.)

People filling the church gave the feeling of being pressed close. Their breathing, their resounding voices when they recited in unison the words of the Hail Mary over and over again. It felt like huge cotton puffs filled in all the space around us. I gulped in, trying to find air to keep me alive. I looked across the pew in front of me. Mother was seated with her eyes closed. Why was she even here? She had spent the day in bed in the dark of her room. Daddy had to escort her on his arm out of the car, into the church and up the aisle. She leaned on him, like he was holding her up. People thought she was crying about the Cardinal, but I know it was her little Cocoa Puff making her sad. Unfortunately the Cardinal wouldn't be able to answer this question: Would we be separated from our baby sister for all eternity just because she wasn't baptized? Can someone that small even be baptized?

We were only on the first decade of the rosary. I knew they were going to drag this out—they usually did. When you've got everybody's attention, you've just got to milk it, that's something I've learned from going to church. Monsignor Boyle was probably going to give some kind of sermon. Christopher Feeney sat with John-the-Blimp over to the side with their hands on their laps. They were both laughing under their breaths, then they sat up, looking serious like they were an important part of this ceremony.

It really bothered me. Christopher Feeney on the altar in front of us all. So we had to look at him, lily white and scot-free of any responsibility for his baby, soaking up all the attention. I took one of the envelopes in the pew in front of me, and one of the sharpened pencils. Usually I would write notes to Jeannie on the envelopes where it said "cash" or "amount" and pass it back and forth, making a joke out of it. Sometimes we invented new words, we were so bored. Today I wrote "Feeney is a baby" then scratched over the "is" and put "has." "Feeney has a baby. Feeney has a baby." I repeated it, so it would seem true. I knew it was. I put the envelope back. Maybe if someone else discovered it, he would have to admit it.

"Holy Mary, Mother of God, pray for us sinners, now and at the hour of our death. Amen." My knees were sweating into the stuffed leather kneeler below me. My shoulder brushed against Jeannie on my right; I was trying to escape the dead body on my left. Jeannie pushed back. I can always count on Jeannie not to give me an inch. I looked across the pew in front of us at all our elbows and arms hanging over the edge one after another, jammed in like sardines. I felt hot, in spite of the marble pillars surrounding us. Maybe I was a fish squished in a can with all my fish brothers and sisters, not quite dead, out of breath from being out of water, but waiting for the lid to be closed forever. Like Stefanucci. I closed my eyes. How could I escape? I felt my heart beating stronger and quicker in my chest and

I was afraid it would burst out.

Just then it occurred to me that the solution to my problem with my reputation had worked itself out when the Cardinal died. He would never visit our classroom, and I would never be exposed in my lies. What a relief. No one would find out that I made up every single story I told about Father Stefanucci. Teresa Feeney would not be able to lord it over me in front of all her friends. I wouldn't be humiliated when the Monsignor & the Cardinal came to our classroom, to ask questions and reminisce about how we all followed the Cardinal's progress through *Reports From The Vatican* delivered by Miss Annie Shea. All of a sudden, this feeling came over me like none of it mattered at all. Instead, I wanted to cry.

I tried to distract myself from breaking into sobs, by looking up at the high ceiling above the columns. There was no one up there but my thoughts. My guardian angel was on a cruise, probably. Blessed Mother could be in Africa, saving someone from the boiling pot, even though at the same time she was cradling the Baby Jesus in a statue on the side altar, right over there. I had no idea where Jesus was, after all this dying he caused. My thoughts were probably sacrilegious. While all the high-ranking men were going on with their sermons about this important dead person lying fifteen inches to my left, I finally had to admit that that thing that had been haunting me was Lily. When I held her small body in my arms and had a look at her strange face. When I met and talked with her adoptive parents, while her real mother sat in her hospital bed, wondering and despairing. All her life Bee Bee would be remembering that other baby and thinking it was her Lily. All her life she would be missing her. All her life, Lily would answer to the name Christine, without knowing why it didn't quite fit.

It was a festering secret; I could barely contain all the anger and sadness I felt about it, but there was no one to tell it to. *Dear Blessed Mother*, I said, but the words bounced back to me. I felt like I was going to burst.

Monsignor Boyle said, "Glory be to the father and to the son and to the Holy Spirit."

We replied, "As it was in the beginning is now, and ever shall be, world without end. Amen."

Our voices died down. All the feet and bodies shuffled as we sat down with a noise that rippled up and down the church. I looked over at the statue of the Blessed Mother, her neck eternally cricked, smiling down at the Baby Jesus.

Then I remembered the photograph getting smeared in my sweaty hands. The photograph of Mother in the hospital gown looking down at a baby in her arms. What happened to that baby? None of us ever heard anything. As far as we all knew, there was no baby; the only thing left of it was the lock of hair in the wax paper envelope. And that baby is our half-sister or half-brother. Mother's heart must have been broken all the way through when her baby was gone so many years ago. First her husband died, then her baby disappeared. Did the baby die? Or, did Daddy make her give it up like he's making Clara give up hers? If we were forbidden to even talk about it, then Mother was forbidden to talk about it, too.

I looked over at her, slumping in the pew, quietly sobbing next to Daddy. I realized her expression was one I had never seen before, like she was far away and there was no way back. Even as she mumbled her prayers, I was afraid of the world coming apart.

There wasn't anything I could do about our little sister up in Limbo forever. There was nothing I could do about Cardinal Stefanucci to bring him back. Or anything for the baby attached to that small hand in the photograph.

Maybe I was only 12-going-on-13, but there had to be something I could do for Clara and her baby.

CHAPTER 29
PROOF

December 5 – Dear Blessed Mother… Thou shalt not bear false witness against thy neighbor. You know what neighbor I'm talking about. It applies to him, too.

I had never been to the Feeneys' house, but I knew just where it was. Walking to school every morning we passed by their street. It was the second house on the left, a big house that stretched low along the ground and somehow managed to look like an elf residence, or the house of the Seven Dwarves. It was nestled among a grove of oak trees that created shade and gave it a cozy, fairytale look. The roof draped down like it was thatched, although it had regular shingles. The windows with lead in-between small panes of glass, weren't stained, just regular see-through with no color. The front lawn was trimmed, the paint had been applied within a reasonable amount of time; in other words, it wasn't peeling. It looked like a normal house in any fine neighborhood.

I stood on the front stoop, and put my finger on the red doorbell button. The sound echoed inside. I heard footsteps, then Teresa Feeney's face peered through the lead glass windows, and she opened the door. Still dressed in her pink pleated uniform skirt, white blouse, black and white saddle shoes. She seemed genuinely happy to see me.

"Annie Shea!" She said. "C'mon in. I was just finishing up my math assignment, but I could take a few minutes off."

She thought I had come to see her, and now that she was being so nice, I wasn't sure I wanted to tell her why I was really here.

"I'll be right out," Teresa said, turning her back on me and disappearing into the house. Her shiny hair bounced around on her shoulders. "Do you want some Kool Aid?"

"No thanks," I said. I peeked around the door. Their living room wasn't whisper-smooth; the floors were hardwood, and the walls had fingerprint smudges in the usual places. For sure toys and books were lying around, but it was way more neat than ours. Teresa came bounding out.

"Where are the rest of the kids?" I asked Teresa. I didn't hear the usual shouting and footfalls and door slamming that is the background ambience of a big family.

"Oh, Mom went to pick them up from school. Everyone stays after for one thing or another, band, drama society, choir. She picks them up around 4:30. I took the bus home 'cause I didn't have anything today. Hey, let's go sit on the wall."

We went out to a cement wall at the front of the property that divided their yard from the sidewalk. It was low enough for us to hop up onto, and it had ivy on it. We climbed up with our legs dangling over the sidewalk. The cement was cool and scratchy under my dress.

"I'm so sorry about Cardinal Stefanucci," she said, sounding genuine. The welcoming tone of her voice surprised me. Then, I had to realize I had never actually had much of a conversation with Teresa at all. Other than that embarrassing thing that happened at Candy's summer pool party. I guess me and Teresa just looked at each other from afar.

"Yeah, me, too." I said. "He was a nice man."

I couldn't think of anything else to say, certainly not what was on my mind.

"Wanda is coming over later," she said. I cringed inwardly with jealousy; Teresa was beginning to take over my best friend Wanda. But then she said: "We're going to go to Sew Nifty to get some material and patterns later. You want to come?"

"No, thank you," I said. My envy evaporated instantly once she included me. It was the kind of thing I would love to have done with the two of them.

I swallowed. "I'm here to see your brother."

"Sam?" (Sam was my age, and for a while there, I liked him).

"No, Christopher. I'm here to see Christopher," I said as casually as possible.

"Christopher? Didn't he go out with Clara?"

"Yeah." I nodded. "He did, but." She looked at me, expecting me to say more. I just stared back.

"I haven't seen Clara for a while."

I shrugged. "I just have something to tell him," I said. Another quizzical pause. She looked into my eyes, giving me the chance to tell her.

Finally, "So you're here to see him, then?"

"Yeah, but I would like to go to Sew Nifty with you

and Wanda," I said lamely. "It's just… I can't go today."

"Okay, well he's here," she said cheerfully. "I'll go get him." She hopped off the wall. So did I. I pressed my uniform skirt down with my hands, wishing I had changed out of it into something more attractive. My hair was probably greasy by now. This morning I noticed an "inner city" zit on my forehead in the space between my eyebrows. I touched it, hoping it had gone down, but it was sore. I sighed. There wasn't much I could do to glamorize myself, and it struck me as odd that suddenly I wanted to.

Christopher Feeney stepped down the front walk. There was something about his stride that made me look at him. He moved towards me like he wanted to see me. He was smiling,

"Hi, Annie!" He called to me from the steps.

"Hi, Christopher," I said. They were the first two words I had spoken to him in my life. Now he was closer, and I detected some kind of pleasant smelling after-shave or cologne. His hair was short and blonde, and his eyes were dark brown. He had a dimple, and if I were going to describe an officer candidate, it would be Christopher Feeney. He'd be stunning in dress whites.

I had been shaking with anger and anticipation when I came up the walk to ring the bell and now I felt all soft and melted down. I don't know what happened, but it sure was curious. I found myself liking him. He seemed so cheerful.

He looked right at me, like I was the only person in the world and he said, "So what can I do for you, Annie? You're Clara's sister. I've seen you a few times—at the opening of Shea Family Motors, I noticed you.

Right?"

Oh, Mary Mother of God, I thought, *he noticed me?*

"It's about Clara," I said, my arms crossed, unsmiling.

"I miss Clara," he said, with an extra sincere sound in his voice, and I could feel my whole body wanting to believe him.

"I think she needs you right now," I said.

"She went up to Ventura for a retreat," he said. "I didn't want her to go."

"Well," I said. Then there was this pause. I didn't have the faintest idea what I was going to say.

"Well?" He asked me. "After all this time, now she needs me?"

"I thought I should come to you, first," I said. "She's been there a few months now, you know."

"I thought she wanted to be a nun."

"Who told you that?"

"Well, why else would you go on a retreat with nuns?"

"Did you ever write to her to find out?"

"She never wrote to me."

"But you could've written to her." Words were leaping out of my mouth with a mind of their own.

"She broke up with me. I didn't break up with her."

"She's not interested in being a nun," I said.

Why was I so afraid to tell him what was God's honest truth? Maybe he loved Clara and really did miss her, like he said. Maybe if he knew, he would be so happy and want to help Clara and want to be the Dad to his own baby. I kept telling myself that I had to tell him. To give that baby a chance to go through life with its real parents. There was only one thing to do.

"I'm coming to you first," I said, "because she doesn't want to give up the baby, but they're going to force her to."

"The baby?"

"She's going to have a baby. She's pregnant. And you're the father."

His shoulders had relaxed and he had his hands in his pockets, but now he pulled them out and stiffened right up.

"What?" he said immediately turning away from me.

"It's almost ready to be born." Now he was pacing the sidewalk.

"She doesn't know I'm telling you this."

Over his shoulder, behind him, a face appeared in the leaded glass window. One of Clara's girlfriends, Mona Allegretti.

"Who else knows?" He asked me, like he was choking. He cleared his throat.

"What difference does it make?" I asked him. I knew exactly what difference it made, but I wanted him to feel the weight of his actions, as Mother and Daddy would say.

"Oh, that's Mona," I said to him, waving, as if he didn't know. I looked back at him like, really? Mona?

"Mona? She's here to… we're in a study group together." He waved his hands in front of his face like he was swatting a fly away. "Biology."

"Have you written Clara? If you miss her, you might write? She's up there by herself."

"Why didn't she tell me?"

"Apparently you're too cool," I said. Another pause. A station wagon turned at the street corner and headed towards us. It was Mrs. Feeney, with the kids. "What are you going to do?"

"What am I going to do? I've just found out about this! I haven't even talked to Clara."

"Yeah, you haven't."

"What do you know about anything?" He seemed angry at me. "I have no idea what I am going to do." He stopped pacing and looked at me squarely. "Does anyone else know about this?"

"Madcap and I went to see her. Obviously Daddy and Mother know she's pregnant, but she hasn't said anything about who the father is. We promised not to tell. But I'm not exactly *telling* you. You're the father. You're an integral part of this." It was the first time I had used the word integral in my life. His eyes were looking all over the place, trying to figure it out. "I really think Clara wants to keep her baby," I said. "Since you're the Dad, you could help her. Daddy said he'd kick her out if she kept the baby. Obviously he wants her to give it up."

"Oh, man," he said.

"Yeah," I said. "Exactly."

"I'm not ready to get married."

"That's what Clara thought. She said you want to 'play the field.' She's probably not ready to be a mother, either." He paced around some more in the silence between us. Mona came out onto the porch. The screen door slammed shut behind her. She waved at us from the top step. The car turned into the driveway. Voices of the Feeneys spilled out the windows as they waved.

"Christopher!" Mona called. "Are you coming in? She was all sweetness and smiles. "C'mon! It's your move! Teresa doesn't like chess." Mona walked right up to Christopher and slipped her arm in his. I guess she was his girlfriend now. My stomach felt like a big lead ball.

"Aaa!" he cried out, pushing her way. "I'll be right there. Go on back in." Now he seemed angry at Mona, even though she didn't do anything but open her mouth and put her foot in it. "I'll be right in," he called after her. I could hear the sounds of the car door opening and slamming down the driveway, and the laughter and chatter of the famous fourteen Feeneys, the most devout Catholics in Pasadena. I couldn't help myself; after Mona, all I had left was sarcasm.

"Listen, Annie. It's just between you and me here." He put his arm on my shoulder, like I was his favorite pal.

"Maybe it is, and maybe it isn't," I said, shaking off his arm.

"You can't let anyone else know about this."

"Why not?" I knew perfectly well why not. It would hurt our reputation as much as it would hurt the Feeneys. It would be a scandal to end all scandals. But I said, "Why can't anyone else know? It's a real baby she's having. I'm pretty sure it's going to want to know who its father is."

One of the little Feeneys, maybe as old as the twins, came running up to Christopher. Boy was he cute. Another blonde.

"Just give me some time to think about this." The little Feeney aimed himself at Christopher's legs for a big hug. Christopher leaned down and hugged him back.

"Hey, buddy! How was school?" The kid grinned up at his brother.

"I got a star! In spelling!"

"A star! Wow. Hey, buddy, give me a minute. I'll be right in." He turned his brother by the shoulders and aimed him at the house.

"I have to help her," I said as the little guy turned and ran.

"Well, just sit on it for now." Christopher said forcefully. "I'll think about it."

"Your baby is going to be born any day now. There isn't much time for thinking." I knew I was pressing him hard.

He stopped moving, staring at something over my shoulder. His face changed as a thought occurred to him. He turned to me.

"How do we know it's my baby?" he said, like suddenly he had this idea.

"Clara said it was your baby. She said it doesn't take much. You would know about that."

"What's the proof?" He asked me.

"What's the proof?"

"Yeah, he said, a little calmer now. "Can you prove that I'm the father?"

• • •

Can you prove I'm the father? I just couldn't get it out of my head. *Can you prove I'm the father?!* All the way home, I didn't see anything but the scuffed toe of my black and white saddle shoes. *Stinkin' diaper!* A big black beetle with a shiny back had the misfortune of strolling across the sidewalk in my path at the very moment I came marching and mumbling insults to Christopher Feeney. I immediately stomped on it, hearing the crack and pop of its magnificent back as its insides smeared the soles of my shoes. *Clara is not a liar!* I wiped my shoes on the short dry grass, but it didn't satisfy me. When I saw the pavement smeared with insect legs, I stomped and pounded it until my foot throbbed. *You don't even care about her!* I pressed the ball of my foot into the sidewalk and twisted at the ankle, embedding the black legs onto the cement. *Coward!* I wanted to flatten Christopher Feeney so flat. Then I remembered him sitting up there on the altar, like he was part of what we were striving to be. I wish I had spit at him.

I had to tell someone. When I got to Madcap's room, suddenly I remembered that Clara swore us to secrecy about Christopher Feeney being the dad. Clara made us *promise.* I was such a blabbermouth! How could I say anything to Madcap now? *Gaaaaaa!* I paced around outside the door.

"Madcap," I said forcefully, bursting into her room. She was sitting on her bed, reading under the skylight. She didn't even look up.

"Not now, Annie, I've got to finish this paper."

"Christopher Feeney wants us to prove he's the father of Clara's baby." *Oh, my God, I'm telling her!*

"What? How do you know?"

"I had to tell him." She sat up and looked at me like *How could you?*

"You did not!"

"Clara needs help to keep her baby. He's the obvious

one to help, isn't he? Isn't he supposed to be responsible for that baby?

"You weren't supposed to say anything!"

"I know."

"Now the word is out."

"What do you mean? I only told *him*."

"He can tell anyone he wants that Clara is pregnant, and he's not the father. It takes the heat off him."

Suddenly I remembered about The Hands. I don't know why. Mostly in the daytime, I forget all about it. I've tried telling Wanda. But it's not the kind of thing you can just "mention." Here it was just Madcap and me, alone in her room. I wanted so much to tell her. But the thought of lying in my own bed sound asleep with my pajama top pulled up, I could feel the energy being pulled right out of me, like the air in a balloon zipping out that little hole with that sucking sound. I slowed right down; a heaviness settled in the pit of my stomach.

Where was God anyway? And all the saints we pray to all the time. And the Blessed Mother! Where was she? How could they ignore The Hands? How could they ignore Christopher Feeney being the dad?

In my mind I was yelling at top volume.

That was better. If I just concentrated on that, I could feel a rage sneaking back into me. I needed the anger. It made me determined.

"I have to tell you something." I sat down on Madcap's bed by her feet, like I wasn't going to move any time soon.

"Aaron and I are going out to a Beach Boys concert, " she said. "Can you cover for me?" It was a weeknight, and we weren't allowed to go out. "I'll be studying up here after the rosary." She emphasized the word studying. "Maybe you can distract them if anyone gets too close? And let me in when I get home."

"You have to listen."

"What?"

"There's something I've been wanting to tell you."

"What, Annie?" she said, kicking her leg impatiently.

"To ask you about, I mean."

"What, Annie? What? Ask me." Her impatient manner reminded me of Mother the night after Dominic got lost at Disneyland when I came to tell her about The Hands. Madcap stared at her book, her finger twirling a strand of hair pulled out from the top of her head. She was only paying attention to me in the most distracted way. I changed the subject, without her even knowing.

"Clara's baby's almost due." I paused. "They're gonna force her to sign the papers, and she'll have to give it up."

"They probably will. It's what they do in cases like this."

"Don't you care?"

"Of course I care! But what can we do?"

• • •

That night I decided to set a trap for whoever it was, before going to bed. The only way to stop him was to catch him and embarrass him when everybody else finds out. I turned the metal wastepaper basket upside down in front of the door and closed the door tightly. I tucked my covers snugly across the mattress and then lay down next to the bed with some clothes folded up for a pillow. I figured, when he opens the door, the metal trash can will make a sound and when he gets to my bed, he's gonna have to yank back the covers. So I'm pretty sure I will wake up.

The next thing I knew, I was gradually aware of a sound at the window, a soft knock at the pane. I hopped up from the floor, tapped the pane and waved at Madcap through the window. I pushed the metal wastepaper basket aside as I went to the laundry room to unhook the metal latch for her. She winked at me and tiptoed upstairs.

But once she was up in her room, I heard footsteps. Creaking down the stairs. I got up from my place on the floor as quietly as I could and climbed up on the upside down basket. I crouched in the dark, balancing on the bucket beside the door. My heart was flying around inside my chest.

The door slowly opened. Gee, he sure was quiet. It was almost pitch black, but I could see his shadowy shape next to my bed. I waited, just to see what he would do. He tried to pull the covers back, but they were pretty tight, so he had to rip at them. I leapt out at him from behind. My weight and the surprise of it pushed him over onto my bed, but both of us immediately tumbled off. He was much heavier than I had anticipated, and when I got close to his head, I understood why.

It was John-the-Blimp! My mouth fell open. *Blimp*?

"Annie?" he said. I couldn't see him clearly, but I can recognize that voice even if he only whispers one word. John? Really? All along I had imagined someone

I didn't know. But it really was my own brother. Then I had a thought that halted me in my tracks. O my God, maybe that's why Jesus hasn't been answering my prayers! John is an altar boy! Until recently, a priest in training. He's probably spent more time in church than I have! He's got more Saint points, and one day, he could become a priest. I tried to grasp it. God was trying to get *his* attention.

It was so unfair! But I was on top of Blimp, squeezing my legs around him as tightly as I could. I grabbed his ear and twisted.

"What are you doing in my room, Blimp? Get the hell out of here and don't ever come back!" I had never said "hell" before in my whole life. My brother was many pounds heavier than I was. He sat up and I fell off with a thud onto the floor.

"Get out of my bedroom! Don't you ever come in here again!" *Why didn't I think of this sooner?* I heard Rosie and Jeannie rustling awake as John turned towards the door. I tore after him.

"I'll get you!" I yelled at him with all my might as he rounded the corner to take the stairs. I managed to grab him around the waist, but I couldn't pull him down. At the bottom of the stairs, we both flailed and fumbled at each other, but he was bigger than me, and one swing of his arm flattened me to the ground. I got up again, racing up after him two steps at a time. At the top, I tackled his feet again and he went down. He kicked wildly, smashing my chin, then scrambled up into his room, slamming the door. I pounded on it and pounded on it. "What were you doing in my bedroom?!" I was screaming as loudly as I could. I wanted to wake up the dead.

Things began to come to life all over the house.

CHAPTER 30
PERFECTLY WELL

December 6 – Dear Blessed Mother, Here's the question. Where have you been?! I'm under siege here. Last night I found out who had been coming into my room at night and feeling me up. If you didn't already know, you'd never believe who. The problem is, he got out of it. He said he heard a noise, and then I mistook him for a robber. (!!!) No wonder I was freaked out, he said. He sounded so sincere, like he was telling the truth. Like he was trying to protect me. He really poured it on, and guess who Mother and Daddy wanted to believe? Then, I suppose logically, I got in trouble for waking everybody up. "You're so dramatic, Annie, now go back to bed." You know what? I DON'T CARE! If he comes back in, I'll bite his hands off.

The next day was Friday December 6th. Only one more school day. My chin was swollen and bruised, but I already knew the bus schedule up to Ventura. I passed Teresa Feeney in the yard before the first bell. It was weird. She had been so friendly. But it was right back to no eye contact, Teresa floating by like she was on display, haughty and perfect.

I watched the hands of the clock above the door before recess, swinging my crossed leg under my desk. Wanda crowded me when the class was dismissed.

"Annie! C'mere." I followed her out of the classroom

to a corner of the schoolyard where the two chain link fences met. There was a game of kick ball going on in front of us, so at first I had a hard time understanding what she said. There was so much screaming and cheering going on. I could tell something was wrong because Wanda was biting the skin on her hands.

"Why didn't you tell me about Clara?" She asked, like she was offended. "I'm your best friend." She was gnawing on her gun finger, making bite marks.

"Why didn't you invite me to go to Sew Easy with Teresa Feeney?"

"I called you. Buddy answered the phone. Obviously he didn't give you the message."

"What about Clara?" I asked, knowing perfectly well.

"You know," she said.

"What about Clara, Wanda?" She was irritating me, insisting. Like she knew. She took her finger out of her mouth.

"Annie! You know all about Clara! She's your sister. She's not on a retreat, she's pregnant." I stared at her as the forbidden words came out of her mouth. I never told Wanda about Clara because it had been really important that no one else knew anything about Clara's pregnancy. Now, Wanda was whispering about it to me. In the schoolyard! There was only one person who could have let the word out.

"Who told you?" I asked her.

"You told Teresa before you told me! I was at her house yesterday after you came to visit. That's all we talked about." Now Wanda started on the inside tips of all her fingers. She bit hard.

"I never told Teresa!" I protested, but my mind was racing all over the place. The only person who could have told Teresa was her own brother, Christopher. Madcap was right; he was already blabbering.

"Teresa said you told her," Wanda repeated, disappointed, like our friendship was on the line. "Why didn't you tell me first?" She was biting the plump flesh on the back of her thumb.

"I would have told you first, but we had to keep it a secret. Really, Wanda. An absolute secret. So Clara could come back to school. Don't be upset. It was Clara's reputation I was trying to preserve."

"So you thought I couldn't keep a secret?" Wanda yelled at me. "You thought Teresa could keep a secret? Well let me tell you this Annie Shea, your sister's reputation is ruined. Teresa and I were talking about it. She said there are three guys who could be the father." I could feel myself getting hot.

"You listen to me, Wanda Nowakowski!" I yelled at her. "I did not tell Teresa Feeney, I told Christopher Feeney, because he's the father."

"Christopher Feeney?" She said, completely taken aback. She looked down at her feet, recovering. "Well, there's some other story going around the school, then. Everyone is whispering about it." Wanda turned into the game of kickball, almost getting hit by the ball that had just been liberated by Todd Zimmerman's shoe.

"Come back here, Wanda Nowakowski!" As I saw her run away from me, her ducktail looked sassy, like it was making fun of me. So I charged her, grabbing her around the waist and toppling her to the ground. We rolled over each other, scraping bare skin against concrete; I couldn't hurt her enough. Wanda is heavier, but I was madder so I socked her a few times, once in the back and once in the arm, and I got hit, too, and I bit her and scraped her with my fingernails and she had me pinned down and we heard the voices around us and finally Sister Everista grabbed me by the back of my shirt collar and yanked me off of Wanda just as I was about to punch her in the face.

"Girls!" She said in a gravelly voice and I thought, *Yeah, we're girls. So what of it?*

CHAPTER 31
EVERY SMALL CREATURE

Dear Blessed Mother. So I guess you've decided not to get involved.

Wanda and I got sent to the Principal's office, but for once, I didn't cooperate. I didn't tell them anything about why we were fighting; it was none of their business. We were both crying and neither of us wanted to make it any worse. By the time we were sent home, it was already noon.

I usually walk home from school, and by the time I opened the back door, it was quiet in the house. Everyone was at school, and the stillness gave the afternoon a sad quality. I listened to the sounds of the day that I normally don't hear at all: a dishwasher sloshing in kitchen in the distance, a bird fluttering around outside my window on the branches of the bougainvillea. Jude and the twins must have been napping in their beds.

I tiptoed down the hall. Mother was having her nap. Either that or she just didn't get up this morning at all. I peeked through her door. The room was dark. I could hear her breathing. So I got my $11.65 from my top drawer and my heavy sweater and quietly went up the steps, straight into Paul's room. Because I was his PX last year, I knew where he kept everything, and

I knew right where the $26 probably was. I hoped he hadn't spent it yet. I was right. It was in the corner of his bookshelf behind some science fiction paper backs, in a wooden box with some keys. The bills were stiff and new, folded up. I counted it and left $1 for his contribution to the sale of the Ambassador. I had never stolen anything before in my life. But at the same time, it was my money. Daddy made the wrong decision giving it to Paul. Daddy made the wrong decision banning Clara to the convent. Wanda's dad wanted to buy the car from me. Wanda used to be my best friend. Everything was totally out of control. I was going to take that money for Clara and no one was going to stop me. I stuffed it into my pocket. Maybe I was on the path to sin, and maybe Daddy was going to belt the living daylights out of me, but I didn't care. The other path just seemed wrong to me. Wrong, wrong, wrong. In every way.

I went back to Mother's room one last time. Not that I wanted to tell her where I was going. I wanted to return the photograph of her and the disappeared baby, and I just wanted to know how she could do it, going along with Daddy about keeping Clara up at the Mission. Clara didn't want to be up there, and they were forcing her. I peeked in. Mother was sitting at the side of her bed, staring at the floor.

"I'm getting up," she said, as if she were talking to Daddy. "I'll be right out to get going on the dinner. Just give me a minute here."

"Mom?" I said. "It's Annie. I don't want to bother you. I just wanted to ask you a question." She didn't answer me. "Just one question." I said.

"I have a migraine, Annie." She said, unmoved.

"Mom, what happened to your first baby?" *What was I doing? How could my voice be forming these words?* "The one that disappeared?" I reached my hand out to her with the photograph. "You dropped this picture of you in the hospital holding a baby. At Cardinal Stefanucci's funeral when your missal fell apart."

Mother looked over at me quickly. My hand was still stretched towards her. She grabbed the photograph out of my hand and looked deeply into it like she was trying to read the fine print. She took a breath in, and my heart beat fast, like a hamster on the wheel. Immediately I wished I hadn't said anything.

"Leave me alone," she said in a clipped tone, straightening up. I heard the way she said that. It twisted something inside me. I pressed her further.

"I just don't see how you can make Clara stay up there."

But Mother was ignoring me. Her head was bent over the photograph, like she was the only person in the universe. This was one of the things that Mother did. She turned the other way, like I wasn't even there. She was so practiced at this, and I was so tired of it. She was deliberately not hearing me! I knew she heard me, I knew she was ignoring me, and I felt like screaming my head off.

"Why are you and Daddy forcing Clara to give up her baby?" I could hear my voice going up in volume. "It's so mean! Clara wants to keep her baby!"

I was still angry about Christopher Feeney, but I felt like taking it out on Mom. She was such a target, sitting in the dark. The outrageous words had tumbled out of my mouth, and now I was like a speeding train with no brakes. "Mother," I said, pushing the knife in, "Did Daddy make you give up your February, 1945 baby, like he's making Clara give up hers?" I felt cruel and powerful, and I knew this would get her. She raised her voice, a tone I recognized from just before getting spanked. This time, I wasn't scared at all. She stood up.

"You have no idea what you're talking about!"

But I knew the photograph was the only clue left about that baby. She and Daddy had hidden the whole thing, like the baby didn't even exist.

"You're trying to hide Clara's baby, just like you covered up your disappeared baby. It's a real baby! You can't make it just go away forever!"

"This is none of your business, Annie." She said, pushing herself up from the bed.

"You say a new baby means there is more love to go around? How can that be? When that baby gets given away to a stranger, where's the love in that?"

"Annie!" she snapped at me, her voice even louder. "That baby could ruin Clara's life. She hasn't even graduated from high school! She can't afford to raise it."

"Why should she have to? Why can't she just move in with us? That baby is just one more tiny mouth to feed. You were going to have another baby yourself, until the miscarriage—you weren't worried about how big its mouth was."

I stood in the doorway, waiting for another touché phrase to leap into my mind. Mother came right up to me, gathering strength into her body. I could almost see her straighten up from inside. I was just about as tall as she was. I pushed my shoulders back and tried to grow.

"Get out of here, Annie," she said firmly. "Before you say something you're going to regret."

"You just pump 'em out so Daddy can brag about how great he is to have so many kids!" I blurted. Instantly, her hand flew at me; I felt a sharp pain across my cheek.

"Don't you ever talk to me this way!" she said, and pushed past me out of the room.

I stomped out of her bedroom like a two-year-old, slobbering and sobbing, my face beet red, my chest heaving. Mother had never slapped me before, but at least she heard what I said. The fight had given me power; I walked as fast as I could down the block to the corner and turned right, up Orange Grove Boulevard. Finally, I was running away from home! I walked quickly so as not to lose my nerve.

It took about a half hour to get to the Greyhound bus station at the pace I was going, and all the way, I stared down at my feet on the sidewalk, having imaginary conversations with mother where I just shut her down with cutting phrases and witty retorts. I was the poster kid for the debating team, until a creeping feeling of remorse seeped into my consciousness, for what I had said. Suddenly small things, like how pale Mother looked and the tone of her desperate sigh came back to me. *You have no idea what you're talking about,* rang in my head. Why wouldn't she tell me about that disappeared baby? Maybe it wasn't hers after all. Or maybe it died.

But by that time I had already bought my ticket and boarded the bus. I sat in my high-backed seat by the large window for a long time as the bus went on the freeways and stopped in the towns on the way to Ventura. For some reason I noticed the small creatures hanging around the stations, like birds, hopping around. A lady walked up the aisle holding a box with a handle, and there was an animal in it. She sat across from me. Once the bus started up again she took a dog out of its cage. It was the strangest looking creature, really small and skinny and shaved to within an inch of its life, with grey and pink skin and bangs that hung over its face between its pointed ears. It sat on the lady's lap, shivering, and I instantly liked it even though it was making a small rumbling sound in its throat like it was going to erupt into a sharp bark. I saw a couple of mangy kittens at one stop, hanging out in the weeds and prancing on things. In Ventura, big, white seagulls dipped on the breeze and that's when I had the thought that before each being comes into the world, its number one job is to get born. A lot of people and creatures seem extremely desperate to get born. We're all pretty desperate in our family, and our Mother was willing. So birth is probably something that's not super complicated, when you have those two factors lined up—desperation and willingness—because a lot of people and creatures have gotten through it.

In order for us to be here, millions of years later.

CHAPTER 32
THE BUS

Dear God the Father. Who's left up there? I can't seem to reach anyone.

When I stepped off the bus in Ventura, the air was cooler and I could smell the salt from the ocean. There was a big white wall clock over the door. 4:00. It was Friday, December 6th, the beginning of the weekend. I walked to the Mission and went directly to the reception desk. One of the nuns told me that Clara was probably at the library. So I got directions, left the convent and walked a couple blocks over there.

Clara was surprised to see me, and I was exceptionally glad to see her. We hugged each other like I was going to the electric chair and this was our last embrace.

"How's the baby, Clara?"

"Shhhh," she shushed me, motioning around her, "We're in a library."

"Sorry," I said, lowering my voice. "Is it coming soon?" I put my hands on her big belly. It was very firm.

"I'm feeling some contractions," she whispered. "I've had them off and on for about five days."

"Has anyone tried to get you to sign the papers yet?"

"Here, I'm having one now!" She grabbed my

hand and put it on her belly. It felt like her belly was vibrating, under the skin. She took a breath in and exhaled. We both stood there, listening with our hands, until it stopped.

"Did you find any one of the girls at the Mission who is going to keep her baby?"

"Annie, the strangest thing. It was staring me in the face. Everyone is here because they are giving up their baby."

"Oh, right."

"They're here so no one will know back home. Otherwise, why be separated from your family at a time like this?"

"That's what I keep thinking." But really, I was thinking how everyone back home knows all about Clara now, because I blabbed to Christopher Feeney.

"They talk to me about adoption every day," she said. "I just nod and ignore them."

"But what are you going to do?"

"I'm not sure. I'm just glad you're here."

"I brought you some money. So you can go to the Y afterwards." I reached into my pocket and pulled out $33. "Sorry, I had to use some of it for the bus."

"Annie," she said, "This is so sweet of you. Really. But I can't take it," she said, pressing the bills into my palm. How are you going to get back home in time?"

"I'm not going back."

"Where are you going to stay?"

"I came here to be with you when you have the baby. So they can't take it away from you."

"They won't let anyone in the labor room except the doctors and nurses. Annie, does anyone know you're here?"

"I got kicked out of school."

"What happened?" she said, sounding like Mother does when I can't thread the sewing machine needle. I started to cry right away. Clara put her arms around me and patted my head. That made it worse. I couldn't stop blubbering. Of course I had to think about why I got kicked out of school, namely, the fight between me and Wanda, which was caused by the fact that Christopher Feeney told his sister Teresa that Clara was pregnant, which was caused by the fact that I told Christopher Feeney that he was the father of Clara's baby. Which Clara made me promise I'd never do. Even though I meant well. The road to hell really is paved with good intentions.

Clara had no idea, but she kept being understanding. It felt so good to have someone hold me and sympathize with me.

"You're such a good student," she said, curling my hair around my ear, like Mother does.

"I was planning on coming up here anyway, ever since your second letter." I tried to stop sobbing, but sucked in the air, three gulps in a row, like the little kids do when they are pathetically inconsolable.

"How could you, of all people, get kicked out of school?"

"I got into a fight with Wanda." When I said that, I could feel a resolve that straightened me right out. It was like the hot feeling when Daddy belted me in front of everyone. I was so angry about what Wanda was doing to Clara's reputation, and how she betrayed all of us, that I got steely. I stopped crying.

"She's your best friend, isn't she?" Clara remembered.

"She used to be."

"Annie, what if I don't have the baby right away? How can you stay here?" She stopped me in my tracks with that question. I hadn't even thought about it.

"Can I stay in your room? There was an extra bed in there."

"The nuns won't let you. I'm pretty sure. They'll call Mother and Daddy. Besides, I have a new roommate."

"Maybe the Y?"

"Oh, here feel this. It's happening again." I held her belly with both hands. This time I could feel movement under her skin all over the big beach ball. She stared straight ahead, almost like I wasn't there. Her mouth was slightly open and she was sort of panting, like she was a dog.

"Wow, that one was stronger!" She enthused, after it was over.

"It's pretty amazing how we all get born, isn't it?" I said, sounding like I could give a lecture on it. Even though the only experience I had was *being* born.

"These early contractions are called 'Braxton Hicks' contractions."

"What does it feel like?"

"When it gets stronger, it's like a cramp, but right now it's just like a muscle moving. They help prepare the body for labor. Look at this," she said, pointing to a black and white drawing in a book with a lot of words. "That's the uterus. It's the strongest muscle in the whole body. Isn't that amazing? But it makes sense. That's what pushes the baby out. This big muscle just squeezing until the baby gets expelled." She started gathering her books and pens.

We took a walk over to the hospital, a few blocks away. I'm not sure if we were headed there on purpose, or if we just ended up there. We strolled through the cemetery with a view of the Pacific Ocean. The bright green grass stretched for an entire city block and sloped down the hill, dappled by the shade of sprawling oak trees. We stepped around the occasional plaques here and there on the lawn. It seemed odd that Clara, who was bringing a new baby into the world, was walking over top of the graves of people long turned to dust. Every few minutes or so we stopped, and she let another one of these Hicks contractions go through her. We came to a bus stop and she sat down for one of them. By the time we got to the hospital, she was breathing very deliberately, with her mouth open.

"I think the baby is coming," she said. She squeezed my hand. I squeezed back. I looked at her. She smiled at me and winked.

"How long do you think it will take?" I asked her.

"It's going to take as long as it's going to take. Sometimes it goes on for like, 24 hours, or even more."

"I wonder if we should check into the hospital, now that we're here?" I said, "We don't have to worry about the priest making you sign the papers, do we? That would have already happened back at the Mission, right?"

"Some of the mothers are forced to sign the papers right after the baby is born."

"Right."

"I can't pay for the hospital myself, and it's all been

arranged through the Sisters of Saint Isabella. So if I check into the hospital, they'll be notified."

"If I'm there, they can't force you."

"They won't let you in the labor room."

"Well, I'll be right outside the door. Just remember that." We were in the lobby of the hospital. Clara sat down on a soft chair. I could see she was having another contraction.

"Tell them you have to ask your sister first."

"I don't want to sign in," Clara said, almost like she was mad at me. "If I can get through this birth without letting them drug me to sleep, I won't let them take my baby."

"Tell them you don't want any drugs."

"Bee Bee said you're lying on your back with your legs up and nothing on your bottom."

"Don't worry about nothing on your bottom," I reassured her. "Bitty didn't have anything on her bottom. You have to let the baby out, and it can't come out if there are underpants in the way."

"I'm not worried about nothing on my bottom. Bee Bee said they tied her arms to the bed. And they covered her face and she had to breathe into a mask."

"Oh."

"The next thing she knew, she was waking up and they were putting drops in her baby's eyes across the room. Then a nurse took her baby away."

"And she never saw her again," I said.

"Well, just once, in the nursery," Clara reminded me. I didn't say anything. I couldn't tell her, even now, that I was the only one who saw Lily.

"Why are we even here right now?" I said. "This is

a hospital."

"Good question," she said. "Let's get out of here."

"Where to?"

"We could sit in the park," she suggested.

"It's almost dark, and there's no one around," it occurred to me. "We need people around."

"What for?"

"In case we need help. Isn't that why you go to the hospital?" I didn't know much about birth, and that was my back-up plan: other people who knew more than I did.

"Listen Annie, I'm not going to the hospital. Women never used to go to the hospital. A hundred years ago, no one went. Women had their babies in the fields."

"Yeah, even nowadays, babies are born in cars by accident. For instance."

"For thousands of years," she said, her voice louder than I would have preferred, "every single baby was not born in a hospital. Birth is a force. That's how come we're all here today, every single person on the earth. Not because of hospitals."

I couldn't figure it out. Cats don't go to the hospital, and they have seven kittens at a time. But humans? They only have one at a time, unless there's twins. Maybe they're afraid the baby might get stuck. Even though I saw Bitty do it, it was still hard to imagine a human baby's head coming out the third hole. I didn't know what to say. I just stared at her.

"I'm not going to the hospital, Annie. We have to find another plan."

"Could we at least be in a place where there's people

around?"

"The library?"

"It closes."

Clara got up. I followed her to the sidewalk. Something splashed on my leg. I looked down. The entire sidewalk around us was wet. It was almost a puddle.

"My water broke," she said. She sounded excited.

"What water?"

"Now the baby can come out." We were standing in front of the bus stop and a stinker wheezed up in front of us and stopped right in front of Clara. The doors flapped open and we were enveloped with the diesel that poured out of the pipe at the back.

"C'mon, she said, there are people on the bus! We could ride the bus." She hoisted herself up the steep bus steps and stood at the top, face to face with the driver. Behind her, I dug into my bag. Clara reached into her pocket and produced a one-dollar bill. The driver, sitting in his cage of shiny steel poles said,

"You look like you're just about ready to burst."

Clara shrugged, smiling. "Any minute, now, I guess. But not yet!" She smiled up at the bus driver and he threw his head back in a gesture which said, *Get on the bus.*

"It's on me," he said. "Where are you going?"

"I'm going where this bus goes," Clara announced.

"This is just a local sputterer," he said, "we take the high roads of Ventura. Up Foothill all the way out to Kimball. And back."

"Perfect!" Clara squealed. "We'll just go for a ride, then."

I had a good look at the bus driver as I ascended the steep bus stairs. (Usually ascend would be a big vocabulary word, but since I'm Catholic, I know words like "ascension" and "conception" and "immaculate" like I know the back of my hand.) He had deep brown eyes and black hair and his skin was as tan as the shell of a coconut. His badge said Santiago. He had a friendly paunch, but it was his voice that sounded reasonable and kind.

"You can sit right up front if you want, in the handicapped seats, M'aam."

A couple of passengers stood and offered Clara their seat. But Clara waddled in front of me, holding onto the metal backs of the seats as she made her way to the back of the bus. Passengers overflowed out of the seats, and of course their eyes popped at Clara. On a bus, it's forced staring when someone comes up the aisle. There's nothing else to look at. Santiago kept idling the bus until Clara reached the bench over the motor and sat down. I was behind her and I could see her dress was drenched, from the water just broken on the sidewalk. At the back, she sat right on that wet dress, smack dab in the middle of the cushions with her legs slightly apart, and her arms holding the two metal bars on the seats in front on either side. I positioned myself in one of those seats where I had a good view of the bus if I looked to my left, and a good view of Clara if I looked to my right.

"Clara," I said. But she was in the middle of a contraction, breathing out through her mouth.

"Annie," she said after she came out of that one. "I could be in labor right now."

I looked at Santiago. Our eyes met in the rearview mirror.

"I'm excited."

"Me, too," I said.

"Thank you for being with me."

"Is there anything I can do?" But I knew there wasn't. Bitty did it all when her babies had to come. In the case of birth, it's all up to the mother.

We moved forward and jerked back for maybe two hours like that in the back of that bus through the streets of Ventura, past the neat homes and small lawns, seeing everything through big, smeared windows and the smell of diesel and the sound of grinding gears making us raise our voices whenever we wanted to talk and the rumbling of the motor underneath our seats. At the top of Foothill we looked out over the city, the sun a dimming orange glow on the horizon. It was almost dark. The streetlights had come on.

"Clara," I said again. "Do you still like Christopher Feeney?"

"Oh, Annie."

"Because you shouldn't."

"You're sweet, Annie."

"He should be so lucky to have you."

"You can't help how you feel about someone."

"Stop feeling anything about him. He's not good for you."

"I can't decide if I want to tell him. When, eventually, he sees the baby." She opened her mouth and exhaled with a deep sound. Luckily the motor drowned it out.

Jeez! I thought. *Why did I bring up Christopher*

309

Feeney?

Just outside the hospital, a young mother with long dark hair stepped up onto the bus. She had her baby tied around the front of her with a cloth, like a kangaroo. She saw Clara right away and sat down next to us.

We both looked at the mother longingly. She probably had a husband and was going home to him now.

"Hello," she said to Clara.

"Hi," Clara said. I looked over at her. A shimmer of sweat covered her neck and face. Her legs were still spread apart in the most unladylike position, but Clara wasn't the least bit self-conscious.

"You're due then?" The mother said. The baby was sound asleep right up against her chest. Clara nodded.

"Are you... can you feel it coming already?"

"I'm having Braxton Hicks."

"Wow, you just missed the hospital stop. Do you want me to... The driver would probably stop for you. I could just tell him you're..." This lady surprised me. She was so demure and shy looking. The last thing I would have guessed she'd do would be tell a bus driver to stop and go back.

"No, no. I'm doing fine," Clara protested. "Did you have a boy or a girl?"

"A girl," the mother said, looking extremely proud of herself. "Marissa."

"Congratulations," Clara said. "She's beautiful."

"Yeah, way to go," I said. I held my thumb up.

"Did you give birth at this hospital?" Clara asked.

"No, we were in Port Hueneme. At the naval

hospital there."

Oh, so she's a Navy wife, I thought. Lucky her. With a Navy husband, who loves her and can provide for her. And probably a really cute dog. Maybe a Daschund. I like those.

"How was it?" Clara said right away. And I thought, what is a bashful lady like that going to say about the birth of her daughter? She's gonna say "fine."

"I don't remember much," the bashful lady said. "I was in labor, like you are. It seemed like the baby was going to be born. Then they gave me Twilight Sleep. When I woke up my little girl was already born!" She seemed pleased with that.

It surprised me. I wanted to know everything about what it was like, but what was there to ask? They had erased her baby's birth from her mind for her whole life. Anyway, it wasn't exactly casual conversation, what really goes on during the birth of a baby. It's another one of those secrets that everybody knows about, but nobody talks about.

I looked at the mother's pretty face. She had thick lips with dark red lipstick. I could see the slight trace of a bruise on her cheek under the pancake makeup. Maybe she walked into a door in the middle of the night when the baby needed a bottle and she was on the way to the kitchen.

"How old is your baby?" I finally asked. It was a pretty safe question.

"Three months," she said, stroking her baby's head.

Wow, three months, I thought. *If we could just get through this birth. If I could just see Clara signing the birth certificate. If the baby woud just come out healthy*

311

and not die, like Mother's did. If only we were at three months already.

"You'll be going to the hospital soon, won't you?" she said to Clara, as she gathered her bag and stood up. She looked worried, and I wasn't sure what was going on.

Clara said, "I don't want to go to the hospital. At least not yet." So we waved. *Have a nice life,* I beamed at Baby Marissa, *with your own Mom and Dad.* Instead of going out the back door, Shy Mama walked up to the front of the bus and said something to Santiago. He looked in the rear view mirror and our eyes met. Then she got off the bus at the top of Foothill with a bunch of other passengers, probably on their way to dinner. Suddenly, I was hungry.

"Clara, you want something to eat?" I asked.

But she had gone somewhere, inside herself, far away. Even though she was right next to me, it was as if I was a piece of furniture she could see out of the corner of her eye; she knew I was there and I had my function, but that was it. We rode together in silence. At the next stop, the bus driver put on the brake and walked to the back, straight to Clara. By this time, Clara was normal again, smiling.

"How are you two doing back here?" He said cheerfully, but I could see concern in his eyes. He was checking us out, trying to decide something. I felt the same way: confusion, urgency, and yet the need to act normal, like there's nothing out of the ordinary.

"We are doing great!" Clara smiled at him confidently.

"You just let me know," he said, and returned to the

driver's seat.

"Thanks, Santiago," I said heartily. And then a question occurred to me. *Is it possible to die at birth?*

I could sense the tiniest feeling in my stomach that had nothing to do with eating. I didn't want the feeling to grow at all. In Clara's presence I had been safe, but now I could see she needed me to be her eyes and ears. It was something I began to realize. I had been counting on her to tell me when we should get off the bus. I didn't know what she had in mind. Did she think that having the baby on the bus would be okay? Suddenly I felt like I needed to protect her. How could she think straight with those contractions going on all the time? Maybe we should go in. Just in case. The bus was on the way back to the street in front of the hospital. I didn't know what to do. In our case, the hospital was a dangerous place. They could steal the baby. They knew what they were doing and they had it all worked out.

"Clara," I said. "Do you think we should go in now? The hospital is coming up. It's the next stop." It was as if she could barely hear me. Like we were on opposite sides of the same pasture that extended across the horizon with mountains in the background. When she heard me, she heard me from far away. Just then she cried out, like she had been startled out of a scary dream. I panicked and pulled the line that told the bus driver to get off at the next stop. Santiago scanned the mirror. I was so glad that I could motion for him to come. He slowed immediately, but it seemed like forever before the bus stopped. Right outside the hospital, Santiago put the brake and the flashers on and jumped down off his seat. Then he ran to the back.

He was a big man, clomping down the skinny aisle, pushing his girth through the few passengers who were left in their seats.

"Here," he said, grabbing ahold of Clara. They struggled down the steps. At the sidewalk, she held Santiago around the neck and leaned onto him heavily, staring at no one, her body relaxed against him as another contraction came and went.

"I'll go get someone," I offered. Now I was afraid. My heart was beating in my throat as I ran through the double glass doors at the entrance to the hospital. At the reception desk, a nurse looked up at me. She had a wide face and a stern look. She reminded me of that famous photo of Florence Nightingale, a smart woman and a brave nurse I admired from history. In the photo, she stared right at you like she never learned to blink.

"It's my sister," I said trying to keep my voice calm. "I think she's having her baby now." By this time Santiago had brought her in, draped over his shoulder. Someone came out with a wheelchair and tried to sit Clara down in the chair. But Clara wanted to stand. Santiago shook her hand and waved at me and ran back to his bus like there was a barking bloodhound at those big feet.

"Thank you, Santiago!" I called after him. Then I remembered what Clara had told me about registering with the Sisters of Saint Isabella.

"I'll have to register her," the nurse said, as if reading my mind.

"I can do that for her," I offered. "She's right in the middle of labor, I think." I looked over at Clara. She was holding onto the back of the wheelchair for support. Her eyes were all glazed over. Nightingale's expression didn't change. In all the pictures taken in the 1800's, people were not reminded to smile.

"I'll need her signature," she said.

"I can sign for her." I cleared my throat, trying to sound official. "I'm her sister."

"No, she'll have to sign for herself."

"What for?"

"To admit her. It's the procedure."

"Oh," I said. "What if she was unconscious when she was admitted? How would you get her signature?"

"She's not unconscious."

"Right." So then she asked who would be responsible for the costs of Clara's stay, and so then I had to admit she had been living at The Mission with the Sisters. Nightingale picked up the phone and dialed a number by heart.

"I have a young mother here who is checking in. She could be in labor already." A pause as she listened.

"What's the name?" the nurse asked me directly, holding the phone to her ear.

"Clara Kathleen Shea," I said feeling an odd sense of pride as I heard my sister's name out loud in the air.

"Clara Shea," Nightingale said into the phone. "Is she one of yours?" She nodded and wrote something down on the pad, and hung up. I watched her carefully as she filled out an empty form.

"What are you staring at?" Nightingale said without looking up.

You. I thought silently. No one could be trusted. I recognized the same skepticism I felt when I thought Aaron Solomon might have been a mass murderer.

"What's her birthday?" The nurse asked.

"February 2ⁿᵈ," I said.

"What year?"

I had to ask Clara, so I walked over to her by the wheelchair.

"I don't want to be here, Annie. I was doing just fine on the bus. Why did you bring me in?" When she said that, I felt a rushing sensation inside me, like a surge of water splashing over the rocks at a waterfall. I was in the middle of the ocean and the waves were breaking over my head in huge swells. I had to make sure I got enough air. Maybe I made the wrong decision on the bus. Now that we were here at the hospital, they could put her to sleep just like that. I had to make sure they didn't tie her down. I had to swim or else we would both drown.

"Mother always went to the hospital," I said. It was the last thought I had before I pulled the line on the bus to stop. Maybe there was a good reason that Mother felt better in the hospital.

"Mother is married, Annie. They didn't want her babies."

CHAPTER 33
THE HOSPITAL

Dear Saint Clare, Your namesake is going to become a mother any minute now. This is an emergency and I'm officially casting myself at your feet. I need some help here, but I think Jesus and Mary might have gone on vacation.

"I'll look out for you, Clara, I promise. Tell them you don't want the drug." Just then another contraction grabbed a hold of her and she fell down onto her knees. I knelt down next to her.

"Right now, they just need the year of your birth so they can register you," I said. Clara got up off her knees. She exhaled.

"1946. I'm almost 18." That was her signal to me. I had to be a strong swimmer for both of us.

Nightingale brought the form out to Clara, but I insisted on reading it first. It had Clara's name, birth date, doctor's initials and the Mission's address. Under "Parent/Guardian" it said, "The Sisters of Saint Isabella." There was nothing on the paper that said "I give up my baby for adoption."

"She's keeping her baby," I said to the nurse, as she handed the paper to Clara to sign. "So she won't sign this if it says anything about adoption." The nurse looked at me, and a thought crossed her face. But it was a thought, and thoughts are silent.

"If you just sign the paper," the nurse said directly to Clara, "we can bring you in and take care of you."

"It doesn't say anything about giving up your baby for adoption," I told Clara. "I read it carefully; I think it's safe to sign. Maybe you should write that in." So Clara wrote, "I am keeping my baby. I don't want to put it up for adoption." She underlined that and signed the paper.

Nightingale went back to her desk. She came back with a thin band in plastic that she fastened around Clara's wrist. I remembered that, from when Mother came home from the hospital. Usually when the baby came home in Mother's arms, the baby had a bracelet, too, made out of beads that spelled "Baby Girl Shea." I guess the hospital gets really busy so people forget their names or something. However, it was a small thing that had the effect of comforting me a little. At least Clara's name would not be lost here. And when the baby came, I would have to make sure they put the same name on the baby's arm.

Another nurse grabbed hold of the wheelchair. She smiled at Clara, and for some reason Clara sat down. Then she started pushing Clara down the hall.

"You can wait out here," the nurse said to me. "I'll take her now."

"I want her with me," Clara managed to say, straining her head around and up to the nurse behind her.

"They won't let anyone in the labor room," the nurse said.

"I know that," Clara said. "I don't care. I want her

with me."

"She can come along while we get you prepped," the nurse said. We went into a small room, and the nurse told Clara to take off her clothes and put on a yellow gown with ties at the back. Then the nurse went out of the room. It was the same kind of gown that Mutter Man was wearing when he fell over and crashed his pole at this very hospital, when we were all here to see Bee Bee. I helped Clara take her clothes off. When her huge stomach was bare it seemed to fill up the small space we were in. I had to touch it. It was so firm. I tried to imagine where the baby was, but it just seemed like a beach ball to me. I was simply amazed at how much human flesh can stretch.

When I leaned over to pick up Clara's pants, I caught a glimpse of her hair, down there, underneath her baby belly. Even though Clara was a brunette, down there, her hair was a dark red. It was weird. For the first time in my life, I felt proud of my red hair.

The nurse came back in the room. She seemed sweet in comparison to Nightingale. She helped Clara get up on the high padded table and eased her onto her back. On either side of the table at the end, two small metal things shaped like a basket on a stick seemed to be standing watch.

"Is this where she's having the baby?" I asked.

"No, we're just going to examine her and prep her for the labor room."

"Are you our nurse?" I asked.

"Well I am your nurse for the next few minutes, at least," she answered. "We're changing shifts and it's time for me to go home." So I named this nurse Nice Nurse, since she was so sweet and I wouldn't be required to remember her name.

"Move your body down to the end of the bed and put your feet in the stirrups, honey," she said with gentleness in her voice.

Stirrups! I thought. *What an odd name for something that has to do with a baby being born.*

As soon as the doctor came in, there was a flurry of activity. Clara was moved onto a bed with wheels and taken to the labor room.

Everything had been going so quickly when we were on the bus, and all of a sudden, it seemed to slow right down. Clara was hurting; I could overhear her in the labor room. I was standing outside the door. Anyone in the whole hospital could hear her; I was sure of it.

"I don't want Twilight Sleep!" she yelled from a deep voice that I never heard before. Then she was quiet. A minute went by. I looked through the rubber crack in the door. All I could see were the backs of the white jackets worn by the attendants. Even though I couldn't see her, I knew Clara was in here, lying on her back, her legs spread apart, her feet up in the air. They were moving over her. Then I heard her again.

"Get your hands off me!" She yelled. I heard more scurrying and straining. The doctors and nurses always spoke to each other quietly, and so from my vantage point, Clara, in contrast, seemed out of control.

Why can't she just ask them nicely? I heard myself thinking. She sounded like she was crazy, even to me.

I felt sick to my stomach. It was my fault for bringing her here. I should have taken her out when Nice Nurse began to soap up her red hair.

"Hair is not sterile," Nice Nurse had said. "Don't worry, it's just the usual procedure." I could see the shaver over there and we both knew what she was planning to do. It seemed like the most humiliating thing that anyone could do to Clara at this moment. I kept seeing Bitty licking the heads of her kittens, with her leg way over her head. I couldn't imagine how shaving might figure in to that. I also knew from having shaved off my own hairs when they first surprised me by growing in down there that shaved hairs are hard and prickly and itchy when they grow back. In spite of this, neither of us stopped the nurse from shaving Clara.

The worst thing was, suddenly I couldn't muster the courage to do anything other than what they wanted, and I wasn't sure it was good for Clara. Once I gave in to signing Clara in, once Clara gave in to being pushed in the wheelchair, once I didn't say anything when they shaved her, it became more and more difficult to assert myself on her behalf.

With each usual procedure, the nurses and the doctors became more and more the authority I was used to obeying. Instead, when a nurse escorted me to the waiting room, I meekly followed her. I sat down next to the one dad there, who was barely able to keep his head up, holding a pack of cigars in his lap.

I sat there for about 10 seconds watching the guy drool onto the lapel of his suit. I knew in my heart that my promise to Clara was the only thing left about me that was still true. I snuck back down the hall to the labor room when no one was looking, and I managed to stay there for a long time, wincing whenever Clara moaned or gritted her teeth or screamed.

"Don't you tie me to this bed!" More sounds of struggle, then Clara was quiet for a minute.

Finally, they were all telling her to push. I looked through the crack, but it was still the backs of the white coats. Clara was grunting and moaning and then I heard a baby crying. I peeked through the crack again. A doctor with a mask over his face held a baby upside down and whacked it across the bottom. The baby started to cry. All I could see was the baby's torso. I stood back from the door. They were going to come out soon with the baby bundled up and take it to the nursery, and I couldn't be seen.

"It's a girl," I heard someone say. More whispering among the white coated nurses and doctors, and the baby quieted down.

"The Mother's coming to, now," someone said. "She won't remember anything."

"You can't let her see the baby."

At last I could do something useful. I would make sure I kept my eyes on that baby. I waited a safe distance from the door so that no one could tell me I was in the wrong place. Sure enough, a nurse came out with the baby bundled up in her arms. She raced over to the nursery. I could hear Clara crying out.

"No, no, no!" She cried. "And then she was sobbing. "Give me back my baby! I don't care! It's my baby!" There was nothing I could do for Clara right now but stand guard over her baby. Maybe she would get some sleep.

I stood outside the big window, like I had when Lily was presented to her adoptive parents. This time the nursery wasn't so crowded. There were seven babies altogether. The nurse unwrapped Clara's baby and I was shocked to see that her hair was red. It stood straight up and gave the baby a surprised look like it had a headful of exclamation points. When the nurse opened the blanket, I could see the little hands balled up in a fist, jerking around at the air like she was in a boxing ring.

I pulled up a chair. I stared at Clara's baby until I couldn't keep my eyes open any longer. I loved that baby so much already, and I hadn't even touched it yet. But it was late. Luckily I had to pee and that kept me awake. I knew the washroom was close by, just around a corner. I looked again at Baby Girl Shea, who was sleeping now. The nurse sat quietly to the side, folding diapers. I ran down the hall. I peed as fast as I could and washed my hands quickly and opened the door.

I heard voices.

"What do you mean Clara has to sign a death certificate?"

It was Mother's voice. *When did she get here?* I shrank around the corner, out of sight, feeling shame for the way I spoke to her in her bedroom when I last saw her. But mostly, I didn't want her taking me home with her until I was sure that Baby Girl Shea was safely in Clara's arms.

"But Mrs. Shea," the nurse was saying, "you signed the papers, giving Clara over to the care of the sisters."

"How did the baby die?" Mother demanded. "What are they saying is the cause of death?"

How did the baby die? That's impossible! A baby can't die in the time it takes me to run to the bathroom and pee.

"The official cause of death is cerebral hypoxia," the

nurse said.

Oh, my God, is Clara's baby dead? I thought in disbelief. *How could The Blessed Mother have let her die?*

"What happens in the case of hypoxia is," the nurse was saying, "the umbilical cord is wrapped around the baby's neck. Usually, it's in the birth canal for a long time like that. When it's born, it's already dead."

"I know what hypoxia is! Did Clara get to hold her baby?" Mother demanded.

"You don't understand, Mrs. Shea. You signed the paper saying you gave Clara and her child to the care of the Sisters of Saint Isabella." But Mother wasn't listening.

"Did my daughter hold her baby?"

The nurse didn't answer. Now Mother sounded angry.

"Did she hold her baby before you took it from her?"

"Your daughter wrote explicit instructions not to adopt the baby. You and your husband were pretty clear about what was best for your daughter. Legally, we don't have any other choice than to record the cause of death as hypoxia."

"What do you mean 'you don't have any other choice'? You just asked my daughter to sign a death certificate for her newborn baby! Do you understand what you are doing?" I have never seen Mother storming angry like that. Usually she withdraws and stops speaking to you when she's mad. This time Mother was spitting when she spoke.

I felt dizzy. What was going on here? How could Clara's baby have died? I saw her come out of the labor room. She was crying and she was breathing and now she's sleeping. I ran back to the nursery. Baby Girl Shea was still sleeping, in the same little crib.

I ran back to the hallway.

"There's no simple way of saying this," the nurse said to my mother. "We already have parents who have agreed to adopt that baby."

"Mother!" I said. Something totally weird was going on here. Mother was trembling like that Chihuahua on the bus. When she saw me, she had a look in her eyes, like she didn't quite recognize me.

"Mother!" I said again. I ran up to her and hugged her. My head came up to her chest, right below her chin. I just fit right in there. Mother put her hand over my face, gently. She started patting my back like I was a baby and she was burping me. It felt so good for her to hold me.

"Annie! I was worried sick about you." She held me so tight and she rocked me back and forth. The feeling was so magic and familiar, from far away. I started to cry.

"Clara's baby," she said. "We have to help Clara."

I pulled away.

"Mom," I said. The nurse stood off to the side, with a form in her hand. She was looking down at the floor. "You can't let Clara sign anything here. They're going to steal her baby."

"She already signed it," the nurse said.

Maybe it was because I was really hungry by then, or exhausted, or because it was so wrong that anyone would take away Clara's baby. Or because I realized that anyone will do anything, no matter what they say.

I moved quickly. I grabbed the form. I tore it in half. And then I tore the halves in half, and the quarters in half until there were little pieces of confetti on the floor.

"Clara's baby isn't dead, Mom," I said, tearing the paper. "Clara's baby is alive," I looked at the nurse, straight in the eyes. "That's the truth of it. She's not dead at all. And you know it."

"Clara's baby is right there," I continued, pointing to the nursery. "She wasn't dead when she was born. I heard her cry, I saw her breathe. I stood outside the labor room right when she was born. She has red hair!" Now Mother was confused. She looked at me like she was coming to, after fainting, and instead of finding herself in heaven, or in church, she found herself in a strange world of deep sea monsters. It is a strange world, I thought, we're just not used to looking at it like it really is.

"She has red hair, Mom," I said, as if that would be enough. I pulled on Mother's hand and dragged her towards the nursery. "Red hair!" I kept saying. Two of us, red heads, scurrying to claim our kin. My niece. Mother's grandchild. Clara's daughter.

When we got there, I pointed out the little girl who was obviously the one. The only one with red hair. Mother opened the door to the nursery. I stood in the doorway. The nurse stood up,

"I'm sorry, you can't come in here," she said. But Mother walked right past her over to the little crib where Baby Girl Shea was sleeping.

"I'm here," Mother said. "I'm here to see my granddaughter."

CHAPTER 34
GREEN PLAID COUCH

Mother said we should sit in the waiting room, and give Clara some time with her new baby. Clara was trying to nurse the baby, but her breasts were humongous, and the baby's lips were really tiny. Clara could have been Mrs. Jolly Green Giant, and her watermelon breasts would have made sense. This was the first time I had seen a naked breast besides my own. It was shocking that breasts can be small enough to look like swollen mosquito bites (like mine) and someday grow into boulders bigger than the baby's head. The baby was brand new, so she didn't know exactly what she was trying to do. Eating is pretty important to a baby, but I couldn't imagine how the baby was going to accomplish what was required.

Anyway, the baby was doing my favorite thing that newborn babies do. Her mouth wanders towards your finger if you lightly touch her cheek. You just dab your finger near its mouth, and the mouth goes in that direction, with the tiny lips trying to nibble on your finger. Then you touch the other cheek, just to see if it works over there.

But it was difficult to leave the room. Every time a nurse came in I looked in her eyes to see if she was plotting some way to get the baby. I didn't know what scheming would look like, but everyone was suspect now. Even Nice Nurse, if she had shown up in the room, might have been part of the plot. My own Mother had been part of it; her signature on the papers meant that the Sisters of Saint Isabella had control over Clara in the hospital. Because Clara was still underage. At least now Mother talked the nurse into bringing the bassinet on wheels from the nursery into Clara's room, right next to her bed. The nurse risked losing her job over this, but Mother just wouldn't take no for an answer. So Clara settled in for the night, holding her treasure with the wandering lips.

The waiting room had a square couch, covered with a green and yellow plaid design. There was a clock right above our heads, and it said 4:10 when we got there. In the morning. I didn't notice anything else because I wanted to lie down all of a sudden. I gladly sat on the cushion next to Mother and closed my eyes. The next thing I knew, my head was in Mother's lap, and I was drooling onto her dress and I could just feel that some time had passed. I looked at the clock. It now said 6:45.

I couldn't believe how special this made me feel. Not the drooling, not the time. The fact that it was just me and Mom and absolutely nobody else. No threat of Jeannie barging in, or Daddy coming home from work, no having to listen to tattling, or whining over lost pajamas. I didn't have to call Mom through the bathroom door or listen to the undignified sound of her tinkle. It was just Mom and me.

Then Mother shifted her weight and started to push me off her lap.

As I sat up, I realized I needed to apologize to her for what I said in her bedroom, the last time I saw her.

Luckily all of us have had a lot of practice apologizing—to each other, to the priests in confession every week. It's always embarrassing, but you know from doing it so often that you can get through it, and the sooner you do it, the sooner it will be over.

"I'm sorry, Mother." I said, hoping that one humiliating "I'm sorry" would be enough.

"Sorry for what?" she asked, sounding groggy. I think she was just waking up too.

"For talking to you that way in your bedroom. Will you please forgive me?" I looked over at her, and the nap feeling descended on me: groggy, cottonmouth and cranky, everything too bright, empty despair, like the world is going to end. Maybe Mother was feeling the same way; she looked exhausted, her face tight and full of tension, like she was going to cry. "I shouldn't have said anything about the baby in the photograph," I added, "I shouldn't have kept the photograph from you." Her face crumbled, and she started to cry.

"Mother, *please* don't cry," I begged her. "Clara gets to keep her baby. You have a grandchild. This is Happily Ever After, isn't it?" But Mother didn't hear me.

I knew I was witnessing something so extraordinary as to be written on a plaque in front of a statue. How could I have imagined I'd ever be in a room with my Mother like this? She didn't seem like my mother right then; she seemed like someone wounded in a war, afraid of the pain she was feeling and full of emotion. It was awkward and frightening. Up until now Mother knew all the answers: how to feel, what to say, what clothes to wear, and what not to do, and more importantly, if you screwed up, who to pray to. She knew what everyone wanted and needed. For Christmas, Easter, birthdays. She had band aids and emergency phone numbers and a stash of new things in her cupboards at all times, an assortment of stuff she got on sale throughout the year, purchased with each and every one of us in mind. She always knew what we were having for supper and how to fix it so there was enough to go around. But here she was, like one of the little kids left in their crib to cry themselves to sleep, desolate and despairing after having sobbed for two hours with no one even noticing. It seemed like she needed someone to touch her, so I reached up and put my hand right square in the middle of her back, and patted her gently, like I was burping a baby. Usually she brushes me off, but this time, she let me.

"It's okay, Mom. It's going to be okay." We both sat there in the strange buzzing silence of that room, smelling the stale cigarettes in the metal-stand ashtray over there, with the round glass dish in the middle, full of tan cigarette butts and gray ashes.

"The baby in that photograph, Annie," she said, "I lost the baby when it was born."

"Oh, Mom," I whispered, feeling an intense sadness, accompanied by an insatiable curiosity. I couldn't imagine what would have made that baby die. The tiny hand had looked perfectly normal. I kept my touch on her back, trying to gather the courage to ask her.

"It was the baby who was going to save my life," she said, very, very quietly.

"What do you mean?" I asked her. When she opened her mouth to speak, the words almost didn't come out. She hadn't ever said these words to anybody; that's what it felt like.

"My husband was killed when I was five months pregnant. But he left me this baby. I don't mean to feel sorry for myself. A lot of widows were desolate because of the war. But this baby." She stopped and took a breath.

"This baby, what, Mom?"

"Was going to be a joy. For everyone. It was not only going to be an antidote to Clifford's death, but also to everyone killed in the war. The baby was life." Even more than what she was saying, my surprise came on the heels of the fact that Mother was stroking my hair. Gently pushing it back over my shoulders. I got this soft feeling in my stomach. My scalp relaxed, my skin felt tingly, I could feel my shoulders let go. Her voice was tired and soft.

"When the baby's head came out, the cord was wrapped around his neck. And when he was finally born, he was blue. They couldn't get him to breathe." She was watching over to her left, like she could see it happening again. "They had him over there, they were doing everything they could. But he died right in front of us." Her hand continued to absently touch my hair.

The poor baby, I thought, but I would have sat there forever, as long as she kept touching me.

Finally she looked at me, like she was Mom once more. Her voice was steadier. She had a few responsibilities again and she pulled her hands back to herself. "When God closes a door, He opens a window, Annie. He never gives you more than you can handle."

"What did you name him?"

"I named him after his father, Clifford."

"Clifford Adamson."

"Junior."

"Clifford *Mary* Adamson?" I asked, feeling a particular insider connection with my half-brother, even though he was dead.

"Junior."

"Did you baptize him?"

Mother tried to speak, but nothing came out.

I didn't know what else to say. The sacraments are ceremonies we understand. I was just trying to get her to talk about something that could comfort her.

"My best friend, Edie, had come to the hospital with me," she finally said. "She and the nurse knew each other from college. Edie came right in after the baby was born and made a case for taking one photograph. Because I had lost Clifford. Because he had given up his life for the war effort. But right after the photograph, they took the baby away. I should have said, 'Baptize him first.'"

Involuntarily, I said "Oh!" And thought: *She didn't baptize the baby? That's not good at all.*

"You didn't know!" I said instantly, trying to cover up my shock. Maybe God would make an exception. Surely He wouldn't keep that particular baby out of heaven just because it wasn't baptized. There had to be a special dispensation for soldiers who have given their lives for their country, and the babies who are born without their daddies.

"No, I don't know what they did with him at all." She stared at the floor, her eyes fixed on a whole world somewhere else. "After nine months of awaiting him while he was growing inside my body, I held him for maybe 50 seconds. I could feel his little soul right through his body; we were still so connected to each other, even though he wasn't breathing. But they thought it might be better for me not to see him, not to hold him." She was shaking her head absently from side to side.

"That's what they did in those days," Her voice trailed.

"Mom," I said, pushing her hair away from her eyes.

"My husband was buried in France. I haven't been able to visit his grave. To say goodbye to him." We sat there on the edge of the green plaid couch, Mother and me, knees touching, the sound of intercom static around the corner. "At least I had the photograph," she added. "I could remember the weight of his body in my arms. I could see his little hand."

CHAPTER 35
BLESS ME FATHER

December 8 – The morning after Emma was born, Mother drove all the red heads back in the VW bus from the hospital. We had to get back right away, because there was no one there to look after the kids, except Daddy. I really felt part of something special. Before, I felt like I stuck out. But that morning I was proud of sticking out. Even though I was exhausted from staying up all night, I felt wide awake with a new kind of excitement that wouldn't stop. I got to hold the baby for a few minutes while Clara had a break and nodded off. We were driving past the ocean, and the day was as sparkly and new on every wave and car bumper as it had been the first time with Madcap and Aaron Solomon. I was sitting in the back seat, with Mother's window partly open, and it felt so refreshing where the breeze touched my skin and blew my hair.

We didn't say much. It was quiet, like we were all the servants in the household of a king, silently asking *How is The King feeling about all of this? What shall we tell The King?* and *What happens when The King finds out?* When we arrived, The King was standing at the door. He had his tie on, and his suit, ready to go to Mass, holding the screen open for us. His face was stern and his eyes were fixed on The Queen Mother the whole time.

We had to pass through the gauntlet of peasants at the castle of the King. The crowds were cheering. All the kids, except for John-the-Blimp, who was already at the church, were dressed in their Sunday best, ready to go. They were waiting for the new royal baby. Madcap wore a short black dress with tights as if she were a beatnik and everyone else was dressed like a normal person; the twins and Jude looking very Prep School in their short ties and little suits.

Princess Clara went in first, with Emma in her arms. The peasants (little kids) strained up to see the baby's face. Mother and I brought up the rear with Clara's suitcase and armfuls of baby stuff. As Clara approached the door, The King and Queen said a message to each other with some kind of look. The Queen seemed determined, and there was a deep layer of sadness in her eyes. But there was also joy. She looked at The King and smiled a big smile. The King just saw the face of the woman he remembered, the one he loved. Then he stood aside as he held the door for the Princess and her new baby, The Duchess of Shea. The peasants filed in behind.

The first thing Clara did was put The Duchess in the middle of our parent's huge bed, covered with the nubby, off-white and slightly worn bedspread. Then she stood back. Her face was filled with such pride. All us happy subjects gathered around the King's bed and thanked God quietly for bringing another healthy baby into the kingdom. I held the hand of Princess Clara, and she squeezed it and she smiled at me. Emma was so tiny, surrounded by all that bed. She made a little sag in the mattress, and her hands opened and closed randomly.

"What kind of a saint's name is Emma?" The King asked, annoyed.

"You're right, Daddy. I don't know of a Saint Emma," I countered, feeling recklessly bold in challenging his majesty. "On the other hand, maybe she will be the first."

"And why not put the baby in the center of your own bed, Clara?" He added, gearing up for a lecture.

So much for the Duchess fantasy.

"Let it go, Martin," Mother said, firmly. "This is our granddaughter."

It was Sunday. The last Mass of the day, the 12:15 noon Mass was about to start at St. Andrew's Church, and Daddy was one of the collectors. Because Clara was still recovering from the birth, she was excused from her obligation so she could stay home with the baby. Mother had the Volkswagen bus, so everybody had to pile in with her.

I felt a hand on my shoulder. It was Daddy.

"You're going with me," he said with a Commander sound in his voice.

Uh, oh, I thought. *Here it comes.*

In the car, Daddy vented. It pains me to think about what he said. I've heard it so many times I could spell it, word for word. Sometimes I wonder why grown ups repeat things so much. When you're a kid, all the time of your life is taken up in the same room with them; you get to see every little detail about them, close up. A hair on the back of their hand, a mole by their lips, the way their hair is parted. Like how Daddy always gets food on his mouth when he's eating and I spend most of the meal trying to decide if I'm going to get him mad by telling him, or maybe this time he wants me to let him know. And then the bit of food falls off his chin and I can finally enjoy my supper. The point is, you get to see them microscopically and hear every thought that comes out of their mouths. Pretty soon, you can predict what they are going to say.

But it was better than being spanked in front of the whole family, so I shut up and waited. Number 1, he said, I had again disobeyed the law of the house by going to Ventura without asking permission, or telling Mother. It was only slightly better that I had taken the bus—"slightly less stupid" was his phrase—at least I didn't get into a car with an evil stranger.

Number 2, I was risking my soul for all eternity. How far away could hell be, if I was only 12 and couldn't even get past the second commandment, "Honor thy Father and thy Mother"?

"I'm almost 13, Daddy." I inserted.

"You're getting too independent, thinking you can make up your own mind about things. The church has come up with some simple rules, like the 10 commandments, and when you disobey your parents, you are sinning," he lectured.

I looked at my hand. It wasn't shaking yet because, what could he do to me in this car? But he had that scary tone in his voice that put me on edge. And what he was saying was like a lot of other things that didn't make any sense. Only this time, it was making me cranky.

Hmmmm. I thought. *So being a parent allows you to do anything, whether it is right or not, and if you're the child, you have to go along? Or you're going to hell? A sin is a sin is a sin whether or not you're a "Father and Mother."* How could it be right that he and Mother had abandoned their own daughter—just to save face in the parish? How could that be something I had to go along with just because I'm a child?

By the time we got to Number 3, Daddy was yelling. It was just him and me inside that car, but it was so loud, the car seemed smaller. I cringed against the door.

"You had no business interfering with Clara's situation! It was an adult matter. Do you understand me? It had nothing to do with you. You willful child! Going up to Ventura on your own, thinking you were saving the bastards of the world from adoption. Who do you think you are?"

I couldn't answer. *The bastards of the world?*

"The last time you tried this stunt didn't I leave enough of an impression on you?" he barked, changing gears and heading into an intersection. "You deliberately disobeyed me! Defying your parents' wishes is another example of your willful disregard for the second commandment."

"Let's call a spade a spade," I heard myself say.

"Don't you dare sass me," he yelled across the car, even though I was only inches from him. "You know nothing about what we've done for you kids. How many people do you know have 13 children? Do you have any idea how much we sacrifice for you?"

All my life, whenever he used this line of reasoning, I felt guilty about being born and causing all his suffering. He didn't have a fancy car, because he had to provide for all the children. The home was always a mess because of us. He didn't get promoted in the Navy because of Mother and a new baby every year. I'm not sure of the other things he did without, but he was aware of them all the time, and he reminded us how much of a stone we were around his neck.

"You act like it's my fault for being born," I said. "Why do you and Mother have so many children anyway?" This thought was like a door opening. And once that door opened, it didn't want to close.

"Don't you talk to me this way!" he screamed, as he turned left in the middle of the intersection. Now we were on the same street as the church. I wasn't afraid of him. My face felt red and a hot feeling shot through my veins. My thoughts were lightning fast: he couldn't even see me; all he saw was the lot of us. I was just another mouth to be fed, a disobedient child with a backside to be belted.

"So you're saying that before we were all born, we decided to be born to cause trouble for you and Mother?" I couldn't believe these questions actually occurred to me, and that I was daring to ask them. But now I wanted to know about the very obvious thing that had been staring us in the face our whole lives. *Why did they have so many children?*

Daddy pulled the car over to the side of the road. I thought he was going to jump out and take off his belt, he was so spitting mad. The problem was, I was mad, too.

"You are still a child!" he bellowed at me in the confines of the car. "You have no right to talk to me like this! You had no right to interfere with Clara and her baby! She has brought shame on our entire family in the parish by bringing that baby home, and you are responsible for that! Who do you think you are?"

I screamed back at him. "I'm almost a teenager!"

"Father Stefanucci is turning over in his grave right now! With that child, born out of wedlock! The example we're giving to all the other families in the parish!"

I thought of the Feeneys and how they would get canonized in comparison, even though Christopher Feeney was just as guilty as Clara for "sins of the flesh."

"Jesus was born out of wedlock," I said calmly. This was the ultimate blasphemy, and I knew it would get him, but I said it anyway. Instantly, he smacked the back of his hand against my cheek; my head throbbed. I grabbed my cheek as I glanced at him.

"Don't you dare blaspheme the Lord and Savior Jesus Christ!" he spat. "It's a good thing we're in this car!"

I grabbed a hold of the door handle and pushed. My feet landed on the sidewalk. I slammed the door and ran down the street towards the church. I wasn't afraid of anyone seeing me. I ran and ran. I was never going to go back to being his daughter. *I'll be a nun, first*, I threatened inwardly. Even being a stupid nun looked better than being anywhere near him. *I'll spend my life praying for your soul!* I didn't care. I could hear the car coming after me and crossed the street. His car passed me.

When I got to the school and the church, I saw the Rambler parked with all the other cars along the road. It was early, but parishioners had begun arriving to fulfill their weekly duty at Sunday Mass. I went in the side door, sweaty from running. The dark vestibule was cool as the marble columns. I pushed open the inner door to the inside of the church.

Daddy was at the back, talking to Father Pierre, who had been standing in the center of the church, greeting the faithful. I didn't realize he had come back to the parish again, from his mission in Africa, but there he was. I was caught off guard by the vision of him. I wondered if he remembered me from before.

I genuflected and chose a pew to the side with no one in it. My chest was still heaving up and down and I didn't want to be anywhere near either of them. My cheek felt hot and swollen from Daddy's blow. I sensed somebody breathing down my neck.

"You are going to go to confession and ask God forgiveness for your sins." I turned away from Daddy's voice. "Father Pierre will hear your confession," he said, the sound of anger still in his voice.

I sat back in the wooden pew, and let it sink in. Father Pierre was standing at the doorway to the confessional. He nodded his head, inviting me in.

Like I was going to tell him I was sorry for what I did! Every cell in my body pounded around inside me, revolting at this idea.

It was the worst possible moment for me to tell some man, whom I hardly even knew, that I had sinned. Especially Father Pierre, who was still as handsome and blonde and movie star as ever. But now, even he seemed like a traitor; he probably agreed with Daddy that I had sinned by interfering with Clara's "situation." My entire being recoiled from the expectation. I sat in the pew, ignoring the both of them.

"Get in there!" Daddy hissed at me. I leaned away from him, towards the wall. Right in front of me, Teresa Feeney and her family filed in and took up two rows at the front. Teresa wore a turquoise dress, light and airy and graceful, as usual. Christopher brought up the rear, holding the hands of two of his younger brothers. He seemed so comfortable and easy in his skin, as if he had forgotten about the whole episode of my visit before Emma was born.

I couldn't bear to look at them.

Then I saw John up at the front, lighting the candles on the altar, his black cassock swishing around his feet. The vision of him mixed with Daddy's humid breath so close made me nauseous. Another twisted bit of thinking banged around inside my head: don't tempt the boys with short skirts, go to hell for impure thoughts, but ignore The Hands. Better than that, put The Hands up on the altar and look at him approvingly for showing up on time without bubblegum on his shoes.

Daddy exhaled over my shoulder. I could smell eggs on his breath. *Okay, I'll go,* I thought, *just to get Daddy off my back.* I stood up in the aisle and genuflected, crossing myself. I turned towards the back of the church and the confessional.

Father Pierre was already sitting in there. Through the grate that divided the confessor from the sinner, I could see his hands on his lap, folded on his brown cassock with his rosary entwined. It didn't feel like Jesus or the Blessed Mother were anywhere in the vicinity. Even my Guardian Angel had abandoned me. I knelt

A THEORY OF EXPANDED LOVE

down, practically choking on the condescension of the situation.

I crossed myself, like I have a thousand times, in preparation for the confession.

"Bless me, father," I said. I paused. I couldn't bring myself to say another word.

"Yes, my child?" Father Pierre asked me.

Normally I would I have said, "For I have sinned." It's the easiest part. It's the rote thing they get you to say to ease your way into telling a complete stranger your weakest moments. Normally I would never leave him there in the dark after asking me that question.

But nothing felt normal. I stood up in the dark confessional. I opened the heavy curtain and stepped into the aisle. I could smell the incense. John-the-Blimp was genuflecting at the bottom of the marble stairs. Mother appeared in the center aisle at the back, the kids trailing behind her, and it struck me that she was like a chicken with her brood following her around the pen, imitating her every move. She was a Mother Hen, and we were just a bunch of chickens.

I put my head down and faced the back, walking past Daddy, who was escorting people to their seats. I kept going, beyond all the parishioners filing into Sunday Mass. Past the statues of Jesus and the Blessed Mother. Past the Stations of the Cross and the baptismal font behind the iron gate. I went outside. It was really sunny.

I squinted against the bright light of the day. I could see everything clearly.

EPILOGUE
DEAR DIARY

New Year's Eve – Remember me? It's been a while but I've decided to write to you again. Directly. So that I can sort everything out myself. There's nothing wrong with Jesus and Mary, but it's pretty hard second-guessing them all the time. I've come to the conclusion that we have to work things out ourselves and there's no point to thinking I have a direct line to God or to the Blessed Mother, any more than anyone else does. I'm just one person in a big family, and it's no different in the world. It's an enormous place, with millions of people, everyone clamoring for something or other.

A lot has happened. Clara had her baby. She's named it Emma. It turns out that Emma was born on December 7, 1963, the 22nd anniversary of Pearl Harbor. In all the excitement, I forgot about Daddy and Father Stefanucci and how that was their special day of friendship.

The other thing that happened is that Mother told us about her lost babies. Everyone was kneeling around the statues up on the mantle on Christmas Eve. Daddy started to say the Our Father. And Mother interrupted him. Everyone looked up. Mother doesn't usually interrupt. In fact, almost never. Just once, this summer, she interrupted him for me. I won't forget that.

"Marty," she began. "I want to tell the children. It's time," she said firmly and quietly. Then she told us we have two more siblings who are in Limbo. There was a lot of gasping and ahhing, except for me. I already knew. She's named the baby girl of the miscarriage. Her name is Ramona, after Saint Ramon, the patron saint of secrets. And she told them about Clifford Mary Anderson Junior. The sunny side of all of this is, maybe if we all pray together, we can bribe God to relent and let them both into heaven, being as it wasn't anybody's fault that neither of them were baptized in the first place.

Right now it's New Year's Eve and Madcap and I are working on the Rose Parade Floats, even though my mind keeps getting distracted with the thought of Emma (who is really my niece). Everyday we go into the warehouse in our overalls and braids and flannel shirt and long johns because it's cold enough to freeze the balls off a brass monkey.

First job we had, we glued black poppy seeds onto a huge ball. We come in everyday at 7:30 in the morning. Today I balanced on a scaffold 15 feet above the cement floor, dipping my brush and spreading the glue on the huge ball of the Cal Tech float. I've got a box of orange mums, every single one of which must be pasted onto the ball with no spaces in between. We're in a huge warehouse with high ceilings and six other floats. The doors are open so that people won't get sick inhaling the fumes. The other volunteers are students at Cal Tech, much older than me, because this is the Cal Tech float. Somehow Madcap and I got added on to the crew. We'll probably be here 'til midnight. There is this one boy who sits next to me on the scaffold sometimes. He's kind of shy and lanky, with yellow curls and big lips that look soft under his fuzzy blonde hairs that are trying to grow into whiskers.

• • •

The queen of the Rose Parade and her princesses came in today in high heels. They were all dressed in lavender pastel suits, straight skirts to the knees, with short jackets and pillbox hats like Jacqueline Kennedy. The queen had a red rose on her lapel. I was looking down on them from my perch on the scaffold. I practiced the Rose Queen wave, in the unlikely case that I would ever become the queen, or even a princess in future years, when I'm old enough to audition—but I still had my brush in my hand, and I accidentally glopped a gob. It hit the bottom of my float and splattered, landing on the back of the high heel of the last princess. She had no idea.

I was seriously tempted to drop the entire glue bucket on them from above. Really. *What kind of girl am I turning into?* I imagined the noise it would make, and the bouncing glue bucket and everyone looking up at me, but unable to find me as I'd be hiding behind the ball. Wanda is also helping on the queen's float. And by the way, she saw the glop, and looked up at me. I stared back. We're still officially not speaking. She wants to get back with me. She's dropped Teresa Feeney because now she understands that Teresa is just hiding behind Christopher's lie about Clara being a slut.

Clara has gone back to school, and she's getting A's again. We all chip in with Emma if she needs her diapers changed or when she's hungry. Mother puts the glass bottles with formula in the pot of boiling water on the stove; then she squirts the milk out of the nipple onto the inside of her wrist to see if it's too hot. But when Clara gets home, she and Emma have this kissing reunion, with Clara doing all of the kissing behind Emma's ears.

She wants to be a doctor, someone who delivers babies, but Daddy keeps telling her she can much more easily become a secretary. "You're smart enough already," he says, "Administrative secretaries make a good living." He tells all of us girls we should be secretaries. Clara ignores him. But I looked it up. Secretary means "keeper of secrets." I certainly don't want to be a secretary, and I don't want to keep any more secrets. Eventually, because of that, and also because it was bothering me, I had to tell Clara my secret, namely that I blabbed to Christopher Feeney about how he's the father.

She surprised me. She said she didn't care what anyone thought of her, including Christopher Feeney. She didn't care whether or not anyone said she was a sinner, or if she was sponging off Daddy and Mother by living at home. Or even that she had a child out of wedlock. She said she's really happy that Emma is growing up surrounded by uncles and aunts as if she were the youngest in the family, because she'll have lots of people who love her and can teach her things. She's thankful to Mother for going against Daddy and bringing Emma home.

I am going to try to be as truthful as possible in 1964. It's hard to realize how much lying goes on with nearly everyone. Especially those people who tell you that lying is a sin. Also I'm not sure why it's a sin if everyone does it. Now I just expect it. It's an ordinary, rampant thing that can't be controlled by the fear of fire in the afterlife. On the other hand, I hate calling anyone a sinner because "there but for the grace of God go I."

• • •

My favorite song on the radio is "I'm Leavin' it Up to You" by Dale and Grace. Whenever it comes on, we all sing along from all the tops of the scaffolds, rocking and swaying to the beat, even though it's rickety and scary up there.

Aaron Solomon is the float supervisor. Madcap and I are his slaves. Well, we're volunteers and it's fun. He has a lot of responsibility; he runs around all day ordering flowers and telling students what to do and talking with the float owners, but still, he takes a break with us and we sit together huddled around a bologna sandwich on white bread with mayonnaise near the space heater in the warm room. Madcap is so lucky he's her boyfriend, and I always see her hand on his knee.

Speaking of lies. I'm sure the priests and nuns didn't even know the truth about Emma. Once Christmas came and went, she just became a fact, Number 14. Otherwise, would the nuns have allowed Emma to be baptized at St. Andrew's Church on Christmas Eve with Sister Maria Dolora's fourth grade class singing Christmas carols as they poured the water over Emma's big forehead? Would they have used a baby born out of wedlock as the Baby Jesus in the crèche? They would not have, but they did. For some people they might require a birth certificate, but when Mother arranged the baptism, would it even occur to them to ask her for proof of parentage? It did not occur to them. Everyone in our parish seems to be making an assumption that Mother is the mother of Emma. I'm not sure how I could tell them all. You can't tell somebody else's truth. I'm not keeping the secret of Emma, and I'm not the watchdog of the truth of Emma, either.

But the Christmas crèche was Emma's first acting job, and she was pretty good. She was the first red headed Jesus ever. And I'm pretty sure, the first female Jesus. So what. If they have so many versions of the Blessed Mother, surely Jesus can have whatever color hair He wants. Of course, the Baby Jesus was a boy and probably an ordinary baby in all other respects, and I remember being on diaper duty while Emma was in the crèche. Teresa Feeney and her brother Christopher were in the church, and I caught them both just baldly staring at the baby as I picked her up. They didn't even look away when my eyes met theirs. I stared them down; Christopher looked away first, more confused than I had ever seen him. Teresa's eyes were wide open, her mouth ajar.

I'm glad that nobody "really" knows. Emma is ours. Otherwise, Christopher Feeney might try to claim her. That family has enough beauty and talent and brains, and worst of all, grace. They had their chance and besides "He who hesitates, is lost." I've seen Christopher wondering about her in church for unbroken moments, as if no one could see that he, a handsome B.M.O.C. (Big Man On Campus), has an abnormal fascination for a small baby girl.

Mother made it official, took away all our doubts, one night at the dinner table when she said, after the

Bless Us Oh Lord… "And take special care of our youngest, Emma." After that we tacked her name on the end of The List (Paul, Clara, John, Madcap, Bartholomew, Annie, Jeannie, Dominic, Rosie, Luke, Matthew, Mark, Jude — Emma) and never bothered to mention to anyone that our youngest was our niece, not our sister. Clara goes along. She is a mother. Her baby has to survive.

More news. John-the-Blimp now has a girlfriend. They met at a dance. Her name is Barbara and she's in Madcap's class. The chaperone separated them while slow dancing to "Hey, hey Paula," with his hand right on her dress, exactly where her breast is. So much for him being a priest. Everybody thought he wanted to be holy. But it was so obvious. He wants to enlist as a sailor. Now I can call him a "deck ape."

Wanda just knocked on my scaffold from below with the end of her brush, and I looked down to see her face smiling up at me. She pointed to her heel, reminding me that I dropped the glop of glue onto the Rose Princess's heel. Then she bent backwards with her hands on her waist like Felix the Cat, like the laughing was killing her. A thing we do. "C'mon down, Annie!" She called up to me. "Take a break!" She apologized already for what she said the day we had that fight, but it's hard to trust her again. Although I probably will. It takes a lot of energy to stay mad at someone who underneath it all, cares about you.

So maybe I shouldn't stay mad at Daddy. But I am giving up 6:30 Mass. I'll miss the early morning air, the stillness of it and the lights on Orange Grove Boulevard fading away as the sun comes up. And being in the car with him. That's over, now that I'm almost practically a teenager. He's still my dad. It's weird how he prays so much, and he still can't listen to anyone but himself.

One thing is for sure: I'm going to keep writing. I've already started with this diary. It's a place where I can say what I see—not just what they want me to see. And when I notice things that everyone can see but nobody admits? I'm going to write them down, too. I'm going to write everyday, so I don't forget that what is in my heart is just as important.

Oh and the "tip" for the first automobile sale at Shea Family Motors? Paul finally noticed the money missing. No one suspects me, and I'm not going to say anything. There's no proof. I'm not even going to confession for it. I'm going to save the money plus my babysitting earnings, in case I need it. Just in case I have to fight for something important and Daddy disowns me for it. The actual $26? I'll just keep it in my... well I won't say where, in case anyone reads this. Wait, I'm going to scratch that out.

DEAR READER,

I hope you enjoyed Annie Shea's adventures in *A Theory of Expanded Love*. I really enjoyed writing it and am thrilled to share my work with readers like you.

I was also born into a very large Catholic family, and I wrote the book to answer a question for myself. I won't tell you the question I sought the answer to, but I invite you to try to figure it out.

While a playwright and performer, my audiences gave me so much with their energy that the work was lifted to another level altogether. One of the best things about feedback from an audience is the surprise of finding things in my work that I hadn't understood were there. I loved how the collective experience of the work gave some people validation and power to deal with their own issues. The whole process is ongoing, unexpected, and alive; as a writer I just begin the discussion.

Having said that, may I ask you a favor? I'd love to hear from you. Please write me directly and tell me what you liked, what you loved, what didn't appeal to you, and why. And keeping in mind that you, the reader, have so much power to make or break a book, I'd really appreciate it if you could put your review on Goodreads, Amazon, or your favorite online bookseller so others can share your thoughts.

Thank you so much for reading *A Theory of Expanded Love* and for spending time with me—and Annie Shea.

Blessings,

Caitlin Hicks

P.S. For more on my journey creating *A Theory of Expanded Love*, please visit me online at caitlinhicks.com

ACKNOWLEDGMENTS

I am lucky to have generous and curious friends who encouraged me greatly from the most vulnerable beginning when I had only a few pages; you listened, you laughed, you loved Annie, you cheered us both on.

To JoAnne Bennison for your frequent and spontaneous laughter, your time to hear me read out loud and consider every paragraph and word in this book. To Ben Low, Kim Lyon, Mary Pinniger, Gary Gronlund, Dolores Houghton and Lis Dixon, for the suppers we shared with friends who eagerly awaited the next installation of the adventures of Annie. To my avid-reader fan, Aggie Sanders, your generous comments from across the continent made me feel I had a best seller from the first few chapters. To Anne Simonet for weighing in on Annie's behalf when disputed words and phrases rang true for you. To John McDougall Goulet for the Prologue. To Sally Simpson, Lolly de Jonge, and Jeannine Fitzsimmons for your generosity, support, and encouragement.

To Rosa Reid, George Payerle, Tracy Stefanucci and Shelley Harrison Rae, for editing support and encouragement. To readers and early reviewers, Sydney Avey, D Lynn Chapman, Linda Szabados, Lis Dixon, and Lance Mason, for generously agreeing to read my book and to give me honest feedback. To Erin Niumata, for sharing your spontaneous gut-response to Annie—when I finally put the book into the world, you were my first test.

To Jaz Halloran, for your professional input on the question of book design. To my sister Mary; you've been an inspiration to me since I was a child; thank you for your "I love you" just before you hang up the phone, for sharing this story, for being alongside.

To Elizabeth Turnbull for your voice over the miles, your diplomacy and excellent suggestions that only served to strengthen this work.

THE AUTHOR

Caitlin Hicks is an author, international playwright, and acclaimed performer in British Columbia, Canada. Monologues from several of her plays were featured in Smith & Kraus' series *Best Women's Stage Monologues* (New York). She also wrote the play, later adapted for the screen, *Singing the Bones*, which debuted at the Montreal World Film Festival to stellar reviews and has screened around the world. While *A Theory of Expanded Love* is her debut novel, she has published several short stories, including *That Rescue Feeling*, which was shortlisted for the John Spencer Hill Fiction Award. She worked as a writer for CBS and NBC radio and has performed her fiction and non-fiction for CBC national radio. In print, her writing has been published in *The San Francisco Chronicle*, *The Vancouver Sun*, *The Milwaukee Journal-Sentinel*, *Fiddlehead Magazine*, *Knight Literary Journal* and other publications. Hicks was raised in a large, Catholic family in Pasadena, California. You can connect with Caitlin online at caitlinhicks.com, @CateHicks on Twitter, and facebook.com/CaitlinHicksTheWritingLife.

A reader's guide will be available
online when the book is released
for sale in June 2015.

An author interview is available online:
lightmessages.com/caitlinhicks

IF YOU LIKED THIS BOOK...

Check out these other women's fiction titles from Light Messages Publishing:

The Particular Appeal of Gillian Pugsley
Susan Örnbratt
From the shores of The Great Lakes to the slums of Bombay and a tiny island in between, this dazzling debut takes the reader on an intimate journey to unravel a family secret that's lain hidden for generations.

How to Climb the Eiffel Tower
Elizabeth Hein
This moving, delightful, sometimes snarky novel about life, friendship & cancer proves life's best moments are like climbing the Eiffel Tower–tough, painful & totally worth it.

A Sinner in Paradise
Deborah Hining
Winner of the *IndieFab Book of the Year Bronze Medal* in Romance and the *Benjamin Franklin Award Silver Medal*. Readers will quickly fall for Geneva in this exquisitely written, uproarious affair with love in all its forms, set in the stunning landscape of the West Virginia mountains.

CPSIA information can be obtained
at www.ICGtesting.com
Printed in the USA
FFOW05n0119280515

9 781611 531312